FUGITIVE HEARTS

STEAM! ROMANCE AND RAILS, BOOK 4

E.E. BURKE

Cover Design by Erin Dameron Hill
Train photography by Matthew Malkiewicz

Published by E.E. Burke
eBook ISBN 978-0-9898192-7-5
Paperback ISBN 978-0-9898192-8-2
www.eeburke.com

To my children, who taught me how to love as only a mother can love.

CHAPTER 1

Parsons, Kansas, March 3, 1874

"Sheriff, I killed my husband."

The honeyed voice was familiar. What she said sounded like pure nonsense. That, or he'd misunderstood.

Frank Garrity raised his head from where he'd laid it on his arms after he got too tired to hold it up. He dragged open eyelids as heavy as wet canvas and squinted at a fuzzy, feminine image clothed in pure white.

God above. An angel.

The smell of cheap cigars and even cheaper whiskey convinced him he was still in the saloon, therefore amongst the living. He'd slipped into another drunken delusion. He only *thought* he saw an angel who'd confessed to murder.

Something about this specter looked more substantial, and far more appealing, than the others that haunted his dreams. A wealth of dark hair cascaded over her shoulders, past the point where the scarred tabletop concealed her lower half, keeping the rest of her a tantalizing secret.

If inebriation brought on angelic visions like this one, he'd have another drink.

He curled his hand around the empty whiskey bottle. Couldn't recall finishing it. Regret flickered, briefly. He didn't drink this much, as a habit. Only on days when guilt overwhelmed his good sense and he could find no other way to obliterate the pain.

God might've sent this angel to warn him not to overindulge.

"Did you hear me?" The angel's dulcet voice wavered. "I shot Frederick."

"Who?" Frank shook his head, confused. The only Frederick he knew lived next door with his wife—

The whiskey-drenched fog cleared.

So did his vision.

Frank jerked his attention to her face and shock struck him square in the chest.

Claire.

She wasn't a vision or an angel. Not the supernatural kind, at any rate. She ran the hotel next door. He hadn't recognized her right off because she didn't have on a dress.

He closed his eyes, then opened them to make sure he wasn't hallucinating.

Nope. She was still standing there, trembling, wearing her nightgown and a thin wrap.

The proper lady he knew wouldn't be caught dead in a saloon, much less looking like she'd just crawled out of bed. Her hair hung in loose disarray. An unhealthy flush beneath her skin coupled with the wild look in her eyes conveyed she might be in distress.

She thrust her arms at him, turning up delicate wrists, pale and blue-veined. Her slender fingers curled inward as if to cradle something fragile. "I-I want to turn myself in."

The poor woman's mind had snapped.

Frank came to his feet so fast his chair flew back. It clattered to the floor, all the louder because the noise broke a hushed silence in the crowded barroom.

No tinkling piano. No clinking glasses. No catcalls. Not even a

2

giggle came from the serving girl, who stood a few feet away, wide-eyed and stock-still.

He stumbled against the table, then wheeled around to where the crazy woman stood with her arms outstretched, like she expected him to slap manacles on her.

By God, he had to get her home before the whole damn town witnessed her madness.

He stripped off his heavy overcoat—her thin wrap didn't stand a chance against the freezing temperatures outside—and flung it around her shoulders. Then he hauled her up against his side and made for the door in as close to a beeline as he could manage.

Not too roostered. He hadn't fallen over, and only weaved slightly.

She slipped her arm around his waist, as if she feared he might fall on top of her, or worse, she could catch him if he did.

"Dang it, woman. Let *me* do the rescuing." He swept her up into his arms as he reached the front of the saloon, where a soot-faced railroader opened the door as courteously as a butler.

A frigid blast struck Frank in the face. He sucked in a sharp breath. *That* cleared his head.

The fragrant, feminine bundle in his arms squirmed. "Sheriff Garrity, put me down! I said you should arrest me, not accost me!"

"Takin' you home," he muttered. He shifted her slight, curvaceous form into a more secure position—she weighed no more than his tack. Then he set off for the hotel, near the railroad depot, on the busiest street in Parsons.

It wasn't far. Just next door to the left. Or was it on the right?

He veered left, focusing on putting one foot in front of the other, and prayed he wouldn't trip and drop her on the sidewalk. Faint light from a quarter moon illuminated the filthy planks. No clouds, no snow, but *jeezus* it was cold. March had roared into Kansas with the fury of a cornered mountain lion.

The frantic woman in his arms finally stopped wiggling and sagged against him. Her teeth chattered, despite her body feeling pretty warm for only being in her nightclothes. She peeked over the lapels of the heavy coat he'd wrapped her up in. "Wh-where are you t-taking me? T-to jail?"

"Home," he repeated.

"But I killed my husband."

Her woeful confession set Frank's teeth on edge. "Right now, all I care about is getting you back where you belong and warmed up. I'll worry about your dead husband later."

She buried her face in his chest.

He hadn't meant to sound so callous. Something terrible must've happened if her sanity had gone this far off the tracks.

Sadness coated his numb heart. Mrs. Claire Daines was the most levelheaded woman he knew. Her visionary brother had put up a fancy hotel out in the middle of nowhere, betting his railroad would fill it. Then Claire had moved out here with her husband and made the place a success, with her gracious hospitality and feminine touches. Every traveler wanted to stay at the Belmont House. The hotel was always full, even in the midst of an economic depression.

Maybe she and her husband had experienced unexpected financial difficulties. The hermit had gone off his rocker and killed himself. She felt guilty. Frank had seen that happen before.

He'd seen too many tragedies that made no sense, which was why he'd stopped trying to figure them out. He did what he *could* do something about. Enforce the law and serve justice. His job didn't include arresting a genteel woman with an overactive conscience.

Frank bumped into an oaken and etched-glass door. "Here we are." He searched for the handle with his fingers, used the toe of his boot to coax the door open. Once they were inside, he put her down.

Half a dozen men milled about the lobby, which was situated between an ornate mahogany reception desk and a carpeted stairway to the second floor.

The distraught woman put her arms around his neck and hid her face in his shoulder.

"Don't worry," he murmured reassuringly. "I won't leave you out here in your nightclothes. Where are your quarters?"

"Upstairs, in the back," came her muffled reply.

The anxious guests converged on Frank about the time a clock started chiming.

"We heard a gunshot."

Chime.

"There's a dead man up there."

Chime.

"Are you the sheriff?"

Chime.

"Thank you. I know. Yes." Frank fired off short answers without slowing down to talk. He'd take Claire to her rooms and learn what happened first-hand before he started interviews.

As he climbed the stairs, the chimes stopped. *Eleven.* When he got a moment, he'd need to jot down the time in the small notebook he carried in his pocket.

The woman in his arms still shivered, despite the air being warmer inside. Maybe it wasn't from cold as much as shock. If her husband had ended his life in front of her, that would explain her fragile state and bizarre behavior.

Frank had been acquainted with the hotel's gracious owner for the past two years. In all that time he'd never seen Claire leave the hotel with so much as a hair out of place.

Her reclusive husband, on the other hand, could be a ghost for all he knew. The invalid never left their suite. He didn't even go to church on Sundays. According to his wife, he suffered from war injuries and had trouble getting out. She took care of him without complaint while running a busy hotel and, more recently, taking in an orphaned boy. "Where's Billy?"

"In bed," she replied quickly.

Odd. Nobody else seemed to be.

Apprehensive guests peeked out of their rooms. They held lamps and candles aloft. The lights cast eerie shadows on their faces and across the rose-patterned paper that lined the hallway.

Frank held the trembling woman closer. Not because he felt more protective toward her than he would any other distraught lady. He'd keep telling himself that until he believed it.

5

When he'd passed the last guest room and a flickering light in a gas lamp on the wall, he came to the first room without a number. Near the end of the hall, a door stood ajar. The owner's rooms.

He hesitated. It might be too much for her if he took her inside and she saw her dead husband again. "Is there somewhere else you can wait while I take a look inside?"

"Jail," she murmured, in a resigned tone.

He huffed with annoyance. "Stop talking about going to jail. You need a doctor."

"I'm not sick."

"Is there a cure for hardheaded?"

With his elbow, he nudged open the door. Cold air escaped the dark room. His nostrils flared at a charred odor. "Smells like something burned."

Frank stepped inside. He set his charge on her feet. She maintained a fixed stare. It reminded him of an expression on the faces of young soldiers who'd gotten their first taste of war.

Without thinking, he cupped his hand on her head and gently stroked her disheveled hair. Desire buzzed through him. He'd never touched her before tonight, but had wondered what might happen if he did. Now, he knew. Didn't come as a surprise.

He dropped his hand to his side. "I have to look around. Wait here."

She didn't speak. He got a nod.

The room was awful dark. He fumbled in his pocket for a pack of lucifers and struck one.

A quick survey revealed singed curtains fluttering over a partially opened window. That explained the chill and the smell. Some papers were strewn around. Nearby, a candle lay on the wood floor in a puddle of water.

The match burned his fingers. Frank shook it out.

Fortunately, someone had put out the fire before it took hold. A blaze could've burned down the building in no time.

He retrieved the candle. After a few matches, he got the damp wick dry enough to light it, wedged the taper into its stand and set it on the desk.

That's when he saw the body.

A man wearing a night robe lay sprawled face down on a floral rug.

Frank squatted by the still figure. He detected a faint scent of gunpowder and a sharper stench that indicated the loss of bodily functions. No pulse, mottled skin, ice cold...

He rolled the dead man over onto his back. The body remained flaccid, which meant he couldn't have been dead for long. Less than a couple hours.

Sightless eyes stared upward. Blood and powder burns stained his white nightshirt around a neat hole drilled in his chest. Whoever shot him had been standing close, but it didn't look close enough to be a self-inflicted wound.

Frank's heart commenced to pound. Every thudding beat resounded in his head and a bitter taste filled his mouth. The effects of the whiskey. He'd seen more than his share of dead bodies, in much worse condition than this one.

He drew a deep breath and released it. Forced his mind to focus. He couldn't allow anything to cloud his thinking—not the smell of death, not the whiskey he'd downed that threatened to come up, not even his sympathy for the young widow.

Mr. Daines had been shot through the heart. His wife had admitted to killing him. One question remained. *Why?*

Frank stood slowly. The poor woman hadn't moved from where he'd left her just inside the door. "Mrs. Daines, your husband's dead," he said as kindly as possible. He figured she knew this, but confirmed it anyway.

Her features twisted in an agonized grimace. Her delayed reaction could mean her husband's violent death hadn't really sunk in until now, regardless of how much she'd talked about it. She would come out of the trance she'd been in and would get hysterical.

Frank stepped into her line of vision. "Don't look at him. Look at me."

She closed her eyes and shook her head. Her dark hair rippled all the way to her knees. He lifted a silky strand out of her eyes, couldn't resist touching it. He'd never seen her with her hair down, much less disheveled, and so vulnerable.

A sense of powerlessness came over him. He had to do *something* to aid her. He adjusted his bulky overcoat around her shoulders and drew it closed to protect her modesty. She'd buttoned the nightgown clear up to her chin.

His heart gave an odd jerk. He lifted his arms to open them to her, then caught himself at the last second. Whether he'd meant to hold her or comfort her, it was so far beyond propriety it didn't bear consideration. He had no excuse other than being drunk, and even that wasn't a valid reason.

Thankfully, she still had her eyes closed and hadn't noticed. As much as he pitied her, or yearned to hold her, it wasn't his job to comfort her. He had a responsibility to find out why she'd killed her husband.

"Can you answer a few questions?"

Keeping her eyes shut, she nodded.

"You shot him?"

Another nod.

"Why?"

The widow put her hands over her face. "I didn't mean to."

An accident. This made sense. He didn't believe she'd kill a fly in cold blood. Engulfed in his oversized coat, she looked so small, not even strong enough to pull back the hammer.

Frank perused the room. A table by the sofa knocked out of place, loose papers scattered on the floor, an overturned candle, all indicated a struggle had taken place.

"Did you two have an argument?" he asked.

She opened her fingers slightly to allow her to peek out from between them. "Yes, no... I-I struck the table when I ran out the door."

Understandable, given her state of mind. "The papers? And candle?"

She let her hands drift to her sides. "I'm clumsy."

He wouldn't have thought that. She had a graceful way of moving, at least that's what he'd noticed. Along with other things he had no business noticing. He also knew her to be scrupulously honest, so he would set aside his doubt. For now.

"Where's the gun?"

"Gun?" She said it like she'd never heard the word before.

"Pistol. Revolver. What you used to shoot him."

"I don't...remember where I left it."

A terrible shock could do that to a person, make them forget. He hadn't felt a gun when he'd carried her over here. He crossed his arms over his chest so he wouldn't be tempted to check. "What *do* you remember?"

She met his question with a blank look.

Perhaps a more direct approach would dislodge a memory. "How did he get shot?"

She frowned, as if thinking hard. "He...tried to take the gun away from me."

Frank assembled a mental picture. "With the barrel pointed at his chest?"

"No...yes...." Confusion, then distress flickered across her features. "I don't remember."

Unease tiptoed up Frank's spine. If they'd fought, she might've gotten scared and picked up a gun, could've pulled the trigger without intending to kill him. "Don't remember? Or don't want to incriminate yourself?"

In the dim room, her wide eyes appeared almost black. He'd looked into them enough times to know they were warm brown flecked with gold. Normally, they snapped with keen intelligence or flashed with dry wit. Tonight, they were dark with fear.

"Here, now, I didn't mean to scare you." He gently put his hands on her shoulders to give her gentle reassurance. The physical contact seemed to shake her out of whatever state she'd slipped into and she twitched in response.

Frank dropped his arms to his sides with a sharp reminder he was supposed to interview her, not hug her. He hooked his thumbs over his gun belt to keep his hands out of trouble. "Just tell me why you pointed a gun at your husband."

Her throat worked convulsively. A moist sheen appeared on her upper lip. She raised her hand to her forehead, swayed.

He caught her as her limbs gave way. As he cradled the limp woman in his arms, he cursed himself up one side and down the other for interrogating her with her dead husband lying there, barely cold. He shifted her weight toward him. The movement pressed her soft breasts against his chest. His body's reaction was sharp and immediate—and inappropriate as hell.

He cast a frantic look around to find a place to put her. A door. Presumably, it led into a bedroom. He'd take her in there. Then he'd fetch the doc before he woke the undertaker.

In the dark bedroom, he could see enough to spot a bed. He settled her on top of the spread. She hardly made a dent in the mattress. After he'd slipped his overcoat from beneath her, he snatched a quilt from a rack near the foot of the bed and draped it over her.

"Mrs. Daines?" he whispered.

Her long lashes fluttered. "Where's Billy?" she asked in a fearful tone.

"Take it easy. He's around here somewhere, I'm sure." The boy wandered the town like a stray cat. His whereabouts was the least of her worries right now.

Frank tucked the quilt up to her chin. When she tried to push the covers away, he caught her hands. Her hold on his fingers felt surprisingly tight. That was fine, if she needed to cling to him for a while longer.

He understood better than she could know. Disbelief and denial, followed by useless remorse and unending guilt. He hadn't pulled the trigger on the gun that killed his wife, but he might as well have. Self-condemnation ate at his soul like an insidious disease.

She screwed her eyes shut, which indicated she remained awake.

He wouldn't get much useful out of her tonight, and wasn't so hardhearted he would try. As it was, she would suffer nightmares. The kind he wouldn't wish on his worst enemy, much less a sweet lady like Claire.

"Don't worry about anything. I'll send for the undertaker, and tell Doc to give you something to help you rest. We'll talk more tomorrow." He closed his calloused palms over Claire's smooth hands. He couldn't picture her holding a gun, much less firing one. Yet, she'd admitted to—

No. She hadn't only said she *shot* her husband, as in, by accident. She had said she *killed* him. That implied something different. Intent.

Frank shook his head at his suspicious nature. He was too used to dealing with liars and murderers. Claire was neither. She was a fine, upstanding lady. A respected woman in the community. What did it matter how she'd worded her confession, considering her fragile state? If she said it was an accident, there was no reason to doubt her.

CHAPTER 2

"Fire!" Claire bolted upright. She caught her breath with a harsh gasp, dropped back onto the bed and curled into a ball. Her stomach roiled. Her head felt fuzzy. Her heart wouldn't stop racing.

Something the doctor had given her to help her sleep must've brought on those awful nightmares. Choking... The smoke? Or Frederick's arm around her neck? The thudding in her chest became heavier, harder, as she touched her fingers to a tender spot.

Fear crested and broke free, coursing through her in a raging river. She squeezed her eyes shut but couldn't block out the images, which seemed too real to be dreamed up.

Her husband's bellow of rage. A loud retort and the stench of gunpowder. Billy's pale, frightened face...

Claire opened her eyes. The air looked clear. She didn't smell anything except her own damp body. She eased off the bed and stood slowly to gain her balance.

Had it happened? She had to find out. Find Billy.

She halted at the bedroom door. The floor in the sitting room, bare. Where was the carpet? A faint smell of smoke. Singed curtains. Furniture pushed up against the walls...

A cold chill passed through her body. She clapped her hand over her mouth to stifle a cry. Oh God, the awful nightmare. It really happened.

The room spun. She staggered to the sofa, grabbed the bolstered arm, and dropped down onto the cushioned seat. Some previous instruction in her mind prompted her to put her head down and take deep breaths. Her dizziness ebbed, but a haunting image remained. Frederick, sprawled face down on the carpet, his dressing gown askew, revealing the back of his hairy legs.

"Our Father, who a-art in Heaven. H-hallowed be Thy name...for-forgive my trespasses...." Claire clutched her hands together to pray. She might as well be talking to herself. God had turned his back on her. He knew she'd secretly longed to escape a marriage that had become unbearable.

Tears blurred her vision until she could no longer see the hardwood floor beneath her feet. She buried her face in her hands. "Frederick, I'm so sorry..."

Why plead with her husband? If God wouldn't pardon her, Frederick certainly wouldn't. He'd make a list of her sins and give it to Saint Peter. If only she hadn't argued and made him angry, they wouldn't have fought. Where had Billy gotten the gun? She didn't think the boy even knew where she kept it. Another sin to add to her growing list.

At the click of the doorknob, she jerked upright. "Billy?"

"Mrs. Kelly, dear. Here to check on you."

The woman she'd hired to do the cooking. A sweet, widowed lady whose grown son helped around the hotel. Good people. Kind. She might've checked on Billy already.

"Come in."

The door creaked and the gray-haired woman peeked around the edge. "How're you feeling, dearie?"

Claire couldn't begin to put into words how she felt. She longed to crawl back into bed and bury her head under the covers. As a child, she'd prayed every night to wake up to a different life. In retrospect, she shouldn't have prayed so hard. "What time is it?"

"Past breakfast." The older woman's cherubic face wrinkled into a hesitant smile as she entered the room. She held a tray laden with food.

Claire's stomach rebelled at the over-rich smell of cooked eggs, charred bacon and browned toast. "Oh dear. I don't think I'm very hungry."

"Don't suppose you are, but you need the nourishment. Try to take a few bites."

Claire kept her face averted from the spot on the floor where her husband had fallen. After the initial thud, he hadn't uttered a sound or moved a muscle. She hadn't imagined death could come so quickly, but she hadn't been able to rouse him. She'd known without turning him over he was gone. Another shudder racked her body.

"Yes, thank you." Somehow, she managed a polite response, despite the terrifying sense of being sucked into a vortex. She began a slow, rocking motion to counteract the spinning sensation. If she succumbed to despair, that wouldn't help Billy. For his sake, she had to gather her strength to face this ordeal.

The cook set the tray on a low table in front of the sofa. "Would you like some more of that medicine the doctor left?"

"No. No more medicine." Claire put her hand to her head. Lightheaded as she was, the last thing she needed was more laudanum, or whatever it was he'd given her. She had to be able to think clearly in order to forestall disaster. "Have you seen Billy?"

"Not this morning. His door is closed. He might still be asleep."

Stay in your room, she'd whispered to him. *Don't talk to anyone until I come for you.*

If Billy had minded her for this long, he must truly be frightened.

A dull ache centered in her chest. She would go talk to him, explain none of this was his fault, impress upon him that he must let her deal with the consequences.

The cook's plump hand came to rest on her shoulder. "Mrs. Daines?"

Claire's eyes popped open. When had she closed them? Her

thoughts kept wandering. It must be the lingering effects of the medicine. "Yes, yes I'm fine."

The cook eyed her doubtfully. "You don't look fine to me. You're white as milk."

"That medicine makes me sick." Claire reached for a piece of toast. "I'll try to eat something."

"Good. You'll need your strength. The sheriff said he'd be back this morning to talk to you. Said you ought not leave again until he returns."

Claire's hand froze halfway to her mouth. Leave *again?* When had she left before?

Her muddled mind pieced together fragments, another foggy memory, also not a dream. She'd rushed to get to the sheriff before someone else did. One of the men she'd passed on her way outside had told her the sheriff was next door. She'd gone into the saloon...in her nightclothes.

Her stomach shrank to the size of a peach pit. She set the toast on the plate, unable to choke it down.

"Missus? You all right?" The concerned voice seemed to come from a distance.

Claire shook her head. She'd been out of her mind. That was the only feasible explanation.

How much did the sheriff remember? He'd been sitting alone with his head cradled in his arms. A whiskey bottle overturned on the table. Drunk.

But not too drunk to scoop her up and carry her back to the hotel. Worse, she'd wrapped her arms around his neck and clung to him. She hadn't wanted him to let her go.

Heat flooded her face. He'd cradled her close. Held her. Touched her hair. His behavior, and hers, ought to disgust her. She waited for the wave of revulsion, then wondered why she couldn't feel anything except numbness and a vague sense of guilt.

"Frederick..." she started.

"The sheriff and the undertaker rolled him up in the rug to take him out." The cook explained this as a matter of fact. She couldn't know how much that would've horrified Frederick, a man who'd guarded his privacy and fretted constantly about being humiliated.

Remorse twisted the knife in Claire's heart. She should have seen to her husband instead of crawling into bed and falling into a drug-induced sleep. She wasn't a good wife. No wonder he had come to despise her.

Hot tears leaked from between her closed eyes. She used to cry all the time after Frederick had returned from the war with his mind broken. That was before she'd learned it did no good. Tears were useless.

She leaned forward and put her fists to her eyes to staunch the flow. Spoke in an agonized whisper. "I never meant to hurt him."

Mrs. Kelly patted her back. "Now, now. Of course, you didn't intend to shoot him. It just...happened."

Her meant-to-be soothing remark carried an unspoken *how* and *why*. Those were questions Claire dared not answer. Not until she came up with a plausible story.

She cringed when she thought about the days ahead. A funeral had to be planned. She would be put on trial. By now everyone in town would be talking and her name would be on their lips. She would rather have her teeth pulled than become the center of attention. Lord above, how would she get through this?

If she telegraphed her brother, Henry, he'd come straightaway. Just like he'd rescued her before when Frederick had lost his job and they were in dire straits. But Henry had a new position, a wife and a baby. It wouldn't be right to burden him with this awful tragedy. He'd already done far more than he should have, and he'd dealt with enough trouble over the past year. No, she wouldn't ask Henry to save her. Somehow, she would overcome fear and grief long enough to take care of things. If not for her sake, for Billy's.

Claire straightened with renewed determination. She used a napkin to wipe her eyes. "Thank you, Mrs. Kelly. I do appreciate your kindness, but I have no appetite. I must get dressed before the sheriff returns. Will you see if Billy wants breakfast?"

With that, she sent the cook away with the tray of food.

The cedar chest in the bedroom contained one black gown, which she'd reserved for funerals. She'd need to purchase another black dress, along with a black hat and veil to take her through the six-month mourning period. Fortunately, the items could be ordered, readymade. If unavailable, she could dye several of her dresses. Given her dismal outlook, she might convert her entire wardrobe to black and be done with it.

She rubbed her arms to stop trembling, and stuffed her guilt deep down where it couldn't hamper her. It was easier to keep her mind from wandering if she focused on the arduous task of pinning up her knee-length hair.

What would be a plausible story? *An accident.* That's what she'd told the sheriff last night. What else had she offered?

A blank gaze in the mirror stared back at her. She couldn't remember what she'd said, other than telling him she couldn't find the gun. She would look for it again this morning. Billy might've taken it to his room.

She secured the heavy twist of hair within a black snood. Tucked a handkerchief beneath her sleeve and buckled a chatelaine around her waist that held her keys.

Now, before the sheriff returned, she and Billy needed to have a talk. If only she could've gotten to him to first. Taken the gun away. To wish things could be different wasted energy. Billy needed all the love and support she could give him. She needed his cooperation to get through the difficulties they'd face in the coming days.

An inquest would be held. Likely, a short one because she'd confessed. If the judge believed her story, and accepted the shooting was accidental, she didn't think she'd go to jail. It wouldn't keep people from gossiping for years to come. She could bear the shame. She'd borne worse.

She stopped at Billy's room and knocked. "Billy? May I come in?"

Maybe he'd gone downstairs to the kitchen for breakfast.

She tried the knob. The door swung open, and her heart lurched. Inside, the room remained dark. No one had pulled back the curtains. The bed covers were smooth and neat, which indicated he hadn't slept there. His hat and coat usually hung on a peg by the door. Both were gone.

She hurried down the back stairs, breathing a prayer. Please, Lord, let him be in the kitchen. He wouldn't run off, not after she'd promised to take care of everything.

Mrs. Kelly met her before she made it down the hall. "We haven't found him yet. Didn't want to worry you. I looked all over, in his usual hiding spots. One of the guests said the sheriff was asking folks if they'd seen him last night."

Claire's heart skipped a beat.

The sheriff.

Surely, he wouldn't have taken Billy to jail. Not unless he'd wrung the truth out of the boy before she had the chance to stop him.

CHAPTER 3

*A*s he exited his office, Frank's breath clouded the cold morning air. He turned up his coat collar and experienced another twinge of conscience. He'd been too busy last night to search for a little boy who had a history of disappearing when he didn't want to be found.

If Billy wasn't hiding somewhere in the Belmont House, he was smart enough to seek out a warm place to spend the night. Perhaps in a closet at the railroad boarding house or the storage area at the train depot.

Frank retrieved a pencil and dog-eared notebook from his inside coat pocket. If he wrote things down, he didn't have to trust his faulty memory. He noted a couple more places for his deputy to check.

The troublesome orphan had run away from every family he'd been placed with. Although it made no sense for him to up and leave a warm house on a cold night. Coincidentally, on the night when Frederick Daines was killed.

Billy must've witnessed the shooting. The boy distrusted anyone in authority, after having numerous run-ins with the law. Stealing, trespassing... At an age when most boys were still attending school, he'd been well on his way to a criminal life when Claire had stepped in. She was one of the few people who believed Billy could become a model citizen. Unlikely, but if anyone could turn him around, it would be the practical, dignified lady who ran the Belmont House.

For now, Billy wasn't the person Frank most worried about. Hopefully, Mrs. Daines would've recovered enough to answer questions and he could write off the shooting as an accident. An awful tragedy. One she would live with for the rest of her life, but wouldn't send her to prison. He couldn't erase her grief, but he could put the unfortunate incident to rest as quickly as possible.

He set a slow, deliberate pace on the short walk to the mercantile and rubbed at the dull throb between his eyes. If he didn't know better, he'd swear an angry mule had kicked him in the head.

The only ass around here is 'yours truly.'

Frank heaved a regretful sigh. He ran his hand through hair that had grown too long on a head that needed examining for signs of stupidity.

Last night made twice in the past four months he'd gone on a bender. The dark episodes that triggered his binges were getting more frequent, not less. If he progressed on a path set by most drunks, he'd soon be wallowing in the mud, ravaged in mind and body.

He dismissed the ugly thought. Right now, his immediate need was food. Once he'd filled his belly, he'd be ready to face a distasteful task. He'd much rather exchange pleasantries than interrogate the lovely widow.

Inside the store, a pot-bellied stove warmed the air. Had his head hurt less, he might've enjoyed the rich aromas created by an assortment of baked goods offered in the shebang. Beneath a glassed counter, a selection of golden-brown hand pies, artfully displayed on a platter. The savory scents sent his stomach rolling.

Frank swallowed hard. He didn't have time to baby his belly with a pot of coffee followed by a nourishing breakfast at the Whistle Stop Café. One of these meat pies would have to do.

Horace Bows, the mercantile owner, bid farewell to a customer and sauntered over. He smoothed his hands over crisply ironed apron, worn to protect his suit.

Bow's General Store, the largest in town, was situated on the main street, close to the depot. He and his wife kept it well stocked with everything anybody could want: dry goods and hardware, groceries, housewares, even beer and bottled liquor. He'd gotten rich because Claire's brother, Henry Stevens, had plopped a railroad out here in the middle of a prairie, then laid out a town around it. Horace had been one of the first businessmen to leap at opportunity.

As far as Frank was concerned, he owed Henry Stevens his undying gratitude for offering a broken-down marshal the job as sheriff. It had been a godsend that saved his sanity, and, for the time being, his life.

"What'll it be, Sheriff?"

Frank dragged his attention from the bottles of home brew on the shelf to the glassed display with the meat pies. He held up two fingers. "Two of your wife's sausage pies."

"She makes the best."

"That she does."

The bell on the door jangled.

Two women bundled in fur coats entered together. Minnie Taylor, a mousy little gal married to the new mayor, and Gertrude Bond, a statuesque lady with pale coloring and piercing blue eyes that could freeze a man at fifty paces.

Last summer, William Bond had taken over the position Henry had resigned as general manager for the Katy Railroad. The Bonds had moved from New York and appeared to have brought most of the clothing in the stores with them.

The two women stopped at a table stacked with bolts of calico cloth. Instead of examining the merchandise, they peered over the top, like curious prairie dogs peeking out of their mounds. When Frank caught them watching him, they dipped out of sight.

Those two must've heard about the shooting, spiced up with the extra parts about Claire going into the saloon and him carrying her out.

The women's schoolgirl antics annoyed him, though it was bound to happen. Juicy gossip passed through town faster than shit through a goose.

"Here you go, Sheriff." Mr. Bows passed the pies over the counter.

"Much obliged." Frank paid him two bits. Just last year, Bows had charged twice that much. With the economy sinking and the railroad in trouble, the merchant had adjusted his prices down. Everyone had been forced to make adjustments, with the exception of a few wealthy families like the Bonds.

Frank had taken a cut in salary so he could keep his deputy on the payroll. He figured he could afford it because he didn't have a family to support and didn't need much. For the moment, just a couple meat pies to stave off starvation.

He unfolded the paper and sank his teeth into the flaky crust. Tasty, and it went down better than he thought it would. He'd not press his luck. The second pie would stay in his pocket, for now. It would make a good lunch if he got too busy to stop at a cafe.

Walt and Dru—two regulars—had taken up their usual position over a checkerboard laid atop a hogshead barrel. This morning, the aging settlers huddled near the pot-bellied stove in the rear of the store. In nice weather, they preferred to sit out front where they could chat with folks passing by. Those two old codgers knew more about what went on in Parsons than anyone else, including the women.

Frank passed by a table stacked with bibbed dungarees, clothing favored by railroad workers, on his way to the back of the store. "Howdy, Walt. Dru…"

"Mornin' Sheriff." Dru hugged a worn Indian blanket around his thin shoulders. The trapper's Osage wife had died the previous winter and he'd taken to hauling that striped blanket around. If it kept him warm, it was more useful than most keepsakes.

"How d'ye do, Sheriff." Walt removed a clay pipe and cradled it in his hand. Smoke curled up around a long, grizzled beard. The fellow had to be sixty if he was a day.

Frank noted, with disgust, his own faded hair had about as much gray, and he was younger than Walt's sons. At least he wasn't bald like Dru.

"What do you know?" he asked casually.

"Reckon you could tell us, seeing as you toted Mrs. Daines back to the hotel in her nightgown after all that commotion last night." Walt's lips twitched.

Dru didn't crack a smile, but the creases around his eyes deepened.

"Don't spread that around," Frank said sharply.

The old fellows threw worried glances at each other. In their rheumy eyes, all amusement had vanished.

Frank adjusted his voice to a polite tone. "Either of you seen Billy Frye?"

The two men shook their heads.

"If you do, let me know."

They acknowledged the request with respectful nods. They'd think twice before they poked fun at a distressed woman who had enough grief to deal with.

No one else was in the store who Frank needed to talk to, so he headed for the door.

Gertrude Bond followed him outside. "Sheriff Garrity, might I have a word with you?"

The new general manager's wife rarely used *one* word. Generally, she spun off a dozen or more, most of them complaints about the local rowdies and how uncivilized Parsons remained in spite of him being in charge of law and order.

If he kept walking, he didn't think she'd trail after him across the street and dirty the hems of those fancy skirts. On second thought, he ought not be rude, even to a woman he couldn't find a single reason to like.

He halted before he stepped off the edge of the sidewalk to allow her to catch up with him. "Yes ma'am. How can I help you?"

He didn't have to look down very far to meet her eyes. She had to be close to six feet tall. The lady towered over other women, and most men, including her husband. Frank had nothing against tall women, but he favored petite gals, in particular one with magnificent chestnut hair.

"I thought you should know about the talk going around." Gertrude kept her voice low. She threw a cautious glance over her shoulder, as if she didn't want her friend, who'd just exited the store, to overhear.

Who did they think they were fooling? They'd whispering the entire time he'd been inside.

He didn't ask *what talk* because he wasn't interested in her gossip.

She kept on anyway. "Mrs. Daines killed her husband in a fit of rage. They yelled at each other and threw things. Everybody heard it."

Frank nudged his hat back, finding it hard keep his expression indifferent. "*You* heard them?"

"Of course not," she snapped. "I wasn't there. I heard about it from one of the guests."

He'd spoken to the guests after he'd gotten Claire settled. Some of them mentioned hearing noises before the gunshot. Nothing specific. Anybody familiar with Claire would know she wasn't the type to go into fits of rage or otherwise. She was one of the most levelheaded women he'd ever met.

Frank hooked his thumbs over his gun belt and adopted the lazy drawl that made everybody think he was friendly and easy going, although he was neither. "Thank you, ma'am, for telling me about the gossip. I appreciate you not wanting to see rumors like that spread around."

The beanpole biddy narrowed her eyes. "It's no rumor. She *admitted* she killed her husband."

Dang. He should've kept walking.

"We don't know the particulars about what happened. Mrs. Daines is in a fragile state, which is why I'd appreciate it if folks would refrain from speculation—"

"Sheriff!"

He jerked his head around, startled by Claire's hail.

The self-made widow, clothed from head-to-toe in solid black, came marching across the dirt street. She hiked her skirts to the tops of her boots and deftly navigated around a steaming pile of manure. Her frown conveyed displeasure and her rapid pace determination. She looked anything but fragile.

"Where's Billy?" she demanded upon reaching him.

That answered one question. The boy hadn't returned. However, it didn't answer why Claire would look at him like she wanted to strangle him.

Frank shook his head. "Haven't seen him."

Her angry glare softened into confusion. "But he isn't...if you didn't... Where is he?"

Still missing, which wasn't good news. "Figured you might know."

The high color drained from her face.

He stepped off the sidewalk into the street, moving close enough to catch her, should she faint dead away, as she had the night before. "Let me escort you to the hotel. It's warmer in there and we can talk." He didn't add, *without an audience.*

Mrs. Bond perched at the edge of the sidewalk. She'd soaked up every word. So had her friend, Minnie Taylor, and a half dozen other women who'd gathered to eavesdrop.

"I have to find Billy," Claire protested.

"We'll find him." Frank slipped his hand beneath her elbow and pivoted her around to head her back the way she'd come.

THE HOTEL LOBBY was busier than a month of Sundays. These people couldn't all be guests, which meant most of them were curiosity seekers. Morbid happenings always drew a crowd.

"Where can we go to have a private conversation?" Frank asked in low voice.

Claire shot a wary look in his direction.

"Unless you want to talk out here?" he added.

"The office." She set a course past the registration desk.

He followed, and kept the oglers away with a glare. He would've ordered them all to leave, except she hadn't given him license to clear out her place of business.

Her office was furnished with a roll-top desk, a bookcase and two chairs. Lacy curtains and a bright rug added feminine touches to an otherwise masculine room. It smelled of paper and ink, and a faint floral fragrance he'd noticed before whenever he got close to her.

Wild roses. Like the ones his mother had brought from Missouri when his father moved them over the border so he could help keep Kansas free. Would the trailing vines still be there, even though she wasn't alive to tend them? One way to find out, take a trip to the old farmstead.

Frank squelched his wistful longing. Going back would only remind him of how miserably he'd failed his family. He didn't need another regret to dwell on.

He closed the door so their conversation wouldn't be overheard. Last night, the new widow hadn't been thinking clearly. This morning, she seemed fairly well recovered, in light of the circumstances. She ought to be able to clear up inconsistencies in what she'd told him last night.

Her fragrance was distracting. He couldn't shut off his senses, but he could keep a businesslike attitude, and remove his hat. "I need to ask you a few questions."

"Yes, of course." Claire took his hat and heavy overcoat, hung them over a wall peg. Her cloak went on the next peg. She untied a ribbon at her chin and removed the ugly black bonnet.

Frank watched her fingers with utter fascination. She had what his mother would've called *artist's hands.* Slim, elegant, deft.

This morning, her hair had been tamed into a smooth roll and confined in a net. If he hadn't seen it loose, he never would've guessed its length and thickness. He imagined how it might feel if he brushed it out with his fingers.

Like silk.

His breath hitched. Then, annoyance set in. This obsession with her hair, and other parts of her, was unfitting, not to mention a damn nuisance. "Why did Billy run off?"

Her fearful glance stopped him. Towered over her with his fists balled, growling questions, would not be the most effective approach.

He released his frustration on a deep breath, then gestured to one of two chairs. "How about we sit down?"

"Yes, thank you." She eased onto the cushioned seat of an armless chair and arranged her skirts. Her back remained rigid—the result of good breeding or a bad case of nerves. One hand went to a broad belt at her waist from which hung a small bag and a set of keys. She toyed with them.

Nerves.

Any woman would be nervous at being questioned. More surprising, the fact that she'd gotten up and out. Ordinary grief would send most women to bed for weeks. She had Billy to consider. She was worried about the boy.

Frank took the armchair. He dug in his coat pocket for his notebook and pencil. If the boy didn't show up, he'd put out a description so others could help locate him. "How old is Billy?"

"He turned twelve the second of November."

Surprising. Frank wrote it down. "Small, for his age."

"I suppose. Having had no children of my own, I wouldn't know for certain." She darted a worried glance out the window that faced the alley. "He's very bright. He didn't know how to read very well when he first came here. By Christmas, he was devouring those dime novels Lucy sends him."

Impressive. Frank would bet it was Claire's doing as much as Billy's. "He was illiterate when you got him, wasn't he?"

"Not entirely. Billy hungers for knowledge. Same as you did at his age, I'm sure."

Frank smiled. She probably hadn't meant the remark to be flattery, but it was far from insulting, and further reinforced his good opinion of her. She looked for the good in others. "My mother would've agreed with you. She always said a curious mind should be encouraged."

The tightness in Claire's expression eased. "Your mother sounds very wise."

"She was." As well as wise, long-suffering, too good and kind for this world, so she'd moved on to the next. While he'd been out to exact revenge instead of remaining at home to take care of her.

Frank dragged his mind out of the unforgiving past, which he could do nothing about. The present was another matter. He had a violent death to resolve. Last night, he'd been close to certain it was an accident. Now, he wasn't so sure.

Still holding the pencil, he rested his hand on his knee. The widow's prickly behavior puzzled him. Granted, she had a good reason to be upset. Except, he got the distinct impression she had something to hide, which figured into Billy's disappearance.

He couldn't—rather, he wouldn't—intimidate her with harsh accusations. At this point, he had few facts to go on. He would have to probe and see where the questions led him.

As far as Frank knew, she ran the hotel with no help from her husband. It wouldn't seem she'd have time to deal with a troubled child. "How come you took Billy in last year?"

"Henry asked me. Several times, actually. He kept finding Billy at the rail yard and worried he'd get hurt. Henry was single at the time and busy with running the railroad. Well, I suppose you know that. Frederick didn't want children. I finally convinced him that Billy had nowhere else to go."

Odd, most men wished to continue their line. "Your husband refused you children or he couldn't give you any due to his injuries?"

She flushed crimson. "Why does that matter?"

It didn't. Unless the shooting wasn't an accident. In which case, she would have a motive for killing her husband. His refusal to give her children might've caused resentment on her part. From all appearances, Claire longed to be a mother. So much so, she'd taken in a wild, half-grown boy. To her credit, Billy had thrived under her wing. He'd gone from a surly hell-raiser to being her devoted admirer. Which begged the question.

"Why do you think he'd run off?"

She pulled a lacy handkerchief from beneath her black sleeve and held it in her lap. "He's scared, I suppose."

"Scared of what?"

Her eyes remained downcast as she twisted the black cloth around her fingers. "Of what he saw."

Now, they were getting somewhere.

Frank shifted to the edge of his seat. "He was in the room when your husband was shot?"

She jerked her head up, as if startled. "No! He wasn't in the room. He came in later, after he heard the gun go off. Then he saw Frederick lying there and he got upset. I was in shock. I-I told him to go to his room. He might think I'm angry with him."

Her maple-colored eyes shone with misery. But she'd twisted that hankie around her fingers so tight one might think she needed a tourniquet. Years of dealing with all manner of charlatans had taught Frank to spot liars. He'd never thought of Claire in that vein —before now.

The realization hit him like a punch to the gut, followed by the sinking sense that he'd lost something rare and precious. An ideal.

Of all the ladies in town, Claire was the one he most admired. In many ways she reminded him of his mother—a devoted wife, a compassionate neighbor, hospitable to all who darkened her door, brave in the face of adversity, hard-working, and honest.

Disappointment welled up, surprisingly bitter. He'd been foolish to place Claire on a pedestal, even if...no, *especially* because of his attraction to her. He'd been a lawman long enough to know that even fine, upstanding ladies would lie, given a motive.

What was Claire's motive? He was mighty tempted to call her bluff. In his experience, liars denied their falsehoods. If he challenged her, she'd clam up and not tell him anything. If he kept her talking, she'd eventually get tangled in the loose threads.

"Where did you get the gun?"

Her spine got a little straighter. "From the registration desk. I keep a pistol hidden there, just in case there's trouble. This can be a rough town. At times. Not so much since you're been here, but I'm not telling you anything you don't already know"

Rambling.

Frank stroked one side of his mustache. Last year, she'd showed him a small Remington she kept in the registration desk. Plenty of outlaws roamed the territory, enough to warrant having a weapon handy for protection. Still, it didn't explain why she felt the need to protect herself from her spouse. "You came downstairs to retrieve a pistol. Were you scared of your husband?"

"No." The muscles in her throat moved as she swallowed. *Another lie.* "I retrieved the pistol earlier and took it upstairs."

"Why?"

"To reload it. The gun went off accidentally."

This didn't fit with what she'd told him last night.

"You mean, it went off when your husband tried to take it away?"

"What?" Her confusion appeared authentic. Maybe she didn't recall what she'd said to him. Shock could do that. He gave her another chance to explain.

"You told me last night you shot him when he tried to take the gun away from you."

She rubbed her temple like she was thinking hard or her head hurt. "Oh, yes. That's right. I must've blocked it out. He wanted me to give him the gun, said he should load it. I told him I didn't think that was a good idea."

This had to be stupidest excuse she'd come up with yet.

"He was a soldier, right? He knew how to load a gun."

Irritation interrupted her grief long enough to show him she didn't appreciate his sarcasm. "Of course, he did. But I didn't leave guns around because..." Her eyes widened as if she'd started down a path unintentionally. "Sometimes he's clumsy."

"You're changing your story, then? Saying he got clumsy, not you."

Her face reddened. "No, that's not what I said at all. While I reloaded, he grabbed the pistol, and it discharged."

"Was that before or after the fire?"

"Fire? I don't remember." She moistened her lips, fidgeted some more with the chain holding her keys. At least she wasn't comfortable with lying, or even very good at it.

His protective streak made an unexpected—and unwanted—

reappearance. Frank balled his fist on his knee and took a firm hold on his bleeding heart. He hadn't been able to keep his wife safe. What made him think he could shelter a dishonest widow who didn't trust him?

One more chance. But she had to come clean.

"Your curtains were scorched. I saw a candle and some water on the floor by the window."

"The candle..." Her attention fixed on the desk behind him. She'd long since stopped looking him in the eye. "It got knocked over, accidentally, while I was looking on the desk for something."

"What?"

"Nothing. Just some papers."

Holy hell, she'd try the patience of a saint—and he didn't qualify.

Frank unfolded himself out of the small chair and adjusted his gun belt. This nonsense had gone on long enough. "If you've finished airing your lungs, why don't we get down to business. You tell me what *really* happened."

CHAPTER 4

*H*overed over her, the sheriff resembled a hawk perched on a fence post, waiting for a mouse in the grass to make its move.

Claire's skin grew damp beneath the widow's weeds. She shivered. Her heart drummed in her chest. The dratted lawman had intentionally tripped her up. To what end, she wasn't sure. Unless he thought she shot Frederick on purpose. Nothing she'd told him would give him any reason to assume she would intentionally pull the trigger.

She adjusted the shawl around her neck in case the high lace collar didn't hide her reddened skin and the bruises from her husband's fingers. Her controlled distress seemed to annoy the tenacious sheriff, if the hard set of his jaw was any indication. Perhaps he thought she didn't act properly mournful because she hadn't wailed her grief for all to see.

He'd have no more patience with a frightened child. Although that wasn't the only reason she couldn't tell him what *really happened*.

Billy had been betrayed so many times by so many people, it was no wonder he didn't expect her to honor her word to protect him. She would, though. And when she did, he would know he could safely return.

With renewed determination, she lifted her chin. "I've told you what happened. It was an *accident*."

He narrowed his eyes, rubbed his forehead. It might indicate he didn't believe her. Or maybe his head hurt. He'd been very drunk last night.

Not for the first time, she wondered what to make of the tall, rugged lawman. From all reports, he rarely swore, didn't smoke, gamble, or visit the dance halls and bawdy houses on the outskirts of the railroad town. His only vice appeared to be his fondness for distilled spirits. Even inebriated, he'd behaved like a gentleman.

Whenever she happened to see him—not as often as she would've liked—he greeted her cordially, yet maintained a proper distance. For the better part of the past three years, she'd fought an unfitting attraction to him. Secretly, she'd been glad he showed little interest in the single women who pursued him, although she understood he'd been married at one time.

Not that she ought to care about his marital state.

She did wonder about his age. Hard years were etched on his face. His sandy hair was streaked with gray, not to mention unkempt. It had grown so long it brushed his shoulders. His craggy features she found compelling, if not what one might call handsome. However, it was hard to tell what he really looked like beneath the bushy mustache and ever-present bristle. She suspected if he cleaned up and got rid of that extra hair, he'd be attractive.

She shouldn't care about his appearance, either.

He tucked his thumbs into his gun belt in what could be considered a threatening posture, except his scowl had softened. "Mrs. Daines, I understood you the first time when you said your husband's death was an accident. But you aren't telling me everything. And don't insult my intelligence by repeating nonsense. You wouldn't load a gun while your place burned to the ground."

She stiffened at the snide remark. "The hotel wasn't burning down. Only the draperies were singed. A vase of water put the flames out. We're not talking about a bonfire."

Her insides quavered. The fire could've been a disaster had Billy not arrived when he did. While she fought to escape her maddened husband's chokehold, the quick-thinking boy had removed flowers from a vase and dashed water on the curtains. That was before he'd threatened Frederick with her revolver. Whether he had it in his hand when he showed up, she couldn't recall. But how else would he have gotten it? She must've left the drawer downstairs unlocked and he'd found it. Another twist of guilt doubled her over.

Maybe the sheriff would leave if he saw she didn't feel well.

His scuffed, mud-caked boots remained planted in front of her. "When you're recovered, accompany me upstairs."

"Why? You went through the room last night. Mrs. Kelly told me you removed the rug, along with...with my husband's body."

"That's true, but I need you to walk me through what happened. Show me where you were when you shot him."

A sick feeling swept through Claire. Additional details? More ornamentation wouldn't improve her story any more than dressing up a pig would make it more attractive. "I've told you what happened. There's nothing more I can add."

The sheriff's features hardened. This cold-eyed stranger couldn't be the same man who'd carried her home last night and tenderly tucked her into bed.

Her gaze slid down to his large hands. Long, blunt-tipped fingers were splayed across his narrow hips while his thumbs remained tucked in his gun belt.

She'd touched those scarred knuckles, felt the callouses on his palms. Hands that rough couldn't be as gentle as she recalled. A shiver passed through her, only she wasn't cold. Her face burned like she was bent over a hot stove.

At last, he moved away. He retrieved his hat from the rack and secured it on his head, smoothing his fingers over the wide brim. Thank goodness. He'd decided to leave.

She breathed easier. "Are we done?"

"No, *ma'am*, we are not done." His drawl became more pronounced when he was annoyed. He shrugged into his worn leather coat. "I'll be back. After I find Billy."

Dear Lord. No. She couldn't let him find Billy before she did. If the boy broke his silence, all her efforts to shield him would be for naught.

She jerked to her feet. "Wait! Don't leave yet."

The sheriff reached for the knob. Hadn't he heard her? Desperate, she lunged for his coat sleeve. He turned his head, slowly. "Is there some reason I should stay?"

If there was a reason, she forgot it completely. His eyes appeared gray from a distance. Upon closer inspection, she could see they were actually pale green shot through with striations of dark blue, like spokes in a wheel. Unusual, and quite beautiful.

One of his sandy eyebrows arched upward in a silent question.

Claire snapped out of the odd spell. Her breath returned in an audible gasp. Shocked at her forward behavior, she backed away so fast she stumbled.

Fast as lightning, he caught her upper arms.

His aggressive move ignited an instinctive response. She shrank away. "Please. Don't hurt me."

He blinked as if she'd stunned him an instant before his harsh features softened into pure astonishment. "What makes you think I'd hurt you?"

"You grabbed me."

"To keep you from tripping over your own feet." He still held onto her arms with a firm, yet gentle, grip.

Her face got hot enough to melt butter. She covered her embarrassment with a sharp retort. "You might've said so."

"Didn't think it was necessary." His eyes narrowed.

She suddenly realized why she hadn't noticed the color before. He squinted. A lot. When he stood outside, when he was thinking. Maybe, like her, he had trouble seeing things up close and forgot to wear his spectacles.

"Did your husband beat you?" The sheriff's unexpected inquiry set off a memory that flashed through her mind.

Frederick had come into the bedroom the previous night to tell her he'd sold the hotel—without consulting her. She'd thrown down her brush in a rare show of temper. Told him he had no right. His powerful backhand had knocked her off the chair.

"I have every right. Or have you forgotten who I am?"

Never would she forget the thoughtful, generous man who'd rescued her from a lonely existence. He wouldn't have lifted a hand to her. But that man had died on a battlefield. Someone who looked like him had returned in his place. A melancholy, brooding stranger prone to destructive, sometimes violent, fits of rage fed by a tortured mind.

"B-beat me? Of course not," she sputtered. "Frederick d-didn't..." She couldn't form the lie. He'd struck her, more than once, only when he wasn't himself. "He wasn't a cruel man."

Thankfully, the sheriff released her. Then he astonished her when he reached up to frame her face with his thumb and forefinger. His regard turned decidedly warmer.

His reaction confounded her, and sent quivers dancing across her skin and cavorting through her insides. Her lips tingled in anticipation. If she didn't know better, she'd swear he was about to kiss her. To her utter mortification, she couldn't make her feet move to back away.

"You don't have to protect him any longer." His low baritone vibrated with reassurance.

Perhaps that was true. Except, she'd been protecting her husband for so long she couldn't imagine doing otherwise. "He wasn't to blame for what happened."

"Are you saying *you* are?" He dropped his hand, which released the invisible bonds that held her in place.

Claire took a step back, stricken with guilt. "That's what I've been saying all along. *I'm* responsible for what happened."

Her affirmation was met with a flat stare. "You believe you deserve to be beaten?"

"Good heavens, no. You mistook my meaning."

"Then say what you mean. Did you shoot him to protect yourself?"

Claire trembled at the stark accusation, which was closer to the truth than the story she'd spun. Except, she wasn't one of those pathetic women who allowed men to abuse her. Most of the time, she could calm her husband during his outbursts. If he did strike out, it was because he didn't know her. However, if she confessed what the sheriff suggested, she didn't doubt he would believe her. He appeared remarkably sympathetic—for a man.

Such a confession wouldn't help. She'd told no one before about her husband's periodic attacks. No jury would absolve a woman for killing her husband just because he raised his hand to her. Most men would believe he was within his rights. If she declared she shot Frederick intentionally, it could lead to longer jail time. Or worse, to the gallows.

The sheriff buttoned his overcoat. She couldn't let him leave before she persuaded him not to search for Billy. God forbid the lawman should find the boy before she did.

She held out her arms in a plea. "Why can't you believe Frederick's death was an unfortunate accident?"

"Maybe I would. If you hadn't lied."

CHAPTER 5

*F*rank strode out of the hotel, fuming. Claire must take him for an idiot if she thought he would swallow that absurd story she'd cooked up. The gun hadn't discharged accidentally. She'd pulled the trigger. He could guess why, after seeing her shrink away, afraid he might wallop her. Although she denied it, the abuse must've been going on for some time for her to snap like that.

Fear also kept her from giving him straight answers. He'd get some if his deputy had flushed out the boy. He angled across the street, barely missed being struck by a buckboard. As it brushed by him, the driver yelled. "Are you blind?"

Frank bit back an obscene reply. He couldn't swear at the farmer for being careless, not when he was the one not paying attention. His mind had been filled with the image of Claire, cringing away from him.

Blast it. He should've noticed her suffering, done something about it. Generally, he picked up on things like that. Abused women were fearful, scared of their own shadows. They hid bruises beneath wide-brimmed bonnets and long sleeves. He hadn't seen any marks on

Claire, and she held her head up. At least, she did whenever he saw her, which he had to admit wasn't often.

His conscience applied another lash. Too much work wasn't the real reason he'd avoided her. Call it lack of moral fortitude or just plain cowardice, he'd kept his distance because he couldn't shake this infernal attraction for a married woman. Not even now, when he suspected she might've purposely killed her husband.

A moment ago, he had nearly kissed her.

If he didn't watch out, he'd let his hankering for her get in the way of doing his job. Just like he'd once let pride blind him to danger. He'd paid too great a price before.

"Mr. Garrity!" The call came from a man bundled in a black overcoat and beaver hat. Elias "Sharp" Taylor, the new mayor. He met Frank as they reached the opposite sidewalk at the same time. "Good morning, Sheriff."

Frank tugged the brim of his hat. He hid his troubled thoughts behind a polite expression. "Morning, Mayor."

Sharp beamed at the moniker. Apparently, he liked his new title better than his nickname, which had been pinned on him during the war when he was quartermaster. He had a reputation for being, well, *sharp* in his dealings.

Taylor had his eye on a seat in the state senate and had hopped aboard the coattails of the railroad's current general manager, figuring Bond would help him get there. Frank didn't trust the new mayor, but he had to show him respect, given his position.

The mayor stroked a luxurious beard. Some grew hair on their face for warmth, others because they didn't care to shave. Sharp thought it made him look more dignified. "You on the way to your office?"

"Not for long."

"That's fine, I'll walk with you and we can talk on the way." Taylor fell into step beside him. His eyes gleamed with avid interest. "What did you find out from Mrs. Daines? Did she tell you why she shot her husband?"

It made sense the mayor would want to know the outcome. Only, he seemed less concerned about Claire's misfortune.

"You know I can't tell you anything about a case under investigation."

"She admitted she shot him."

"Did you hear her say that?"

"No, but Mr. Bond did. He said she announced it in the saloon in front of you. In her unmentionables."

Was it against the law to sew people's lips together?

"She didn't announce anything. When she came to find me, she wasn't thinking clearly. I don't think she had any idea what she said." Frank lengthened his stride, intending to leave the shorter man behind.

The mayor doggedly kept up. "Is that what she claimed? She went crazy?"

Frank jerked to a halt. "That's *not* what I said."

Sharp leaned in with a sly smile. "I heard she caught him with another woman."

The crude insinuation sent Frank's anger soaring. "Since when did our mayor turn into a gossipy old lady?"

Taylor drew back with a surprised expression that quickly turned offended. "I heard you were rude to the ladies this morning, as well. You ought to arrest that brazen woman for murder instead of throwing stones at respectable citizens."

Respectable citizens? More like dim-witted sheep.

Frank pulled in his horns before he gave the town more grist for their gossip mill. "I've found no cause to believe she murdered him. If anything, he..."

"He what?" If Sharp was a dog, his ears would've pricked up.

Now Frank wished he'd sewed his own lips shut. "Nothing. I can't talk about the case. She'll appear before the judge. He can decide if there's enough evidence for an indictment."

"But you will arrest her?"

These folks were worse than coyotes scenting a carcass.

"For Pete's sake, Sharp. The poor woman just lost her husband. Don't you think we can let her bury him before we lock her up?"

Taylor had the grace to look chagrined. "Of course. That would be the Christian thing to do. And don't get me wrong, I have nothing against Mrs. Daines."

"Why would you?" Frank couldn't imagine why the mayor would have an ax to grind. How could anybody dislike Claire? She was generous and kind to everyone. Up until yesterday, she had been one of those *respectable citizens* he'd mentioned.

Frank took his leave of the mayor to seek refuge in his office. He'd hardly gotten inside when his deputy arrived.

"Good mornin' Sheriff." Gideon issued the greeting without a smile. Then again, he rarely smiled, not even when he was in a cheerful mood.

"Morning. Nothing good about it. Yet. Did you find Billy?"

"No, sir." Gideon removed the cream-colored, wide-brimmed Stetson. A gift from a grateful friend. It pleased Frank that he wore it with pride. "The porter said he didn't show up at the depot to help out like usual. Checked the rail yard. Nobody there seen him either."

"Or they aren't saying. They might think they're doing him a favor by hiding him."

"Possible. You might get more if you was to go out there." Gideon hadn't admitted he'd done a poor job. He'd simply acknowledged the fact that some folks didn't cooperate with a colored man just because he wore a badge.

Frank didn't give a damn what they thought about Gideon's skin color. He'd picked the man because he was the best one for the job. The soft-spoken former slave had been at the front of the line to sign up with the First Kansas Colored Infantry, which had been formed by Frank's commander, General Lane. Frank had seen how fiercely those men fought. He'd vouched for them when his jealous peers wrongly accused them of cowardice. He and Gideon had become fast friends. Gideon had helped him track down the scoundrels who'd killed his wife.

Past aside, the deputy had more than proven his worth by keeping thugs off the streets and rousting outlaws and rustlers. He knew how to handle those twin Colts, but he wasn't a hothead. The town was fortunate to have a man like him around.

"I doubt those railroaders will tell me anything more than they told you," Frank said, wearily.

Railroad men were a tight-knit lot. Protective of anyone in their circle. Billy had joined the fraternity at a young age when he'd started hanging around them. "I'll have a talk with the yard manager. You check to see what trains left this morning. Find out who was on them. Somebody's seen that kid. He didn't just disappear."

Gideon gave a nod and vamoosed. Another reason to like him. He didn't waste words.

After his deputy left, Frank sank into his chair with a tired sigh. He rubbed his hand over the back of his neck where the muscles had tightened into knots.

For the most part, the people of Parsons were good, decent folks. They provided him with a fair salary and a roof over his head. In turn, he kept the peace and made sure justice was served. The arrangement suited him. Most days, he liked his job. This didn't happen to be one of them.

Part of the problem could be him. He'd lost the proper perspective, had let the case become too personal. He pulled out the top desk drawer and withdrew a photograph taken the day he'd married Sarah Jane Mitchell in the parlor of her parent's home.

He touched his thumb to her image in a brief caress that caused his chest to tighten. Sarah had been too good for him. She'd loved him far better than he was able to love her. The day they married, he'd sworn to protect her, with his body, if necessary. Then he'd failed to live up to his promise. Anytime he got to thinking he might want to make another promise like that, he took out this photograph and disabused himself of the notion.

The memento went back into the drawer.

He couldn't promise Claire anything, much less protection. At best, he'd gather enough evidence to convince a judge not to bring her up on charges of murder. However, he couldn't let attraction, or even affection, prevent him from fulfilling his duty. When he'd taken this job, he'd sworn to uphold the law. That was all he could afford to care about.

CHAPTER 6

*B*y the afternoon, Claire ceased waiting for Billy to return and went out to the rail yard to look for him.

A train's whistle split the air, followed by the hiss of steam. As she drew closer to the switchyard, the cacophony grew louder. Several locomotives puffed and roared like great iron beasts. Boxcars and freight cars rumbled and clanked as they rolled along parallel railroad tracks.

One train chugged northeast in the direction of Sedalia, likely on its way to Chicago. Another left the yard in the opposite direction toward Indian Territory, and beyond that, Texas.

Her instincts told her Billy was hidden somewhere in this tangle of tracks and railroad buildings. He loved this place more than any spot on earth. He went on and on about how he would one day work various jobs on his way to becoming an engineer, or a *hogger,* as he called them.

A sharp breeze snatched at her hood. She drew the warm lining closer to her face. Then made a core with her mittened hands and blew into it.

The sun had attempted to warm the air, but the wind wasn't cooperating. Cold weather would prevail through March, if the old farmers were right. She prayed Billy had curled up inside a warm building last night and not in one of the deserted rail cars.

She held her skirts higher than usual to step across multiple sets of tracks, as she worked her way to the far side of the switchyard where the roundhouse was located. Billy loved being around the steam locomotives. He spoke of them as if they were living creatures. Indeed, with their noses poked out of the arched openings, they looked like horses eager to start a race.

Machine shops, tool sheds, and a foundry with a tall brick chimney flanked the massive roundhouse. Henry had overseen the construction of the vast rail yard, including the splendid roundhouse. She was proud of her brother for climbing out of poverty to reach success with the railroad, and even prouder of the choices he'd made more recently.

For years, his sole ambition had been to build a railroad empire and rule it. Being the most determined soul on earth, he'd triumphed over every obstacle in his path to success. He would've stayed and fought a scandal had he not done a dramatic about-face when he found another, better dream. He'd married his true love, and had left to start a new life with her. He and Lucy had a baby daughter. His letters were filled with plans and hopes for their future.

Claire blinked at the bite of tears behind her eyelids. Her dreams had died long ago. With Frederick's death, so had her purpose. Drowning in self-pity wouldn't help him or anyone. She couldn't fix her mistakes, but she could give Billy a better life, which would provide her with a new purpose. As long as managed to protect Billy and stay out of jail

She halted to allow a steam engine to pass on the tracks in front of her. The locomotive, painted cardinal red with yellow trim, puffed black clouds as it passed, pulling behind it a string of boxcars that looked to be mostly empty.

Until the financial crisis had gotten a chokehold on the economy, the Katy couldn't buy enough cars to contain all the wheat, corn, coal and cattle that moved along its tracks. Despite the hardships, hopeful immigrants continued to arrive in Kansas. Their dogged faith in making a better life for themselves had saved her hotel.

A switchman in greasy bibbed denims jogged alongside the slow-moving train. He waved with a hand minus two middle fingers. The loss of digits, even limbs, was a risk attendant to the job. She'd heard Henry talk about the perilous task of "coupling" cars. It had given her the shivers. As did his descriptions of brakemen on the run atop trains to get to the wheels they had to crank to bring the heavy cars to a stop. And the engineers who fought to keep locomotives from careening off the rails when those brakes snapped.

Just about any job with the railroad was fraught with peril. Yet, no other career held the same appeal to an adventurous boy like Billy. He idolized the workers and would do anything to become one of them. Sweep floors. Run messages. Wipe down grimy engines. He'd even started learning the telegraph so he could fill in for the operator. Because it seemed a safer option than others, Claire hadn't objected. Henry had started out much the same way.

"Howdy, Miz Daines." The switchman used his remaining thumb and forefinger to tug the short brim of his cap in a respectful greeting.

"Good afternoon, Mr. Foster." To the rest of the men, he was *Fingers*. Out of respect, she didn't call them by their nicknames.

He gave her a lazy smile, but his clear blue eyes snapped with quick intelligence. "What brings you out here on a cold day like this?"

As if he didn't know.

"I need to find Billy. He ran off last night. I thought he might've come here."

The switchman rubbed his hand over his chin, appearing to think about her request. He didn't fool her. He knew something. Whether he would tell was another matter altogether. The railroad workers looked out for Billy. While she didn't always agree with their methods, she couldn't fault their good intentions.

"He's not in trouble from me, I can assure you. I'm only interested in his wellbeing. I'd protect him with my life."

"Aye, I know how you feel, ma'am. Got a couple rascals of my own at home." The wariness in the switchman's eyes softened. "Mr. Tobias caught Billy curled up in an empty box. He ran off afore we could catch him."

Claire's heart lurched. Her child had spent the night in a cold, dirty railcar? God knows where he'd gone from there. "You let him get away?"

"Not me." The switchman laid his damaged hand over his heart. "Talk to Pat Tobias."

"I will," she said firmly. "If you see Mr. Tobias, tell him I won't rest until I find Billy—"

"Uh oh." The switchman nodded in a direction over her left shoulder. "You got company."

She twisted, saw the sheriff fast approaching.

Turkey feathers. He must've followed her.

"I'll be sure to tell Paddy what you said." The switchman spun on his heel. In a smooth motion, he grasped the rail of the last car as it passed and hopped aboard. As smoke billowed over the caboose, the scamp smiled and waved his three fingers at her.

Too bad she couldn't make such an easy escape.

Sheriff Garrity's long legs ate up the tracks between them. She wasn't a tall woman by any stretch of the imagination, but he made her feel positively tiny. He and her brother were of a similar height, but the sheriff's lankiness disguised his powerful build. She found herself too often thinking about what he might look like unclothed.

He held on to the brim of his black hat. The wind would've snatched it away otherwise. He'd wisely buttoned up his overcoat, wore a scarf and leather gloves.

A worrisome thought flashed through her mind. Had Billy remembered to take the new scarf and gloves she'd given him for Christmas? The poor child had arrived with nothing but the ragged clothes on his back. By scrimping, she'd been able to purchase him a warmer wardrobe without Frederick noticing the missing funds.

She hugged her cloak tighter, tapped her booted foot against the gravel while she waited for the sheriff. Running would provide the added advantage of keeping her blood flowing, but she couldn't get away in these skirts. He'd eventually catch up with her.

Better to meet a problem head on, as her brother was fond of saying.

"Thought you might come out here. Find out anything?" The sheriff didn't bother with idle chitchat, which actually relieved her from coming up with any.

"No, Sheriff, I have not. What have you discovered?"

The creases beside his eyes deepened. Accusation. Annoyance. His emotions were difficult to decipher when he wore the same face all the time. "The men out here told my deputy they haven't seen the boy around for a couple days."

Claire tucked her cold hands inside her cloak and surveyed the busy switchyard, as she contemplated whether to share what Mr. Foster had told her. She liked Frank Garrity. Actually, more than liked him. Besides finding him attractive, she admired his quiet strength and considerable intelligence, which most people missed because he put on a lazy act.

The taciturn sheriff had a reputation for being tough and unbending when it came to the law. That toughness might not extend to children, but why risk finding out? If she could get rid of him, she could come back later and talk to Mr. Tobias. Find out what he knew. Best case, she'd gain his assistance to locate Billy. "I have no idea where he might be. If you've already checked, I suppose there's no reason for you to stay out in the cold."

THE SPUNKY WIDOW delivered her dismissal, then started back across the switchyard in the opposite direction from where she'd been headed.

Frank trailed her. The gravel between the ties crunched beneath his boots. He was sorely tempted to kick the stones, if not pick up a handful and throw them. She must think he had rocks for brains. She wasn't about to give up her search. Not the woman who'd kept after an illiterate boy until he'd learned to read.

"Headed back to the hotel?" he called out.

She tossed the answer over her shoulder. "It's customary for grieving widows to remain confined at home and go out only when necessary."

"That didn't stop you from your errands earlier."

He knew because he'd followed her. After she conferred with the undertaker, the rest of her morning had been spent searching the depot and visiting the railroad boarding house.

When she reached a set of tracks, she hiked up her hems to gingerly step over the rail in between two ties. He lengthened his strides to catch up. What had she been thinking to come out here in that get-up?

He offered her his arm.

She eyed him warily.

For Pete's sake, he was being a gentleman. He hadn't been a gentleman earlier when he'd cupped her face in his hand. Had she noticed he'd come within a hair's breadth of kissing her? No wonder she didn't want him close.

That was just too bad. He planned to stick closer than a flea on a pup until he discovered what she was hiding.

"You aren't exactly dressed for roaming around a rail yard." He kept his arm extended.

Finally, she slipped her hand around his forearm. Proper behavior. Except for his response to it.

Her shiver passed through his arm. He darted a surprised glance in her direction. Her pinched expression didn't convey anything more than discomfort.

She'd never given him any indication that she shared this awkward attraction. She must be cold. The rail yard was built on a high plateau where nothing blocked the ceaseless wind—and this one had teeth.

He laid his hand, encased in heavy leather, over her smaller one, covered in a thin mitten. Her hand trembled. He could swear he wouldn't hurt her, or Billy, for that matter. She would only believe him if he demonstrated more restraint.

He squeezed her hand gently to reassure her, and reminded

himself to be patient. She hadn't answered straight when he'd asked why the boy had run. He would try a different approach. Engage her in sympathetic conversation.

"Billy hasn't made it easy for you, has he?"

She flashed him a questioning frown then looked straight ahead. "I didn't expect him to be easy. Not after he was cast aside and treated as though he's worthless."

Another thing Frank had come to appreciate about Claire. Her empathy and kindness went more than skin-deep. "You've got a big heart."

"No bigger than yours."

"If it's bigger than a walnut, it's bigger than mine."

Her lips slid into a hesitant smile. She thought he was joking.

"I understand what Billy's been through," she said softly. "Both my parents were dead by the time I was six. Henry—he was fourteen at the time—had to go to work to support my two older sisters and me. Of course, he couldn't provide us with a home. We were split up and passed around to different relations. Most of them viewed me as a nuisance."

She delivered the revelation in a factual tone.

It had the impact of an artillery shell.

He hadn't known she was orphaned, and at so young an age. She'd lost her family, her security, had been sloughed off on people who didn't care about her. God, it tore him up just thinking about it. The circumstances he'd lived through were different, no more or no less painful. His response, however, hadn't been to take in a troubled youth.

The depth of her compassion stirred feelings he'd buried—and intended to *keep* buried. He could admire her without an emotional entanglement.

She took hold of her fluttering cloak and huddled against his side. He drew her closer to keep her warm. Now that she'd opened up, she might begin to trust him enough to tell him the truth. "What about your husband? You said he didn't want children."

"Frederick agreed to let me take Billy. As long as he behaved."

"Billy and your husband didn't get along?"

"I wouldn't say they didn't get along. Billy stayed away from Frederick."

"He was afraid of him?"

"No, the two of them rarely saw each other." She pulled the hood closer to her face, hiding whatever her expression might reveal.

"Was there a reason for that?"

"Not one that matters anymore. Frederick didn't like having children around. They made him nervous. He tolerated Billy for my sake."

As she stepped over a rail, she stumbled.

Frank caught her. He curled his hand around her small waist. After steadying her, he released his hold, though he was sorely tempted to run his hands over her hips. That kind of behavior would earn him a slap, not her trust. Once again, he offered her his arm. If she knew the kind of willpower it took, she'd appreciate his restraint.

As they reached the edge of the switchyard, he returned his attention to the nagging questions. The uneasy relationship between her husband and foster son might have something to do with events leading up to the shooting. "Did anything happen between Billy and Mr. Daines?"

She withdrew her hand from beneath his and stepped away. "What are you suggesting?"

"Suggesting? Nothing. I'm asking. Was there an altercation? An argument? Some sort of misunderstanding that resulted in somebody getting a gun?"

"How many times do I need to tell you? Billy had nothing to do with it. You can choose to believe me or not, but I have no more to say on the matter."

"Take it easy, Claire, I'm haven't faulted you or Billy. That doesn't mean I'll turn a blind eye to the truth, which you haven't seen fit to share."

"Thank you for your kind assistance, Sheriff. I'll take my leave of you." She put him in his place, then whirled away and started down a narrow road.

The uneven path could be treacherous, the weather just as wicked.

Frank caught up with her. "Where's your buggy?"

She kept her eyes forward. "Why would I waste money to rent a buggy?"

"Because it's a long walk back to town. You aren't dressed for being out in the weather." To prove his point, he grasped her wrist and held up a hand covered in a flimsy knitted mitten. "These aren't warm enough. You ought to be wearing fleece-lined leather."

She wrenched her hand out of his grasp. "I am not ignorant of how to dress for the weather. My leather gloves wore out. These will do until I can replace them."

As she marched off, Frank shook his head in confusion. She didn't have enough money to buy gloves? He had no idea the hotel wasn't doing well. It was always full.

He made a quick decision. Jogged over to the foundry where he'd hitched his horse. He wouldn't let her walk two miles back to town in this cold, windy weather.

Claire scurried to the far side of the road as he approached on horseback. He rode ahead a few feet, stopped and dismounted, then led the horse over to where she stood.

She backed away. Had she forgotten that a couple minutes ago she'd been huddled up next to him?

"Come over here. I'll help you up. You can ride back with me."

"I am not riding with you. That would be improper."

Offering assistance was the most proper thing he'd done. Rather than argue, he draped the reins over the horse's neck. "You ride. I'll walk."

His bay gelding turned its head. Ulysses' dark limpid eyes reproached.

"He's telling you to make up your mind."

"I already told you, I'm not riding. Why would you think I could sit a saddle in a dress?"

"Some women do."

"Not wearing a bustle."

After making her somewhat valid point, she started off down the hill.

Frank strode up beside her with Ulysses dutifully ambling behind.

She jerked around, then executed a little hop away from him. "What are you doing?"

"What does it look like? I'm walking with you."

"Why?"

He released a weary sigh. He ought to mount up and vamoose, catch up with her later. Except, he didn't much like the idea of leaving her alone to walk all the way back to town. Parsons had gotten fairly civilized, but no place was free of scoundrels.

"Mrs. Daines..." He wouldn't call her Claire. Not after she'd made it clear she didn't appreciate his too-familiar use of her name. "There are men you ought to fear. I'm not one of them."

She responded with a look of surprise. "I don't fear you, Sheriff."

"That so? Then why do you keep skittering away?"

She tossed a wary look over her shoulder. "Does your horse bite?"

"Ulysses?" Frank couldn't hold back a dry laugh. "He might take a bite if he mistakes you for an apple."

Claire's frown told him she didn't find his joke funny.

"You're afraid of my horse?"

"He's very large."

By gum, it hadn't entered his mind she would be scared of horses. Being around them was second nature to anyone who'd grown up on a farm. If she'd lived in cities all her life and wasn't used to the large animals, he could understand why she might be intimated. "You walk here on this side. I'll keep the horse away from you."

She heaved a sigh and gave in. He felt like he'd won at Keno.

Now that he thought about it, he only recalled seeing Claire on foot. It wasn't usual for townspeople to walk everywhere. Parsons wasn't that big. But she might choose to walk because of her fear of horses. In the army, he'd run across a few men who'd feared the big animals. He knew how to help her get past her fear enough to gain more freedom. "Have you ever driven a buggy?"

"Of *course,* I've driven a buggy. I don't like riding horses, but I'm not helpless."

"You're about as helpless as a porcupine with a litter."

"Did you just call me prickly?"

Having been a soldier, he'd learned the importance of knowing when to retreat. "No ma'am, that was a compliment. On your protective nature."

"If that's your idea of a compliment, I can only imagine what you consider an insult."

"Probably best you don't."

After a long walk, they plodded into town. His horse couldn't accompany them down the sidewalk and she'd sealed her lips for the time being. He halted at the intersection and touched the brim of his hat. "I'll leave you here."

She acknowledged his departure with a nod. "Thank you for the escort."

Well, well. She sounded grateful and didn't appear quite so tense. He might be making progress.

"My pleasure." Frank meant it. He enjoyed every minute spent in her company, even when she was being stubborn and wouldn't give him straight answers. She'd come around. He had to be patient, continue to exercise restraint, and above all, remain objective.

Eventually, he'd get to the truth. He always did.

CHAPTER 7

The next morning, Claire was no closer to finding Billy than she had been the evening before. Pat Tobias, the engineer who'd seen him last, had left on a run to Texas and wouldn't be back for three days. No one else had spotted the boy. She wondered if Billy had convinced Pat to take him along.

She didn't share her suspicions with the sheriff. Instead, she asked several of the railroad workers to keep their eyes open. If Billy hadn't returned after Frederick's funeral, she would find out which direction he'd gone and go after him.

In the meantime, she had to mourn her husband.

A black wreath hung on the front door of the hotel. Black crepe draped the interior. Public rooms were decorated with black beribboned baskets of lilies and morning glories. Mr. Murdoch, the undertaker, had provided paper flowers in lieu of real ones, which were unavailable this time of year.

Since dawn, she'd held vigil in the parlor beside her husband's body. His coffin had been lined with black silk, draped with crepe and flanked by flower arrangements.

Frederick was dressed in a formal black suit with his dark hair neatly combed to one side. His hands were folded serenely over his chest, the ever-present worry lines smoothed into a peaceful expression. He appeared far less troubled in death than he had been in life.

Mr. Murdoch had suggested having his picture made as a memento. Claire declined. Instead, she displayed a velvet-covered case with a photograph. Frederick, proudly wearing his uniform shortly after enlisting. That man was the one she wanted to remember.

The visitation dragged on through the day, with a brief break in the middle so she could get something to eat. She couldn't manage more than a few bites. Numb with fatigue, clothed in solid black to the ends of her lace gloves and long flowing veil, she felt like a sleepwalker in a nightmare.

She'd lost track of time. All clocks in the hotel had been stopped on the time of Frederick's death. It must be late afternoon, though the crowd hadn't diminished. If anything, more people showed up. They weren't here to mourn her husband, who socialized with no one. They had come to gawk at her.

A solemn man with a bull-like neck approached the coffin. He awkwardly clutched a black dress hat against his broad chest. "He looks real peaceful."

Claire did a double take before she recognized the Katy fireman in his Sunday best. His face was usually wreathed with soot from stoking the boilers on the big engines.

Earlier, a surprising number of railroad workers had stopped by to offer their condolences. Good, kind men. Her brother had cared about the railroaders. He'd made sure they were treated well and paid fairly, unlike their current boss. Their kindness to her showed they hadn't forgotten the former general manager's concern for them and their families.

"Thank you, Mr. Elliott. It means a great deal to me that you stopped by to pay your respects. Have you, by chance, seen Billy?"

"No ma'am. Truly sorry I can't help you."

He moved along, leaving Claire to wrestle with despair. If Billy wasn't in town or at the rail yard, where could he be? She didn't want to consider the possibility that he'd sneaked onto a train headed for Texas, as he'd done once before. That time, Henry had caught him. Billy might not be so fortunate this time.

"Make way, make way..." The mournful wail came from behind the line of mourners. They parted like the Red Sea. Gertrude Bond paraded across the room wearing a black silk gown trimmed sumptuously in velvet, with a matching bonnet and a lace fan. She never missed the opportunity to make a fashion statement.

On a gold chain around her neck hung a delicate glass vial. Why the lachrymatory? She wasn't family, wasn't even a close friend. She had as much need of a tear-catcher as a crocodile.

She paused in front of the coffin, flanked by her followers, which included the mayor's wife.

One of the bitterest pills for Claire to swallow was seeing former friends, like Minnie Taylor, switch loyalties after Henry had left town and a new general manger took over.

His flamboyant wife drew the fan to her shapeless breast with a loud sigh. "What a terrible, terrible loss. An honorable, respected man. Cut down in his prime."

The room fell into silence. Some gave her sharp looks. No one, however, rebuked the harpy for her rudeness. Instead, they turned away and pretended not to notice. Due to her influential position in the community, no doubt.

In a brief fantasy, Claire stuffed her black handkerchief into the other woman's mouth.

Things were bad enough without a spectacle.

She gave a cool, yet polite, reply. "Thank you for coming by to pay your respects."

Gertrude maintained a mournful expression, practiced enough to appear convincing. "Do allow me to convey our deepest condolences for your loss. I'm sure your heart must be broken. With your husband gone, what will you do?"

Claire bit down on a saucy reply. This wasn't the time or place to be discussing her future, and she certainly wouldn't fill Mrs. Bond in on her plans. "I'm afraid I can't think past the moment."

"Of course. You're beset with grief. A very great burden to bear alone. Family can be a comfort. Have you sent for your brother?"

Oh, Gertrude would love that. She took every opportunity to remind people that the *former* general manager had left under the shadow of *scandal*. She'd even gone so far as to suggest it was Henry who had defrauded the railroad instead of his assistant, George Caldwell, the man who'd murdered the investigator and very nearly killed Henry.

Claire had written to advise her brother and sisters of Frederick's death, but not the manner in which he had died. With the trouble she'd caused her siblings over the years, she didn't want to add humiliation to the list. "My family has been informed," she said simply.

"Will you go to live with them?"

Why did the wretched woman care?

"Why should I burden them? My home is here."

Gertrude looked down her nose. "You wish to remain in Parsons?"

"Why wouldn't I?"

"To avoid jail, I suppose."

Claire's face grew hot. She couldn't stand this abuse another minute. She put her shoulders back and faced her tormenter, albeit through a black veil. "Out of respect for my husband, please take your leave."

The other woman dipped her chin. "As you wish. I meant no disrespect to *Mr.* Daines."

Claire kept her head high as Mrs. Bond and her black-garbed covey sailed away, conversing in loud whispers.

"Can you believe it? She threw Mrs. Bond out for telling the truth."

"The hussy went to a saloon in her unmentionables."

"And admitted she killed her husband."

"She ought to be in jail."

The remaining visitors cast fearful glances in Claire's direction. Perhaps they were worried she might shoot *them*—or Mrs. Bond. Ah, that was an option she hadn't explored. If she were to hang, it might as well be for a crime she'd committed.

She reached beneath the veil to loosen the lace collar so she could breathe easier. No one could see. Even if they could, a loosened collar was nothing compared to wearing one's *unmentionables* into a saloon.

Her stomach knotted tighter. She had to get through the funeral, then the hearing before the judge, and the worst would be over. Unless the judge, like the sheriff, refused to believe her story. If that happened, the nightmare would worsen.

CHAPTER 8

*B*uggies and wagons lined the hitching rails up and down the street. Ladies in black gowns crowded the sidewalk outside the hotel. In the lobby, more women had gathered in tight knots to talk in low whispers.

Frank caught enough to cinch his suspicions about why all these folks had showed up for the viewing. *The Black Widow.* She was the topic of conversation all over town.

For two days, the story of Claire's audacious confession in the saloon and speculation about her motives had filled the front page of the *Parsons Sun.* Nothing this interesting had happened since last spring when they'd dug up the first of eleven mutilated corpses behind the Bender place. Since then, Parsons had settled into boredom. The newspaper was all too eager to find a new scandal.

He gave wide berth to a bustled black skirt, but he wasn't able to slide past without drawing the woman's attention. She turned with an inquisitive expression.

"Sheriff Garrity. Good afternoon."

"Ma'am." Frank lifted his hat in a general greeting to the woman who'd spoken and the three others with her: the mayor's wife, Mrs. Bannerman, who owned the hat shop, and Mrs. Callahan, the wife of a local Grange leader. All four were influential members of the community, as well as notorious gossips.

Mrs. Bond's lips stretched in a thin smile. "Are you here to arrest Mrs. Daines?"

Add *bloodthirsty* to the list. Claire stood a better chance in front of a firing squad.

"I'm here to pay my respects."

Danged if Mrs. Bond and the other biddies didn't look disappointed.

"Of course," she murmured. "That's why we've all come by, to pay our respects."

"Glad to hear it. You have a nice day." Frank lit out for the parlor before he said something he might later regret. He couldn't condemn the women for voicing the question when the mayor and town council had urged him to jail the widow. He'd put it off as long as he could. If Claire didn't start talking soon, he'd have no choice but to lock her up.

He removed his hat as he entered the parlor, used his fingers to comb down his hair, which got unruly after he washed all the oil out of it. He'd gotten a haircut and a shave and put on a suit. He didn't want to disrespect Claire by showing up looking as dirty as a dog. He doubted she'd notice his efforts. He hadn't done it to impress her. Much.

Frank counted heads and came up with two dozen. Mostly women, along with three or four men, all crammed into the small sitting room. The coffin had been set up in a corner, perched on two chairs, with Claire seated close to it.

Generally, women took care of each other during times like these. Claire wasn't surrounded by a passel of friends. She sat there all by herself while visitors filed past her dead husband. He couldn't tell if she'd seen him yet. Her face remained hidden behind a long, dark veil.

The room had been drenched in black fabric. It hung over the windows, the mirror above the mantle, the clocks, tables, chairs. Black ribbons were tied around baskets and bundles of flowers. He'd had been in more than a few death rooms, but this one… Well, Claire had outdone herself with the dismal display.

A dour woman, also in black, approached the widow. Frank recognized her immediately. *Mrs. Thrasher.* She didn't like saloons, billiards halls, dance halls, gaming halls or boarding houses. She didn't care for the railroad because it ran on Sundays, or the hotel because it served travelers who needed someplace to stay on Sundays. Mrs. Thrasher routinely held prayer meetings out in front of each of the many establishments she disapproved.

Could mean trouble.

"May I pray with you?" Mrs. Thrasher asked Claire.

She tipped her head in what looked like a nod.

The older woman gripped the widow's shoulder and clamped her other hand on Claire's head. "Oh Lord, I beseech you!" She always prayed loud enough for the whole town to hear. "Give this woman strength to bear up beneath the weight of this terrible tragedy. Even if she brought it on herself."

What the heck kind of prayer was that?

"Repent!" Mrs. Thrasher bellowed. "Repent, and ask the Lord to forgive your great wickedness…"

Self-righteous windbag.

"Excuse me." Frank squeezed past a robust matron in front of him, pushed aside the other onlookers crowded around the coffin. He reached Claire just about the time Mrs. Thrasher had worked up a full head of steam.

"Amen," he said in a loud voice.

Old hatchet face glared at him. She didn't take her hand off Claire's bowed head. "I am not finished—"

"Sounds to me like you are. Did it sound like that to the rest of you?" Frank looked around the room.

The other visitors gave each other uneasy glances, yet remained silent. Only the fellow in the coffin had an excuse for not speaking up.

When Frank turned around, Mrs. Thrasher wagged her finger in his face. "Sheriff Garrity, you've got no call to interrupt me while I am endeavoring to save this woman's soul."

Frank forced her to back up and planted himself in front of Claire, who was in less need of saving than him. Or the Pharisee in front of him. "I'm sure Jesus is grateful for your concern over this woman's soul. But you'll recall he warned about removing a log out of your own eye before you pick specks out of somebody else's."

"Don't preach to *me*, you sinful drunkard." She whirled away and stalked out of the room. After a moment, the others slunk away, one by one, like dogs with their tails between their legs.

"Good riddance." Frank didn't give a damn what those folks thought about him, but he wouldn't let them disrespect Claire. She didn't deserve their rudeness or disdain. She warranted pity, at the very least. Except, pity wasn't he felt right now. He was angrier than a nest of hornets.

"Sheriff Garrity?"

The veil obscured Claire's features, which prevented him from clearly seeing her face. Maybe he'd embarrassed her. Should've thought of that before he stormed the gates.

As a rule, he kept his temper under control. He knew better than to take sides in an argument. He ought to remain objective, especially where suspects were concerned. But when he'd heard that nasty biddy spew her poison, his intentions to remain impersonal dissolved faster than ice on an August night.

CLAIRE REGARDED the sheriff with grateful astonishment. Frank Garrity, whose duty might be to arrest her, had come to her defense instead. Of all people, he was the last one she would have expected to fight her battles.

Then again, he had always behaved like a gentleman. Today, he also looked like one. Instead of his usual worn jeans and leather vest, he had on a dark gray suit and matching waistcoat. A starched white collar with the points turned down set off a black silk tie knotted in a perfect bow. He'd polished his boots and combed his hair, which had been cut several inches shorter. His face was clean-shaven. Even the bushy mustache was gone.

He stared down at her with a frown that conveyed confusion, worry, and possibly, a hint of panic. His expression reflected more emotions than she'd ever seen him display. Strangely enough, she had Mrs. Thrasher to thank for stripping away his guard. That alone was worth being the target of one of her salvation prayers.

"Didn't mean to stir things up," he started on an uncertain tone.

"Don't apologize."

Before she could thank him, he spun away.

"Please! Don't go."

He retrieved one of the chairs lined up against the wall. Positioned it next to hers, sat down and leaned forward with his arms on his knees. "I'm not going anywhere."

"Thank you." She heaved a breath of relief. Bearing this alone had been harder than she'd imagined, and she had been close to breaking down when he stepped in.

A friend in need is a friend indeed.

The old adage proved true. Before Frederick's death, she would not have dared to call this man her friend. As it turned out, he might be the only true friend she had left.

Her breath caught on an unexpected sob. She'd made it through the entire day without succumbing to tears, and now she was crying?

"You all right?" With just three words, he managed to convey empathy, compassion and concern that went beyond mere kindness. Sheriff Garrity continued to surprise her. Each time she saw him, he revealed different facets of his personality, like a rough stone slowly being polished until it became a gem.

She swallowed the urge to cry. "I'm very grateful for your defense of my character."

"Don't mention it."

Did he regret his actions? If so, she couldn't blame him. He wasn't in a position to offer her protection, much less friendship.

He held his hat in both hands, as if he might be in a hurry to put it on. The wide-brimmed Stetson was a cleaner version of the type he wore every day. His transformation certainly meant nothing more than a show of respect. She appreciated the effort, nonetheless.

"Are you having second thoughts?"

"For getting rid of the hypocrites?" He glanced over his shoulder. "No. They ought to leave you in peace so you can mourn your husband."

Once again, Claire was glad for the veil. Not to hide her tears, but to conceal her dry eyes. Her soul should be writhing in grief, her heart broken. Yet, all she could feel was guilt, digging its spurs into her heart. "I'm afraid I must admit to being a hypocrite, too."

"Aren't we all?"

"My comment wasn't an acknowledgement of universal sinfulness. What I mean is..." She couldn't confess to guilt instead of grief. He might take it as an admission of premeditation. "I've had years to mourn my husband. One more day won't make much difference."

Her cryptic remark was met with a puzzled expression.

Claire clutched the handkerchief in her lap. If she didn't proceed with care, she'd dig herself a deeper hole. Still, he'd risked a great deal to come to her defense. Her heart told her he wouldn't intentionally harm her. He knew she hid something, and he wouldn't let up until she gave him a plausible explanation.

She touched the side of the coffin. Her husband's officer's epaulets, his sash and sword, would be buried with him. She wanted to bury everything he'd brought home from that awful war. Let him be remembered as a hero, not a madman. However, keeping Frederick's secret wouldn't help Billy. As she'd found out, she couldn't protect her husband and her son, too.

"Did you fight in the war, Mr. Garrity?"

He shifted in his seat to face her more directly. "I did. Under General Lane."

She knew little about the Kansas regiments, having not moved here until well after the war. But she'd heard about the Kansas Senator's fierce raiders. "Frederick served in the army, as well, with a regiment from New York. He never balked at doing his duty. He returned home...different."

"War changes men."

"I don't mean that kind of different. When Frederick returned, he wasn't..." she struggled to find the right word. "Himself."

That still didn't explain it.

"The man I married was reserved, but amiable and even-tempered. After the war, he became moody, easily agitated. He would explode in anger at the slightest provocation. Bright lights, loud noises, sometimes even smells would set him off. He would break out in a sweat and tremble."

"Soldier's heart."

"You've heard of it?"

"I've seen it."

She doubted he'd seen anything like what she'd lived with.

"The doctors claimed his condition was one of the worst they'd seen. He had wild delusions. He'd think he was back on the battlefield. He even heard the guns and cannons." Claire fisted her hands in her lap, recalling her frustration with physicians who offered no treatment or hope. "He'd become paranoid, think *I* was the enemy."

A look of enlightenment dawned on the sheriff's face. "That's what you meant when you said he didn't know what he was doing when he hit you."

"Like I said, he wasn't himself."

The sheriff cast a thoughtful look in the direction of the coffin. "Same thing happened to a man in my company. After the war, he couldn't stop his mind from going back. He went loony. Eventually shot himself."

Claire didn't balk at the blunt remark. Mr. Garrity had just given her an opening to say Frederick had done the same thing. Her husband once told her he would be better off dead, but he lacked the courage to take his own life. She shuddered to think he had purposely lunged at Billy, hoping the child would pull the trigger. Whatever had been in his mind at the time, saying he took his own life would taint him as a coward. She couldn't do that.

"If your friend suffered like Frederick, I understand how he might've become hopeless. My husband's illness affected him so badly he couldn't work. After he experienced several episodes in public, he refused to go out anymore. We visited all manner of doctors. Quacks. Anyone who purported to have a cure. Nothing helped. We were nearly destitute when Henry offered to bring us here and set us up in the hotel business. I thought it would give us a chance to start over, and that he might get better."

"He didn't."

"No."

Her heaviness lifted. She hadn't realized how ponderous her burden had become until she'd allowed someone to share it.

From the thoughtful expression on the sheriff's face, it appeared he might believe her, which was also was a relief. With less need to hide, she lifted the sheer fabric and placed the veil over the bonnet. Cool air bathed her face as she took her first deep breath in hours.

That odd smell lingered. It came from the formaldehyde they'd used to preserve the body, as Mr. Murdoch had explained. She tried to not to think about it and instead focused her attention on the sheriff's face, which told her nothing.

Next to her brother, Mr. Garrity was the most inscrutable man she'd ever met.

He also happened to be very handsome. Just a haircut and a shave had transformed him. His eyes appeared lighter, greener. His lips, now that she could see them, were well formed. He had a slight cleft in his chin, which hadn't been visible beneath the bristle.

Her heart sped up.

With no little effort, she dragged her attention away from the man sitting next to her to the one in the coffin. She was wicked indeed, to be admiring the sheriff with her dead husband in the same room. As his wife, now his widow, she owed him respect. Perhaps if she'd loved him more, he would've gotten better. The thought had tortured her for years. Now, it would torture her for the rest of her life.

"Those bruises, is that what happened? He had one of those spells and attacked you?" The sheriff's question surprised her.

She touched her bare neck. Drat, she shouldn't have loosened her collar or removed the veil, and she shouldn't have talked to him about her problems.

Too late. He'd pried open the box. All those bad feelings wanted out.

"We did argue that night."

The reason for their spat wasn't important. She'd acted foolishly when she'd gone through his papers, and, in a fit of anger, torn up what appeared to be a bill of sale.

"I could tell a delusion was upon him from the look in his eyes."

That's where she always saw it first—in his eyes. The fearful confusion, the panic, and then a terrifying detachment, right before he left her for some place she couldn't follow.

"He became agitated. Then he grabbed me around the neck from behind, and started talking gibberish. Called me a Reb. I tried to calm him. Usually I could. This time, nothing worked. I don't recall when the candle was knocked to the floor."

"When did you get the gun?"

The sheriff's question stopped her cold. She'd been so caught up in the retelling she hadn't remembered to adjust the details.

"He...he'd taken it away from me while I was reloading it, like I said before. When he grabbed me, we fought. I wrested the gun away from him. In the struggle it went off."

In the long pause, Claire realized what was meant by the phrase, *deafening silence.*

Had the sheriff picked up on some inconsistent detail? The drumming of her heart resounded in her ears.

"You said he had you in a chokehold from behind."

She closed her eyes and cursed her stupidity. "I managed to twist around."

More deafening silence reverberated in her ears.

"Isn't Billy's room next to yours?"

"Yes."

"He didn't hear all the commotion?"

She threaded her fingers in her lap to prevent her hands from shaking. "As I told you before, he came in *after* the gun went off."

"The gun you were loading. With your husband in the room."

Her stomach plummeted. If she said, *yes*, she appeared stupid or uncaring. Well, she was stupid for having thought up that excuse. She'd never loaded a gun in front of Frederick. She never left a gun anywhere close to him for fear he might use it when he was in a deluded state. But it was too late to renege on her story. She couldn't think of a good way to explain it either, so she remained silent.

"Is that what you plan to tell the judge?" the sheriff asked in soft, almost kind tone.

Claire hesitated. If the judge thought her judgment poor, it wasn't the worst thing that could happen. She could live with it, along with the rest of the lie. She moistened her lips. "Yes."

"Nothing more to add? Nothing you want to change?"

She shook her head, a slow back and forth motion, because really, she wasn't sure.

The sheriff released a long sigh that left no doubt as to his disappointment. "The judge will be here next week. You ought to get yourself a lawyer."

CHAPTER 9

In the heart of Indian Territory, hidden in a grove of cottonwoods along a meandering creek, Jasper Byrne observed a line of black clouds that marred an otherwise clear blue sky.

"There she is," he said to his men. "Right on time." He held the reins taut as Bandit shifted restlessly. The gelding jerked its head up, nostrils flaring. Smelled the smoke or had picked up on its rider's excitement.

The hunt was about to commence.

Despite reservations about his chosen lifestyle, Jasper couldn't resist the thrill. Robbing a train was like going into battle, both terrifying and exhilarating at the same time. Like other unhealthy obsessions, it would one day kill him and send him to hell.

The puffing engine reached a curved a section of track where it slowed down. A man in railroad bibs waved a signal light, indicating construction ahead. The real signalman was bound and tucked away for the time being.

Jasper had learned this neat trick from irate settlers in Kansas, many of whom still waged an undeclared war against the railroads. As had virtually every tribe in Indian Territory.

He wasn't fighting a war. He needed money, craved excitement, and had few other options. Outside of killing—which he'd cut down on considerably after General Watie had surrendered in '65—thieving was what he did best.

As the approaching train slowed to a crawl, his muscles tightened in readiness. He raised his hand. Then he slashed the air and let loose with a war whoop.

Seven riders charged out of the trees at a full gallop. The horses' hooves thundered on the dry, packed earth.

A drought had only added to the misery of poor folks who tried to scratch out a living. Money was tight. Jobs were scarce. But the men who owned the railroads got rich. Jasper intended to relieve them of some of their wealth and redistribute it.

One of the most seasoned, fearless men—some might call it *mad*—went straight for the engine. Charley and Proctor would disarm the engineer and firemen and take control of the train. As they came even with the cab, they returned fire then covered each other as they boarded.

Dave and Lester peeled off in the direction of the caboose, where the brakemen were holed up. Moments later, the brakes squealed.

As the train slowed, Jasper charged his mount at the mail car where the safe would be located. He didn't bother with pawing through passengers' purses and bags. Petty thievery wasn't worth the risk. Why chance an encounter with some nervous Nellie with a gun, when he could get his hands on a large amount of money with minimal effort.

"Stay with the horses. Cover me," Jasper ordered the two men behind him before he leapt onto the platform.

In less time it took to smoke a cigar, he'd busted through the door, disarmed the guard, and convinced a terrified clerk to open the safe.

Strike quick as a rattler and get out. The best way to avoid getting caught—or killed. It didn't hurt that the railroads didn't expect such a bold move. It was almost *too* easy.

He hefted the heavy leather pouch over his shoulder and exited the mail car.

Tom had control of the horses, as ordered. Candy, who usually paid better attention during a robbery, had collected an extra souvenir. A towheaded boy snagged by the back of his coat.

The kid flailed his fists while the much larger man lifted him up and laughed. "What should we do with this critter? He tried to sneak up and shoot me."

"Put him down," Jasper ordered. "We don't have time for this nonsense."

Candy lowered the boy to the ground and tossed the small handgun to Jasper.

Expensive piece. What was a boy doing with it?

"Since when did the railroad start hiring midgets as security guards?" Jasper cracked.

It was a pretty good joke. Tom and Candy seemed to appreciate it. Shorty didn't find it funny. Looked like he might bare his teeth and bite.

Where had the little wildcat come from? His clothes were filthy and he stunk to high heaven.

"What were you holed up with, a bunch of hogs?" Jasper asked the kid.

"Hogs make better company than stinking outlaws," the boy returned.

Smelly, smart-mouthed, and a thief to boot.

Jasper held up the confiscated weapon. "Nice piece you got here. Reckon you stole it. That makes you an outlaw, too."

"Give it back. It's mine."

"Not anymore," Jasper tucked the fine little pistol into his coat pocket. He could use an extra gun. Besides, the kid needed to be taught an important lesson. "Word of advice, Shorty. Don't point a weapon at somebody unless you know how to use it."

The boy's freckled face drained of color. His sky blue eyes got bright like he was tearing up. Then he blinked and adopted a fierce glower. "I *know* how to use it. I *killed* a man."

Jasper released a low whistle in mock admiration. Damn if this kid didn't remind him of himself at that age, full of piss and vinegar. "Then you better get goin' before the law shows up."

With a snigger, Candy released him.

Shorty hesitated. Then he whirled away and took to his heels. Not back to the train, where somebody might be able to help him, but in a mad dash for the trees. His tan coat flapped behind him like broken wings.

Odd. The closest town had to be ten miles away. Even with all that dirt, the boy didn't look like he belonged to any of the locals. Indians were too poor to outfit him in a fleece-lined coat. And that bold claim about killing a man. What reason would he have to shoot somebody?

Jasper could come up with several possible answers, none of them good.

Tom swung onto his horse. He wheeled his mount around. "Are you coming?"

"Yeah." Jasper stared at the trees where Shorty had disappeared. He tried his damnedest to ignore an uncomfortable tightness in his belly.

The boy would find help somewhere.

Or not. This wasn't friendly territory. Especially for a smart-mouthed white boy.

Jasper tightened the reins as Bandit began to dance. Wasn't this a fine time for his conscience to show up after all these years? He had enough to say grace over without chasing after a runaway. Heck, he'd run away from home and he had turned out fine.

All right, maybe not so fine.

"Go on, I'll meet you at the cabin," he told his two friends.

He touched his heels to the horse's sides. Blame it on curiosity. He'd find out what Shorty was up to, and then decide what to do about it.

BILLY SPRINTED into the cottonwood grove. His heart pounded so hard it felt near to bursting. He panted hard as he dodged trees, trying to lose the man pursuing him on horseback.

The varmint had already taken his gun. What more could the outlaw want from him?

He charged through a clump of bushes. His heel hit a soft spot in the dirt. He went down hard on his backside then went slipping and sliding down an embankment, with dirt showering him. He flailed for something to hold onto. Roots and sharp rocks slashed at his hands. His plunge stopped when he rolled into a dry creek bed. He ended up on his back, out of breath, bruised, his hands stinging like the very devil.

The blue sky went dark when something sailed over him. He curled into a ball and put his arms over his head.

The horse and rider landed with a crunching thud on the opposite side of the creek bed. Curses rent the air, along with some strange words Billy had never heard before.

The outlaw came off his horse in one fluid movement. He stomped over to where Billy remained curled into a shivering ball, dreading the bullet that would end his life.

A dead leaf clung to the man's collar-length black hair. His lips were pressed into a hard, thin line. His slouchy hat had gone missing. Perhaps it had flown off during the chase. Losing his hat must've soured his mood.

"Can you get up? Or did you break your fool neck?"

His harsh, raspy voice made him sound monstrous, like one of those villains in a dime novel. The worst kind of outlaw.

Billy shuddered. He'd felt braver earlier, when he'd been outside a train filled with people, even though none of them had bothered to help him. Now, no one was around to save him. Not even if he screamed.

Birds that had flown away at the commotion settled back into the trees, warbling about being disturbed. They'd be no help.

He half expected the other outlaws to show up. But the bow-legged thug and the black-haired savage didn't make an appearance.

The bad-tempered outlaw propped his hands on his hips. "You hurt, Shorty?"

Billy rolled to his feet and backed away. If he weren't so scared, he'd give this outlaw a whipping for calling him names. He wiped his damp hands on his coat and tried to look mean. "What d'ya want?"

"You're bleeding."

Billy looked down in surprise. Bloodstains on his coat. He lifted his hands and stared at his lacerated palms. His hands had stung earlier. Now, they were on fire. And there was no water in the creek to douse the flames.

The ground seemed to tip to one side. He stumbled, threw his hands out to break his fall.

The outlaw grabbed him by the shoulders before he pitched to the ground.

"Lemme go!" Billy fought a dizzy, sick feeling and struggled to get away. Fear clamped around his heart and hot tears pricked his eyes. "Please. I didn't do nothing."

"Take it easy." The outlaw put Billy on his butt in the gravel. "Stay here. Let me get something to clean those cuts."

While the outlaw dug through his saddlebag, Billy remained still. After his head cleared, he considered running. He glanced nervously to where the man stood a few feet away. The outlaw might shoot him in the back. Or run him down again. Best stay put until he figured out a better plan.

The man's horse flicked its white tail. Its snowy coat had brushstrokes of black and orange. The paint hadn't walked off when his owner dropped the reins. Billy hadn't seen a horse that well trained since he'd spied on a group of Kiowa braves with their ponies.

"Are you an Injun?"

The outlaw squatted beside him while he opened a canteen. His eyes narrowed. "Afraid I might take your scalp?"

Billy noticed a bone-handled knife in a sheath on the man's belt and his heart thudded. "You ever scalped anybody?"

"Not lately." The outlaw took hold of Billy's hands, turned them up, and poured water over his palms.

Billy hissed through his teeth at the pain.

"Hurts now. You'll thank me later. Don't want dirt in them cuts. They'll fester."

The man was dark like an Indian. He had that look about him, too—the hard features and angry eyes. He frowned as he untied a faded blue bandana. Raised, discolored marks ringed his neck, as if something had cut or burned him. Or maybe somebody had sewed his head back on. Like in that story about the doctor who made a monster. No wonder his voice sounded odd.

He dampened the scarf and used it to dab away the sand and dirt on Billy's palms. An outlaw acting nice was scarier than one acting mean.

Billy couldn't stop shaking. This man could be like that old bummer who'd befriended him and then tried to touch his privates.

The outlaw stuffed the bandana into his back pocket. "Pull out your shirt."

Take his clothes off? Billy shook his head emphatically.

The man's knife came out of its sheath with a deadly whisper. "I can take the shirttail or your scalp. You choose."

Terrified, Billy tugged his shirttail out of his pants. He held his breath as the man sliced off two strips, then wrapped his hands. The outlaw didn't ask him to take off any other clothes, much to his relief.

"Are you a medicine man?"

"You got more questions than aces in a gambler's deck." The outlaw held out the canteen. "Here. Take a sip. Don't drink it all. The creek's dried up. That'll need to last."

Cool water soothed Billy's parched throat. He wanted more, but he didn't want to anger the outlaw, so he took only one more swallow before he returned the canteen.

"How long since you had something to drink? Or anything to eat?"

Did a stolen cookie count?

"This morning."

"In the boxcar?" Still squatted, the man rested his arms on his knees and gave Billy a good look-over. He'd been decent so far. That didn't make him trustworthy. "Did you run away from someone?"

"What of it?"

"Where's home?"

Billy hedged. If he told, the outlaw might rob the hotel. "Not far."

One side of the outlaw's mouth lifted in what looked like it might be a smile or the beginning of a snarl. "What should I call you. Besides Shorty?"

Oh no, he wasn't telling anybody his name. For all he knew, it was already on one of those *Wanted* posters in the sheriff's office.

"You ain't told me your name," he countered.

"Jasper."

Billy gingerly took the man's outstretched hand and shook it. "That's a funny name for an Injun."

"I'm only part, on my mother's side. My Pa was Irish. Which isn't much better by some folks' way of thinking." He reached into his coat pocket and brought out something wrapped in brown paper. Unfolded it.

Billy's mouth watered. "Is that cheese?"

"Want some? Or are you still full from that big meal you ate this morning?"

"I could make room."

Jasper handed it over. "You eat up. I've had my share."

The cheese tasted tart and delicious. Billy didn't eat it all. He broke it in half and put the remainder in his pocket. No telling when he'd find food again. He'd be on the run for a long time.

His dream of becoming a railroad engineer was over. He tried not to think about it so he wouldn't cry.

The outlaw stood and brushed his hands on his dusty black trousers. He cocked his head almost like he was listening for something. Billy didn't hear or see anything out of the ordinary—the wind riffling dead leaves on the ground, a squirrel scampering across a tree limb.

"If you won't tell me your name, I'll have to call you Shorty."

"Then I'll call you Gravel Mouth, cause that's what it sounds like when you talk."

The teasing gleam faded from Jasper's eyes. He snatched the bandana out of his back pocket and tied it around his scarred neck.

An uncomfortable silence fell between them, which gave Billy time to consider his hasty retort. He'd hurled insults at the boys at school who'd called him a *puny orphan*. Later, Mrs. Daines had hugged him and said it wasn't so. She'd told him he ought to turn his cheek and let folks slap him. He'd told her that advice didn't sound very smart. She said making somebody else feel bad wouldn't make him feel better. Seems she was right.

"Time to get outta here. They'll be sending out a posse as soon as that train reaches town." Jasper's whistle sounded just like a bird. The horse, which had wandered off to nose around, came plodding back.

The outlaw gathered up the reins. "If you got nowhere else to go, you can come with me."

Billy's first instinct was to let the man leave and try to find a place to hide. Except, something the outlaw had said stopped him.

They'll be sending out a posse.

The railroad owners wanted train robbers caught something fierce. They offered big rewards.

What if *he* brought in the train robbers?

Why, he'd be a hero to the railroad. It would make Mrs. Daines proud, too. Maybe enough to forgive him and tell the sheriff he didn't mean to kill her husband. Then he'd be back on the path to his dreams.

Jasper had done him a good turn. *Do unto others* was something else Mrs. Daines had taught him. Did it apply to outlaws?

He curled his bandaged hands in his lap, not wanting to look at them or think about how guilty he'd feel later. That shouldn't matter. Jasper robbed trains. Every railroader knew those were the lowest kind of outlaws. Lower than someone who'd killed a man without meaning to.

"Hold on. I'll go with you." Billy got to his feet, his mind made up. He'd ride out with Jasper, discover what he could about the outlaws. Who they were. Where they holed up. Then he'd figure out how to set a trap.

CHAPTER 10

A handful of mourners had gathered with Claire at the graveside. Most were railroad workers and their wives. The wind and gathering clouds had kept everyone else away. Or the low turnout was due to her rapidly deteriorating reputation.

A few fat drops pattered on top of the pine box at the bottom of a neatly dug grave. The minister quickly finished his prayer. Claire bent to scoop up a handful of damp earth mounded by the grave. She tossed it onto the coffin. The clod landed with a resounding thud.

"Goodbye, Frederick." Her only comfort came from knowing he was reunited with his family in heaven. He would be happier there. So much happier than he had been here, with her.

Mrs. Kelly looped her arm through Claire's. "It's rainin' dearie. You know what that means. His poor soul is a-flying to glory."

That old superstition was meant to console the grieving when dark clouds threatened a funeral. However, rain in the midst of a drought did seem a hopeful sign.

Frank Garrity's presence could also be an omen. He had accompanied the funeral party and trudged up the road to the graveyard in his best suit. Claire assumed it was his best, as he had worn the same suit twice—to the visitation and to the funeral.

The sheriff had stood on the opposite side of the grave holding his hat in his hands while scriptures were read and the prayer delivered. As the other mourners began to disperse, he'd replaced his hat, picked up a shovel and joined two grave diggers.

During the wake, the sheriff had appeared at an opportune moment and offered his protection. Now, he was helping again. Considerate *and* compassionate. What other fine traits did he hide behind that taciturn demeanor?

Mrs. Kelly hugged Claire's arm. "You're sad now, and that's proper, but you must remember the good times. Those memories will keep your heart from sinking too low."

"Our courtship," Claire responded. One of the few good times.

Mrs. Kelly drew her away from the graveside as the three men continued to fill it. "That's a good memory, then. How did you meet?"

"Frederick lived next door to the family I stayed with in St. Louis. He and his father started a freighting business to sent building supplies out west. He found out that I was good with calculations and asked if I would help with the books."

"An excuse to be near you, I'm sure."

"No, I'm afraid there wasn't anything romantic about it. Frederick offered me the job because he had difficulty putting numbers in the right order. I doubt he would've proposed if I hadn't made my interest obvious."

"It's good to be needed."

Claire nodded. Truth be told, her husband's needs had exhausted her. Had she been stronger, she wouldn't have become resentful. She never should've married him. He'd deserved a better wife. One whose love never wavered.

The three men patted the mound with the backs of their shovels. As if to spite them, a strong wind kicked up and scattered the top layer of loose earth. The wind also chased off the rain. It seemed as if God had changed His mind and heaved a great breath to blow the clouds away.

The curse on the land would continue, as would the drought in her heart.

Frederick was gone. Billy had run off. She had few friends left, and her family was far away. She'd never felt so alone.

"How long were you married?"

Claire supposed the conversation was meant to keep her mind occupied. Widows had been known to swoon from grief. She longed to lift her skirts and run. Only, there was no escape. She had to face her mistakes and protect a child who depended on her. "Twelve years."

Mrs. Kelly drew back with a look of surprise. "Why, you must've been a girl."

A very unhappy girl, desperate to be loved.

"I was sixteen when we wed." Claire noticed the sheriff, leaning on his shovel, eavesdropping. Disappointment cooled the warmth he'd inspired earlier. She should've known why he was really here—to snoop around.

Last night, he'd coaxed her into revealing her husband's secret. No doubt, doing his *duty*. Well, he'd learned nothing useful. Being a young bride wasn't a criminal offense.

His false sympathy was all the more hurtful because she'd almost believed they shared something special and formed a rare friendship. She'd even dreamt about him.

Mrs. Kelly gave Claire a motherly pat on the shoulder. "I know it's hard now to imagine things will get better, but they will. You'll see."

Claire didn't share her friend's optimism. The sheriff might not be keen to see her go to jail, but he would do his job, regardless. All the more reason to stick to her story and pray the judge would believe her. For the sheriff most assuredly did not.

Mrs. Kelly took her leave to return to the hotel. The cook had prepared enough food to feed an army, even though it didn't look like one would show up.

Just as well. Claire had no desire for company.

She bent down at the head of the grave and positioned a wooden cross bearing Frederick's name, the dates of his birth and death, and a citation of Psalms 23. This would serve as the only marker until a headstone could be put into place, hopefully within a few weeks.

Next to the cross, she placed a bouquet of dried flowers tied with black ribbon. When spring arrived, she would bring fresh flowers to adorn the grave. Perhaps family members of others buried here would help her paint the fence around the graveyard and clear the weeds. Tending her husband's grave wouldn't make up for not loving him enough, but it was one way she could honor him.

She stood and brushed the dirt from her hands. Now that the funeral was over, she would be expected to remain confined at home for at least a few months. How could she stay sequestered as long as Billy was still out there alone?

Only a few mourners remained, Pat Tobias being one of them. The burly engineer, dressed in an ill-fitting suit rather than his usual bibbed denims and striped cap, started in her direction. Her pulse quickened as he approached her.

Thank heavens, the sheriff was busy putting his shovel away in the back of the wagon and wasn't paying attention. If he saw the engineer talking to her, he would suspect something was up.

"Ma'am, my condolences on your loss," Pat Tobias tugged the brim of his hat. "Fingers told me you was lookin' for Billy."

She lowered her voice. "Do you know where he is?"

"No, ma'am." Regret flickered across the engineer's weathered face. "Caught him sleeping in a stock car day before yesterday. He ran off before I could catch him. One of the brakies said a boy jumped a train headed south. Might've been him."

A train headed south.

Billy had once told her if he couldn't be an engineer, he'd go to Texas and become a cowboy. That's what he must've done. Taken the train to Denison.

Lord knows what kind of trouble he might get into. He could be accosted on his way through the Territory. Indians might take him captive—she'd read about that happening. Or he could be killed by any number of vermin running amok in that lawless land.

She couldn't wait around, hoping he might come home. She had to go after him.

The sheriff walked back to the front of the wagon, once again he watched her intently.

After thanking the engineer, she kept her head bowed.

Regardless of her anxiety, common sense told her to be patient. Return to the hotel, keep to her room, do nothing to rouse suspicion.

In the morning, she would sneak out and catch the first train south before the sheriff realized she was gone.

Pat Tobias. Another person to add to the list of people to question. The engineer had talked to Claire at the funeral. He might've gone over to console her, but it wouldn't hurt to find out what he knew about Billy's whereabouts.

Frank tied his horse to the hitching rail in front of his office. The downpour hadn't materialized, just a few drops. Winds coming from the south had warmed the air, a welcome relief after that cold snap. Milder temperatures meant Billy wouldn't freeze if he happened to be roaming around outside. That should ease one of Claire's concerns. Her other problem would be more difficult to resolve.

What had her life been like married to a broken man? Based on what she'd revealed, it must've been akin to being strapped to a lit stick of dynamite—unable to get away, knowing it would one day explode and kill her. A wonder she hadn't snapped before now.

Murder? No. Claire wasn't cold-blooded. Even if she'd intentionally pulled the trigger. Unfortunately, Billy's testimony could send her to jail—or to the gallows. Just thinking about that possibility made Frank's blood run cold.

Across the street, the undertaker assisted the widow from his wagon. Several onlookers had stopped to gawk. Frank waited until she got safely inside the hotel. He could do only so much to shield her. Sadly, enforcing the law wouldn't protect her, but it was what he was sworn to do. Duty demanded he go after the boy and put him on the stand. His heart told him to wait.

He heaved a troubled sigh and entered his office.

The Katy's new general manager, who sat in a chair in front of the desk, came to his feet. William Bond straightened his suit coat. He liked to tell everyone he knew President Grant and purchased suits from the same tailor. Unlike Grant, Bond favored flashy ties and gold stickpins. He'd slicked his hair with some kind of oil that made the office smell like a boudoir.

"Afternoon, Mr. Bond," Frank said politely.

The stuffy little man consulted the watch in his hand. "About time you arrived to work. Where've you been?"

"At a funeral. Where were you?"

Bond slipped the watch into the pocket of his waistcoat. "Oh, yes. Mr. Daines' funeral, that was today, wasn't it? Sorry, I couldn't make it. Too much work."

The fact that the general manager hadn't been at the funeral didn't bother Frank as much as the man's casual excuse. Even if he and his wife weren't close to Claire, common courtesy dictated he show respect. Especially given her standing in the community, and as a relative of previous general manager.

From the moment the Bonds had arrived six months ago, they'd shunned Claire. Frank assumed they were jealous of how loyal the railroad workers remained to Henry Stevens and his family. Bond would do well to take a lesson in how to earn respect. The current general manager had released workers and cut pay. Granted, the economy had gone sour, but Stevens would've cut his own salary first. He'd damn near bankrupted himself to make the payroll.

Frank hung up his hat on the way to his chair. "Something I can do for you?"

"Yes, Sheriff, there is something you can do. Have you forgotten one of our trains was robbed day before yesterday?"

"Nope. My memory is fine, thank you." Frank shifted forward and rested his arms on the desk. The stout little Napoleon was getting on his nerves. Nevertheless, he was obliged to consider whatever Bond had to say.

He retrieved his notebook from the desk drawer, unstopped the ink well and picked up a pen. "Any new information I ought to know about?"

Bond's eyes became angry slits. "Need I remind you, investigating crimes is *your* job, not mine. Or are you too busy handling business over at the saloon?"

Frank tightened his grip on the pen. "My job is to investigate crimes committed in Labette County. Your train was robbed in Indian Territory. I have no jurisdiction there, as I told you before."

"Are you saying you won't do anything?"

"That's not what I said. I've telegraphed the federal marshal, notified the Indian authorities. If those outlaws come up here, we'll go after them."

Bond slapped his palm on the desk. "Form a posse. Send that deputy after them, if he's up to the job. Kill the vermin."

Frank came up out of his chair and loomed over the pompous asshole. "You want to hire men to go hunt down your outlaws, be my guest. Neither my deputy nor I are your employees. We serve the people of this county."

"You won't for long." Bond muttered, as he snatched his overcoat from the chair. "The county commissioners aren't happy about your choice of deputies. Or the fact that you seem more interested in protecting a murderer than arresting one."

"Murder? There's no evidence of murder."

"Claire Daines admitted to killing her husband and she's still walking around free. The shameless hussy ordered my wife out of the hotel. I heard you humiliated Mrs. Thrasher when she tried to say a prayer over the sinful wretch. Do you plan to wait until she disappears, like that Bender woman?"

Frank fisted his hands at his sides. He was inches away from grabbing Bond by his fancy suit and heaving him out the door. "Rumor has it the Benders are buried in a shallow grave. Considering nobody's seen them or turned them in, despite a sizable reward, I'm inclined to believe it."

"The governor doesn't believe it. And he wonders why you're still employed here as sheriff, and that useless deputy. I'm beginning to wonder the same thing."

Bond slammed the door behind him.

"Son of a... Tarnation!" Frank sent the papers on his desk flying. Hell would grow icicles before he bowed to Bond's intimidation. His deputy had more than proved his value. There were plenty of folks who could vouch for that, including the banker whose life Gideon had saved during a hold-up. As for those murders at the Bender place...

Frank swore again. He stalked over to a wallboard decorated with *Wanted* posters. They fluttered like leaves as he rifled through them to search for the ones that had hung there for nearly a year. Crude drawings of a beetle-browed German and his hatchet-faced wife, their chuckleheaded son, and the beautiful, charismatic daughter who'd lured men to their deaths.

For months, he'd searched for those killers. He had meticulously gathered evidence, been diligent to follow every lead. No one could fault him for that. Bond's implication that he'd botched the case was nothing more than an empty threat.

Still, Bond had him over a barrel. His refusal to arrest Claire was tantamount to refusing to do his job. She'd admitted to the killing. He had reason to believe she'd done it intentionally. Billy was the key to proving one way or the other whether she'd acted in self-defense, and the boy was missing.

Frank paced behind his desk. Never had he turned his back on his duty. He had always upheld the law. Even when his family became the target of vengeful cowards. His wife and unborn child had paid the price. If he refused to serve justice now, it would be like admitting their sacrifice didn't matter. He'd fail them. Again.

Claire didn't deserve to be punished for what amounted to preserving her life. That wasn't justice, even if it followed the letter of the law. He had a few more days before the judge arrived to gather evidence that would prove Claire had no choice. That she'd pulled the trigger to save her life. The case could be made. But to do it, he had to find Billy.

CHAPTER 11

*T*he boarding bell clanged. A moment later, the locomotive spewed black smoke, readying to leave.

"All aboard!" called the conductor on the platform.

A brisk wind swept smoke over the passengers waiting to embark. The man next to Claire coughed and closed his eyes.

Tiny cinders caught in the cream-colored netting wrapped around her hat and face. She brushed them off. As the smoke cleared, she took another furtive look around.

No sign of the sheriff.

After the funeral, she'd remained cloistered in her room. As soon as morning had arrived, she'd told the cook she was indisposed with a sick headache, and had asked if Mrs. Kelly's grown son would manage things for a few days.

She'd dispensed with her widow's weeds—too easily spotted in those—donned a well-worn travel suit, wrapped sheer netting around her hat and over her face, and had slipped out the back door and down the alley.

Once more, she looked around, then shifted her satchel from her right hand to the left so she could grasp the railing to mount the steps up to the railcar.

Her heart fluttered faster than the wings of a baby bird about to take flight. One could argue her escape from Parsons was as ill-advised as that little bird's leap from the nest. But she had no other choice. She had to fly.

Try as she might, she couldn't quell her fears. Besides eluding the sheriff, she was setting out alone for the first time in her life. She'd never gone anywhere entirely on her own, much less to a place reputed to be wild and dangerous.

Before her brother had moved away, he had told her if she was ever in trouble she should go to the sheriff and he would help her. Henry believed Frank Garrity to be upstanding and dependable. From what she knew of the sheriff, she agreed. Just because she could trust Mr. Garrity with her life didn't mean she could trust him with her secrets.

Inside the car, passengers raced for the best spots, all of which were soon gone. Claire took the first open bench. A moment later, a tired-looking woman in a faded calico dress squeezed onto the seat next to her, followed by a little girl in an aproned frock and a boy, also in homespun clothing. On her lap, the mother held a crate containing a chicken.

The bird squawked once. Then it fluffed its spotted feathers and settled down.

Claire scooted closer to the window to give the family more room. She knew coach cars were crowded, but hadn't expected to be hip-to-shoulder with her fellow passengers, much less their fowl. *Ah well,* she could put up with being crowded. It was preferable to be gawked at and ridiculed.

Once she reached Denison, she would look up Mr. Munson, one of Henry's trusted allies. He would help her locate Billy. On the trip home, she could coach him about what to say if questioned. Everything would work out for the best if they both told the same story.

A whistle sounded. The car lurched then slowly moved forward.

Claire made another cautious appraisal of the cabin. Her fellow passengers looked to be mostly farmers and their families. A soldier sat in the back row. His chin had already dropped to his chest. The brim of his hat concealed his face.

No sign of the sheriff.

She turned around and released a relieved sigh. One hurdle crossed. She'd managed to get out of town without being followed.

For the next several hours, she watched out the window. Some people complained about the sameness of the scenery. They didn't look carefully enough. Winter had turned the earth brown, but the variations were innumerable. As were the shades of gray lurking in the heavy clouds that hovered over the vast prairie. Soon, the sun would kiss the faded land and produce a profusion of wildflowers.

Out of a clump of buffalo grass, a prairie chicken took flight with a flurry of wings. Farmers from the east had been lured west by the rich Kansas soil. The lush grassland that protected and fed abundant wildlife would soon produce food for settlers.

According to Henry, the railroad construction crews had feasted on wild turkey and deer, even buffalo, as they'd pushed south. The buffalo were being exterminated, as were the Indians, whose lives depended on the great beasts. This seemed a great injustice, one she felt powerless to change. She could, however, save a child who'd been wronged.

With a weary sigh, she leaned back and unwrapped the netting from around her hat and face. The cool air on her skin felt good. No need to hide anymore. They'd left the station and no one she recognized was around. She folded the sheer cloth and tucked it into the satchel on her lap.

"Excuse us for crowding you, Miss."

The woman next to her handed the chicken crate to the boy.

Claire hadn't meant to make the woman feel uncomfortable. "Don't worry for a minute. We're close enough that we shall all be friends by the end of this journey."

A smile transformed the woman's raw-boned features. She removed her wide-brimmed bonnet and tucked it beside her. She'd braided her fair hairs into long lengths wound around her head. Pretty, yet practical. Her daughter's hair was similarly styled. The little girl couldn't be more than six, the boy looked a couple years younger than Billy.

"I'm Mrs. Wilcox. Faith." The woman introduced herself and gestured to her brood. "My children, Daisy and Samuel."

The children peered around their mother at Claire.

"Nice to meet you. Please, call me Claire." She purposely didn't give her last name as a precaution.

"Where are you headed, Claire?" Faith asked.

"Denison." Claire prayed Billy hadn't ventured farther. The Katy line ended there, but Texas went on and on.

"We're goin' to Texas, too," Samuel announced with excitement.

"To meet my husband," Faith added. "He found us a place down there."

Claire smiled at the shy girl who peered around her mother's arm. "I'm sure you're looking forward to being reunited with your father, aren't you Daisy?"

The golden-haired child hugged her cornhusk doll. "My Papa sings to us."

An intense longing bubbled up from a deep well in Claire's heart. She couldn't remember much about her mother or her father, only bits and pieces of their life together. Scraps. Not enough to form a quilt. She'd missed out on the closeness of a family while growing up. Passed around to different homes with indifferent relations, often separated from her brother and twin sisters. Even after she'd married, her heart still yearned for something it didn't have. She was still searching for it.

She smiled at Daisy. "I'm sure you and your dolly enjoy hearing your daddy sing."

"We do miss him, but we couldn't keep the farm here." Sadness tinged Faith's admission.

They were one of many families who'd recently pulled up stakes and left the stricken region.

Claire attempted to lift her neighbor's spirits. "I've heard good things about Texas. They ship out a great deal of cattle and cotton."

Faith released a long sigh. "Sure hope it's a good place. Things got so bad up here, what with the drought and money being so tight and a cold winter. We had to sell our livestock. All we got left is this chicken."

The boy wrapped his arms around the crate as the bird became restless. "Ma, all the smoke bothers her."

His eyes were red-rimmed. The smoke bothered him, too, but he was more concerned about their hen. It was the only creature they owned. How terrible for them if something happened to it.

Claire dug into her satchel and withdrew the netting. "Here, wrap this around the crate and see if that helps."

"Oh, no, I couldn't. It's too fine," Faith protested.

"Please. I'd like for you to have it."

"Thank ye, kindly." With tears in her eyes, the farmer's wife handed the netting to her son, who draped it over the slatted box and tucked in the edges.

The bird made a clucking sound.

Samuel's eyes lit up. "Phoebe likes it."

Oh heavens, they'd named the chicken. Even more reason to protect it.

"I'm glad she approves." Claire's own spirits lifted at being able to help. She'd never had a pet, not even a favorite chicken. When she was eight, she'd discovered a kitten in the barn and took it inside to hold it. Her mean cousin drowned the poor little tabby. From that point on, she'd guarded her heart against getting too attached to creatures. Now, seeing how a chicken gave the children comfort, she wondered if perhaps a pet would be a good thing for Billy. She'd prefer a puppy to a chicken. Especially in the hotel.

"Is your family in Texas?" Faith asked.

"No, I'm making a short trip." Claire didn't have the energy or inclination to fabricate more. "To pick up my son."

"Your husband lets you travel alone?" Faith's glance was more worried than reproachful.

"He passed away."

"Awful sorry to hear that. How old is your boy?"

"Twelve."

"Samuel's ten."

Claire congratulated herself for guessing right.

"You got other children?"

"Sadly, no." Claire didn't add that she'd yearned for children and prayed earnestly. But even years ago, when Frederick had been coming to her bed, she hadn't been able to conceive. She'd sought out doctors. They'd told her there was nothing they could do.

Faith regarded her with sympathy. "You're young still, and pretty, and there's plenty of men out here. I reckon you could have your pick whenever you're ready."

The sheriff's image popped into Claire's head. *Frank Garrity?* Heavens, no, he wouldn't be putting a ring on her finger. Shackles around her wrists, maybe.

She couldn't deny having a strong attraction to him. When he'd held her close, the air fairly crackled, or so it seemed. A wild current raced through her veins when he touched her, even if only to offer his arm. She couldn't seem to control it. Another reason to stay away from the sheriff. As well as his unfortunate fondness for strong spirits.

She smiled at Faith. "Thank you for the compliment. I'm in no hurry to wed again."

Even after her prescribed mourning period was over, she wouldn't marry again. If she was frugal, she could be independent and provide for Billy. They wouldn't have to trust their future to a man who might one day let them down.

Claire shifted her bag on her lap and withdrew a book, along with the spectacles she used for reading. She wasn't used to sharing her private affairs with others. Now, more than ever, she would be wise to keep her own counsel. "If you don't mind, I think I'll read for a while."

The train made numerous stops through Indian Territory. Mid-afternoon, Claire delved into her satchel for one of the ham sandwiches she'd packed. She shared her dried apples with the children. Toward dusk, she closed her eyes.

A loud clatter woke her.

Out the window, tall, hand-hewn timbers flashed by. A bridge. She could see little else in the dusk. The distinct clacking of wheels on a track built over trestle timbers went on for some time. Then it sounded like they were crossing a second bridge.

Three Forks.

Claire tensed as the car swayed. Was it the bridge that moved? Her breathing grew ragged.

A long section over one of three rivers had collapsed the first time Henry's men constructed it. Timbers, ties, rails and workers were sent hurtling two hundred feet into the river. Her brother had called the incident his *Waterloo* because the tragedy had devastated and nearly defeated him. But Henry hadn't quit. Neither would she. Somehow, she would find Billy and bring him home, and they would be a family. He needed her as much as she needed him, and she wouldn't let him down.

Faith reached over and clasped Claire's hand. "I don't like this much."

"Nor do I. We'll soon be on the other side."

In another moment, the train reached firm ground.

The next stop would be Muskogee, in the heart of Creek country. The town offered little more than gambling halls and dovecotes. Few whites lived there. Mostly "bloods and breeds," as the railroad workers called them.

After the train stopped, she had to find a place to relieve herself. She'd like to find a cup of coffee, if she had time, but then she would get right back on the train.

THE KATY FLYER rumbled into Muskogee a few minutes shy of midnight. A band of local roughs greeted the arriving train. They whooped it up and fired their revolvers as the locomotive came to a stop. An armed engineer and his fireman charged out after the drunks, who went tearing off down a wide, muddy street, howling with glee. Muskogee was just as Frank remembered.

93

He holstered his gun and hopped down from the rear exit of the passenger car. Took a moment to twist his back to relieve muscle cramps he'd gotten from being cramped up in between two drummers and their cases.

Back in Parsons, he'd slipped onto the train at the last moment. He'd worn his old Army hat and coat and had kept his head down so Claire wouldn't recognize him.

After the funeral, he'd gotten the strong feeling she might go looking for Billy, so he'd made preparations. Good thing he did. She'd shown up at the depot when first train of the morning arrived. Must've learned from that engineer Tobias where she could find the boy.

Frank moved to a shadowed corner beneath a roof that extended over the platform. In a spot where Claire wouldn't see him if she departed the train. He squinted in the drifting smoke, which turned to a gray haze in the light from mounted signal lamps and lanterns carried by the conductor and brakemen.

Now that the welcoming committee had left, the passengers ventured out. The locomotive hissed, releasing more steam.

"Ten minutes," the conductor called out.

"The café's closed," muttered one of the drummers. "Where do we get a cup of coffee?"

Not here. The only establishments open were saloons, gaming halls and whorehouses. Pretty much all there was in this place.

After the others had departed the train, Claire ventured off. She clutched an ugly carpetbag to her chest and set off with a purposeful stride toward the corner of the building.

Frank trailed her. He wouldn't expect to find Billy here, so where was Claire headed in such a hurry? He found out when he reached the edge of the station.

An outhouse.

The ramshackle privy appeared to also be used by patrons of a saloon next door, if the steady stream of drunks was any indication. They scattered when a bevy of tired women and fussy children descended. Claire took her place at the end of a long line.

Frank leaned his shoulder against the clapboard siding. He wasn't about to let her out of his sight for her safety, as well as peace of mind. Given the wild greeting and the wandering drunks, he didn't imagine she'd tarry long.

He could've arrested her at the station. Probably should have, then gone after Billy on his own. She wouldn't give up the boy's location willingly, and he didn't have time to guess. He'd follow her, find Billy, take them both back to Parsons. Put them in jail together, if that's what it took to prevent them from doing something stupid like run away.

He'd tried being reasonable and friendly, and that hadn't worked. Heavy-handed wasn't his preferred method, especially with women and children. But he might have to put the fear of God into Claire and Billy to get to the truth. He'd do his damnedest to help her find a way out of this mess, but she had to trust him—and they were running out of time.

When she finally emerged from the outhouse, the other passengers had already heeded the last call for boarding.

A warning whistle sounded.

She jerked her head up and looked directly at him.

Caught off guard, he froze half a second before he turned around. Had she recognized him? It was pretty dark out here. Chances were good she hadn't really looked at his face.

He walked toward the train at a nonchalant pace. In a moment, she'd race past, wouldn't miss that train. If he kept his head down, she wouldn't recognize him.

Gravel crunched behind him. Hurried steps. He slowed, waited. The steps sounded fainter, as if they were receding. Then, there were none.

He ventured a quick look over his shoulder.

She wasn't behind him.

Frank whirled around. The platform had emptied. Where they hell had she gone? He would've seen her if she'd boarded the train.

He dashed behind the station. Not there. Circled the building, and came back around about the time the engine let out a blast of steam, which obscured his vision. No more subterfuge.

"Claire! Where are you?" he yelled.

The train chugged as it pulled away from the station. He stood there a moment, waiting. He half expected her to dash out and attempt to jump the train. He waited, as it pulled away and the sounds from the saloon became more distinct. Raucous laughter, music, arguing voices. A scream.

Frank's blood froze. Had she run into the saloon to hide? He whirled around and strode past the station. Fear crawled up his throat as he approached the canvas and wood structure.

The sound of an argument grew louder. Wasn't inside the saloon, it came from a crowd gathered in the street. They thronged around something—or someone.

Dread wrung Frank's insides. *God no.* This couldn't be happening. Not again. A moment's inattention had cost him everything once before. And he'd thought he had nothing left to lose.

He broke into a run.

"Claire!" He called her name and plowed into the mass of onlookers. Instinctively, he reached for his revolver then stopped. If he pulled a gun, these crazy bastards would start shooting.

He shoved a bulky, black-haired drunk out of his way.

In the middle of the street, two men were going at each other with fists flying. Around them hovered the sweaty, whiskey-soaked crowd. Men cussed, hollered and made bets on who would walk away and who would be buried in the morning.

Frank heaved a relieved sigh. Claire wasn't involved. Just a couple idiots.

"Hey, asshole." Someone spun him around. The man he'd pushed out of the way. Big as an ox and red-faced with fury. He slammed his mallet-sized fist into Frank's face.

Pain splintered behind his eyes. He staggered backwards, momentarily blinded. Before he could retaliate, another man leapt on him.

"Give him Jesse!" someone in the crowd yelled.

Frank tore the man off his back and heaved him at the lumbering drunk. He swung at anything that moved, his fists making contact with soft flesh and hard bone. He lost count of how many punches he'd given and taken. He had to stay on his feet or he'd never make it out of this alive.

The moment he saw an opening, he escaped the chaos.

He staggered down the street, struggling to breathe after being punched in the stomach. He'd lost his hat in fracas, but wasn't about to go back to fetch it. He'd lost his common sense the minute he'd let fear get hold of him.

Frank put distance between himself and the furious roars. He stumbled through the wide-open doors of yet another saloon. When he caught up with Claire, by God, he'd—

Someone grabbed his arm and spun him around.

CHAPTER 12

$\mathcal{C}$laire threw her arm over her head. "Don't hit me!"

The sheriff raised his fist, his face bloody and his hair windblown. With that vicious snarl, he was almost unrecognizable. He jerked his hand back with an oath. "God above, I almost—"

"We have to get out of here." She snatched his sleeve and tugged him out the door.

She'd been crouched behind a bush next to the station when he'd run past. For some inexplicable reason, he'd charged into that drunken brawl, yelling her name. The agonized desperation in his voice had wrung her heart.

As the last cars rolled by, she had a second to choose whether to run for the train or stay to help the hapless lawman.

Her choice may have sealed her fate.

Frank wiped the back of his sleeve over his bloodied lip. Somehow, he'd escaped from the melee. But the shouts and curses coming from down the street sounded like they were getting closer. She had to get him out of here, somewhere safe, before he got dragged back into the fight.

She spotted the perfect place across the street. Some enterprising businessman had turned three railroad sleeping cars into a boarding house. They were set upon an island made of railroad tracks and fronted with a white picket fence—a veritable oasis in an inhospitable desert.

"Come with me." Claire picked up her satchel and took the sheriff's hand. He allowed her to tug him along as a child might lead a wooden duck on a string.

As the noise from the street fight grew louder, he pulled his revolver from its holster.

Good Lord. If she didn't get them to safety fast, they'd be caught in a shoot-out.

She approached the door to one of the rail cars where she saw light through the window. "Wait right here. And don't fire that thing."

Frank faced the street with the gun at his side. Cocked.

Claire mounted the metal steps leading up to the door and banged furiously. "Is anyone here? Please let us in."

After a moment, the door swung open. A short, stout gentleman with shoulder-length white hair looked out. "Hello? What have we here?"

"Forgive me for disturbing you. The sign says this is a boarding house."

"Pioneer Boarding Cars, to be exact." The man leaned outside enough for her to see the rifle he tried to hide behind the door. He eyed her protector with a dubious expression.

No wonder. Frank looked as though he'd been dragged, face down, over the railroad tracks.

"Sir, we missed our train, and—" She took a breath to remain calm. "We need a safe place to stay."

The older gentleman moved back and opened the door wide. "Come in, quick."

Claire retrieved the sheriff from his post. He holstered his gun, thank goodness.

Inside the railcar, red calico ruled. The brash color adorned walls, windows, the sofa and chairs, in every imaginable pattern. Green oilcloth covered the floor.

Their diminutive host shut the door and turned the key in the lock with a click. He lifted onto his toes to place his rifle on a set of antlers mounted on the wall. Then he turned and made a sweeping bow. "James Barnes, at your service."

His green suit with a crimson waistcoat matched his surroundings. Odd, but interesting.

"You have saved our lives, sir. I thank you. I'm Mrs. Daines." She gestured to the sheriff. "This is my...companion."

She'd almost lied and said he was her husband, for propriety's sake. In a lawless town like this one, no one would care.

"Our train stopped. We weren't able to board again in time, and it left. As you can see, Mr. Garrity has been sorely abused. I'm sure we can catch another train tomorrow. In the meantime, would you have two rooms?"

The proprietor clasped his hands together with a look of consternation. "Ah, Mrs. Daines. I am sorry. I only have one car available. I'll throw in dinner."

The sheriff limped up behind her. "You take it."

Claire stiffened. He had no right to order her around. Besides, where did he plan to sleep, in the street? She kept her attention on their host. "How is each car arranged?"

"With a sitting area and two berths."

"Do you have anything we can use to separate the space?"

"Each car has a screen that can be used to create a dressing area. For the ladies."

How many ladies made stops in Muskogee? *No.* It didn't bear asking.

"That will work. We can set up the screen between the berths. We'll take the room."

"Just a minute." The sheriff drew her aside and lowered his voice. "Get this straight. We aren't sleeping in the same room."

Her face grew warm. She glanced at their host, who had looked away, though he must've heard the sheriff's remark, which made it sound as if she'd offered to crawl into bed with him.

"In many establishments, travelers sleep with nothing more than a sheet between the beds. I don't see how this can be construed as any different," she answered in a harsh whisper.

"You stayed in any?"

"Well, no. I haven't traveled much." She hadn't traveled at all. But she wasn't about to admit it. "Do you know of another decent place in town where we'll be safe?"

His scowl deepened.

"As I see it, you can be fussy or you can be comfortable. Take your pick."

"What about your reputation?" He slurred his words, likely because his lip had swollen from a cut. One of his eyes remained half-shut and the flesh around it looked red and puffy. He had bruise on his chin and dried blood beneath his nose. The poor man was a mess, and he was worried about her good standing? In a town populated by heathens and drunks?

"One more dent in my character won't matter." She tenderly cupped his cheek.

At her touch, his disapproving expression settled into stoic acceptance.

"And I trust you're a gentleman," she added. More to remind herself that she was a lady. This desire between them, thus far ignored, was like hot embers beneath a pile of ashes. The least little disturbance would set it ablaze. Unfortunately—or perhaps fortunately—he was in no condition to do much about it.

She followed the proprietor with the glum sheriff trailing after her. The idea to use railroad cars as a boarding house and diner was a very clever one. If business in town took a turn for the worse, he could move his establishment. Too bad she couldn't move her hotel to a new town, start over fresh. It was an idea worth considering, after she found Billy.

Inside the vacant car, Mr. Barnes lit two oil lamps, one mounted on the wall and another on a table. Besides the small table, the furnishings consisted of two chairs and a lumpy sofa, all decorated with the ubiquitous red calico. Two berths could be folded down from compartments on either side of the ceiling.

"Very homey." The most honest compliment she could come up with. "Where did you find this much calico?"

Mr. Barnes grinned. "I got lucky. A local shopkeeper went out of business."

He'd saved money. That much was true.

"You two get comfortable while I fetch you something to eat." Mr. Barnes handed her the key and whisked out the door.

The ensuing silence made her feel awkward. If she displayed nervousness, the sheriff might decide to leave her in the car and seek another place to recuperate. She suspected there wasn't another place. Unless he went to one of the brothels. That idea bothered her more than she wanted to admit. They would both be safer here. She could make this arrangement work.

Claire echoed their host's suggestion. "Make yourself comfortable."

"Whatever you say." The sheriff's dry retort rubbed her wrong. He hadn't come up with a better option.

Before she could respond, he turned away, apparently intent on ignoring her. He peeled off the soiled officer's coat. At one point, he'd worn an Army-issued hat. His old uniform, perhaps.

"Very clever, that outfit," she acknowledged. "That was you in the back of the car."

"Yep."

"Hiding."

"In plain sight." He sank into one of the armchairs, drew his revolver and rested it on his thigh. His antsy behavior made her anxious.

"I should've looked more closely." Her disguise hadn't fooled him. "How did you recognize me?"

He tipped his chin to look at her with a quirk on his lips that might've indicated amusement on a man who hadn't been beaten. "Your shape. I'd know it anywhere. No matter how much netting you wrap around your head."

She resisted the urge to touch her face to see whether it was as hot as it felt.

Shortly, Mr. Barnes returned with water, two washrags and towels. He even gave her a tin with salve. He also provided butter sandwiches and hot tea. "This is all I have to offer tonight. In the morning, we'll serve a big breakfast.

"Thank you, this looks wonderful."

Claire closed the door behind Barnes and slid the bolt into place. Her stomach growled.

First things first.

She dipped the cloth in the porcelain washbowl, wrung it out, and went to where the sheriff had sprawled in the chair. With as much care as possible, she cleaned his face then applied salve to the cut on his lip. "You'll sleep better if you don't have dirt and blood all over your face."

He cracked one eye open. The other was too bruised to bother. "Don't recall saying I'd be sleeping."

Annoying man. She wanted to both hug him and box his ears. Instead, she dampened the second, clean cloth, folded it, and laid it over his injured eye.

The sounds from outside had died down. Thankfully, no one had followed them over here.

She reached for the weapon he held and gently removed his fingers. "I'll put this gun on the table. You can get to it if you need it."

For years, she'd been both caretaker and protector for her husband. In a sense, she had rescued the sheriff, too. "You don't have to stay awake to protect me. Those men out there won't be in any shape to bother us tonight."

"Not protecting. Guarding."

That didn't sound good. Had he implied she was his prisoner?

"And just where would I go?"

"Wherever you went the last time you vanished."

"I didn't vanish. When I saw you, I realized you had followed me. I thought you might try to stop me from boarding the train, so I evaded you." Claire took the soiled washrag to the basin to rinse it. She'd use it to wipe off. Let him have the clean one for his eye.

She removed her coat and laid it over the back of a chair.

A creak came from behind. Before she realized he'd gotten up, he grasped her arm and spun her around.

"You ran away from me," he accused.

Was it a crime to flee a lawman who'd followed her? If so, she'd deny it.

"I have no reason to run."

"You're after Billy. If you care about his safety, tell me where to find him."

"If I knew where to find him, I'd tell you." At some point in time. Not immediately. "All I have to go on is what a witness told me. Billy jumped on a train headed south."

"Stop lying, Claire." The sheriff's grip on her upper arms tightened, though not painfully.

A different kind of pain centered in her chest. She ached with regret for what she'd put this fine man through. He considered her a suspect and a liar, yet he'd charged into a drunken melee to protect her. She'd never felt so ashamed, so unworthy. "It's not a lie."

"You've lied from the beginning."

Because the truth was too risky. Even if she told a jury that her husband had attacked her, it might not be enough to guarantee Billy's freedom. He'd shot an unarmed man. They would take him away. Put him in jail.

Her heart throbbed and swelled with an emotion fiercer than all the other emotions buffeting her. No one would hurt her Billy, not as long a she drew breath. She had promised to be his mother, and a mother shielded her children. Even if she had to lie.

Claire released a ragged breath. Unable to look the sheriff in the eye, she stared at his chest. His vest hung open. The buttons had been torn away. She touched a bloodstain on his shirt. He'd taken quite a beating. He'd also busted a few heads, from what she'd seen.

Frank Garrity didn't strike her as the type of man to leap into a fight without provocation. He'd gotten involved, and hurt in the process, because of her. He cared about what happened to her. She suspected he cared about Billy, too. He wasn't simply doing his job. He was trying help them.

Contrition squeezed her heart. She longed to trust him, yet she didn't dare. The upright lawman wouldn't stand by silently while she lied to a judge. He would put Billy on the stand. The truth would be discovered. Then, she could no longer protect her son.

Frank struggled to breathe. Not on account of the ache in his midsection. The problem was Claire's hand on his chest. She put her forefinger on his shirt near a button and stroked it. Every brush sent a charged current through him. He couldn't move, couldn't do anything but hold onto her.

He slid his hands up her arms, a stolen caress. "You can't keep running. Let me help you."

The light brush from her finger halted. "You believe I fled from justice? I didn't. I plan to return as soon as I find Billy. You don't have to arrest me."

"If I wanted to arrest you, I would've done so before now."

"Then why did you say you were guarding me?" She gazed into his eyes as if the answer might be there.

God forgive him. It probably was. He couldn't outright admit to this overwhelming need to protect her, which went against his common sense, not to mention his vow to uphold the law.

"I can't let you leave without me." His voice came out rough with desire. He could no longer hide it. Not with her so close and touching him.

He couldn't resist the urge to cradle her head. If only she'd trust him, he'd help carry her burdens. He'd take all her worries and stuff them in his saddlebag. He'd do damn near anything to keep her safe. Somehow, she'd crawled into that empty place he called a heart. He couldn't evict her. Truth be told, he didn't want to.

As he gently stroked her face with his thumbs, a dreamy look came into her eyes. Her lips parted, as if begging to be kissed.

He'd gladly oblige.

The moment their lips touched, she came out of the trance and pulled away. Because he still held her, the movement dragged him forward, which triggered a painful catch in his side. He put his hand there. His palm came away damp and sticky. No one was more surprised than him, except perhaps her.

"You're bleeding!"

"Looks that way."

"Why didn't you tell me? Sit down and let me tend to it." She locked her hands around his upper arms and pushed him back in the direction of the chair, all the while avoiding eye contact.

She wanted to treat him like an invalid, assume a role she was comfortable with, dismiss this thing between them.

Smart, on her part.

"It's just a scratch. Not a mortal wound."

"If you haven't looked at it, how would you know?"

"Because I'm not dead." However, the injury stung and his side ached, so he conceded for the moment and sat down.

In less than a minute, she'd taken off his vest and shirt. The blood-soaked fabric stuck to his side. When she pulled it away, it felt like she'd stripped off a piece of his hide.

He grunted in pain. "That hurts worse than leaving it alone."

She didn't appear repentant. Maybe she'd done it to get back at him for kissing her.

"If a wound isn't cleaned properly, it will putrefy and you could die from infection."

God, he loved it when she got bossy.

"That little scratch won't kill me." He pointed at his mouth. "But I might keel over from this cut on my lip. You should take a closer look."

Her cheeks turned a pretty shade of pink. "Lift your arm. Let me see where you're hurt."

Might as well humor her. She wouldn't stop fussing if he didn't let her tend to him. She had a nurturing streak a mile wide.

She knelt beside the chair and examined the injury.

He looked under his uplifted arm at the cut, which oozed blood. Somebody had tried to knife him. Came damn close to gutting him.

He sucked in a deep breath to counter a rush of lightheadedness. "See? Doesn't even need stitches."

"You're lucky. Whoever did this could've put a knife between your ribs."

"That's a sunny thought."

"I'm only pointing out what might've happened."

"But it didn't. Stop worrying." He patted the top of her head. What he really wanted to do was take down her hair and comb his fingers through it. She jumped to her feet before he could put his plan into action.

She pursed her lips in what was probably meant to convey annoyance, but it only made him think about kissing her. "Who else is around to worry about you?"

"Nobody's around to worry about me." As soon as the words were out, he wanted to retrieve them. He wasn't sure why he'd said that. He hadn't meant it like it sounded. Pathetic.

His barren existence wasn't her problem. It was just the way it had to be. His life was too dangerous to bring another innocent woman into it. Even if he couldn't stop thinking about her.

For the first time in a week, he longed for a drink. "You see any whiskey around here?"

"Mr. Barnes brought butter sandwiches and tea." She made a slow perusal of the sleeping car and then shook her head with sigh. "We could ask if he has whiskey. Distilled spirits can help stave off infection."

"Among other things." Like painful memories and inconvenient urges.

She went to the washbasin and wrung out the rag. Acted like she hadn't heard him, or maybe she'd decided to allow the awkwardness to pass without comment.

He kept his mouth shut as she knelt beside him and went to work on the cut.

He expected pain. Her tender touch hardly stung at all. She smeared the salve with her finger, stroking gently. Every touch, a caress, which created a different kind of agony.

She caught her lower lip between her teeth. "I'm sorry. Did that hurt?"

"No." He captured her hand so she wouldn't keep touching him and he wouldn't end up shaming them both. "That's good enough."

She withdrew her hand from his grasp. "Next time, before you charge a crowd of drunks, make sure you know for certain the damsel needs to be rescued."

"Then the damsel ought to stop running."

"You don't have to follow me."

"Yes. I do." Twice, he'd failed to protect people who were important to him. Whether Claire liked it or not, she'd become important to him. Sadly, he couldn't do a damn thing about it *except* to protect her, and he wouldn't fail.

Claire stood and wiped the greasy salve off her hands with the bloodstained washrag. "Why don't you help yourself to the sandwiches and tea?"

His stomach rumbled at the mention of food. "You want some?"

"After I wash up." Without further explanation, she dragged a calico-covered dressing screen from the corner of the room over in front of where the washbasin was set up on an oilcloth. A few minutes later, her jacket appeared over the top of the screen, joined by a dainty white garment she wore next to her skin.

He imagined it smelled like roses, was tempted to find out.

Soon came the sounds of water splashing in the washbasin.

Although he couldn't see her, he had a good imagination. Too good.

In need of a distraction, he got up and went to the door. The cut in his side didn't burn much. Maybe the salve had helped. Or her soft touch.

He opened the door.

"Where are you going?" She sounded worried.

He wouldn't worry her more by telling her the real reason he'd sought the cool air. "Wanted to check outside."

"And?"

He peered in the direction of the saloons. "Streets look empty, except for a few drunks."

The brawl had petered out. He'd seen the same type of disturbance explode into a riot. They'd gotten lucky. He closed the door and latched it.

The splashing started up again.

Frank paced. He scrubbed his fingers through his hair. Fresh air hadn't done the trick. Freezing water might. Or he could try food. It took two seconds to devour his half of the sandwiches, which he washed down with a cup of lukewarm tea. He would've preferred something stronger, though it was probably a good thing he couldn't get his hands on any liquor. Horny and inebriated didn't make for a good combination.

He unbuckled his gun belt and draped it over the back of the chair. Drunk or not, he'd never take advantage of her. She must know this, or she wouldn't feel comfortable bathing while he was in the same room.

Well now, that gave him an idea. She'd clammed up, said she couldn't tell him everything. If she would take her clothes off with him in the same room, she ought to be able to trust him enough to confide her secrets.

He approached the screen, stopping short of being able to see over it.

The splashing ceased. She peeked over the top and her eyes narrowed. "Don't come any closer."

Mighty tempting, but no.

"You must have a little faith in my self-control, else you wouldn't feel comfortable washing up with me in the same room."

"I have faith in you because you're a gentleman."

"Hm. I wouldn't go that far."

With a look of alarm, she snatched the lacy top.

"Don't worry. I won't come around there." The devil in him couldn't resist adding. "Not unless you invite me."

By her quick, jerky movements, he could tell she dressed in a hurry. A moment later, she emerged from behind the screen with the jacket buttoned up to her chin, which was a real pity because she had a pretty neck. Which still showed the marks where her husband had tried to choke her. Had the scoundrel lived, Frank might've killed him.

"Why did you come over here before I was dressed?" she asked.

"To make a point." He gently wrapped his fingers around her wrist and drew her to him.

Her eyes got as big around as sunflowers. Surprisingly, she didn't pull away. She didn't even resist when he put both arms around her.

So small, like a sparrow. He could tuck her head under his chin. She smelled fresh and clean, which made him more aware of his filthy state—and his dirty mind. If she had any idea of the fantasies she inspired, she'd grab his gun and shoot him. Well, she wouldn't, but she ought to.

Her hand came to rest on his bare chest. His body's reaction was instantaneous and hot. Instead of pushing him away, she curled her fingers in a gesture of childlike trust.

The noose around his heart tightened.

"What point are you making?" she asked in a soft voice.

He had a point? Funny. He couldn't think about anything except how perfect she felt in his arms. He dropped a kiss on her hair. Then he recalled why he'd ventured this far into danger. "Tonight you put your life and reputation into my hands."

She tipped her head to look up at him. Her eyes glistened, each emotion reflected like facets on a diamond—longing, fear, regret. "I know, and I do trust you. But I won't ask you to sacrifice your integrity in order to help me."

He caught a tear with his thumb as it slid down her cheek. Ah, the problem wasn't a lack of trust. He should've known. Claire didn't do anything for her sake. She'd shielded a crazy, abusive husband to let him keep his pride. She'd taken half-wild, illiterate boy under her wing to raise him as a gentleman. Now, she tried to save a lawman's heart from the tough decisions that came with his job. How could a woman so compassionate, so caring, kill anybody?

She wouldn't.

Claire would never shoot another soul, accidentally or otherwise. Violence wasn't in her nature. However, she would sacrifice everything, even her life, for someone she loved. In fact, she'd said as much.

The key she'd just given him opened a lock. Her behavior made perfect sense now. The continued evasiveness, her determination to prevent him from interrogating the boy, her frantic flight to find the child before anyone else did.

Frank put his finger beneath her chin and gazed into her eyes, where he found the painful truth. "Billy fired the gun. He's the one you're protecting."

CHAPTER 13

Frank's blunt statements shook Claire out of her stupor. For a blissful moment, she'd forgotten he was a lawman, first and foremost. Her better sense had taken flight when he'd gathered her against his chest—a very broad, naked chest.

Unlike her husband, the sheriff's lanky build was all muscle. His fair skin had more than a few new bruises along with old scars. Even bruised and battered he was a beautiful specimen of manhood. He'd cuddled her close and lured her into trusting him. Without meaning to she'd given up her secret.

"Let me go." She wriggled out of the warm cocoon he'd created with his arms. False protection. Panic sent her heart racing. "Get away from me."

"Claire." He spoke gently, as one might soothe a frightened child. His gaze glowed with kindness, understanding, and—God help her—affection.

She couldn't trust whatever it was she saw there. Billy would pay the price for her foolishness. "You're wrong. He wasn't even in the room. I'll swear to that."

"Lying to a judge is a serious crime," the sheriff reminded her.

"So is shooting an unarmed man," she reminded him.

"He's a boy. They won't hang him for trying to protect you."

She couldn't imagine any decent soul would sentence a boy to hang. The very thought chilled her blood. However, given Billy's truancy and numerous brushes with the law, he might be jailed or sent off to some awful place where she'd never see him again.

She lifted her chin, determined to stay the course. Mr. Garrity couldn't prove Billy did anything. It was his word against hers. "He won't hang because he's not guilty. I am."

The softness in the sheriff's gaze turned to flint. His hand, held out in a gesture of supplication, dropped to his side. "There's no point lying about it. The truth will come out as soon as we find him."

She trembled with fear. He had so easily pried open her heart and stolen her secrets. She had to be stronger. Clever, like her brother. "I've *told* you the truth."

The sheriff stabbed his fingers through his hair and turned away to pace the length of the sleeper car. She was no less frustrated. Her attraction to him had muddled her thinking. No, not just attraction. Affection.

She'd grown fond of Frank Garrity in a remarkably short time. Or maybe that fondness had been there longer, lurking in her heart. His infrequent visits to the hotel always lifted her spirits and she'd looked forward to them. Even as a widow, she couldn't give those feelings free rein. She would never again give anyone the kind of control over her life she'd given to Frederick. Hadn't she seen how Fate could change a man from benefactor to beast?

The sheriff heaved a great sigh, either acknowledging defeat or with complete exhaustion. "Let's get some sleep. We'll talk about what to do in the morning."

"I agree." She wouldn't be here in the morning so it wouldn't matter. After he fell asleep, she'd sneak out. Not even her fear of what awaited her outside would keep her in here. As much as she regretted deceiving this good man, she dared not stay. The sheriff would take her back to Parsons then go after Billy on his own.

He bent down to pick up his shirt and vest with slow, careful movements. Not with his usual fluid grace. Muscles bruised by the beating he'd taken were starting to get stiff. He'd feel worse by morning, which might slow him down and give her time to get away.

What an awful thought. She didn't wish him ill. On the contrary, she wanted him to be safe and well, and to find some measure of happiness. She'd seen and heard enough over the past two years to know that something from his past tortured him.

His drinking bouts were undoubtedly tied to whatever demon rode his back. She'd lived with a tormented man and recognized the signs. The sheriff did a better job controlling his temper and didn't appear to be prone to violence, as Frederick had been. Regardless, she wouldn't get close enough to him to find out for certain.

She took hold of the screen and lugged it over between the two sleeping areas.

"I'll take this berth." She indicated the one closest to the door.

He said nothing, presumably content with her choice.

Claire set about preparing for bed. She put her satchel on the floor where it would be convenient for her getaway. A footstool had been provided. For someone taller, it might've helped. For her, it took great effort to hoist herself—and her skirts—up into the bed. At last, she accomplished the feat.

The mattress might've at one time been fluffy. Not anymore. She lay down on a lumpy pillow that smelled like bacon grease. With a grimace, she tossed it aside and folded her hands beneath her head. She wasn't comfortable, but it didn't matter. She wouldn't be here long.

"Would you be so kind as to douse the lights before you retire?" She couldn't stop a yawn. Her eyes were heavy.

The light winked out.

After a moment, a thump sounded from below the berth.

She dragged her eyelids open and leaned over the edge of the bed, but was unable to see in the dark. "Did you fall?"

"No."

"What are you doing down there?"

"Sleeping, as soon as you stop jawing."

Confused, Claire propped herself up on her arm. "Why sleep on the floor? There's another berth."

"Easier to keep watch from here."

She flopped onto her back with a huff. *Keep watch*, indeed. She should've known. He'd been too quick to acquiesce to her wishes.

That sheriff, so blasted persistent. Like her cousin's coonhound. Old Blue would not stop hunting even after he got too old to see or hear. The dog would put his nose to the ground and off he'd go, without a hope of catching anything.

Mr. Garrity wasn't blind or deaf, and he certainly wasn't old. He was, however, injured, and had to be exhausted. She'd wait until he fell sound asleep then figure out how to get away without falling on top of him.

He might be persistent, but she was resourceful. After all, she had convinced her guardian not to shoot that useless old hound. She'd tricked her cousin into thinking the dog could root out vermin in the barn. She and the cats got rid of the mice while Old Blue napped.

FRANK FOLDED his arms behind his head with a smile, then winced when the cut on his lip protested. That little huff she'd made cinched it. She planned to sneak out while he slept in a comfy berth across the room.

Claire would not slip off the hook so easily this time. He knew her ways. More important, he knew her secret, and refused to allow her to continue this farce. She might be willing to bet her life on it, but he wasn't. The judge hadn't earned the nickname *Stretch* because he was tall and skinny.

Frank heaved a tired sigh. Tonight, he had to get some rest. Tomorrow, he would sit Claire down and tell her plainly what would happen if she lied. She would get locked up and Billy would still have to face the judge and tell his story. There was no getting around it.

Above, she moved restlessly. The berth creaked. She couldn't twitch without making noise, and he was a light sleeper. He'd also moved the footstool. She would have to jump to get down. That would wake him up if nothing else did. Short of flying out a window, she could not escape without his notice.

For a second, he'd considered crawling into that berth with her. If he did, neither one of them would get any sleep.

He stared into the darkness, painfully aware of his aroused state, made worse because she was so close. And willing. The way she'd looked at him earlier told him as much. With a little patience, he could woo her into his bed.

He frowned at the direction of his thoughts. Unproductive, not to mention inappropriate. Claire was a lady. He didn't dally with ladies. Not even if they happened to be willing widows. If he bedded her, the right thing to do would be to wed her. He wasn't about to save her life, only to risk it again.

Fatigue finally took him under. He drifted off with the image of Claire in his arms.

Sometime later, a noise woke him.

He blinked, disoriented in the dark. He'd rolled up the curtains to let in sunlight so he wouldn't oversleep. Based on the minimal amount of light in the room, it had be very early, pre-dawn.

The bare skin on his arms prickled with cold. He drew up a blanket. "Claire?"

No answer. Not even a rustle or a creak.

His stiff muscles put up a fuss as he rolled over. When he got to his feet, he couldn't suppress a groan.

He squinted at the lump in the bed. Claire appeared to be huddled beneath the blanket, likely freezing. The cold air blew in through an open window near the foot of the bed.

A window that could only be operated from the inside.

Frank jerked off the blanket. She'd piled it up around a pillow. He stood there a stunned moment, staring at the empty berth. How the hell had she slipped past him?

"Dammit!" He tried the back door. Still bolted shut. The door at the front end of the car—also locked.

Frank stared in disbelief at the open window, the only way out. He must've been *unconscious* to sleep through the racket she would've made crawling out the window.

"I'll wring her neck," he muttered, as he yanked on his shirt. He hurriedly buckled his gun belt. She had to be out of her mind to go out alone in this cesspool.

His conscience jerked another knot in his chest.

Claire had never been out of her mind. Hadn't she told him she would do *anything* to protect Billy? To her way of thinking, she had nothing more to lose by going after him.

She was too blasted innocent for her own good. The dangers out there, she couldn't begin to imagine. She needed a protector.

And he'd fallen asleep on the job.

He grabbed his coat and unlocked the door.

If anything happened to her, he would never forgive himself.

CHAPTER 14

he door at the front of the rail car slammed shut.

Huddled behind the sofa, Claire released the breath she'd been holding. The sheriff had awoken moments after she'd slid out of the berth and dropped to her toes on the floor, a few inches from his feet.

He would've found her had he taken the time to search the car instead of rushing out the door. She would be more satisfied with her cleverness if she didn't feel so bad about it. She'd caused poor Frank no end of misery.

He'd given her few choices. She couldn't let him bring Billy in for questioning. This meant she had to go alone. Find Billy. Make sure he had a safe place to hide until the court proceedings were over. Somehow, she would convince the judge the shooting had been an accident without involving her son.

She reached beneath the sofa, hauled out her satchel and exited through the door opposite the one the sheriff had taken.

Outside, a soft gray sky heralded the arrival of dawn.

Claire peeked around the edge of the car. Four saddled horses were hitched outside the saloon. No one wandered the streets.

Good. She could avoid the drunks.

The morning train wouldn't arrive for another hour, at least. In the meantime, she'd find a place to hide. Somewhere she could watch for an opportunity to sneak aboard without being seen. A warehouse across the street situated near the depot would be good spot.

She took another furtive look around then dashed across the street and keep running until she reached the door at the rear of the building.

Padlocked. *Drat.*

The crunch of gravel from behind warned her of someone's approach. She whirled around to bolt, and ran right into the sheriff. He clamped a tight hold on her arm before she got her feet into motion.

She sagged with weary disappointment. Chances had been slim, at best, to be able to evade him while they remained in town. She would have to find another means of escape.

His ferocious frown softened with what looked like relief. "What the devil did you plan to do out here?"

"I should think that'd be obvious."

He heaved a sound of frustration. His meaning, well, *obvious.* She'd ruined his morning. Not to mention the trouble she'd caused last night when she had run from him. The damning evidence was right there on his face—a bruise beneath his left eye, the scabbed cut on his lip. Brown bristles darkened his cheeks but didn't hide his washed-out pallor.

She held her case in one hand. He held her other arm, which was a good thing, or she might've done something stupid like caress his cheek.

"Why are you so all-fired determined to do this by yourself? Why can't you trust me?" He demanded answers she couldn't give.

She longed to accept his assistance. Heaven knew she needed help to locate Billy. Moreover, she could use a friend to stand beside her through the upcoming ordeal she'd have to face. Except, Frank Garrity, the lawman, was set in his ways. He wouldn't go along with her plan to lie to the judge so there was no point to confiding in him.

She sighed with regret. "There's nothing you can do. Let me go."

His scowl deepened. "Not on your life. I am not letting you out of my sight again."

She jerked her chin up. "You have no right to force me to come with you."

"If I take you into custody, I have every right."

"Oh, for heaven's sake..." He didn't mean it. Well, he might. He looked angry enough to arrest her if she pushed him over the limit of his patience.

If only they could come to an agreement, except she was too tired to offer one. Her earlier rush of energy had drained, leaving her empty, exhausted, and feeling slightly ill. Her satchel suddenly weighed more than if she'd stuffed it with bricks. She shifted her hold on the case so she wouldn't drop it. The movement caused her to sway.

He grasped her shoulders. "Look at you. You're worn slick."

"You look worse than I do."

"I don't doubt that." He didn't return her wry smile. At least he didn't appear angry anymore. "Will you come back with me willingly? Or do I have to throw you over my shoulder?"

"If those are my only two choices, I'll walk."

He secured her arm through his. When he set off, she had to move quickly to keep up with his long strides. She knew better than to try to run away. He'd make good on that threat, and she didn't fancy a return trip to the sleeping car slung over his shoulder.

Outside the nearest saloon, three men in black attire loitered, smoking. Heavy holsters sagged at their hips. They resembled the gunslingers in those dime novels Billy loved to read. One of them glanced over, then got the attention of the others.

They swaggered into the street.

"Hey pretty lady, is that horse's ass bothering you?" one called out.

She swiveled her head around and acted like she hadn't heard.

"Don't talk to them." The sheriff's voice dipped low. "Keep walking."

"I know that," she whispered. He must think she had mental deficiencies.

He slid his arm around her waist and picked up the pace.

The three men cut them off in the middle of the street. They had to stop, attempt to run around them or barrel through.

Her escort hesitated.

She'd never seen the bold sheriff hesitate before. Something about the way he acted, almost as if he recognized them. Although his hard expression didn't show it, she sensed he also feared them. She'd never known anyone with more courage than Frank Garrity. What sort of men would scare him?

"What's your hurry?" The one who spoke had the blackest eyes she'd ever seen. Looking into them was like staring into the darkness of a sealed room.

The soulless man smiled. That was even more terrifying. "Mister, your little friend there don't look like she wants to be with you. Why don't you hand her over?"

Claire clung to the sheriff's arm. She might wet herself if he pushed her away.

"My wife isn't feeling well. Let us pass." He delivered the lie smoothly at the same he tucked her behind him.

Their adversary no longer smiled. His hand drifted to one of the revolvers in its holster on his hip. "I said, hand her over."

Frank had already dropped his free hand to his weapon.

Claire's heart fluttered into her throat. Three against one? These devils would kill him to get to her and he knew it.

She considered asking them nicely to step aside. They weren't the type to respond to polite requests or reason. One look told her what they wanted. What her cousin had wanted years ago when he'd attacked her in the barn and torn her dress. She'd gotten so scared, she'd—

Wait. Hadn't her *husband* said she wasn't feeling well?

"Ohhh!" she groaned loudly. Apparently, it startled him because he didn't stop her when she staggered in front of him and wove toward the leader with her hand outstretched. "Oh, sir, please...*please* help me! I-I'm terrible sick..."

"Claire, come back here," the sheriff demanded.

If he would play along, they might avoid getting killed.

She reached the gunslinger and grabbed his sleeve, as if she needed his strength to uphold her. "Oh God, *help* me. Get me a doc. I got the...*cholera*."

"Cholera? Christ!" The black-haired outlaw couldn't shake her off fast enough.

She gagged and retched, couldn't force anything out of her stomach, so she spit a wad of saliva on the ground and let it drip from her lips.

"Shee-it! Brad, she's pukin'!" one of his companions blurted. "She'll infect us. We'll die!"

His two cowardly cohorts turned tail and ran.

Claire dropped to her knees and threw her arms around her would-be rescuer's legs. "Mister," she wailed. "Help me!"

"Let go of me, you stupid bitch. Get the hell away." The man called Brad shoved her onto her side. He took a step backward, then spun and fled like demons were after him.

The scoundrels couldn't get to their horses fast enough.

As the three troublemakers thundered away, Frank bent down and scooped her up, satchel and all. She wound her arms around his neck and buried her face in his shoulder, still moaning, in case someone might be watching.

His expression remained grim while he carted her across the street back to the sleeper car where they'd spent the night. Without a word, he mounted the steps, swept her inside, and set her on her feet. Then he slammed the door shut and latched it.

Her moans turned to laughter. She didn't find anything about the situation funny. In fact, she couldn't control her laughter after being scared witless.

Her protector turned on her. He wasn't laughing. Apparently, he didn't experience relief in quite the same way.

Another nervous giggle escaped. "I'm sorry," she said. "I can't help it."

"You could've gotten yourself killed with that little stunt." His rebuke struck with the force of a slap, which dried up any inclination to laugh.

She dropped her satchel before she hit him with it. "That wasn't a *stunt*. I saved your life. Who was that man, anyway? I could tell you knew him."

"I don't know him. I recognized him from a poster hanging in my office. Brad Collins is one of the meanest outlaws in the Territory. He's a crazy half-breed who'd kill you without blinking."

She swallowed a lump in her throat. Good thing she'd listened to her instincts, even if the sheriff wouldn't admit she'd done the right thing. "Well, how was I to know? You didn't introduce us."

Something hot flashed in his eyes.

"Why are you so angry with me?"

"Because you don't have a care for yourself," he roared. "You go off and do things that can get you hurt. What gave you that idea?"

"My cousin. He trapped me in a barn when I was thirteen and tried to—" She didn't see the need to go into details. "Well, I knew what he wanted, and it scared me so badly, I threw up on him. I thought if I acted sick, mentioned cholera..." She shrugged. "Everybody's afraid of cholera."

The sheriff's face lost some of its dark anger. He still had his hands clenched at his sides. "Blast it, Claire. Those animals might've shot you down like a sick dog."

A flush rushed into her face. She hadn't really thought about that possibility. "What would you have me do? Stand there and watch you get killed? If I hadn't distracted him, he would've shot you."

The sheriff took a menacing step forward. "How do you know I wouldn't have killed him first?

"The others would've killed you before you could react."

"Or I would've shot them, too."

She held her ground. He would not make her feel bad for caring about him or for protecting him. "That's bravado talking. You knew they could kill you. That's why you hesitated, and why you put me behind you. I couldn't let you face them, knowing there was every chance they would gun you down. I'm not willing to take that risk."

"Neither am I." He grabbed her shoulders and dragged her up against him.

His mouth came down on hers and their lips fused.

Had he kissed her with anger, she would've pulled away. But this wasn't anger. This kiss had the same desperate edge as the hunger of a starving man, and it awakened her own deep hunger. A hunger she hadn't been aware existed.

Until now.

Oh, yes, she wanted this kiss...had wanted it for a long time.

She slid her arms around his neck, threaded her fingers through his hair. Thick, yet soft, some strands silky, others coarse, the contrast fascinating.

He moved his hands over her body as if he needed to reach everywhere at once. He murmured her name while he rained feather-soft kisses on her forehead and cheeks before returning to her mouth.

The faint, nearly forgotten stirrings she'd experienced in her marriage bed were like warm embers compared to this roaring blaze. It burned down her weakened defenses. The sudden sense of vulnerability would be terrifying if he weren't holding her close. So close, she could feel his heart thud with the same passionate response.

She kneaded his hard shoulders, caressed the ropey muscles in his arms. When he'd held her before, against his naked chest, she'd longed to stroke his warm skin.

He shrugged out of his coat, unbuttoned his shirt, drew her hand inside. The man must be a mind reader.

She touched him with quivering delight. His skin wasn't just warm, it was hot, and smooth. Even the short hair covering the solid planes of his chest felt smooth and soft, not crisp or coarse. With increasing excitement, she explored his upper body. Had she been thinking about what she was doing rather than reveling in the exquisite pleasure of touching him, she would've been horrified. Men were aggressive and dominant by nature, women, submissive.

Instead, he submitted to her touch. The turnabout freed rather than frightened her.

He kissed her deeply, slowly, as if they had all the time in the world. She didn't have the sense of being hurried along through the necessary preliminaries that would lead to a predictable end. Frank seemed to enjoy the kissing and fondling as much as she did.

These heated caresses weren't like the touches they had shared earlier. Then, she'd been acutely aware of his body, even eager to learn it, but not scorched by passion's fire. Now, she wanted to shed her clothes, let the cool air drink up some of this heat. Purr like a kitten while he rubbed his calloused hands over her skin.

Frank Garrity could show her what true passion felt like. She wouldn't call it love. They hadn't known each other long enough. She didn't want a permanent entanglement, which came with too many risks. Promises were as unreliable as tarot cards. She didn't need those, either. Her need came from a baser urge. Sexual fulfillment. She'd been cheated out of it because of Frederick's illness, and, frankly, his disinterest.

In an unspoken plea, she pressed herself against Frank's chest. Her body grew heavy. Her skin tingled, and her intimate parts ached.

A warning growl rolled up from deep inside his chest. He pulled his lips away from hers with obvious reluctance, cupped her cheek with the greatest tenderness. "If we keep going, I won't be able to stop."

The black centers of his eyes subdued the lighter color around them. Within those stormy depths lurked a force more powerful than anything on earth.

Passion.

Desire swept over the edges of her self-control like waves filling a dingy afloat on a wild ocean. She trembled at the sense of being pulled under. Yet, she was unafraid. She ought to burn with shame rather than brazen lust. She'd be branded a wanton if anyone found out.

No one need find out. Frank Garrity had more than proved he was a gentleman. She trusted him to keep her reputation safe. He wouldn't look down on her for her unladylike yearnings. After all, he'd coaxed them to life.

Her heart trembled like fluttering wings. A nestling about to take flight. *Stop and be safe or let go and fly?*

She circled her fingers around his wrist, perched at the edge of the unknown, trembling with fear and excitement.

"Don't stop."

CHAPTER 15

$\mathcal{F}$rank's heart pounded so hard he was sure Claire could feel it. They were pressed together so close not even a blade of grass could pass through. Where she clasped his wrist beneath her cool fingers, his heated pulse galloped. That wasn't the only evidence of his heightened state of arousal. As a married woman, she'd know and understand the signs.

Her luminous eyes warmed with longing. Something he'd only dreamed of seeing there. Now that he'd gotten his wish, he felt like a criminal. He'd stolen her affection and she didn't even realize she'd been robbed.

She reached up to touch his face, rubbed her thumb over his bristled chin. "Frank?"

His heart constricted at her use of his given name. Spoken softly, entreating. He wondered how it would sound cried out in the throes of pleasure.

"Will you...not stop?" Her halting tone conveyed uncertainty, not timidness. She was braver than any woman he'd ever known. At the same time, she remained a lady, and she'd gone far out on a limb to coax him to her.

She couldn't know the nature of the beast she lured. He'd let her touch him, had submitted to the excruciating pleasure without demanding anything, even though his nature was exactly the opposite. He'd put on a good show of being magnanimous, but the real man was selfish and lustful. He had so much blood on his hands they'd never come clean. He had no more a right to drink in her sweetness than the Devil had license to feast at Heaven's table.

Yet, he sensed Claire needed something from him. For reasons he'd never understand, she'd granted him the power to give it to her. She'd gone from a lonely childhood into a lonely marriage. He could tell from her kiss, she'd barely tasted passion. Now, she was asking for it. Begging.

How could he deny her?

His resistance collapsed beneath the barrage of tenderness and affection. He'd show her more than passion. He would show her what it felt like to be treasured. To be adored.

As he drew her against him, he leaned down and placed a kiss on her mussed hair, which smelled, as always, of roses. He removed hairpins from the quick knot she'd fashioned in her haste to escape. She wouldn't get away this time.

"Beautiful," he murmured, as he combed his fingers through the silken mass.

She placed a soft kiss at the base of his throat. "Thank you. I'm too vain about my hair."

"You've got every reason to be vain. It's not a sin to recognize a gift."

She tilted her head to look up at him. "I'm glad you like it."

He smiled at her gracious acceptance of his compliment. Claire was every inch a fine lady. He had to keep reminding himself. Desire fought the bit, yet he had to control it so he didn't frighten or hurt her. Take his time, show her pleasure, give her satisfaction. Leave her feeling cherished.

With reverence, he went to work on the buttons down the front of her jacket. She remained still. Trusting. Waiting, while he removed her top. He unhooked the waistband of her skirt and helped her shed the petticoats beneath. Thankfully, she hadn't bothered with bustles or crinolines. Methodically, he stripped away the corset, shift and lacy drawers. Until she stood gloriously naked, except for gray cotton stockings held up with black garters. A shocking reminder that she was a widow.

He'd never seen a sight so erotic in his life.

His body throbbed impatiently. He knelt and rolled down her stockings, slipped them off her feet as she balanced herself with her hand on his shoulder. All the while, she didn't speak a word. She trembled and blushed, but bravely went along.

He got to his feet, taking a moment to drink in her beauty. The blush spread from her face to her body. She didn't do what he feared she might and cross her arms over her perfect form. She allowed him to look at her—and look he did.

His gaze traveled over the gentle slope of her shoulders to her small breasts, tipped with rosy nipples, down her narrow waist to the flare of her hips.

With her long wavy hair and sweet curves, she resembled a picture of Aphrodite he'd seen years ago in a painting at the home of a southern sympathizer. He'd stolen it during a raid. The spoils of war. He'd wanted that painting badly, but his commander had confiscated it. The beauty probably hung in some Army barracks out West. But what did he need with a painting? He had his very own goddess in the flesh.

Frank struggled to control an intense urge to lay her down and bury himself inside her. Every cell in his body yearned for it. But this wasn't about quenching *his* thirst. Even though he wanted it as much, if not more, than her, he was doing this for Claire. She'd been starved for so long for physical affection. He could tell by how she touched him. She deserved to be given the gift her husband had not been able to give her.

He reached out and touched her cheek, drifted his fingers down her elegant throat, played over her delicate collarbone, and at last, cupped a perfect breast. With his thumb, he brushed the peak.

She gasped, wide-eyed, and her color deepened. On an exhale, she cast her gaze to the floor, giving in to shyness.

"Don't be embarrassed. You're beautiful." He tried to keep his tone gentle. In the breathtaking grip of lust, his voice dropped to a rough rasp.

"Do you...do you think you might let me...undress you?" she asked, breathlessly.

Oh, he would like nothing more than to have her strip him. "'Course you can. You can do whatever you want—when we're ready for that."

He scooped her up into his arms and carried her over to the mattress on the floor. It wasn't much, but it was better than bare wood or the thin rug. He dragged the blanket off the berth to add another layer of softness and placed her in the center. "Wish there was a feather bed in here."

"Me, too." She gave him a rueful smile. "Except, I might start sneezing. Feathers tickle my nose."

"That so? I'll remember..." He'd remember everything about her. What she told him, what she liked, how she responded. He'd take those memories to his grave.

He leaned over and began to kiss her. At the same time, he stroked her body, easy and gentle, to get her used to his touch. She welcomed him with open arms, her generous nature evident in this act as it was in everything she did. She didn't have a selfish bone in her body. This might be the one and only time she'd ever given in to her own needs.

She whimpered with excitement when he fondled her in all the intimate places he knew would arouse her. His body throbbed and ached. He'd never wanted a woman this badly. As he coaxed her response, he fought the urge to take her too soon. He wanted her as hungry for him as he was for her.

He couldn't fool himself any longer into thinking this was only about giving Claire something she hadn't experienced before. He would get something in the bargain, and in doing so, take advantage of her innocence. She wasn't untouched and virginal, but she might as well be. He sensed she hadn't been awakened to real passion. And what he was about to do would bind her to him. Then, one day soon, he'd cut the ties.

He hesitated, his mouth a mere inch from her breast, his breathing ragged, as desire and guilt squeezed him in a double vise. This was the wrong moment to stop, but he couldn't go on, knowing how deeply he would wound her.

"Claire," he gasped, lifting his head. "Can't promise..." was all he could get out.

He saw a flash of pain in her eyes before they darkened with acceptance. "Neither can I. So let's not make any."

Long buried emotions seeped up out of some dark place in his soul and scorched his heart. At the same time, lust gripped him with such force it took his breath.

She drew him to her to press a kiss on his mouth, even bolder than she'd been before. Her tongue touched his, telling him in no uncertain terms what she wanted. Without promises.

He couldn't stop now even if he wanted to.

As he returned her kiss, he banished doubt along with the unhappy thoughts of the bleak future that lay ahead of them, and focused only on pleasing her.

SUNLIGHT STREAMING through the railcar window shone on her lover's hair, turning the strands silver and gold. Claire ran her fingers through the thick, unruly locks.

All the time he had kissed her—on her neck, her breasts, her belly, and lower, in places that made her blush—he kept saying she was beautiful. He was, too. Beautiful as only a self-assured, mature man could be. He hadn't yet given her an opportunity to explore his body as thoroughly as he'd explored hers. She wouldn't wait much longer.

Her body hummed with sensual energy. She felt truly alive for the first time.

Frank had awakened her passion. She could no longer think of him as *the sheriff*, or simply *Mr. Garrity*. Not after he'd kissed and stroked her in every possible way, and in some ways she hadn't thought possible.

Past intimacies were distant memories. Her husband hadn't touched her since she couldn't remember when. They'd coupled early in their marriage, less frequently as the years dragged on. But he had never worshiped her body with ardent kisses and caresses. He had never touched her to her very depths. She had known a wife's duty, but not a woman's pleasure.

Not until now.

Frank returned to her mouth. His lips were damp and salty, and tasted slightly musky. Was that how she tasted? One wicked thought led to another. How would he taste?

Eager to have him as naked as she was, she tugged at his shirt. He allowed her to draw it over his head. Then she reached for the waistband of his trousers. At her bold advance, his lazy, slow-as-syrup seduction became a fast, fumbling, shedding of clothes in between frantic kisses.

He rolled to a sitting position and yanked off his boots, threw them across the room, followed by his socks. Standing, he shucked his trousers and drawers simultaneously. She barely got a glimpse of his jutting arousal before he was back on his knees, dropping into her open arms.

"Claire, sweetheart."

She loved the way he said her name—as if he ached with longing —followed by a drawled endearment. Emboldened, she ran her hands down his long back. He didn't have an ounce of fat or soft flesh, just hard, lean muscle. She grew breathless with excitement and reached between them, wanting beyond reason to touch him intimately. She knew enough to know he'd like that.

"May I?" she whispered in his ear, as his tongue traced the edge of hers.

"So polite. How could I refuse?" He nipped her lobe and raised his hips.

Below his flat abdomen, in a nest of hair, she found what she sought. The part of him that felt as smooth as silk over iron. She clasped him tight. No, it wasn't as inanimate as something like metal. His staff pulsed and filled with a powerful life force.

Her body wept in response.

She wanted to please him as much as he'd pleased her, and had some idea about how that might be accomplished. With a firm grip, she moved her hand down and then up with gentle squeeze, and was rewarded with his groan.

A twinge of uncertainty made her hesitate. This was another new intimacy. Her husband hadn't expected her to touch him. Nor had he taken time to touch her. Everything was done beneath the sheets with their nightclothes lifted. Proper. What she was doing now would be considered highly improper, wicked even. But she had fallen too far to stop.

"Am I doing this right?"

Frank's warm breath gusted against her ear. "If you get it any righter, I'll lose control."

The self-contained sheriff losing control? My, that would be interesting. Although he'd come close to losing his temper with her, he hadn't been at the end of his tether. If he did lose his vaunted control, she might get a glimpse of the man hidden behind his carefully constructed persona.

She stroked and caressed him until his breath came in ragged gasps. He held himself propped on rigid arms, allowing her full access so she could fondle him. The muscles in his chest were bunched, his jaw clenched, his lips pressed into a thin, determined line.

At last, he lowered his head, groaning. His hair fell into his face. The bridge formed by his arms began to give way. "Can't take any more..." He sounded reluctant to admit it. Yet, he still seemed in control.

When he started to shift away, she wound her arms around his neck, panicked he might've changed his mind and would take this delight away from her. "Don't leave."

He stilled, his expression strained, yet with such tenderness in his gaze. "I'm not going anywhere."

"Good. Because I don't think I can let you go." She bit her lip, but it was too late. The truth was out.

She'd assured him she expected no promises and would give none. Deep in her heart, she knew she wasn't being honest. She wouldn't be giving him her body if she hadn't committed her heart.

He didn't seem to pick up on the deeper meaning. Rather he claimed another kiss, then nudged her knees apart and slipped two fingers deep inside the slick recess leading to her womb. It felt as if he'd touch her soul. Her muscles responsively clenched around his fingers, and her breathing quickened.

She held his gaze, captivated by the shifting shades of green and gray, as he slid that larger part of him inside her and began to move. Her heart jumped at a feeling of fullness, the sensation of being stretched beyond her limits. Alarmed, she clutched his shoulders.

He gently grasped her hands and lifted them over her head, threading her fingers with his. In that instant, she became frighteningly aware of her utter vulnerability. The power he had over her. If he wanted, he could plunge in and take her, regardless. She was at his mercy.

He lowered his mouth to brush his lips over hers. "Trust me."

There was little she could do to resist him even if she wanted to. Still, he'd asked her to yield and made it clear he wouldn't proceed without her permission. She released her pent-up breath and relaxed the muscles preventing him from fully entering. "I do."

She buried her face in his neck, believing with all her might he would never hurt her.

He entered inch-by-inch, letting her become used to him, waiting for her muscles to loosen before pressing further. He bent over and suckled her breast. Took the stiffened tip between his teeth in a gentle bite before he soothed the sensitized tip with his tongue. Still holding her hands, he began to thrust. Slowly at first, and then with an increasing pace until he set a steady rhythm.

Claire arched her back. She strained against his hold, desperate to touch him. He kept her hands pinned while he tortured her breasts and impaled her, again and again.

Her heart raced. She told herself not to panic. He hadn't hurt her. He gave her pleasure—exquisite, maddening, mindless pleasure. All she had to do was to trust him, as he'd asked, and let him take her where he would. She curled her fingers tight, held his hands, and released her will. She gave him what he wanted. Her surrender.

Desire wrapped her in silken leads and took control. Her hips lifted and rolled, in perfect time with his movements. They became a single entity, joining, merging into one. Together, they flew into the sky. Higher. Higher. Her body instinctively knew what to do, and she strove for it with all her might.

Her release slammed into her. So strong, so overwhelming, it took her breath and her conscious thoughts.

A moment later, he shuddered and moaned. Then he jerked out of her, spilling hot seed against the inside of her thighs and on the blanket.

His reaction, so unexpected, jarred her. It burst her euphoric bubble and left her vaguely dissatisfied and confused.

Her brain took over. He'd pulled out to prevent getting her with child. She nearly told him it wasn't necessary. She couldn't conceive. What was the point? Frank had made no promises. He didn't intend to marry her. They wouldn't have an ongoing relationship. She couldn't bear it.

When the last aftershock quivered through him, his fingers flexed and opened, releasing hers. He collapsed on top of her, helpless and spent in her arms.

Control shifted. A sense of incredible power coursed through her in the aftermath of their lovemaking. She pressed a tender kiss to his neck. As his breathing slowed, she caressed his smooth, damp back. The moment might've been perfect—if he loved her.

He stirred, rolled over.

This meant, what? They were done?

When she started to sit up, he pulled her into his arms. "Not yet."

Gladly, she acquiesced.

He cradled her head in the crook of his shoulder. She rested her hand on his chest, swallowed the lump in her throat, and tried hard not to think about what she'd done or why.

It would be easier to analyze her mistakes when she wasn't cuddled up next to one.

He threaded his fingers through her hair and smoothed the long strands over her arm. The tenderness in his touch brought tears to her eyes. He didn't speak, so she assumed he didn't know what to say any more than she did.

After another moment, he kissed her head. "We need to get dressed to catch the next train."

The magic had ended. Time to return to reality and get back to her life, which at the moment was in shambles. She had no one to blame except herself. Frank had offered to stop, but she had asked him—no, begged him—to ravish her.

With her face turned away so he wouldn't see her tears, she left the shelter of his arms. For some reason, she felt more exposed putting her clothes on than taking them off. While they dressed, she kept her back to him.

She finally worked up the nerve to face him.

He was fully clothed and watched her with an expression that verged on cautious. Perhaps he was worried she would melt into a puddle of tears or he feared she'd make demands of him. She'd do neither. She wasn't as fragile as he believed her to be. Very early in life, she'd learned how to cover her hurt and go on.

Her only concern had to be Billy. This morning, that near fiasco had convinced her Frank was right in one respect. She had no business going after a missing child alone. She wouldn't succeed without the help of someone who had experience at tracking people down. Frank wouldn't let her escape anyway, so she might as well accept his assistance.

She checked the buttons on her jacket even though she knew they were closed. "We must go to Denison. That's where we'll find Billy."

"What makes you think he's there?" Frank impatiently smoothed his hand over his mussed hair.

She longed to finger-comb the wayward strands into place and straighten his collar. He needed a woman's touch, even if he didn't think so. "Once, he told me he wanted to go live in Texas. He loves the railroad. I imagine he might be at the rail yard, hoping to pick up odd jobs."

Frank surprised her when he came over and drew her into his arms. For a long moment, he held her close and rubbed his hands in comforting circles on her back. Somehow, he knew she needed to be held.

Her propped-up courage fell apart. She clung to his coat and buried her face in his chest, fighting tears. Look at her. Not even a widow two weeks, and she'd fallen into the arms of another man, had done things with him she hadn't even thought of in over twelve years of marriage. Did that make her wicked, desperate, or both?

"We got things to talk about," he said solemnly. "Right now, we don't have time. Let's go to Denison. Find Billy. Then get back to Parsons and meet with the judge. You have to tell him the truth, Claire. Promise me you'll do that."

Frank Garrity was a good man, a kind man. But as a man, he would never understand a woman's heart. Or a mother's love.

She stepped back, out of the shelter of his arms. "I believe we agreed. No promises."

CHAPTER 16

*B*illy held tight to a long root poking through the crumbling earth at the edge of a steep bank. The air smelled heavy and damp, and a faint gurgling came from a creek below. He carefully let himself down, using the toes of his shoes to search for footholds.

Soon, he spotted a crevice in the rocks where water gushed out. The spring he'd been sent to every day for over a week. Today, a heavy fog hung over the creek and crouched in the low branches of bare trees.

The mist looked ghostly.

Billy shivered. He had spied four graves on his way here. This was Cherokee land. Their dead might haunt the place.

As soon as he'd filled two buckets, he hurried back to the cabin.

The outlaw's hideout in Indian country lay hidden between what Jasper called "the hills." They looked more like mountains to Billy. At the moment, he paid little attention to the gray peaks. He moved fast to avoid any encounters with unhappy spirits.

Jasper had declared the locals wouldn't bother them and the law couldn't find them out here. That made it safe.

Billy didn't feel safe. Not with ghosts or with the live varmints who'd stayed behind after the rest of the gang lit out. Tom Bluejacket didn't talk a lot. Candy gabbed too much. Those two were as useless as tits on a bull. All they did was laze around, drink, play cards—and give orders.

At the hotel, Billy's chores had included filling the pitchers in the rooms. He didn't have to walk very far to fetch water, and he sure enough didn't have to contend with ghosts. He'd complained about the work. But after waiting hand-and-foot on the outlaws for the past week, he'd decided his life at the hotel weren't so bad.

Only, he couldn't go back to the hotel. The missus wouldn't want him, and her man's ghost was sure to haunt the place. The best he could hope for would be to get a *pardon*. He'd heard about it from the railroaders. An outlaw who'd been wanted for a massacre back during the war had got one. A rich woman who knew the governor had arranged it.

Billy didn't know anyone rich, much less friends who knew the governor. The only way he'd get a *pardon* would be to bring in the train robbers and become a hero. He still hadn't figured out a plan. It wasn't as easy as it seemed in those Ned Buntline stories, where Wild Bill rode in, guns a-blazing, captured the bad men and killed the savages.

Billy didn't have a gun anymore. He didn't ride well enough to round up a single buffalo, much less an outlaw gang. Plus, he couldn't bring himself to kill anybody again, not even savages. It made him mighty hopeless about the whole idea.

Still, he couldn't just give up. Not if he wanted to become an engineer.

He lugged the buckets and his heavy heart back to the lean-to that sheltered the horses. Water sloshed onto his shoes.

Bandit nickered and nipped at his hair.

"Stop it. That ain't hay." Billy pushed the horse away. That ornery cuss sure did live up to his name. Bandit would steal anything resembling food.

Billy set the buckets aside. "So, you're hungry, eh?"

The horse nickered and sniffed Billy's ear.

He laughed, forgiving the earlier offense, and stroked the velvety nose. "Dumb horse. My ear doesn't look like a carrot."

Billy found a pitchfork. He tossed sweet-smelling hay into Bandit's stall. He'd need to put down fresh straw after he cleared away the manure. Another job Jasper had given him.

He fed the other two horses. They weren't as friendly, so he didn't pet them.

The only other structure on the cleared land, besides a cabin with spider webs and bird nests in the rafters, was the covered stalls. Wasn't big enough to be called a barn. Jasper said the old barn had burned down.

Billy couldn't see why anybody would want to live here.

The outlaws cooked in a fire pit outside the house. Most mornings, Jasper made breakfast out of whatever he happened to bring back from his trips out to the woods.

The scent of cooked meat drifted over. Smelled delicious.

Billy squatted down beside Jasper to see how breakfast was coming along. The game had been skinned, gutted and neatly threaded onto sticks. Didn't have heads or tails, so it was hard to tell what they'd been. "What's that?"

"Rabbits."

"Did you shoot 'em?"

"Used a snare."

Billy had never learned to hunt. No one had ever cared to teach him. "Will you show me how to set one?"

"Might as well. I'll teach you how to cook, too. Then you might earn your pay."

"You haven't paid me anything."

"Because you haven't earned it."

"But, you stole that money. You didn't earn it."

"How about you stop clattering and turn these skewers. Make sure the meat cooks even."

Billy did as he was told. Whatever Jasper showed him was bound to come in handy when he got around to living on his own. He couldn't steal food like he'd done before. Not if he wanted to work for the railroad one day.

Jasper stood and brushed his hands on his trousers. "You ever help your Ma cook?"

"I don't got a Ma." This wasn't exactly true. Mrs. Daines had said she considered him her son and planned to adopt him. She'd hugged him every night and tucked him in, fussed over him if he didn't eat. It had taken some getting used to, but he'd come to look forward to those moments. He blinked when his eyes started to sting. The wind was blowing smoke into his face.

"You didn't hatch out of an egg," Jasper commented.

"I lived with a lady and her husband. He's the man I shot." Billy had already admitted to the killing. He didn't reckon Jasper would turn him in after offering to shelter him.

"Why did you shoot him?"

"He was hurting her."

Jasper nodded. "Sounds like he had it coming."

Billy bit back a denial. He should've found some other way to stop her husband. He still had nightmares about the killing. Only, in the dream, the crazy man didn't fall. Wild-eyed and foaming blood at the mouth, Mr. Daines grabbed him by the neck. Just as the dead man's fingers closed around his throat, he'd wake up. It was awful.

Billy kept his attention on the skewers so Jasper couldn't see the fear on his face.

Fat dripped from the cooking meat into the hot coals. Small bursts of flames sent smoke into the air. Billy took a deep whiff. "Smells good."

"Better than canned beans?" Jasper arched his eyebrow like he couldn't believe it was so.

A smile tugged at Billy's lips. He tried not to laugh at the outlaw's bad jokes or find enjoyment in his company. But it was hard not to like Jasper. For some reason, Jasper liked him, too. Or he had a different reason for taking on a helper. The other two didn't do any work.

"Mm. Something smells mighty good." Candy lumbered onto the

porch of the cabin. He stretched out his arms, yawned, then scratched his backside. The buttons on a faded blue shirt stretched over his big belly. Suspenders as red as his hair dangled on either side of his baggy trousers. He waddled past Billy on his way to the woods. "Be back in a bit. I gotta go commune with the Lord. Better not eat my portion, Shorty. Or I'll skin you and cook you."

"You'd make a bigger meal," Billy shot back.

The fat outlaw kept walking. He must not have heard. Or didn't consider the insult worthy of reply.

Tom Bluejacket emerged from the cabin with a whiskey bottle in his hand. He was what Jasper called a "blood," which meant he was full-blown Indian. Jasper was a "breed," which mean he was only half Indian. Both men had dark skin and black hair. Other than that, Jasper pretty much looked like any other white outlaw. Tom wore a fringed shirt, deerskin trousers and beaded moccasins. He even had a feather in his hatband.

Billy wasn't so afraid of Jasper anymore, or even Candy, but he got nervy around Tom, especially when he started talking about his preference for scalps from fair-haired boys.

Tom darted a furtive look around as he reached the fire pit. "Did you hear it?"

"Hear what?" Billy stood up. He tried not to act anxious.

"*Tskili* cried in the night."

"That owl visits every night." Jasper bent to tend the spitted rabbits and acted like he didn't care about *Tskili*, whatever that was. Maybe a ghost owl.

"You don't believe what the old ones say?" Tom remarked. "That owls are witches in disguise?"

Billy jerked a worried look at the wooden-faced Indian who'd made the remark. "Witches? Where?"

Tom stared out at the woods like he hadn't heard the question. "This place is haunted."

"I saw ghosts. Down by the creek," Billy reported.

"That's just fog." Jasper's explanation sounded reasonable, and that was what it looked like. But one couldn't be too sure.

Tom lifted the whiskey bottle to his lips. He had a sharp odor, like those liquored up cowboys who sometimes came stumbling out of the saloon and into the hotel looking for a bed. He finished drinking before he spoke again. "The spirits are restless."

Jasper gave a scornful huff. "The only spirits around here are the ones in that bottle."

"You don't believe in ghosts?" Billy decided he'd better educate Jasper. "Mr. Tobias, he's an engineer. He swears he's seen haints out at the old Bender place. He says it's those murdered folks. Their ghosts want vengeance."

Tom nodded, real solemn-like. "Spilt blood demands atonement."

"Atonement?"

"Revenge."

Billy's arms prickled. He, for sure, wanted to know if there were vengeful ghosts about. He jerked this thumb in the direction of the graveyard. "Who's buried over there?"

"My Ma and Pa, a baby sister, and my granny," Jasper replied.

"This here's *your* place?" Billy had been sure it was an abandoned farm before the outlaws took over. The buildings were in sore need of repair. Maybe that's why Jasper had robbed a train. "Now that you got money, are you gonna fix this place up and live here?"

"Don't plan on it."

"Why not?"

"Ghosts," Tom suggested.

"Bad memories." Jasper's harsh tone didn't invite more questions.

Billy couldn't stop. He had to know. "What happened?"

"Pay attention." Jasper directed Billy's attention to the skewers. "Don't let our breakfast burn."

"I won't." Billy turned the meat. "Will you tell me what happened?"

"Maybe." Jasper didn't launch into the story right away. He took a pouch of tobacco out of his vest pocket and rolled a cigarette. "How old are you?"

"Twelve."

Jasper held his cigarette to a burning coal until the end glowed.

He took a long drag and blew a cloud of smoke over the fire. "Happened early in the war. I was a year older than you are now. Soldiers rode in one night and killed my Pa."

Billy's breath caught in surprise. He knew men with the railroad who'd been soldiers during the war, but he didn't think they had killed Jasper's Pa. At least, he hoped not. "How come they did that?"

"Said he was a southern sympathizer." Jasper spit flecks of tobacco on the ground. "They were set to kill me, too. Tried to hang me."

So, that's how he'd got those scars.

Billy stared at the faded bandana Jasper wore around his neck. "How did you get away?"

"My mother gave up her virtue. In exchange, they let me live." Jasper relayed the story in a flat voice, like he didn't care.

Billy knew that couldn't be true. Just hearing it turned him inside out. No wonder Jasper didn't like to talk about it.

He didn't like to talk about his Ma, either. Folks had told him she was wicked because she'd given her virtue away and sold herself to men. He'd never understood why she'd done it. Now, hearing about how Jasper's ma had saved her son, he wondered if maybe his mother had sold herself for the same reason. If so, her actions would be heroic, not wicked. His heart didn't hurt as bad when he thought about it like that.

He glanced over at Jasper, who remained crouched with his arms on his knees. His hands hung down and the cigarette dangled from his fingers. Relaxed, but not really. His jaw was set, his mouth held tight, and his eyes were narrowed. He looked downright mean.

Mr. Daines had looked like that sometimes. At first, Billy had assumed it was him. But Mrs. Daines explained that her husband had gotten resentful and bitter about his situation. Those emotions made him unhappy and ate away at his soul. Maybe that's what had happened to Jasper, too.

Billy didn't know what to say to make Jasper feel better, other than to share his story. "My Pa got kilt, too. Not by soldiers, I don't think. He got shot in a card game. My Ma gave up her virtue, too. On account of me, I reckon. She died when I was real little. I don't remember anything more than that."

"We're the same, you and me," Jasper said matter-of-fact.

Billy nodded. That was pretty much what he'd been trying to say. "Both orphans."

"Outcasts."

Outcasts was a word Billy had heard once in a story Mrs. Daines had read to him. "Like them lepers, you mean."

"Lepers?" Jasper appeared confused. Maybe he'd never heard of them.

"In the Bible. Mrs. Daines used to read it to me before I got to where I could read by myself. There's this story about some lepers. They were *outcasts* because there was something wrong with them. Nobody wanted them around. Well, nobody except for Jesus."

Behind him, Tom huffed.

Billy's face got hot. He didn't understand what was so funny, and it bothered him when people made fun of him.

"Shut up." Jasper's rebuke appeared to be intended for Tom. He flicked his cigarette into the fire and clapped Billy on the shoulder. "You got it right, boy. We're *lepers*. You, because your Ma was a whore. Me, because mine was Indian, and white folks think all Indian women are whores. What we are can't be cured. Best you just accept it."

Billy shrugged off the friendly gesture. Accept that he was an outcast? If he did, he might as well give up on his dream of becoming an engineer. The railroad wouldn't hire an incurable leper.

A log fell into the fire and sparks flew. Smoke billowed, stinging Billy's eyes and nose. Just like that log, his dreams burned up. He didn't want to be an outcast, but he feared his new friend was right. He couldn't change what he was, what he'd always be. Worthless.

He'd gotten hopeful while he lived with Mrs. Daines. She'd told him he could achieve whatever he wanted if he put his mind to it. That was before he shot her husband. Now, she and everyone else would go back to believing he was bad. He'd pretty much proved it, and nothing he did could change that.

He waved the smoke away from his face and swallowed the urge to cry.

"Is it time to eat?" Candy hunkered down by the fire pit, adjusting his suspenders. He always showed up when it was time to eat and vanished when there was work to be done. Without waiting for an answer, he nabbed one of the skewers and pulled off the blackened rabbit. He tossed it, steaming, from hand to hand. "Woohee, that's hot."

"Then you ought to wait 'til it's cooled before you grab it." Tom snatched at a leg and the carcass came apart.

While the two haggled over one of the puny rabbits, Jasper took up the other skewer, blew on it, then ripped off a haunch and handed it to Billy.

The meat was stringy, but it tasted a whole lot better than canned beans.

Jasper went to work on his portion. He tore the meat with his teeth and wiped his fingers on his trousers.

"Mrs. Daines would have a fit if she saw me eat like that," Billy remarked.

"Like what?"

"Using my teeth instead of a fork, wiping my hands on my clothes, talking with my mouth full." Billy listed off the sins. He wouldn't have known or cared about manners six months ago, so he could understand how Jasper might not be aware.

"She says you got to know manners if you want to be a gentleman. Took me a long time to learn everything. I could forget real easy." To prove the point, he attacked the haunch with his teeth.

"She's a proper lady, then. So was my Ma."

"But you said your Ma was an Indian. They don't know manners."

"Shows what you know. The Cherokee who left their homes in the east knew more manners than the white soldiers that forced them out here. My granny was a proper lady, so was my Ma." Jasper drew out a clean handkerchief from his back pocket and handed it to Billy. "Here, use this to wipe your hands. Don't forget everything you learned or you'll have to start over."

146

Billy's stomach sank. If only he could start over. "I can't go back. I'm an outlaw now."

Candy's laugh sounded like a pig grunting. "Shorty, you ain't big enough to be an outlaw."

Heat streaked through Billy up to the tips of his ears. He leapt to his feet with his fists clenched. "Yeah? Well you're nothing but a fa—"

"Sit down, boy," Jasper commanded.

Billy did, still simmering.

The fat pig stood and wiped his mouth with his sleeve. One day— Billy vowed—he would wipe that smirk off Candy's face.

"We're goin' into town to find some women," Tom announced. "Wanna come with us?"

Billy knew they hadn't invited *him*, but he didn't care. He'd rather hang out with ghosts than those two coyotes.

Jasper shook his head. "Got things to do around here."

"Like what? Plant corn?" Candy snorted, though he was the only one laughing. He had to laugh at his own poor jokes. Tom never laughed at anything. Jasper only occasionally half smiled.

Tom and Candy strolled off in the direction of the lean-to.

"I'm glad they're leaving," Billy said.

Jasper tossed the bones he'd picked clean into the fire pit. "Candy's right, you know. You're too young to be an outlaw. Besides, you aren't bad enough to join our gang."

Billy got to his feet, determined not to let Jasper brush him off. If he couldn't become a railroad engineer, he might as well accept who and what he was and embrace his destiny. "*You* could teach me."

"Teach you?" Jasper stood and kicked dirt over the smoldering embers. "What? How to be an outlaw?"

"Why not? You're an expert at it."

CHAPTER 17

A band of cowboys, whooping and waving their hats, drove a herd of longhorn cattle down the middle of Denison's busiest street. The beasts bawled and kicked.

Pedestrians scattered. Hapless riders guided their mounts onto the wobbly boards that functioned as sidewalks. Wagons loaded with supplies crowded the hitching rails. One unfortunate driver lost part of his load. The flour sacks burst open, sending a white cloud into the air before the substance was churned into the mud and manure by pounding hooves.

Claire watched the chaotic proceedings from the safety of the newly constructed sheriff's office. The smell of animal dung mingled with a scent of fresh pine from the unpainted walls. She prayed Billy wasn't anywhere near that stampeding herd.

He hadn't been where she thought he would be. Not at the rail yard or hiding inside empty freight cars. They'd checked the train station and the nearby cotton compress facility, which was being converted into a slaughterhouse.

She rubbed her burning eyes. Lack of sleep had caught up with her, but she dared not stop to rest. She had to find Billy, not give in to her needs, though she'd done just that this morning. She'd wasted precious time dawdling in an illicit liaison. No wonder God had cursed her. She was too sinful and selfish to be a good mother.

"Mrs. Daines?" Frank's proper address touched off a wave of wistfulness.

She longed to hear him speak her given name in that melting drawl, which only proved she'd lost all sense of propriety. She should be glad he still treated her with respect after she'd thrown herself at him like a strumpet.

He stood next to a plethora of *Wanted* posters tacked to bare boards. His shoulder against the wall, arms folded over his chest, one leg crossed over the other ankle and propped up by the toe of a scuffed boot.

His posture conveyed unconcerned ease. His tight-lipped expression told a different story. He might regret what happened or worry she wouldn't hold up her end of the bargain.

No promises.

"Did you hear Sheriff Hall's suggestion about a reward?" he asked.

She concealed her despair with annoyance. Frank had been relentless. He'd insisted she shift the blame for her husband's death onto Billy. She'd told him, repeatedly, she would not change her story. If she offered money for Billy's return, she might as well announce his guilt to the world. "His name doesn't belong on one of those posters. He's not a criminal."

"Ma'am, I wasn't suggesting that." The local sheriff used a deferential tone meant to butter her up. He rested his hip on the edge of a battered desk, the only furniture in the room other than a large gun cabinet secured with iron bars and a padlock. "You said he's missing. You don't know where else to look. Put out a notice. Offer a reward to anyone who has information on his whereabouts. The more people who search for him, the better. Money is a strong incentive."

Sheriff Lee Hall—appropriately nicknamed *Red*—had a fierce reputation for law and order. According to Frank, he was also an experienced, determined tracker.

His suggestion they put up a reward wasn't a very impressive demonstration of his skills.

Claire wasn't convinced it was a wise move, either. "If we put Billy's picture on a poster and he sees it, he'll go into hiding so deep we'll never find him."

"Why? What's he done?" Sheriff Hall asked.

"He hasn't done anything." She darted a worried glance at her companion, whose bland expression gave nothing away.

Frank wouldn't support her story, but at least he hadn't blurted out his suspicions. She could've kissed him for that. But no. No more kissing.

She hugged her arms. Ineffectual protection. He read her too easily, was even more accomplished at seduction. Or had she seduced him?

Heat flared beneath her cheeks. She dragged her attention back to Sheriff Hall. The sooner she found Billy and returned to Parsons to smooth things over, the sooner her life would get back to normal. Which didn't include extra time with Frank Garrity.

"Billy has a history of running away when something goes wrong." She launched into her prepared speech. Might as well practice for her appearance in front of the judge. "My husband was killed in a tragic accident. While I was cleaning a weapon. Billy witnessed—" Wait, that wasn't what she'd said at first. Nervousness had eroded her memory. She made the correction. "Witnessed the body. He saw my husband lying there, dead. He's only a child, barely twelve. He was understandably distressed. I was beside myself, as you can imagine. Without thinking about how he might take it, I told him to go to his room and wait there. He might be afraid I'm upset with him. As I said, his first response is to flee."

Claire breathed through her nose so she wouldn't gulp deep breaths. She'd gotten through the story with just a small hiccup.

Red Hall rubbed his chin. Like Frank, he had fair skin, and more freckles than Billy. "Did he have any run-ins with your husband?"

Her breath caught. Frank had warned her no one would believe her. He wouldn't come to her rescue. She was on her own. "Nothing serious. The usual things you'd expect. Billy is rambunctious. Frederick was sensitive to loud noises. He occasionally rebuked the child for being too loud."

"Did he abuse the boy?"

"No." She'd intervened before that could happen.

If she hadn't been with Frank every moment since they left Muskogee, she'd swear he had put Sheriff Hall up to this. The two lawmen thought alike.

"Billy's relationship with my deceased husband is not the reason he ran away. He's had a very difficult life. He's distrustful. He needs to know I want him to come home." Her voice wavered as her emotions rose dangerously close to the surface.

Oh Lord, she was so tired, and worried and scared. She shifted her gaze out the front window and fought to maintain her composure.

A fiery ball teetered on the tin roof of a boarding house, as if the sun were reluctant to set and miss out on all the fun.

A thought popped into her head. One that made so much sense it should've come to her before now. "We should check the hotels."

"Why would he go there?" Sheriff Hall asked.

Frank answered before she could open her mouth. "Mrs. Daines runs a hotel. Billy helps her. He might try to get work. We'll check it out before we catch a train back to Parsons. In the meantime, I'll put up two hundred, cash, as a reward."

He not only wore the coat of a military officer, he behaved like one, taking charge and issuing orders. Well, she wasn't one his soldiers.

"I told you I don't want—"

"You want him found. So do I." Frank pushed off the wall, straightening to his full height. As he approached her, the harshness on his face softened. "We can say he's missing, don't have to mention the shooting."

"I *told* you, he had nothing to do with it." She took a deep breath to cap her anger. Fatigue interfered with her ability to reason. If a reward could speed up the process of finding her son, she'd agree.

But she'd stick close to Frank. He could not be allowed to talk alone with Billy before she prepared the boy for the interview.

She directed her next response at Sheriff Hall. "All right, we'll offer a reward. I'll add another two hundred. That should get someone's attention."

"Four hundred dollars?" He let out a low whistle. "Bet he'll turn *himself* in for that kind of money."

She could hope. Billy wasn't motivated by money. Food would work better. "You could have it say we'll include cherry pie with the reward. Billy will do most anything for cherry pie."

"I'd have to agree with him." Sheriff Hall came off his perch. He went behind the desk and pulled out a drawer, from which he withdrew paper and pencil. "We'll get this out first thing tomorrow. Make up some posters. Put it in the newspaper."

"Thank you for your help, Red." Frank shook the other man's hand. "Let me know if you hear anything. I'll get you the name of our hotel after we find a place to stay."

Sheriff Hall made a rueful face. "*If* you find a place. Cattle season's started. Rooms are scarce."

THE ROWDY CROWD in the streets spilled into the hotels and boarding houses. Filled every nook and cranny. By the time Frank escorted Claire into the last place in a respectable part of town, his feet ached, his head hurt, and his stomach growled worse than a bear fresh out of hibernation.

The Red River Inn looked to be full, too. Men in leather chaps and spurs stood around in groups, yapping and smoking. Some were draped over chairs while others sprawled on a sofa. The two-story hotel had become a temporary bunkhouse, catering to saddle tramps.

The combined smells of kerosene, whisky and cattle were far from pleasant. Smoky lamps were responsible for the first odor, an adjacent saloon the second. The cowboys had brought the stockyard with them. The way they ogled Claire reminded Frank of dogs with their tongues hanging out.

She appeared oblivious to the hungry pack.

He tucked her hand into the crook of his elbow before he approached the registration desk. "We're looking for—"

"Nope. No rooms." The pasty-faced clerk at the registration desk cut him off. Tapped a pencil on a large register that lay open with nary a line that hadn't been filled.

Frank answered as pleasantly as he could after being on his feet all day with nothing to eat. "We've been to every hotel in town. You're the last one."

"Have you tried the boarding houses?"

"The decent ones."

"We got no rooms available." The clerk kept up the tap-tap-tap, telegraphing his impatience.

Frank cast a worried glance at Claire, who clung to his arm. *Poor thing.* Another minute, and she'd drop in a heap on the moldy carpet. He'd land right next to her if he didn't find a bed soon.

He released her hand for a moment, leaned over the counter and grabbed the clerk by his string tie. Looked him dead in the eye. "Check. Again."

The clerk leapt back when Frank released him. His spectacles slid down his nose. He pushed them up with one finger. His Adam's apple traveled the length of his skinny neck. "All right, mister, hold your horses."

He hunched over the hotel register, ran his finger down the left column, turned a page filled with names, darted a look at Frank and went right back checking. Finally, he crossed through an entry, straightened and adjusted his tie. "One room just came available."

One room. Frank suppressed a groan. Even comatose, he couldn't keep his hands off Claire, and he'd already put his hands on her enough. With *no promises.* He couldn't continue to bed a decent woman without doing the proper thing, but he couldn't marry her, so... "We need two rooms."

"*One* is all we have." The clerk backed away. Short of crawling over the counter, Frank couldn't reach him.

Claire curled her fingers around his arm. He tensed at her touch.

"We'll take it," she said softly.

He released a pent-up breath. What could he do? She had to sleep. He'd find somewhere else to hole up. Men had options women didn't.

The clerk pursed his lips in disapproval.

He had some nerve. His other guests were horny cowboys, not Sunday school teachers. Frank's anger rekindled. "You got a problem? The lady asked for a room."

The stuffy little sap took up his pencil. "What's the name?"

Frank curled his hand into a fist on the counter. Mr. Prissy didn't need to know her name or anything else about her. "Garrity."

She cut him with a frowning glance, showing the first sign of good hearing since they'd walked in. Didn't call him out. He reckoned he'd hear her objections once they reached the room. He had no plans to marry her, though she didn't seem to expect it, which annoyed him.

The clerk finished writing with a flourish. "That'll be five dollars. In advance."

Claire went for her satchel.

"I'll take care of it." Frank dug into an inside coat pocket for the pouch with his money. She had plenty of other things to spend her cash on. He needed nothing, save the basic necessities, like food. "Bring us dinner."

"I'd like to have a bath. I can pay for it."

An image popped into his head of him lathering her breasts. Sweat broke out on his forehead. He'd leave before she started undressing.

"Make sure the water's hot," she added.

With the heat his body generated, he could warm it up with his finger.

While the clerk scribbled their order on a piece of paper, he shook his head, as if they'd asked for the moon.

Frank pushed a gold eagle across the counter. "That'll more than cover everything, including the room."

The clerk handed him the key.

Upstairs wasn't much better than the lobby. The room smelled like one of those unwashed cowboys. A bed, covered with an old Army blanket, sagged in the middle. Other furniture consisted of a washstand and one cane-back chair. Holes were worn in a rug centered on the rough plank floor.

Claire had to be thinking about how poorly this place compared to the Belmont House. If she was disappointed, she didn't show it. Another admirable trait. She wasn't a complainer and made the best of whatever situation confronted her. Few women could come through what Claire had endured with such grace.

Frank tossed his overcoat on the chair and went to the window. When he lifted the pane, his nose was assaulted by worse odors than those inside. The stockyards were one street over. "We got a nice view of the cattle pens."

"That's one place we haven't looked yet."

He pulled his head in. "We haven't checked all the outhouses either, but I don't reckon he'll be there."

She slowly lowered her satchel to the bed. Perhaps afraid the rickety thing might fall apart. "He told me he'd become a cowboy if he couldn't be an engineer."

"Then we'll check the stockyards."

Moisture welled along her lower eyelids. Tears were more than understandable, given their uncomfortable truce and uncertain situation, coupled with Billy's disappearance. "What if...what if something's happened to him?"

The unhappy thought had crossed Frank's mind numerous times, but he didn't want her to think he'd given up. He took a step closer, struggled to maintain the distance. His defenses had been weakened from fatigue, worry, and an endless well of longing. "Billy's a survivor. He's out there, somewhere. We'll find him. The reward will help."

She blinked. Tears coursed down her cheeks. "How can you be sure?"

"Nothing's certain. It's the best next step."

Her features twisted with despair. She put her hands over her face.

He couldn't stand it. In two strides he reached her and pulled her to him. She gripped the lapels of his overcoat with her face buried against his chest. Her silent weeping was worse than if she'd wailed her grief.

"He-he thinks I don't love him." Her muffled voice wavered. "Frederick r-refused to sign the adoption papers. He agreed to do it, but he procrastinated. Billy must believe I don't want him because I didn't honor my promise."

Frank held her tight. Her grief tore him apart. "Billy doesn't think that. Last time I saw him, he bragged about being adopted as soon as all the papers got signed. He understands. He knows you love him. You showed him that every day."

"I never had a chance to be a good mother."

"Don't say that. You *are* a good mother, Claire." Frank's heart ached to offer her the things she longed for. Things she deserved like a home and a family. As a lawman, he couldn't guarantee her safety, and he wouldn't risk her life.

"I meant what I told him. I won't give him up."

Frank rubbed her back, soothingly. Sounded like she'd regained her courage, which was a good thing. She'd need it to get through what was still ahead of her.

When he found Billy, he had to take the boy to appear before the judge. Not even the *Hanging Judge* would condemn a twelve-year-old. Without a doubt, Billy would be taken away from Claire. She'd lied and covered up the situation that led to the shooting. Not to mention, Billy had killed a man. He might've been defending Claire, but that wouldn't matter to the folks in Parsons. He'd be shunned, treated like a criminal. He couldn't stay without his life being ruined. He had to go.

Frank wouldn't say all that. Not now. He had to gain Claire's trust in him first. Only then could he convince her to tell the truth so they could find a way out of this mess. Then, he would help her put her life back in order before he stayed out of it for good.

CHAPTER 18

*C*laire relaxed in Frank's embrace, grateful for his solid presence and tender comfort. She hadn't thought he would hold her even if she needed to be held. He'd kept a careful distance all day, touching her only to assist her as any gentleman might.

He'd been very honest with her about his intentions. She could only assume he'd decided to put an end to their relationship for both their sakes. Despite knowing it was for the best, her misery had mounted by the hour, made worse by her weariness and her fears about Billy's safety. By the time they'd arrived in the room, she'd been on the verge of tears.

As his large hands made slow, comforting circles on her back, she burrowed into his chest. She hadn't meant to break down in front of him or use it as a ploy to entice him. But now that his arms were around her, she wasn't strong enough to let him go.

He made her feel like a whole woman when he ushered her into that place where nothing mattered but mindless passion. For a time, she forgot the heartaches, her mistakes as a wife, and her failure as a mother.

He tugged at the ribbons holding her bonnet. Would he undress her again with slow deliberation, as if he savored every moment?

Desire rose like water in a flooded creek. She leaned into him, slid her arms inside his coat around his waist and splayed her fingers across his back. His hard, unyielding body offered a safe harbor in the midst of the storm.

His arms fell away. He hesitated a fraction of a second before he moved to set her bonnet on the bed beside her satchel.

Her illusion dissolved.

Frank wasn't her haven and never would be.

Shaken, she backed away, hugging her arms, her vulnerability bare for him to see. She'd felt less exposed when she had been naked.

His expression flattened. He did that when he didn't want her to know what he was feeling. He might be longing for the same things she wanted, but he had fears and doubts.

She looked away, chided herself for trying to read him, which would only lead to more disappointment.

"You ought to get some rest." Before, his voice had been rough with concern. Now, it had a dull tone. He'd withdrawn again. "I got to find something to eat, and a place to sleep."

He took up his overcoat from where he'd tossed it over the chair. Like Billy, he ran when he felt threatened. It stung her pride. She wouldn't accost him. He needn't flee from her desire.

She dried her eyes with a handkerchief before she straightened to face him without tears. "There's no need for you to go. You ordered dinner. Stay here and eat. We can work out an acceptable sleeping arrangement."

"You ordered a bath." He buttoned his coat.

She squared her shoulders, gathered the tattered edges of her dignity. "If it makes you feel safer, when the bath arrives you can go downstairs."

Surprise flashed across his face. "Me? I'm not the one who needs to feel safe."

"No? Look at the way you buttoned up your coat. Like you're afraid I'll rip it off you."

"Claire, you got it all wrong. Blame me, not you. I'm not the marrying kind, but I don't want to treat you shabby. That's why I need to stay away. So I won't be tempted. You're a hard woman to resist."

"You seem quite capable of resisting. I'm the weak one." How shameful, knowing she would go into his arms right now if he touched her.

He edged closer, put on an apologetic expression. "You got nothing to be ashamed of. There's not a thing wrong with having urges. It's perfectly natural."

Her cheeks grew warm. "Don't talk about urges. That makes it sound crude."

"That's not... I meant no offense, only that you ought not feel bad about something that's—"

"I understand. You don't have to spell it out. And yes, of course, you need to leave."

If she had the least idea where Billy might be, she would leave too. She'd go out searching for him, despite being bone-tired.

She'd find nothing but trouble if she wandered around an uncivilized town after dark. Tomorrow, bright and early, she would resume her search, with or without Frank.

"When will you be back?" She moved to the bed and opened her satchel to look for her book.

"If you'd like, I'll check on you in a couple hours."

"You didn't plan to return tonight?"

He didn't meet her eyes. "Thought it best if I didn't sleep here."

The only other places that might have a free bed were one of the many brothels tucked behind the respectable part of town.

Claire's heart constricted at a mental picture of Frank tangled in the arms of a soiled dove. He'd leave her to go lie with a whore. To take care of those *perfectly natural* urges.

"Fine. Don't come back."

He stood there a moment. Long enough for her to wonder if he'd changed his mind and would stay. Not so long that she had time to work up the nerve to apologize and ask him. He brushed her skirts as he walked past.

At the door, he paused. "Keep this locked. I *will* be back."

By the time Frank made his way to the busiest part of town, dusk had fallen. The moon hung in a gunmetal sky. A few stars had popped out. The long-horned cattle were gone, traffic was back to normal, and sidewalks were crowded with rowdy cowboys. Most were headed in the direction of a tent town, located a short distance behind other amusements.

All manner of sinful enjoyment could be had in Denison's darker district—gaming, dancing, drinking and whoring. Out of curiosity, Billy might've decided to check it out.

Frank hadn't mentioned his suspicion earlier. He wouldn't have taken Claire with him anyway. He would check around after he rustled up something to eat. Then, he'd get back to the hotel.

His instincts warned him against leaving her alone for too long. Too many things could go wrong. After her bath, she might take it into her head to go look for Billy. Fortunately, she was dead on her feet and would need to rest a bit and get something to eat. He'd be back before she worked up enough energy to set out. He could haul that chair out by the door and keep watch.

Claire's sharp request that he not return stung. She had every right to be angry. When he'd tried to explain why he couldn't remain in the room with her, he'd stepped on his tongue and nothing he said came out right. If he hadn't given in and bedded her before, she wouldn't be so hurt now. He didn't know how to fix things, except to keep his distance, but he couldn't win her trust if he ignored her. Damn, he'd made a mess of things.

Frank left the boarded walk when he came to the first tent. The city fathers wouldn't spend money on sidewalks in this part of town. His shoes squished in the pungent mud alongside a row of shacks. Oil lamps were hung on hooks by the doors. The lights flickered through colored glass, casting a red glow against the unpainted wood.

It wasn't just cowboys out here tonight. While visiting the working girls, railroaders left their signal lamps outside so they could be located in case train schedules changed. When the lamp was lit, it meant the owner was busy.

Farther along, strains of fiddle music filled the cool night air along with the savory scent of steak. The sounds and smells appeared to be coming from a large frame and canvas structure with a hand-painted sign mounted above the door.

The Lone Star.

He'd lost count of how many establishments used the popular name for the state of Texas.

Frank veered inside. He surveyed the combination saloon and dance hall. Customers crowded a bar constructed from barrels and railroad ties. On a makeshift dance floor, sawdust filled the air, kicked up by energetic dancers. Mostly men.

In these parts, males outnumbered females easily twenty to one. If men wanted to dance and couldn't find female partners, they danced together. A piece of red cloth pinned to their sleeves indicated which fellow took the woman's role. They weren't practiced dancers, but what they lacked in skill they made up for in enthusiasm.

Any other time, Frank would've enjoyed the entertainment. Tonight, he was tired and hungry, and in a hurry to get back to the hotel to check on Claire.

Every seat at every table appeared to be taken, with the exception of one. In a far corner, at a table occupied by a lone man.

By the time Frank reached the table, he'd recognized the burly, dark-haired lawman hunched over a large steak. A U.S. marshal, ironically named Marshall Stokes. Made it easy to remember.

"Mind if I sit, Marshall?"

"Yeah, I do mind." Stokes glanced up. His surly frown lifted in surprised recognition. "I know you. Garrity. You're a sheriff now. Parsons, Kansas, if I recollect right."

"Nothing wrong with your memory."

Stokes straightened. His demeanor became a hair less impolite. "What brings you here?"

"Thought I'd ask you to dance."

The marshal didn't crack a smile. Or if he did, it wasn't visible beneath the black mustache. The tough-as-nails lawman spent most of his time scouring Indian Territory. He'd chased down numerous scoundrels and scalawags holed up there. That kind of work would kill anybody's sense of humor.

Twelve years ago, Frank's life had been similar. Only, he'd tracked down border raiders and bushwhackers for the army. That was when he'd first met then-Lieutenant Marshall Stokes, who'd been almost as rash, but not as thirsty for revenge.

Frank grew tired of waiting for a polite invitation and pulled out the empty chair. "I'm on the lookout for a boy that's gone missing."

Stokes's expression turned speculative. Then he went back to work on his steak.

Frank ordered. Soon as his steak arrived, along with a bottle of whiskey, he tried to focus on the food instead of the worries that nagged at the back of his mind.

After his stint in the Army, he'd become a lawman. An unbiased instrument of the system. If someone broke the law, regardless of who they were, they were apprehended and faced judgment. He'd never balked at doing his job—until Claire had confessed to killing her husband.

Even if he hadn't figured out her ruse, he couldn't see how justice would be served if she got locked up—or worse. And arresting Billy for defending her didn't seem right, either. No matter what choice he made, both of them would suffer. He couldn't protect them and perform his duty.

Frank pushed his empty plate away and downed another drink. If he left the bottle, he wouldn't be tempted to finish it. He fished money out of his pocket to pay for his meal and the liquor, then filled the marshal's glass. "Have a drink on me. Got to get back to the hotel."

Stokes took a sip. "Before you go, tell me about this missing child."

It made sense to enlist the federal Marshal's help. If Stokes happened across Billy, he would bring him in.

Frank gave him the description he'd used for the reward poster.

"His name's Billy Frye, twelve years old, freckle-faced, tow-headed, stands about four-foot-eight. He might be wearing a tan, fleece-lined coat. Last seen in the Parsons switchyard. We suspect he jumped a train headed south."

The marshal set down his glass. "Sounds like the kid I'm looking for."

Frank straightened in surprise. "Did Red Hall tell you about Billy?"

"Haven't seen Red yet. Just got to town. I'm working on a case. A string of train robberies. The latest one occurred last week a few miles north of the Kansas border. Involved a Katy train."

"Yeah, I heard about it. What's that got to do with Billy?"

Stokes leaned back in his seat. "Don't know if it has anything to do with him. One of the passengers reported seeing a boy run away from the train into the woods. He had blond hair, a tan coat. One of the outlaws rode off after him."

A pit opened up in the bottom of Frank's stomach. That would be one explanation for why they hadn't found Billy at the rail yard in Denison. He could've left the train for some reason when it was held up. Why would outlaws chase him down?

"You know who robbed the train?"

"Jasper Byrne and his gang."

Frank rubbed his hand over face. Things had just gone from bad to worse.

Jasper Byrne's long string of crimes had started during the war. He hadn't been much older than Billy. He'd ridden with Rebel trash. The same kind of men Frank had chased down and killed—or hanged from a nearby tree. After the war, the half-breed hellion had moved from raiding farms to robbing trains. There was no reason he'd know Billy or have any use for him.

"We've been hunting these snakes for years, but they're slippery. And the Indians cover for them," Stokes continued. "Before now, we hadn't heard anything about a boy being part of the gang. If he's your runaway, he might've decided he liked the adventure."

"Or they chased him down because he saw too much."

"If they wanted him dead, they could've shot him."

The marshal had a point.

Frank's dread deepened. If Billy had gotten tangled up with a gang of thieves, intentionally or not, it would make matters worse. The judge might decide the troubled boy was incorrigible enough to be tried as an adult, in which case he could end up charged with murder.

Fiddle music started up again. The celebratory strains couldn't drown out a funeral dirge playing in Frank's head. If he told Claire about this, she'd never come clean. He wasn't sure how long he could keep it from her. But he sure as hell wouldn't take her along while he tracked down those outlaws to find Billy.

He poured himself another drink. He'd drown his doubts with whiskey. It wouldn't solve anything, but it took the edge off the pain.

He had to convince Claire to return to Parsons. Which meant, he had to lie to her.

CHAPTER 19

$\mathcal{C}$laire woke with a start at a thump outside her door. She blinked in the darkness.

She didn't remember falling asleep. Actually, she didn't even remember lying down. She'd sat on the bed to comb out her hair after washing up.

Someone could be here to retrieve the wooden tub with two inches of lukewarm water. It wasn't enough for a bath, even if one happened to be a duck.

Another knock.

She fumbled around for matches, lit the wick in an oil lamp and went to the door. With all those cowboys around, she wasn't about to open it.

"Hello? Who is it?" she called out.

"You all right?" came the reply.

She recognized the voice, and it made her far too happy. The sheriff had walked out on her after informing her—again—that he wasn't the marrying type.

Although Frank had promised to return, she hadn't expected to see him until morning. With some hesitation, she cracked open the door. "I'm fine. I was asleep."

He held his hat in his hand. His hair was mussed, his face etched with fatigue, and his eyes were bloodshot. He hadn't slept. Or perhaps he'd just woken up.

"What time is it?" she asked.

"Not sure." He fumbled with a pocket watch then turned the crystal toward the light in the hall. "Eleven."

"You didn't stay out all night."

"Didn't say I planned to."

Relief trickled through her. Given his protective streak, he might've gotten worried about her. Or, he'd changed his mind and decided a willing woman was preferable to one he had to pay. If so, that was too bad for him. She wouldn't issue an invitation.

Her conscience pricked. He'd done nothing to offend her other than leave, which didn't make him a scoundrel. In fact, he'd given her fair warning. If he had bruised her pride, it was her own fault.

She opened the door to allow him to enter. "Have you had dinner?"

"Steak. All those cows are good for something. And you?"

"I'm not sure what it was. They covered it up with gravy."

He lifted her satchel off the chair, tossed her coat and jacket on the bed. "You can go back to sleep. I'll be right outside if you need anything."

While she slept, he would sit in the hall for the remainder of the night. Truly, she was ashamed of her earlier suspicions. She stopped him before he'd reached the door. "That's honorable, but unnecessary."

"It is necessary."

"Why, because you've been drinking?" She smelled whiskey on his breath. He'd been more inebriated the night she'd tracked him down in the saloon, and he'd treated her with utmost respect. Even if he took advantage, she still wouldn't fear him. Foolishly, she would welcome him with open arms.

"You can't sit up all night and keep going tomorrow. We both need rest." She put her hand on his vest. "I trust you, Frank. You'll need to trust me, too."

Without waiting for a response, she locked the door. After she'd crawled onto the bed, she scooted to the far side to make room for him. "Turn down the light, will you?"

After a long moment, she heard the scrape of the chair on the floor, followed by a rustling sound. Perhaps he'd wrestled out of his coat.

The light went out. Then the bed shifted as he lay down next to her. She hugged the far side and tried not to think about his warm, firm body or how much she wanted to be held. Even if she didn't sleep a wink, she would let the poor man rest.

The next time Claire opened her eyes, she saw Frank's broad chest, which rose and fell in a slow rhythm. Her head lay on his shoulder, she'd reached out to hug him. Was she the one who had moved or had he?

She lifted her arm, careful not to wake him.

He sighed and brought his arm around her. "Not morning yet."

The light outside their window proved him wrong. She didn't point that out. Instead, she stayed put and spread out her fingers over his shirt.

He stroked her hair, toying with loose strands around her face, touching her lightly, as if she might break. She wasn't that fragile. But if it pleased him to think so, she wouldn't disabuse him of the notion.

Wistful contentment lapped at her heart. Once they rose from bed, this sweet intimacy would end.

She closed her eyes before tears escaped. Grief and loneliness had driven her into his arms, but it wasn't fair to either of them to continue this charade.

Her sole concern had to be for Billy. Once she found him, she still had to deal with the turmoil surrounding her husband's death, as well as her grief and guilt, and this awful sense of failure. In many ways, she'd been a poor wife. She would work harder at being a good mother.

She dearly wished her own mother had lived long enough to teach her how. As it was, she knew next to nothing about raising children, save what she'd learned by watching others do it. Frederick hadn't wanted children because of his condition. Perhaps Frank had no interest in children either. Or he had lost one, along with his wife. That might explain his reluctance to have another family.

"Have you ever had a child?"

His hand came to rest heavy on her shoulder. Just when she thought he might not answer, he spoke. "A newborn daughter. She died with my wife."

His soft-spoken answer wrung Claire's heart. He'd been married, looking forward to a baby. A time that should've been the happiest in his life. "It must've been awful to lose both of them in childbirth."

He released a slow breath. "Wasn't in childbirth. My wife was shot. The doctor tried to save the baby, but she died, too."

Shock jolted Claire. She lifted up on her arm to look at him. "What kind of fiend would shoot a woman, much less one expecting a child?"

Frank stared back at her with a dull gaze. "He was aiming for me."

"Oh my God. Oh, Frank, that's awful." Claire tried to put her arms around him to hug him, but he held her away from him and his expression turned hard.

"I killed a man. An outlaw. His two brothers came to my house, gunning for me. A stray bullet struck Sarah. I knew there was a chance they might try to ambush me. I should've sent her away until I caught them."

So, this was what tormented him. Guilt drove him to drink too often and too much.

"You blame yourself."

His eyes reflected soul-deep despair. "Her safety was my responsibility."

The ache in Claire's chest worsened. His refrain sounded horribly familiar because she'd heard it in her head, over and over. Responsibility. She bore responsibility.

She couldn't find words to soothe Frank's pain or to give him the assurance that he would one day feel better. She understood his hurt too well to pretend that peace would come easily, if ever. "That's a terrible burden. I wish there was some way I could make it lighter."

He cupped his hand on her jaw, rubbed his thumb over her cheek. "Aren't you hauling around enough? You ought to know better than to think I'd let you carry my burdens, too."

What little resistance she had left dissolved at his touch. The defenses she'd built up over the years, layer by layer, gave way. The protective barrier could no longer hold back the flood. Tenderness, affection, yearning—feelings she couldn't even name—swirled into the empty chambers of her heart. The sensation took her breath away.

She shook her head, though there was no denying it.

Foolish, foolish woman. She should've known this would happen.

Love had stormed in, uninvited.

FRANK HELD Claire's hand while she mounted the steps to the passenger car. He kept a sharp watch for the local sheriff or the marshal. If either man showed up, they could unwittingly put an end to this ruse.

"You're certain Billy is in Parsons?" Claire asked him again.

"That's the message I got last night." Frank hadn't come up with a better story to convince her to return willingly.

He glanced worriedly at the clear blue sky. The weather had been as dry as tumbleweed in a dust bowl, so there was little chance lightning would strike.

"You should've told me before this morning," she chided.

"Wasn't thinking straight. I was tired." Both statements were true.

From the moment he'd stretched out next to her on that tiny bed, his thoughts had scattered. If he hadn't been so exhausted, he would've taken her in his arms long before morning. As it was, she hadn't done more than mumble when he drew her over and tucked her head onto his shoulder.

Claire hesitated on the top step. "Why do you keep looking up? Are you worried about the weather?"

In a manner of speaking. He half expected God to hurl a bolt and strike him dead for telling a bald-faced lie. "The weather down here is less reliable than in Kansas."

He escorted her to the rear of the car. "You mind if I sit near the window?"

"Not at all. Smoke and cinders blow in. You're welcome to them." She scooted onto the bench next to him then adjusted her skirts before she situated her bag on the floor by her feet. Her eagerness to be off, her teary-eyed relief when he'd told her Billy had been found, made his guilt ten times worse.

He turned his face to the open window, unable to look her in the eye.

Early this morning, in bed with Claire in his arms, he hadn't wanted the moment to end. He'd gathered her to him while she was still asleep. She'd come without hesitation. He knew it would be the last time she would let him touch her, and he'd found it damn near impossible to let go.

For some reason, she'd asked him about children. He hadn't talked about what had happened to his family to anyone who didn't already know the story. Mostly because it hurt too much, and nothing anybody said ever helped.

Claire's sensitive response had pierced his heart. He drank in her kindness like it was sweet water, bubbling up from an endless spring.

In return, he'd lied to her. What he was about to do would break her heart and destroy her faith in him. He despised himself more than he thought possible.

A whistle sounded. As the train pulled out of the station, smoke poured through the open windows. Bits of ash snagged on his clothes. The dense cloud would prevent her from seeing the reward poster for Billy tacked to the side of the depot. She might question why the sheriff had gone ahead and put it up.

Frank observed the car wasn't full. Northbound trains hauled mostly freight and cattle. Trains headed south were filled with passengers and mail, and were frequently targeted by outlaws. Based on what the marshal had told him, Jasper Byrne and his gang seemed to know when the payroll cash would be transported. Someone had to be tipping them off.

Billy wouldn't know anything about the payroll. In fact, it made no sense the boy would be involved with those thieves. He worshiped the men who worked on the railroad, longed to be one of them. They hated outlaws even more than they hated the disgruntled settlers who tore up their tracks.

"Did the message say if Billy went back to the hotel?" Claire's question pulled Frank out of his musings.

Not used to lying, he hadn't prepared a detailed story.

"No."

"Who sent it?"

"Deputy Branch."

"Did he say if Billy's all right?"

Oh sure, drag his deputy into the lie and have Claire hate both of them. Gideon didn't deserve that. He hadn't deceived a sweet, decent woman who'd offered him affection and understanding.

Frank rubbed at his chest. The damn thing ached worse than a rotten tooth. "The message didn't say. Let's assume he's at the hotel, safe and sound."

"What are you not telling me?"

"There's nothing more to say. It was a short message."

Her suspicion didn't waver. He did the only thing he could think of to distract her—scooted closer and put his arm around her shoulders, which elicited a look of alarm.

"What are you doing?"

"Trying to calm you down."

"I was calm *before* you put your arm around me." She shifted away, but she couldn't move far without falling off the bench.

Frank put his lips near her ear. Her sweet fragrance tortured him. "What's your favorite flower?"

"What?" She twisted around and peered at him, anxiously. "Have you been drinking?"

"Not a drop since last night."

"Too much strong drink can lead to hallucinations. You shouldn't imbibe to excess. If you can't resist, consider stopping altogether."

Oh no. They were *not* discussing his drinking habits.

He straightened, but left his arm draped over the back of the bench. This way, he could brush her shoulder with his fingertips, to keep her off guard. And because he couldn't resist touching her. If he confessed to the addiction, she'd probably advise him to stop touching her altogether. He'd rather give up whiskey.

"I'm not seeing things. I just asked what kind of flower you like. My favorite is trailing roses. My mother planted some that grew up the side of our house. Your perfume reminds me of them."

She looked stunned.

"What? I don't look like the type to talk about flowers?"

"Or perfume. I don't wear any. I use water infused with rose petals to wash my hair."

"Rosewater?" His mind conjured a blissful fantasy of joining her in the bath to rub soft, fragrant rose petals over her skin.

He touched a shiny, braided loop not covered by her cozy bonnet. She flushed a delightful shade of pink. "You're blushing," he murmured, "and your lips are rosy."

If he bent down, he could kiss—

"Not *here*," she gasped in a horrified whisper, and dipped her chin.

Her reaction shook him out of the sensual daze he'd slipped into. He sat straighter and gripped the bench so he wouldn't touch her. He had no business kissing her, much less in public. When she discovered his lies, she would believe, rightfully so, he'd used her.

Guilt flayed his conscience. Claire wouldn't despise him as much as she'd hate herself for being gullible. She wasn't to blame for anything. Her only fault was caring—for her husband, for Billy, for a lying lawman.

Curse him. He couldn't help being drawn to her. Like a plant reaching for the sunshine. He'd basked in her light and warmth, had started to heal, and hadn't even realized it until now. When it was too late.

"Claire..." her name came out in a low plea. "I..."

Love you.

Good God, no. He couldn't tell her how he felt. That would be an even worse betrayal, to tell her he loved her when all along he planned to break her heart by going after Billy without her.

Her eyes shone with anticipation. After an awkward moment, hope faded, replaced by sadness, understanding. "Tell me about the roses, and where you lived growing up."

He was tempted to hand her his gun and tell her to shoot him. That's what she ought to do when she encountered a snake.

"My mother transplanted trailing roses from our home in Missouri. We moved to a farm just over the border in what was at the time Kansas Territory." Frank could see in his mind's eye the profuse vines, heavy with blooms. His mother's lined, weathered face, her proud smile. "They spread up the porch supports and on a trellis on the side of the house. I can remember how they smelled when the window was open and there was a breeze."

For years, the scent of roses had reminded him of his mother. Then, he'd met Claire. Her sweet fragrance reminded him of all he'd lost. Made him long for things he wasn't destined to have, like a stable home and a family.

His spirits sank further.

"Are the roses still there?"

"Don't know. I haven't been back since she died ten years ago."

"You don't have family living there?"

No one lived at the deserted farm. He didn't know why he hadn't sold the place.

"My sisters live in Missouri with their husbands and families. They're quite a bit older than me. They married before my parents moved to Kansas in fifty-seven. Both my folks are gone."

For years, Frank had kept the window to his past firmly shut. Because he felt safe with Claire, he opened it. "A year after we moved, southern raiders crossed the border. They rounded up a dozen free-state men, including my father. Took them to a ravine and shot them. Murdered them, because they opposed slavery."

Claire's eyes were deep pools of sympathy. She had a gift for being able to connect with another person's pain. Or maybe it was something special between the two of them. Whatever it was, it had the same effect on him as bathing in a sun-warmed lake.

"How old were you when your father was killed?"

"Sixteen."

"That's too young to lose your father." A small crease marred her smooth forehead, a sign she was thinking. "You're thirty-three."

She said it like she'd compared him to Methuselah.

"Hard to believe with all this gray hair." Not to mention the extra years carved into his face. He sure felt like he'd lived three lifetimes.

She touched her hair self-consciously. "I'm sure I look older than twenty-eight."

"Not by a minute." What a relief to be able to make an honest statement.

Her eyes shone with gratitude, even as her lips twisted in a rueful smile. "Let's just say we've both put a lot of living into our few years."

She'd been a young bride tied to a broken soldier. He'd spent half his life pursuing justice, which had turned out to be an elusive ideal rather than a hard and fast principle.

"Living isn't what I'd call it."

Her expression turned somber. "Did losing your father make you pessimistic?"

"It made me bloodthirsty. After my father was killed, I lied about my age so I could join up with the Kansas militia. We raided, looted, and hit back twice as hard. Not very heroic. Or effective. By the time the war ended, I'd spilled enough blood to satisfy even me."

As he spoke, her eyes grew larger, looking wounded. Yet, it seemed as if her hurt was on *his* behalf. He hadn't intended to stir her sympathy with that story. Rather, he wanted her to know he'd ruined his life a long time ago and wasn't worth her affection.

"Did you become a sheriff after the war?"

"For a while I chased war criminals. Then I decided I might as well wear a tin star."

She searched his face. He sensed she could see things he'd prefer to keep hidden. His weakness for her being foremost. "What did your father do for a living?"

"He was a farmer."

"You never had any desire to return home to farm the land?"

If possible, the ache in his chest got worse. "My mother begged me to come home. I was too busy exacting revenge. The day finally came when I realized I'd never gain justice by spilling blood. By then, she was dead, and it was too late. The farm holds too many bad memories."

She put her hand on his arm. "You could always create new ones. Better memories, I mean."

It was on the tip of his tongue to say if the new memories included her, he would jump at the chance. He longed to hold onto the contentment he found beside her. His natural selfishness urged him to give in. Give up his job. Offer to take Claire away and make a fresh start. Maybe even go back to the farm.

His conscience reminded him he wasn't free to offer her anything. He was already married—to justice. It didn't matter whether justice turned out to be a cold bedfellow. He had chosen it, and the law, and was bound by duty.

Besides, she'd distrust him after she got home and realized he'd lied to her. And she'd hate him when he brought Billy in to testify to the truth.

Frank swallowed a fist-sized lump lodged in his throat before he dismissed her tempting suggestion—with another lie. "I'm not much interested in settling down."

CHAPTER 20

The moment the train arrived in Parsons, Claire set off for the hotel, eager to find Billy. Frank told her he had to check in with his deputy and would see her again soon.

He'd been acting strange the entire trip home. At first, evasive, then overly friendly, and finally, silent and uncommunicative. It had exhausted her trying to figure him out. She had to stop dwelling on the frustrating man and focus solely on keeping Billy safe.

If he'd returned to the hotel, he must not have admitted to anything. He had a survivor's instincts and was a practiced liar. She could school him on what to say so they could make it through the hearing without incident. If she and Billy agreed on the story about the gun accidentally discharging, who could refute it?

Claire kept her head down as she hurried along the sidewalk. Was it her imagination or were people staring at her? She didn't have on the customary widow's weeds, something she would correct immediately.

She slipped in through the front door. Thankfully, few guests were in the lobby. Billy might be in his room. On her way to the stairs, she glanced over at the registration desk. Then halted, startled.

Gertrude Bond and her sixteen-year-old son, Clive, who'd routinely tormented Billy at school, sat behind the registration desk.

What were those two doing *here*?

Claire marched around the counter. "I beg your pardon, where's Karl?"

Mrs. Bond shrugged. "I have no idea where young Mr. Kelly might be found. He and his mother no longer work here."

"What do you mean, they don't—?" Claire drew herself up with indignation. "How dare you come in here and act as if you own the place."

Gertrude Bond's thin-lipped smile reminded Claire of a man-eating reptile she'd seen at a circus. "Oh, but I do own the place. Your husband sold it to us."

Claire took a step backward. *No. No, it couldn't be.* The night Frederick had died, she'd torn up what looked like a bill of sale. Or had it been something else? "That...that's not possible."

"Excuse me." A bearded man in a business suit approached the counter. "I believe I have a room reserved."

Mrs. Bond nudged her aside. "We can discuss this later if you'd like. I need to see to our guest."

Claire flushed hot, then cold. She'd walked into a nightmare. These horrid people had waited until she'd left town, then they'd swept in and stolen her home like vicious blue jays descending on a robin's nest. There had to be something she could do to prevent this monstrous theft. Henry would know what to do. She'd send him a message immediately.

The odious woman handed her a key. "No one knew where you'd gone or when you would return. We took the liberty to move your personal things into that spare room where the boy was staying."

A light flickered in the dark tunnel Claire had entered. "Billy? He's here?"

Clive Bond snickered. "Of course not. We wouldn't let that little thief stay in our hotel."

How dare he malign Billy? These two were lower than the lowest outlaws. Fouler than egg-stealing vermin.

Claire's pent-up frustrations and fears, the anger and grief she'd suppressed, erupted in a volcanic rage. She shoved Mrs. Bond aside, snatched up the registration book and began to beat the pimple-faced youth away from the registration counter. "*You* get out of here."

He yelped like a scared pup and threw his arms over his head. "Mama, help!"

Sharp fingernails dug into Claire's shoulder. "Stop this instant, you heathen."

Claire whirled around and smacked the other woman in the face with the book. "Get out!" she screamed. "Get out of my hotel!"

As she brandished her weapon, the two vultures backed away. They screeched for someone to fetch the sheriff.

The visitor at the counter retreated with his hands up. Other guests scurried out the door.

Good, let them leave. Let them all go and leave her alone.

Her breathing grew ragged. Her chest ached and her eyes stung.

Frederick had betrayed her. Billy had left her. Frank didn't want her. She was alone. Completely, wretchedly alone.

Hell would freeze over before she gave up her home.

"You can't steal my hotel. I won't let you." Claire slammed the book on the counter. She fumbled with the drawer in a mad search for the pistol she kept handy in case of robbery. This outrage qualified as a crime, as far as she was concerned.

The gun had gone missing. Where had she—? *Billy.* He still had the gun. He'd used it to shoot Frederick. Which was *her* fault because she'd left it where he could find it.

She cried out, enraged, grief-stricken and brokenhearted. "Where is he? Where's Billy?" She swung around to the remaining two people in the lobby. "Where's my son?"

How long she stood there, weeping and calling for Billy, she didn't know. She couldn't see past the tears streaming from her eyes. Someone called her name, as if from far away. His voice sounded familiar. Soothing.

The moment Frank touched her shoulder she turned, grabbed his coat and clung to him. He was her friend. Her lover. Her refuge.

"I'm sorry, Claire." His voice grew rough with regret. "I have to arrest you."

~

REGRET DIDN'T BEGIN to describe the emotions clawing inside Frank's chest when he ushered Claire into one of the holding cells situated behind his office.

He shouldn't have left her alone.

His plan had been to recruit his deputy's help to keep her in town while he slipped away to search for Billy. Before he could work out his next step, Gertrude Bond had dragged her sniveling son into his office, hollering something about Claire going mad and attacking them.

By the time Frank reached the hotel, Claire was wandering around the lobby, weeping, calling for Billy in halting, gasping sobs. A frightened guest reported she'd gone after Mrs. Bond and her son with the hotel register then said she would shoot them.

Frank had no choice but to arrest her. For *her* own safety.

He spread a clean blanket over the cot. Couldn't do much about the smell from the previous occupant. A small, barred window let in a little light, but also cold air. He shrugged out of his coat and tucked it around her shoulders, as he spoke softly. "I'll be back in a bit. Won't be long. We'll get this sorted out."

She sank onto the cot without answering. Stared straight ahead with a blank expression.

"Claire?" Frank squatted in front of her. He gripped her arm to get her attention. "Look at me. Everything will be all right."

The disdainful look she turned on him made him wish he hadn't asked for her undivided attention. "Where's Billy?"

He released her. She wouldn't want him to touch her. In fact, she'd probably spit on him when he told her the truth. "The U.S. Marshal thinks he's with a gang of train robbers."

Her expression turned horrified. Slowly, awareness dawned on her. "You *knew*," she accused in a hushed voice. "You knew and you *lied*."

It was too late for apologies or explanations, even if he owed her both.

"For your protection. I had to get you to come back with me. I knew you wouldn't return willingly if you found out about Billy being holed up with those outlaws. I'm sorry I had to lie."

"You *had* to lie?" The raw hurt in her eyes was worse than her cold silence. "No one has to lie. You *chose* to lie. You begged me to trust you, then you deliberately deceived me."

He would've preferred she use a whip instead of words. The lash would hurt less. He could beg her forgiveness, except he didn't deserve it. For her sake, it would be better if she continued to hate him. Hatred would keep her from sinking into despair.

More words were useless at this point.

He closed the cell door behind him and left her to return to his office, which had become busy as a beehive in just a few minutes.

William and Gertrude Bond, their lawyer, and the mayor, Sharp Taylor, had stormed into the office, with everybody talking at the same time.

Gideon moved off to one side. He'd wisely allow the sheriff to handle things.

The red-faced lawyer waved a piece of paper under Frank's nose. "We have legal documents that give my client ownership of the Belmont House."

Frank snatched the paper away. He glared at the document, which meant nothing to him, other than proving the Bonds had dotted the *i*'s in this farce. "You waited until she left town and then moved in? Why didn't you say anything about this earlier?"

Gertrude Bond piped up before her husband could answer. "We thought it more civil to wait until after the funeral. Then she disappeared. How were we to know she hadn't fled justice? When I tried to explain, she attacked me."

The elegantly dressed woman tucked a stray blond hair—the

only one out of place—behind the silk ribbon securing her feathered bonnet.

"Doesn't appear you were done any harm," Frank pointed out.

"Only because the crazed woman couldn't find her gun," her husband interjected.

"You should've arrested her when I told you to." The mayor straightened his coat and puffed up his chest like he was an important person, rather than an insignificant toad. "She poses a danger to our town."

Frank entertained the thought of stuffing his fist down Sharp's throat. "Mrs. Daines is about as dangerous as a toothless hound."

"That woman *shot* her husband. She attacked Mrs. Bond and our son without provocation. She's a menace." William Bond snatched the deed out of Frank's hands. He handed it to the balding attorney standing next to him, then drew up to his full height, which still wasn't as tall as his wife.

He tried to look Frank in the eye, but had to crane his neck to do so. "When I last spoke with Mr. Daines, on the night before he died, he told me he feared his wife would kill him. We'd finalized our agreement when he said, 'S*he'll kill me for doing this.*' Those were his very words."

Frank's shock was surpassed only by the anger that flooded him an instant later. "Even if he said it, men say stupid things like that all the time."

"Obviously, he wasn't a stupid man. He knew his wife to be capable of violence."

Frank balled his fists. He sorely needed a punching bag. Perhaps Bond's face. "Why didn't you come forward with this information before now?"

"As Gertrude said, we wanted to wait until after the funeral. Out of respect." Bond adjusted the gold stickpin on his tie. The rich railroad baron didn't think he had enough money. He had to steal from a sweet widow and accuse her of murder. Hell wasn't hot enough for his type.

"*Respect?* You wouldn't know the meaning of the word."

"That's a grave insult, sir."

Taylor leapt in, as if on cue. "If you can't execute the duties of your position, Sheriff, perhaps you ought to step down."

Oh, they'd like that, wouldn't they? These rats were in cahoots. They'd cooked this up together. Or Bond had falsified the documents and told the mayor what to say. Taylor didn't have that much imagination.

"I'd be happy to execute my duties, which, by the way, include investigating schemes perpetrated against an innocent woman. One who has no one left to protect her from opportunistic vultures." Frank came around his desk. He hadn't felt this violent since he'd started chasing bushwhackers.

Taylor, Bond, his wife and the lawyer all took a step back.

Frank jerked a tight rein on his fury. He gestured to the front door. "See yourselves out. I have business to discuss with my deputy."

"You'll regret throwing us out, Sheriff," Bond cautioned.

"I've asked you to leave. Politely. If, or when, I throw you out, you'll know the difference."

Mrs. Bond paused with smug triumph on her face. "If you release that woman, she'll flee justice, as she did before. I'm sure you don't want the record to show you allowed *another* murderer to escape."

Frank seethed at the taunt. Unfortunately, he had no proof to refute Claire's foolish confession, and she'd complicated things by losing her temper. At this point, he'd have to proceed with caution in order to protect her, even if it didn't look that way.

"She's not going anywhere," he ground out.

With a satisfied nod, Mrs. Bond followed the rest of the uninvited visitors out the door.

Frank slammed it shut behind her. Hot enough to breathe fire, he turned to his deputy. "Take my gun away if they come back. I can't promise I won't do something I regret."

Gideon's dark eyes reflected sympathy. "Things don't look good for Mrs. Daines."

Frank released an aggrieved sigh. He had hoped he could quietly fetch Billy home before anyone found out where he'd been or what he'd been doing. Bond's revelation had upped the stakes. It was imperative he find the boy and fast. Unfortunately, it also meant Billy's sins would have to be exposed. "She didn't kill anybody."

"But she said—"

"I know what she said. That's not what happened. We have to find that boy."

CHAPTER 21

*J*asper spent the morning teaching his charge how to set snares. He'd learned how from his Cherokee grandfather before the old man had gone on to the happy hunting grounds.

After they finished with the snares, they went fishing. He showed the boy how to clean and cook his catch.

Afterwards, they sat on the porch and he had a smoke while Billy worked on various types of knots he'd been taught. Thus far, it had been a quiet, surprisingly satisfying, day.

"How are you coming along on those knots?"

Billy threw down the rope with a huff. "When am I gonna learn how to be an outlaw?"

Never.

Jasper had decided he would teach Billy useful lessons that would keep him alive longer. Eventually, he'd turned the boy loose, after Billy tired of all the hard work.

"An apprentice doesn't ask those questions. He learns what his teacher wants to teach when he wants to teach it."

In the week since his men had ridden off in search of whores, Jasper had recruited Billy to help him with a number of tasks.

They'd cleaned out the cabin, filled missing chinks in the log walls, repaired holes in the roof, and fixed the porch rail, among other things. He didn't intend to live here—with a price on his head, he couldn't stay anywhere for long—but it felt right to put the family home back in order. In fact, for the first time in years, life felt normal. Almost good.

Around noon, Candy and Tom arrived with news that spoiled everything.

Jasper rocked in one of the porch chairs while he read the notice Candy had given him. He'd sent Billy out to the woods to check on the snares so the boy wouldn't find out what was going on. He'd run if he knew.

"Ain't no question. Shorty is worth four hundred dollars. We just got to figure out how to turn him in without getting caught." Candy rested his ample hip on the rail, which creaked underneath the weight.

Jasper frowned at him. "Can't you sit in a chair? I just fixed that porch rail."

Candy conceded to the request and dropped his big ass in the other rocking chair. Baxter Beeman was called *Candy* for a good reason. He liked sweets too much.

Tom leaned against a post with his arms crossed. His slight weight wouldn't collapse the support. "You could ask Sally to turn him in."

His cousin knew better than to suggest such a thing.

"No. She doesn't need to be involved." Jasper flat refused to ask his younger sister for more favors. He'd already asked too much of her over the years.

She had lied for him, hidden him and patched him up. He would leave her in peace, while continuing to funnel money into a bank account he'd set up for her and her daughter. They could use another four hundred dollars.

"Hell, for that kind of money, *I'll* risk it." Candy leaned forward in the rocking chair to rest his arms on his knees. He'd gotten flushed with excitement or liquor. Either turned his face red.

"You'd risk your neck for forty dollars, which is why I don't let you make any decisions that have to do with money."

"How hard can it be?" Candy grinned.

He smiled more often since getting that gold cap on a front tooth, which had gotten broken off in a fight. Too brash for his own good, yet loyal to a fault.

Loyal men were hard to come by.

"That's why I don't let you do the thinking, either." Jasper planned the jobs and managed the execution. The other two weren't smart enough. He wouldn't want them to plan a family picnic, much less a robbery.

What a sorry lot they were. But they'd been together from the start, had each other's backs. No one else gave a damn about them.

"All right," Candy slapped his knees and straightened. "You decide who goes and collects. But we split it, right? Just like always."

"Yeah. We'll split it. If I collect." Jasper leaned back to ponder what he ought to do.

Billy claimed to be an orphan. He'd said he shot his guardian's husband. Why would they offer such a large reward for his *safe return*? Oddly enough, the notice made no mention of the shooting. The boy could be lying. Or there was more to the story than what he'd shared. Or...

The reward could be a smokescreen. Someone on the train might've noticed Billy, and the outlaw riding after him.

Jasper sighed. In hindsight, it would've been better to leave well enough alone. At the time, he hadn't taken time to think about it. He had heeded an inner voice. He'd better stop listening to that do-gooder. It would get him killed.

He looked between the two men awaiting his decision. "We don't know why they offered all that money for an orphan. They might've figured out we have him. Want to flush us out."

Tom looked unconvinced. "How would they know we have him? You haven't taken him anywhere but here."

"Someone on the train could've seen him, and seen me when I rode after him. I don't want to walk into a trap."

Candy released a huff. He sometimes confused caution with cowardice. "What're you sayin' Jasper? You'll just let all that money slip away?"

Under normal circumstances, *no*, he wouldn't turn down a chance for easy money. But betraying a boy who trusted him didn't set right. He couldn't turn the kid in without first discovering who wanted him and for what purpose.

Jasper pushed out of the chair. "I'll slip into Parsons. Find out why they're so anxious to get him back."

"You?" Tom looked alarmed. "There's a big price on your head. If somebody recognizes you—"

"They won't. Those *Wanted* posters don't look a thing like me. I'm a lot handsomer." He joked about it, but he knew he would have to take care not to be noticed. "I'll see if my contact can help us."

"This contact of yours, who is he?" Tom asked.

Candy leaned forward, as if he thought he might learn the secret.

"You know I can't tell y'all that." Jasper wasn't so stupid he'd give up critical knowledge. Not even to his most loyal men.

Six months ago, when he'd been hanging out around Vinita with no money and few ideas about where get some, he'd met a white man who had offered him work. Typically, whites didn't venture into Indian Territory to recruit employees. This fellow claimed he wanted men who wouldn't ask too many questions.

The jobs were small, at first. Mostly vandalism against the railroad. Then his contact suggested he'd be willing to provide information about when the payroll would be moving. In return, Jasper would keep his mouth shut about where the information came from and turn over a small percentage to his benefactor.

Not being the trusting sort, he had done his own investigation and had discovered the surprising identity of his contact. This knowledge gave him power and some degree of protection. He would keep the secret as long as it benefited him to do so.

"What makes you think this contact won't betray you?" Tom asked.

Jasper shrugged, as if he weren't concerned. "He hasn't turned on me yet. No reason for him to do it now. He's got too much to lose if I blow."

"Not if he has you killed," Candy pointed out. Unnecessarily.

Jasper knew the risks. He never went into anything unprepared. "I'll be back within the week. Then we'll take the kid in—if it's safe. You two stay here. Keep an eye on Billy. Don't hurt him. And whatever you do, don't lose him."

When Billy returned from checking the snares, Jasper had up and lit out. According to Tom and Candy, *the boss* had gone to scout a new job, which meant to plan a robbery.

It wasn't fair. Jasper had finally decided to do something interesting, and he'd left without his *apprentice*.

"Hey Shorty, you gettin' hungry?" Candy remained planted in the rocking chair on the front porch. The lazy oaf wouldn't rustle up dinner. He wanted someone else to do it.

Billy hunkered down on the front step with his arms on his knees and didn't offer. He'd starve first.

"I shore did work up an appetite."

Doing what? Sitting? If Candy was so hungry, why didn't he get off his fat butt and get himself something to eat?

The other chair creaked. Tom Bluejacket was just as lazy, even if he wasn't fat. "Sun's setting. Now would be a good time to go fishing."

Billy wasn't moving from this spot. "Why don't you two go?"

"Can't. I got to finish this." Tom rocked slowly. He'd whittled every so often on a piece of wood that appeared to have no definable shape or useful purpose.

"Tell you what. You catch us a mess of fish and we might let *you* eat some." Candy slapped his knee and hooted.

He amused no one but himself, but that didn't stop him. For some reason, he'd been in a jovial mood ever since he and Tom had returned from town.

Billy still couldn't figure out why Jasper had left him in the company of these two idiots. The outlaw was supposed to show him how to be a train robber. Instead, he'd learned how to hunt and fish, and Jasper had talked him into helping with repairs on the cabin. All that work hadn't been bad. Mostly because it was fun to be in the company of a man who seemed to have all the time in the world to teach him things. It wouldn't change his mind about being a farmer, if that was Jasper's plan. The confounded outlaw hadn't even *talked* about robbing trains. In fact, he'd acted like he didn't care if he never did another job.

Someone cuffed Billy on the back of the head.

He leapt up and whirled around with his fists raised. "Stop that!"

"Oh, no! I'm *so* scared." Candy spoke in a high, quivery voice with his hands held high. He doubled over with laughter.

"You're in charge of dinner tonight, Shorty." Tom kept right on shaving that stick.

Billy entertained a rude thought involving the stick and where it might be placed. "I was in charge of dinner last night."

"And you'll be in charge of dinner tomorrow night," Candy shot back. "You want to be part of the gang? You gotta make yourself useful."

"You and Tom don't do anything except sit around and drink Jasper's liquor."

"It ain't Jasper's liquor. We share everything, even Steven." Candy slipped his forefinger in the round handle of a narrow-mouthed jug, lifted it up to his shoulder and took a swig. He wiped his mouth with a dirty shirtsleeve. "Now get goin' before it gets dark."

Billy simmered. He could refuse, which would provide brief satisfaction. But then they'd beat him and he'd have to do what they wanted anyway—or leave. If Jasper were here, Candy and Tom wouldn't dare beat him. He'd have a talk with Jasper when the outlaw got back. These two loafers should have to earn their keep.

After another moment, he got up slow and went inside the cabin to fetch a sack for the fish. He spotted a saddlebag hanging from a peg near the door.

A wicked idea took hold.

Billy tucked the saddlebag under his arm and ran out the back door. What a good laugh he'd have when Candy found his saddlebag filled with stinky fish. Oh man, it would be worth the beating.

For the rest of the afternoon, Billy hung out down by the creek. He wasn't in a hurry to get back and fry up somebody else's supper. If they didn't like it, they could come down here and catch their own dang fish.

After a while, he opened the saddlebag and pulled out a folded piece of paper. Perfect for wrapping the fish once he got around to catching some. He opened the paper, which kind of reminded him of the *Wanted* posters in the sheriff's office.

Reward. Missing boy.

Billy's stomach knotted. He quickly scanned the fine print. Mrs. Daines had made him learn how to read. If he hadn't, he wouldn't know he had a price on his head.

The significance of where he'd found the poster dawned on him. Candy and Tom had brought this reward notice back with one intention. They hadn't acted on it because they never did anything without Jasper.

And Jasper had left.

The last line condemned him.

Contact Labette County Sheriff Frank Garrity.

Billy tried to breathe and couldn't. Jasper's betrayal stuck in his throat like a fishbone. The outlaw wasn't scouting a potential robbery. He'd gone to Parsons to collect the reward.

No wonder those two fools were in such a good mood. Every time they looked at him, they saw the four hundred dollars they'd split three ways.

The double-crossers.

Billy scrubbed away angry tears. He wouldn't cry on account of those no-good, low-down belly crawlers. Mrs. Daines had an acceptable reason to give him up. He'd killed her husband. Jasper had brought him out here and acted friendly. Then put him to work like a slave, and now planned to sell him. What the railroaders had said was right. Men who held up trains weren't to be admired. They were dishonest. Rotten right down to the core. Even Jasper. He'd turned traitor at the mere mention of money.

What time was it?

Not the time to sit around and nurse hurt feelings. Wouldn't do no good. Never had.

Billy rummaged through the saddlebag to see what else it might contain. He found a small sack of coins. What good fortune. He'd need money to get home.

He didn't want to be an outlaw no more. And he wouldn't stick around here, waiting until those liars bundled him off to Parsons. He still had a chance to become a hero and get a job with the railroad—if he could catch up with Jasper.

Billy set out at a trot toward the sinking sun. The railroad lines were in that direction. Jasper hadn't told him how far. He'd go straight, *as the crow flies*, and eventually find the tracks. Hitch a ride on a northbound train.

He'd sneak back into town, locate Jasper. Then he'd tell the sheriff where to find an outlaw with an even *bigger* price on his head.

CHAPTER 22

*T*he jail cell had a small window with iron bars, which overlooked a barren field where gallows were constructed when necessary. None had been needed since late last year when Henry's former assistant, Mr. Caldwell, had been hanged for the murder of a railroad investigator.

Claire was painfully aware she'd risked the same fate when she confessed to killing her husband. But considering a possibility and looking one square in the face were very different matters.

"Mr. Bond claims your husband said you would kill him if he sold the hotel." The lawyer's remark from behind her penetrated her morbid musings.

"Yes, the sheriff told me what he said," she answered without turning around.

God help her.

All her energy had to be directed toward remaining clam, collected. She hadn't been either when Frank had brought her in here yesterday. Stunned, heartbroken, then furious at his deceit.

After she had licked her wounds and reflected, she'd accepted the obvious. The sheriff had simply done his job. She was the one who'd forgotten her common sense and fallen in love. Didn't mean she'd forgive him for lying to her.

She continued to stare out the window. "Frederick might've made the remark in jest, though I doubt it. His condition affected his sense of humor, as well as his reason. He had an unnatural fear that plots were being hatched against him. He also accused the cook of trying to poison him, and I can assure you Mrs. Kelly prepares wholesome meals."

At her attorney's silence, she finally faced him.

The serious, dark-haired lawyer leaned heavily on a cane he used for balance.

Her manners had flown out that window.

"Please, do sit down, Mr. Moore." She gestured to a chair the sheriff had thoughtfully provided. Frank had also placed a mattress on the hard cot and brought in a washstand. He'd done everything he could to make her comfortable. Everything, except release her.

"Thank you." The lawyer used his cane and lowered himself onto the seat.

According to what he'd told her, he had recently immigrated to Kansas. From where, she didn't know. Somewhere in the South, based on his accent. He mostly handled land disputes, which often put him in opposition to the railroad. This could be an asset or a liability, depending on whether the jury had more settlers or railroad men. Regardless, he'd been the only attorney in town willing to take her case.

He pushed his sable hair out of his eyes. Despite being too gaunt, he had even features, and could easily be called *handsome*.

For some reason, Claire thought about her sister's preference for dark-haired men with soulful eyes. Hannah would enjoy meeting Mr. Moore, although it was doubtful the two would have the opportunity to make an acquaintance.

He leaned his cane against his leg. Took out a notebook and pencil from a case he'd put on the floor. "Were Mr. Bond and your husband well acquainted?"

"Frederick wasn't well acquainted with anyone, except me." She walked the breadth of the confined area. "I invited the Bonds to a dinner shortly after they arrived in town. Henry and the railroad directors had a falling out, but I was prepared to bury the hatchet with the new general manager for the sake of peace. When the Bonds returned for another visit, I was surprised Frederick was willing to see them. As I told you before, my husband feared social settings. I took his interest as a positive sign. I didn't suspect Mr. Bond might be manipulating him into signing away our rights."

Thus far, Mr. Moore seemed quite intelligent and very much a gentleman. She prayed he could help her avoid being hanged, among other things. "Will you be able to make the Bonds return my hotel?"

"Shouldn't you be concerned about gaining your freedom first?"

"Do you doubt I will?" Claire ceased pacing and clasped her hands together in front of her.

"Won't you sit down, Mrs. Daines?" Mr. Moore indicated the cot.

She was too nervous to be still. But if she remained standing, propriety dictated that he should do the same. He couldn't stand, hold a cane, and take notes.

"Yes, thank you." She ran her hands over her skirt. Without her chatelaine with its keys, her hands had nothing to do. Most women knitted. Being in charge of a hotel, she had no time for that. She might attempt it in here if she could coax someone into bringing her yarn and needles.

She tried a deep breath to calm her jitters. "The sheriff said I must remain in jail for my own sake. Until the judge arrives for the hearing. He has odd notions about protection, don't you agree?"

Mr. Moore's sympathetic expression turned reproachful. "Sheriff Garrity agreed to release you on bond. If you will sign an affidavit swearing to the fact that your foster son fired the gun."

Claire released a long sigh. She actually hadn't requested a lawyer. Frank had recruited the man in an ongoing effort to pressure her into admitting her innocence. "I won't swear to that."

The lawyer studied her for long moment. "You'll be in a better position to reclaim your property if you're not in jail."

Mr. Moore made a compelling argument. Hopefully, he would be just as persuasive at the upcoming hearing.

If she betrayed Billy, the judge would take one look at the boy's troubled past and his current association with outlaws, and condemn him. Even if Billy didn't get sentenced to hang, he would be locked up. Or sent to a home for derelict children. Regaining her life wasn't worth ruining his.

Claire lifted her head with a clear conscience. "I did not murder my husband, Mr. Moore. The gun went off by accident, as I've told both you and the sheriff."

The lawyer heaved a heavy sigh. That wasn't the answer he sought and they both knew it. They'd gone over her statement several times already. She wouldn't change the facts. Given Mr. Bond's revelation, things didn't look good for her. She would admit that much.

"One more thing..." Mr. Moore rubbed his hand over his knee. From what she could deduce, he had false leg shoved into a boot. Perhaps the damaged limb still pained him, which would be a shame. It wasn't something she should ask about, as it would embarrass him. "Sheriff Garrity sent a telegram to your brother."

Frank had threatened to notify Henry if she didn't.

"Did he respond?"

"He's on his way here."

Claire dropped her chin to her chest and heaved a discouraged sigh. She hadn't wanted to involve Henry. He'd left Parsons to put a painful past behind him. If he returned, all the muck would be dredged up again.

On the other hand, Henry cared about Billy. He'd been the one to suggest she take the boy, and would be willing to look after him if she ended up in prison—or worse. "Thank you, Mr. Moore. I appreciate everything you've done."

"If you have nothing further to add, I'll take my leave." The lawyer pushed to his feet using his cane. He put on his black hat then knocked on the bars to alert the sheriff their conversation was done.

The door leading into the sheriff's office opened. Frank unlocked the cell to allow the lawyer to leave. His expression remained grim when he returned. When he entered the small space, it seemed to shrink in size.

Her back struck the brick wall behind her. She hadn't realized she'd moved away.

He apparently had, which might account for the disappointment on his face. He must know she didn't trust him. Would never trust him again. "You could walk out of here, Claire. All you have to do is tell the truth."

"No matter what I say, I look guilty."

The utter irony of her situation wasn't lost on her. She could shout her innocence from the treetops. No one would believe her. Not after she'd admitted to being the culprit.

She wouldn't escape a murder charge without a confession from Billy.

Frank paced the cramped cell like a caged tiger. An uninformed observer might think he was the one imprisoned. "We'll have you out of here as soon as we find Billy."

Fear constricted her heart. "Are you going after him?"

"Not until after the hearing."

"When is that?"

"Day after tomorrow."

Day after tomorrow might end up being the worst day of her life. Or the second worst day. She threw an anxious glance outside at the spot where the gallows would be built, should she be convicted of murder. If she were to hang, that day would definitely be the worst.

Claire hugged her shawl. It wasn't cold enough in here to be shivering. Part of her wanted Billy found so she would know he was safe. Another part wished he'd remain hidden for his own sake. "If you find him, you mustn't force him to testify. He's done nothing wrong."

"Running from a crime is wrong."

"Billy isn't to blame."

"This isn't about blame. It's about justice."

"Justice?" She was tempted to spit on the floor. "You can speak of justice after I've lost my home, my freedom, possibly my life, based on the word of a schemer?"

"Bond won't get away with his lies. I won't let him."

She didn't doubt Frank's determination. It wouldn't be enough. It never was when money and power were involved.

She whirled away to look out the window so she wouldn't see her fear reflected in his eyes.

His hands hovered at her shoulders.

Claire held her breath, at the same time, she cursed her weakness. She knew better than to want him. If only her heart would listen to her head.

He grasped her shoulders. His warm hands provided more comfort than a fire on a winter's night.

Fire could also burn and destroy.

"You're a survivor, Claire." His voice dropped to a husky whisper. "Like those trailing roses my mother brought with her to Kansas. They lived, even bloomed, in spite of heat, cold, drought."

He turned her around and captured her chin. He'd dropped the sheriff mask and his expression revealed gut-wrenching desperation. "Why won't you tell the truth? Why would you throw your life away?"

Frank understood so many things about her. Why couldn't he grasp the most important one?

"Because I need to protect Billy. That's what a *mother* does. It's what your mother did, and she would tell you, if she could. Children, like roses, need someone to look after them. Someone to care for them."

He folded her against his chest with a groan. "I care about *you*."

"I know you do," she choked out. He'd shown her in many ways how much he cared. As a fierce protector who could also be gentle. He exercised power with restraint. Honest, most of the time. Brave, all the time. Fair-minded. Committed to upholding what was right and just. He possessed the traits she'd looked for in a man, but had never found.

Frank wasn't perfect, not by a far stretch. But he was the man whose shape she knew in her heart. Here, in his arms, with her cheek pressed against the lapel of his vest and her nose buried in his chambray shirt, smelling of leather and laundry soap, she had found, at last, the place she belonged.

She splayed her fingers on his chest. Closed them over the cold metal of a sheriff's badge.

The hopeful winds, which had lifted her spirits, stilled. Her wings faltered. She couldn't sustain the dream any longer and plummeted back to reality.

He might care for her. Yet, it didn't change who he was or what he had to do. His rock-solid honor was one reason she loved him. It was also the reason they couldn't be together.

Frank Garrity had declared his commitment to pursuing justice under the law. The law would not give Billy either justice or mercy. She had the power to give him both. If she had the courage.

"You once told me you felt responsible for your wife and child. You would die for them if you could do it over again, wouldn't you?"

Frank put his face against her hair. "It's not the same."

"It is the same. It's exactly the same." She clung to him, frightened. Needing his firmness, his resolve. Desperate for him to stand beside her and uphold her so she could pass the hardest test her heart had ever faced. "Please, Frank. Don't fight me on this. Help me to be strong."

CHAPTER 23

Claire would let herself hang before she put Billy on the stand. If she wouldn't save herself, someone had to do it.

Frank stopped outside the mercantile to read a new brass plaque outside the door. *G.W. Moore, Attorney at Law.*

He'd won several land disputes against the rich and powerful railroad. The old settlers swore he walked on water.

Sounded like the kind of lawyer Claire needed.

Frank took a set of stairs up to a door that stood open.

Moore sat in his modest office, which was equipped with a desk, a bookcase filled with thick volumes, and two chairs. Dignified, but not showy.

The lawyer came to his feet behind the desk. Papers and legal books were scattered across its surface. More papers and books were in boxes on either side.

"Good afternoon, sheriff. Please, have a seat. Pardon the mess. I'm still getting moved in." The lawyer's soft drawl set Frank's teeth on edge, even after all these years.

Men who sounded like Moore had attacked his home and murdered his father. An aristocratic Southern accent didn't mean Moore had done anything wrong. Although the scuttlebutt around town had him pegged as a former slave owner. Frank had an abiding dislike for men who presumed they had the right to possess another human being. For the time being, he'd put aside his personal dislike and do business with the Devil if it saved Claire.

"Don't care to sit." Frank drew back his coat and hooked his thumbs over his gun belt.

Moore's gaze flickered over the Colts, unimpressed or unconcerned. "What can I do for you?"

"What can you do for Mrs. Daines, is what you mean," Frank corrected. "That's what I hired you for."

Yesterday, Claire had begged for his help. God, he would do anything for her, but he could not do as she asked. He couldn't stand by and watch her hang.

He'd hoped being in jail would dissolve her resistance. It hadn't worked. Neither had reason. Or threats. Or pleas. He was clean out of ideas, and she was running out of time. Moore better have a plan. "Claire won't blame Billy."

The lawyer shifted in his chair to lean back, perhaps so he wouldn't have to crick his neck to make eye contact. "Did you expect she would?"

"I figured you might talk some sense into her. She seems more determined than ever. Told me to stop pestering her. Said I ought to understand."

"You'd die for them."

Frank's heart constricted as her words came back to him. God yes. If it were possible to go back in time, he would take his wife's place. Claire's situation wasn't the same. Sarah and the unborn child had been innocent bystanders. Billy made a choice to pick up a gun. Claire might feel responsible, even guilty about him getting involved in a domestic quarrel, but she wasn't at fault for what happened.

"Are you certain she didn't kill her husband?" Moore asked him.

"As sure as I'm standing here."

The lawyer crossed his arms over his chest. His rolled-up shirtsleeves revealed tanned, muscular forearms. Surprising, for a skinny fellow who spent his days indoors, pushing a pencil. "Well, then. If she won't speak in her own defense, you'll have to speak for her."

Frank let out a disbelieving laugh. This wasn't a plan. "How can I speak in her defense? I'm supposed to present facts about the crime. Not give my opinion of the accused. All I have is a hunch, based on what I suspect. It'll be my word against hers."

Moore nodded. "That's right."

"What the hell kind of defense is that?"

"A better one than what she has now."

Frank shook his head. He couldn't believe what he was hearing. This was the best Moore could come up with? "No wonder you boys lost the war."

"Let's not bring my friends into this," Moore said smoothly, with a hint of dryness in his tone.

Frank couldn't pace in the cramped office. He moved from behind one chair to the other. "What about Bond's shenanigans? Don't you find it odd that Mr. Daines would sign his hotel over to a man who took his brother-in-law's job?"

"Mrs. Daines told me her husband didn't care for her brother. He resented having a hotel thrust on him. He may have found satisfaction in selling it to Mr. Stevens' replacement."

Frank halted abruptly, surprised, and more than a little angry. "You're supposed to uncover dirt on Bond. Discredit him as a witness. Not strengthen his statement."

"And you're supposed to be looking for a missing boy," Moore pointed out in an irritatingly friendly tone.

"The hearing's tomorrow. I can't leave before that. I sent my deputy after him." For some reason, this came out sounding like a weak excuse.

Gideon's tracking skills equaled, if not exceeded, his. Not to mention, he wouldn't leave Claire to a pack of wolves.

"Other than testifying, locating Billy is the best thing you can do for Mrs. Daines."

Frank pointed his finger at the useless lawyer. "The best thing *you* can do is come up with a better plan than putting me on the stand to spout my *opinions* about her innocence."

"What do you think I'm working on?" Moore motioned with ink-stained hands at the documents and legal books scattered across his desk. "Do you have any idea why Mr. Bond would want a hotel?"

"Because he's a greedy bastard."

"That's your opinion?"

"No, it's a fact. He cut everybody's pay but his own. Ask the men who work for him. He let crews go, cut back on maintenance, fired his security officers. And, he seems to think I ought to police his trains in my free time."

"Austere measures in a bad economy?"

"Or somebody higher pulling his strings."

"Someone who would want the hotel?"

"Maybe. It might not have anything to do with the hotel." Frank removed his hat to plow his fingers through his sweaty hair. *Confound it.* What had he missed? "Bond and his wife were both anxious to see Claire locked up. I don't know why."

Moore rubbed his chin thoughtfully. "You said her brother ran the railroad."

"Henry Stevens *built* the railroad. He served as general manager until he quit last year. After an investigator turned up some discrepancies with the books. They discovered that Mr. Stevens' assistant had skimmed money from ticket sales. George Caldwell got spooked and killed the investigator. Came close to killing Stevens, too. Blamed him for the whole mess. It was quite a scandal. Mr. Stevens left his job. A jury convicted Mr. Caldwell for murder. We hanged him in November—" Frank caught his breath, as the gears in his brain jerked into motion. "Ah, shit. Why didn't I think of that before?"

"Think of what?"

"The connection. Between Henry's troubles and what's happening to Claire. She's Henry's sister. If somebody wanted revenge, but couldn't get to Henry, they might target someone he holds dear."

Awareness dawned in Moore's eyes. "Mr. Bond wants revenge?"

Frank secured his hat and moved in a small, tight circle behind the chairs. "Maybe not Bond. Henry would've picked up on a direct connection and warned Claire. It could be somebody above the current general manager. Someone with a grudge against Henry. He once told me he's made a lot of enemies. Might even have something to do with that Caldwell business."

"What about Mr. Daines?"

"What about him?"

"Would he have been party to whatever Bond was up to?"

"Don't think so. Based on what Claire told me, his mind wasn't right. Bond could've figured that out and taken advantage of his discontent." Frank smacked a fist into his palm, imagining Bond's face in it. "God, I'd love to—"

"I'd advise against that. For the moment. Let's talk to Mr. Stevens when he arrives. He knows the railroad and the players. He may be able to identify the spider who's spinning this web." Moore stood, a bit unsteady, until he grabbed the cane by his desk and regained his balance.

Must've lost his leg in the war. Hadn't lost his mind, though. Not like Claire's husband, poor bastard. Frederick Daines had been a casualty long before Billy pulled that trigger.

"You keep working on Claire's defense. I'll nose around and find out what I can about Mr. Bond's background." Frank much preferred taking action to talking a thing to death.

"Sheriff, a moment." The somber tone in the lawyer's voice made Frank pause at the door.

"Yeah?"

"As you said, the hearing is tomorrow. It's doubtful we'll have all the pieces assembled by then. I expect the judge will lay a charge of murder against my client, unless you can convince him to do otherwise. You should clean up. Get a shave. A haircut wouldn't hurt. Put on a suit. We don't want Mr. Bond to be the only witness who makes a good impression."

CHAPTER 24

*B*illy got lucky. A train had stopped because some Indians decided to herd their cattle across the tracks. While the engineer and a conductor argued with two blanket-clad drovers, no one noticed when he climbed up the side of a boxcar.

After the whistle sounded and the train got underway, he settled in on the top. He sat cross-legged, humming, enjoying the wind in his hair, and the spectacular view.

"What the devil are you doin' up here?"

Billy felt a jerk. He twisted around so fast he nearly lost his balance.

A windblown brakie held a club in one hand and had Billy's coat fisted in the other. Brakemen used their clubs to turn metal wheels that operated the brakes, not as weapons. Unless there were outlaws about.

Billy offered an uncertain smile. Fortunate for him, he wasn't an outlaw yet, and he knew this particular brakie. "Hey, Charlie."

The man's eyes and weathered forehead crinkled at the same time. He seemed more concerned than angry. "Small Fry? I shoulda known it was you."

Billy released a relieved sigh. The nickname, which he hadn't liked before, sounded like music to his ears. His railroad friends had called him that ever since he was knee-high to a toad. It was a term of endearment, rather than ridicule. Much better than *Shorty.*

"Where you been?" Charlie demanded. "The whole town's lookin' for you. We feared you was dead."

"Nah. I been hidin' out in the Territory," Billy explained. He wanted to remain honest, yet offer as little detail as possible so the railroaders wouldn't think he'd gone bad by hanging out with outlaws. "I'm hitchin' a ride home."

Home sounded good. It also made him sad. He'd never had a permanent home. Never really belonged anywhere, and didn't reckon he ever would. Not unless he could somehow get a job with the railroad. Being on a train was where he felt most at home.

"You ought to be thrashed for scaring everybody. Now c'mon." Charlie motioned with his chin toward the back of the train. "You can ride in the shack with us."

The shack, or caboose, was where brakemen stayed when they weren't coon walking along the top of trains. To be issued an invitation was an honor Billy wouldn't refuse.

He trotted along behind Charlie, had to take running leaps to clear the distance between the cars. The brakie didn't even look over his shoulder. Railroaders watched out for each other, but they didn't coddle greenhorns.

Billy wasn't no greenhorn.

As the long line of cars rumbled along, the occasional swaying didn't bother him. Neither did the wind rushing past, which made his coat flap.

He must look like an awkward bird trying to figure out its wings. If a strong crosswind caught him unawares, he'd tumble over the side of the railcar and those wings wouldn't do him a bit of good. He knew the dangers enough to be careful. He wasn't near as scared atop this train as he was at the prospect of returning to Parsons.

When he got there, he'd have to talk to the sheriff. How would the lawman react? Billy wasn't sure. After all those times he'd gotten into trouble for running away or for stealing things, like food.

The sheriff and him had made their peace when he'd moved in with Mrs. Daines. Still, he didn't think Sheriff Garrity trusted him or even liked him very much. 'Course it was hard to tell if the sheriff liked anybody, except for Mrs. Daines. His voice got softer when he talked to her and his frown weren't so severe. If she were to put in a good word, maybe.

Billy's chest got tight. No, he couldn't ask for her help. Nor could he beg her forgiveness. Not yet. Not until he turned in the outlaws and become a hero. Then, he could face her without so much shame. Tell her how sorry he was for what he'd done. She might not love him anymore, but she was kind and generous. If she thought he'd turned his life around, she might eventually forgive him.

By the time he climbed down to the caboose, his heart raced and his blood sang. He felt like an honest-to-goodness railroader as he followed Charlie through the door.

Inside, a small table had been set with a checkered cloth and a handful of wilted wildflowers stuck in a tin cup. Two berths were made up with clean white sheets and folded blankets. Lace curtains fluttered over the windows.

Didn't look very manly.

Billy snickered.

Charlie twisted around. His wool jacket pulled tight across his wide shoulders. There wasn't nothing girly about the strapping brakie. He might decide to use that club if he got offended.

Billy put on an innocent face. "Did your wife decorate the shack?"

Charlie's black mustache twitched like he'd smiled, but it was hard to tell because his lips didn't show beneath the bushy facial hair. "Not my wife." He motioned to a scrawny fellow in baggy coveralls who sat on the lower berth, eyeing Billy from beneath a too-large cap. "My daughter."

That was a *girl?*

"This here is Billy Frye," Charlie told her.

"Mac," she said.

Billy cocked his head. "Pardon?"

"My name. It's Mac."

"Never heard of a girl named Mac."

She rolled her eyes like he was the stupidest person on earth. "Short for Mackenzie. Our surname."

"Oh, sure," Billy said quickly. He should've figured that one out. He'd forgotten Charlie's full name. What was his daughter doing dressed up like a railroad worker, riding around in a caboose reserved for *men*?

Billy wandered over to the ladder, which led to a lookout where the brakemen could keep an eye on things and watch for signals. Typically, two brakemen worked a train. "Where's the other brakie?"

"Pete's out." Charlie went to a counter and picked up a plate. "You hungry? We got half a sandwich left."

"I sure won't refuse." Billy mumbled his thanks around the first bite.

"We'll be comin' to Vinita soon. Got to go up top. You stay here with Mac." Charlie exited the caboose, leaving Billy with the strange girl.

Not knowing what to say, he sat in one of the two chairs at the table and finished the sandwich. He had to wipe his hands on the edge of the tablecloth because he didn't have a napkin or even a handkerchief.

The girl's expression remained guarded. Maybe she didn't know what to say either.

"Where you headed?" she asked, finally.

Billy didn't feel comfortable conversing with girls. But her father had done him a good turn, and Mrs. Daines had told him it wasn't polite to ignore people's questions. There was no law that required him to give long answers. "Parsons."

"You live there?"

"Used to."

"Where?"

Great days, she sure was nosy.

"The Belmont House."

Her eyes got big as coneflowers. She picked a newspaper off the bed and held it out. "Do you know this lady? The Black Widow?"

Billy took the newspaper. He looked over the headline and began to read. Most words didn't give him trouble anymore, but this story confused him. He couldn't be reading it right, or the reporter had got all the facts wrong. Mrs. Daines hadn't shot her husband. The article said she had. Not only that, she'd gone and admitted it to the sheriff.

He frowned. She'd lied. And she'd instructed him to *always* tell the truth. Why would she confess to something she didn't do? Why did everybody think she was a killer? She wouldn't kill a fly.

"Well? Do you?"

He jerked his head up. His heart jumped with alarm. "Do I what?"

"Do you know her? That lady who shot her husband?"

"She didn't sh-shoot—" he stammered, then caught himself before he tripped up and admitted he was the guilty one. "I mean, I don't know her."

Mac stared at him like he was an idiot.

He didn't want to talk about this anymore. Not until he'd found out what was going on. If Mrs. Daines had confessed and they didn't think he'd done it, how come they offered a reward for him? Four hundred dollars was a lot of money. Nobody had ever paid a cent to get him back before.

He put his hand in his coat pocket and touched the folded notice he'd found in Candy's saddlebag.

"What've you got there?" The girl scooted off the berth like she would come after him.

Billy took his hand out of his pocket. He handed her the newspaper.

"No, I mean in your pocket. You were digging for something."

"You're awful nosy."

"Nosy? I asked you a simple question" The girl came so close he leaned over in the chair and about turned it over. "You got no call to be rude."

"Oh yeah? Well, I got bigger problems than remembering to be polite to a girl who don't even look like a girl." Billy scooted the chair back, pushed her aside and climbed the ladder to the look out. He'd put up with enough from her, Charlie's daughter or not.

He peered out the narrow window at the top of the lookout. Those low clouds rolling in could turn into a ripper of a storm. If given a choice, he'd rather get caught in a tornado atop a train than face what he was about to walk into.

If he didn't say anything, nobody would have to know he'd killed a man. He wouldn't have to go to the sheriff or tell him about the outlaws or risk getting killed by Candy or Tom for betraying Jasper. He could go back to the roundhouse, offer to wipe down the big hogs, work his way up to being an engineer. He could keep his mouth shut and get away with murder.

Billy had to squint to see Charlie. The brakeman was bent against the wind as he grasped the brake wheel.

The train squealed. It resisted being stopped.

Billy's conscience squealed, too. He could ignore it. Eventually, the nagging noise might stop. Then, he'd be free to do what he wanted, go wherever he wished.

Without brakes, a train would charge down the tracks, out of control. Ram into another train. Or jump the rails on a tight curve.

He would crash, too, if he kept resisting the brakes. If he kept on running when he ought to stop. Mrs. Daines had confessed to something she hadn't done. Deep down, he knew the truth. He was the killer. If he didn't go back and straighten things out, he'd also know he was a coward.

CHAPTER 25

*L*ater that night, after Frank had locked the front door to his office, he pulled open the bottom drawer in his desk, took out a bottle and poured himself a whiskey. He'd needed a drink all day. Actually, several.

He ruffled his fingers through his shorter hair, then smoothed his hand over his clean-shaven face. At Moore's suggestion, he had visited a barber. His notes were in order. He'd written key points to jog his memory. He could he poke holes in Claire's story and set Billy up as the gunman. He knew she was innocent. Tomorrow, he had to convince the judge.

Frank drained the first drink and poured a second.

If he was right, and some big bug pulled Bond's strings, things could get very ugly. The railroads were the most powerful entities in the country. The men running them, the richest and most corrupt. Claire had proved to be a strong woman, but she wasn't strong enough to face this danger on her own.

After she got cleared of murder charges—and he would see to it that she did—she would need protection. Her brother had made too many enemies. Not to mention, Henry had a wife and baby to worry about. Claire's sisters weren't around. What could they do to protect her, anyway? She didn't have anybody else.

After the third drink, Frank slowed down.

Him. She had him. He'd mulled this over ever since he'd left Moore's office. He could take care of Claire. Granted, the risks with his chosen profession hadn't gone away. But weighing what *might* happen if he wed her against what was *likely* to happen if someone didn't protect her, he kept coming around to the same answer. She'd be safer if they married and he took her somewhere her enemies couldn't find her. He could be careful and ensure she stayed out of the way. He wouldn't make the same mistakes he had before. He was wiser now.

Or was he just talking himself into this because he wanted her? If she was his wife, it meant she'd be in his bed. Every night.

No. It wasn't lust that drove him. Claire needed him, even if she didn't think so, at the moment. Which was why he'd needed the drinks. To bolster his courage when he went back there and asked her to marry him.

He corked the bottle. Wiped his hand over his face and took a deep breath. He could face the meanest killers in the country without flinching, but couldn't work up the nerve to confront one small woman. She'd tied him completely into knots.

Frank picked up the oil lamp and carried it back to the cells. The light illuminated the cot where Claire lay huddled beneath one of his quilts. He hoped she'd gotten comfortable enough to sleep after he'd brought down the feather mattress that used to be on his bed. He ought to sleep on nails, anyway.

She didn't move.

He could wait and ask her later. After all, he couldn't let on that they had an intimate relationship if he wanted the judge to believe his testimony.

On the other hand, he had a good reason to gain her agreement now. She might not be as eager to marry him if he waited until she got released to ask her. Freedom would give her a false sense of security. She would fight to get her hotel back, which would draw dangerous attention. Married to him, she wouldn't need a hotel.

He turned the key in the lock. The click echoed off the walls.

She bolted up and the quilt fell away. She still wore her dress. Most of the petticoats that had filled out her skirts were draped over a chair. A braid as thick as his wrist hung over her shoulder. "Frank? Why are you here?"

Not, *it's good to see you,* or *I'm glad you're here.* Just, *why?*

As if he needed a reason. He couldn't stay away from her.

He set the lamp on the floor. Then he went over to sit beside her on the mattress.

None of the other smells completely masked her intoxicating scent. Who needed whiskey when he could come back here and get drunk smelling her? Same thing happened when he touched her.

He lifted her plaited hair and let the sleek braid slide through his palm. The sensation made him dizzy. An answering desire flared in her eyes a second before she hooded them. With a slow, cautious movement, she retrieved her braid.

"What are you doing?" she asked in a hushed tone.

"Why are you whispering? There's no one else here."

The other cell was empty and would remain that way as long as she was here. If he needed to lock up rowdies, he'd put them in an old stone building the railroad had once used to store explosives. No one would bother Claire or hurt her so long as she was in his care.

This urgent need to protect her reminded him of his purpose for coming to her.

He ran his tongue over his lips, which had gone bone dry, as had his mouth and throat. Mother of God, he needed a drink. He'd left the bottle in the next room.

He couldn't say why marriage scared him so bad. Other than his concern about exposing her to danger as the wife of a lawman. Maybe he feared the risk to his heart. He hadn't thought he had a heart left to give. He still wasn't sure it was worth much.

"Marry me." His proposal tumbled out, almost slurred because he said it in such a hurry.

Surprise was too mild a word for the startled look that crossed her face. "*Marry* you?"

The way she said it made it sound like he'd asked her to wash his dirty socks. She might end up doing that, but he wouldn't demand it. For now, he hadn't asked her to do anything more than tie the knot. He'd hoped she might be at least halfway interested.

Maybe she expected a proper proposal.

Frank dropped to his knees and grabbed her hands.

She jerked them away and shot off the cot. Stared at him with a horrified expression. "What's wrong with you?"

"Nothing's wrong with me." He found it mildly annoying that she thought he'd lost his reason. This was the sanest thing he'd done in over a week.

With a sigh, he propped his hand on the cot and got up from the awkward position. If she thought kneeling indicated he was crazy, he'd stand. "I want you to be my wife."

She backed up against the brick wall.

He advanced. Slow, yet relentless. Once he set a course, he didn't alter his direction and this was no different. He would overcome her nervousness or distrust or whatever stood in his way. "Now, I know you're sore because I lied to you, and I'm sorry. I truly am. I won't ever lie to you again."

"That's a relief." She defended her chest with crossed arms.

This would take some finesse.

Frank rested his hands lightly on her shoulders. The conversation would go much smoother if he touched her. Better yet, he ought to kiss her. He bent his head.

She twisted out of his arms and bumped up against the washstand.

"Careful. Don't break my mother's pitcher."

She looked behind her like she hadn't noticed it before. "You brought your mother's water pitcher in here? Why would you do that?"

"Because you needed it."

"But Frank, your *mother's* things, those are precious."

He didn't contradict her because she was right. She also needed to know he valued her more than any possession. "Claire, I would give you anything I have."

Her eyes rounded, then became bright with moisture. Tears weren't what he was going for, unless they were the happy kind.

"No need to get choked up about a water pitcher. You can cry when the preacher pronounces us man and wife."

She didn't even crack a smile. Just moved her head back and forth. "Frank...don't..."

"Don't what?"

"Don't confuse me."

"I'm not trying to confuse you. I'm asking you to marry me. Appears I'm doing a dang poor job of it."

She put her hands on his chest. As if that would stop him. "You've been drinking."

"Just a couple. Nothing to worry about."

"But I do worry. I'm concerned about your fondness for spirits. It can become a weakness."

It hadn't entered his mind she might think he was *weak*. Or maybe she'd been listening to that Baptist preacher who ranted about the evils of strong drink and had signed up with the teetotalers. The best way to handle crazy was with calm reason. He adopted a sensible tone. "Since when do a few drinks make a man weak?"

"Since the time he started losing count." Her soft-spoken remark triggered something akin to guilt, which irritated him. He had nothing to feel guilty about. He knew how much he could handle and when he ought to stop.

"Claire, I had three drinks." He held up as many fingers. "I can count. And I'm not so addled I can't tell when you're changing the subject."

She shook her head again. "This isn't a good time to discuss marriage."

He let his hand drift down the back of her arm. The resulting shudder made it clear she wasn't immune to persuasion, which gave him hope. "I'm here. You're not going anywhere. It's as good a time as any."

Her frown telegraphed doubt. "What made you change your mind? You told me *no promises*. You said you wouldn't marry again after what happened to your wife. You even said you didn't want to settle down."

An honest answer would be tricky. He'd vowed not lie to her again, which left him few choices. He could tell her straight out he feared she was in danger and wanted to bring her under his protection. It made perfect sense to him and had compelled him to act on his feelings. But a woman wouldn't think it was a very romantic reason to get married.

Problem was, he was the least romantic person he knew. He'd never been able to string together sweet words and not have it come out sounding ridiculous. For him, actions worked better. He cupped her face in his hands and pressed a gentle kiss to her forehead. "Am I allowed to change my mind?"

"I...I suppose."

He gently smoothed strands of her hair that had come loose and pressed a kiss to her temple before he forged a light trail down her cheek. "And we enjoy each other's company, wouldn't you say?"

"Ye-yes, but..."

Her trembling uncertainty encouraged him. He targeted the next attack on an unguarded spot. Her neck.

"I...I haven't been a widow for very long," she stammered while he ran his lips over smooth, fragrant skin. "It wouldn't look proper to marry again so soon."

"Plenty of widows out here get hitched again quick," he whispered into her ear. "Nobody thinks twice about it."

Claire turned her face away. She grasped the lapels of his vest and held him close. "Frank, I can't think."

"Then don't think. Or if you do, think about this." He turned her face to him and kissed her full on the mouth.

Her lips, as soft as rose petals, opened on a sigh.

In no time, the kiss turned hot and desperate. He plundered her mouth. She, in turn, plundered his. He loved that she held nothing back, at least when it came to kissing. He still had to get past her concerns about marriage. The more he kissed her, the more appealing the idea became, and he had found her appealing enough even before he kissed her.

He came up for air, sucked in a great lungful. "Say you'll marry me."

"After the hearing...I'll give you my answer," she said between gasping breaths. Her fingers worked their way across his chest. For some reason, she dodged, even as she caressed him.

It wasn't possible that she only wanted him to scratch a physical itch. Women like Claire weren't the type to dally. Whatever held her back, he would overcome.

He grazed her lower lip with his teeth before he continued. "We don't have to tell anybody right away. Best if we don't. At least, not until after the hearing. But I want your promise that you'll marry me after this business is over."

"I can't."

"Yes, you can, You're just being stubborn." He kissed her again. Deeply. Longingly. She waged a foolish war. One he knew he'd win because she wanted this as much as he did.

In between kisses, he laid down the rules of engagement. "If you want...to keep kissing me...you got to marry me."

She broke off the kiss. Then braced her hands on his shoulders when he tried to continue. "I'm not the one who's in a hurry."

"If we're suited—and you know we are—why wait?"

"Because you might change your mind again."

He dropped down to one knee. "I won't change my mind. I give you my word."

Distress flashed across her face. "Get up, Frank. Groveling isn't what I want. I could be charged with murder. I wouldn't saddle you with that."

She looked meaningfully out the window.

Despite his warning that she could hang if she didn't come clean, he rejected the notion of Claire meeting such a fate. He'd move heaven and earth to prevent it.

"You won't be convicted."

"How can you be so sure?"

For one, he planned to find Billy and get him on the stand. If he told her as much, she'd turn him down flat. Besides, there were other things she needed to know. He wasn't sure the knowledge would improve his chances, but it would be irresponsible to leave her in the dark and in danger. "Your brother made enemies over the years."

"What does Henry have to do with this?" Her chin came up and that glare dared him to disparage her brother. "He's an honorable man. A good husband and father."

"You don't have to convince me. I like Henry. But not everybody does. Mr. Caldwell tried to blame him for the railroad's financial problems. The directors suspected him enough to sic an investigator on him. Somebody might still hold a grudge."

"That's ridiculous. There is absolutely no evidence Henry did anything wrong. He has nothing to do with this."

"Then why does Mr. Bond have an ax to grind? He's got no reason to take your hotel. It's not worth that much, as far as the railroad is concerned. Haven't you wondered why he wants it so bad? And why he's so eager to make trouble for you?"

On her face, surprise, uncertainty, and finally, fear. "You think Mr. Bond has a grudge against Henry?"

"Not Bond specifically. Henry would know if he was an enemy and he'd warn you. I think it's somebody above Bond. Somebody with power over him. They're striking at the easiest target. You." Frank gathered her into his arms. She came to him as if it was the most natural thing in the world. He nuzzled her hair, and with his lips near her ear reassured her. "Don't be afraid, Claire. I swear, I'll protect you."

She wrapped her arms around him tightly. "No, Frank. You can't become involved in this. I won't let you. You could be hurt."

His frustration boiled up. "Dang it, stop trying to save everybody but yourself!"

She looked up at him with tears streaking her face. "How is it all right for you to sacrifice yourself, but when I do it, it's wrong?"

"Marriage to you is not a sacrifice. Believe me."

"If you married me and someone came after me, you would try to stop them. Even if it cost your life. Am I correct to assume that?"

"Yes, but—

"Then I won't marry you."

He tightened his hold on her. Her response shouldn't surprise him. She looked fragile, yet she was tough on the inside, and as hardheaded as a team of mules.

By God, he was tougher. She sure as hell wouldn't stop him.

He gripped her shoulders and looked her right in the eye. "Whether you say *I do* or not, I *will* go after whoever's trying to hurt you. Do you understand? I won't allow anybody to harm you. And I won't keep silent and let you put a noose around your own neck. I *will* protect you, in spite of everything you do to prevent me."

CHAPTER 26

A sound like a knock woke Frank. He'd dozed off at his desk, so it could be he was hearing things. He lifted his head off his arms and listened. Maybe the wind had rattled the front window. It was still dark outside, had to be late.

He turned up the wick on the oil lamp and capped a half-empty bottle. He would lock it in a drawer so he wouldn't be tempted to finish it off.

A second knock. Hesitant, as if the person outside wasn't sure he was at the right place, or didn't really want to be let in.

Frank got up, shaking his head at the unknown caller's timidity. Why didn't they just go home and go to bed? Decide in the morning.

He checked his gun out of habit. Fully loaded. Then he unlatched the door and opened it. He had to look down to see the caller.

"Howdy, Sheriff." Billy lifted his hand in a half-hearted wave.

Gideon must've tracked him down.

Frank leaned out and peered past Billy. Not a soul on the street. No horse at the hitching post. "Where's Deputy Branch?"

Billy shrugged. "I dunno."

Hell of a thing. The boy had come back of his own free will.

Frank stepped aside and motioned for Billy to enter.

The boy's shoulders slumped. He dragged his feet. When the door closed, he jumped like he was nervy.

He still wore the outfit Claire had described, the fleece-lined coat, brown trousers and checkered flannel shirt. Looked like he hadn't taken them off, despite rolling around in dirt and straw and what smelled like manure. His neck was several shades darker than his face, and his hair had enough oil to grease an axle.

Claire would be appalled. She'd also be so happy to see him she'd hug him even if he smelled like horse piss.

Frank hesitated. Not yet. He couldn't let Claire talk to Billy until after he heard what the boy had to say. "What brings you here?"

"You gonna arrest me?" Billy's expression remained guarded.

If he had something to confess, Frank wanted him to do so without being coerced. "Is there a reason I should?"

"There's a reward out for me, ain't there?" Billy eyed the *Wanted* posters.

Apparently, he'd seen the notice. His conscience must've filled in the reason. Telling the truth might encourage him to do the same.

"You aren't wanted for a crime, if that's what you're asking. Mrs. Daines is worried about you. She offered money so other people would help us find you."

Billy stuffed his hands into his coat pockets. He looked positively miserable. "She can't want me. Not anymore."

This boy had no idea how dear he was to that woman in the cell.

Frank dragged his hand over his hair. He'd rather let Claire handle this. Except, he couldn't send Billy back there. She could influence him to lie.

Deep emotions were as dangerous as murky lakes, and just as terrifying. Despite being a poor swimmer, Frank overcame his fear and waded in. For Claire's sake, as much as for Billy. "That's not true. She told me lots of times how much she wants to adopt you. She hasn't changed her mind."

The statement drew a look of pure disbelief.

Understandable, considering Billy had shot her husband and left her to hold the bag. She had every right to resent him, yet she didn't.

She loved him with a love that was pure and true. The kind everyone longed to possess, yet couldn't, because it wasn't something to be bought or earned. That kind of love was a precious gift, and she had given it to Billy.

Frank struggled with envy. What he wouldn't give for Claire to love him so completely. "Mrs. Daines has a big heart. Once she decides to take you into it, she won't throw you out, no matter what."

Doubt rested on Billy's brow. "How can you know that?"

"Because she's here. Locked up in a cell."

Billy pulled something out of his pocket, a torn piece of newspaper. He carefully unfolded and handed it over. "They say Mrs. Daines confessed she shot her husband, then you tracked her down and arrested her."

The boy thought he was heartless. Frank didn't disabuse him of the notion. He couldn't let on he'd gone soft on Claire and take the pressure off Billy. Not when he was so close to getting to the truth.

"She did admit to it."

Billy's complexion seemed to pale. Though it was hard to tell in the dim light and with all those freckles, not to mention the dirt.

The child's distress stirred Frank's sympathy. He'd been blessed with good parents, even if he'd lost them far too soon. Billy had been abandoned repeatedly until Claire took in. The boy might not grasp the depth of her love, but it was obvious he understood the significance of her sacrifice.

Billy blinked a few times. He sniffed and wiped his nose with his shirtsleeve, trying hard not to cry.

Frank knew the feeling well. Gut-wrenching regret. Instead of giving in to tears, he got drunk. He conceded he had less courage than Billy.

"You got the wrong person in jail. *I'm* the one you want," Billy said in a low voice. A visible tremble shook him.

As frightened as he was, he'd come back willingly to face what he'd done. His action demonstrated both grit and character. If Claire could get past her fears, she'd be proud of him.

"Come, sit down." Frank pulled over a chair for Billy. He sat in the other chair rather than behind the desk, which would be too intimidating. "Why don't you tell me what happened," he said softly.

Billy scooted back in the chair. He took a deep breath, as though he needed to screw up his courage. "My room is next to theirs. I heard them arguing. They argued a lot. But that night I heard a noise, like somebody dropped something or fell. I got worried and went to check. When I opened the door, I smelled something burning."

"What?"

"A fire. It was climbing up the drapes. But Mr. Daines didn't notice. He had his arm around his wife's neck. She was fighting him, trying to get away. I reckoned he was scared of the fire. He went crazy sometimes. So I grabbed a vase of flowers. Used the water to put it out. But he didn't let her go. He kept choking her." Billy's expression went blank like he'd gotten lost in his story. "That's when I saw the gun."

Frank started. Claire had told him she'd brought the gun upstairs. In her version of the story, she was holding it. He'd assumed Billy had retrieved it from downstairs. "Where did you see it?"

"Partly under a newspaper on the desk."

Hidden.

"You picked it up?"

"No. I told him to let her go. She couldn't talk. Her face had got all red like she couldn't breathe. I yelled at him, *'Let her go or I'll shoot you!'* That's when I grabbed the gun. He threw her aside and came after me. His face was all screwed up. He had spit around his mouth. He looked like a monster. I-I thought he'd tear me apart."

"Did you fire the gun?"

The boy's eyes filled with tears. "I cocked it. I-I don't remember pulling the trigger. I guess I did. The gun went off. It jerked my arm back. Then...he fell."

Billy released a huge breath.

He'd gotten rid of a heavy load.

Frank's first instinct was to clap the kid on the back and thank him, not lock him up. That crazy bastard would've killed Claire if the boy hadn't stopped him.

This story fit with the scene that night. Also, with what Claire had said about her husband's delusional attack. Only a few facts were off. Billy had put out the fire. Claire didn't mention that. She wouldn't have, if she didn't want anyone to know Billy had come into the room while she was being attacked. It wasn't a troubling difference. Something else was.

"You said you saw the gun on the desk under a newspaper?"

Billy nodded.

"Did you see Mrs. Daines take it upstairs?" This fact concerned Frank. Given Bond's damning statement, the judge would question Claire's intentions.

Billy shook his head. "Earlier, I saw Mr. Daines come downstairs. I ducked around the desk so he wouldn't see me. He didn't like me. He went through the drawers. Took out her pistol. I don't know why. I wish I'd mentioned it to her. But I didn't think about it until later."

Had Frederick Daines planned to shoot his wife? Who could say what was in his mind? The important thing was that Billy could testify *she* hadn't gotten the gun.

"Where's the gun now?"

Billy looked down at his feet. "I lost it."

"Where?"

"I hitched a ride on a train. Had a run-in with some outlaws. They took it." He rubbed the toe of his shoe on the floor.

Whether his reluctance to tell the whole story came from fear or a misplaced sense of loyalty didn't matter. He had to be made to understand the danger of withholding information. His troubled past and long history of poor decisions wouldn't sit well with the judge. There was no telling what his honor might decide to do, even if a good argument could be made for leniency.

"The U.S. Marshal told me you'd joined up with train robbers." Frank exaggerated to see how Billy would respond.

The boy jerked his head up, looking panicked. "I-I didn't join. Just said I wanted to, so they'd trust me. I planned to bring 'em in."

He thought to round up a pack of outlaws? *Unbelievable.* Then again, twelve-year-old boys imagined doing a lot of unbelievable things.

"Why would you do that?"

"To make everything better," Billy said with utter sincerity.

The boy's simple explanation sounded a little foolish. Yet, Frank had entertained the same belief when he was just a few years older than Billy. After his father had been murdered, he'd set off to make things right. Even after his wife was killed, he wouldn't give up his commitment to justice. Somehow, he got it in his head he owed it to his parents, and then, to his wife and baby girl.

He could catch a thousand outlaws, and it might make things safer, but nothing he did would put things right—whatever that was. What he'd done, the mistakes he'd made, he couldn't reverse. Neither could Billy.

Frank couldn't be soft. It wouldn't do either of them any good. "Did you participate in any crimes? Steal anything? Shoot anybody else?"

Billy moved his head back and forth, emphatically. "No sir, I did not. All we did was fix up a rundown cabin."

"We?"

The boy looked down at his feet and didn't answer. For someone who claimed he was ready to turn himself in, he sure was reluctant to give up his rascally friends.

Frank stood up and stretched. He retrieved one of the *Wanted* posters and handed it to the boy. "That's an old picture. Maybe you met him? Jasper Byrne."

Billy studied the poster. He shook his head. The anxious look on his face said different. He'd met the notorious outlaw. It sounded like he'd been living with the ferret for the past few weeks. Surprising. Few people could get close to Byrne. According to those who knew him, he had a handful of allies, three friends, and not a soul he trusted.

"I-I don't think..." Billy started nervously.

"He can't hurt you," Frank assured him. "If you tell me where to find their hideout, I'll take care of bringing them in. Make sure the judge knows you cooperated. Byrne won't come after you. I can promise you that."

Billy kept staring at the poster. "What'll happen to him?"

His tone of voice spoke volumes. The boy wasn't afraid of Byrne as much as he was afraid *for* him. If the two had developed a friendship, that was too bad. Frank couldn't, and wouldn't, sugarcoat the outlaw's fate.

"If he's convicted of half those crimes, he'll probably hang."

Billy remained silent, but his face reflected the agony he felt.

Frank wasn't without sympathy. He'd seen men he liked go to the gallows. But he wasn't responsible for their choices. That was something Billy needed to recognize. "What happens to Jasper Byrne isn't your fault. He's made bad decisions and has to face the consequences."

"But, aren't we supposed to forgive people?"

Sounded like something Claire would read from the Bible.

"That's God's business," Frank stated. It was easier to leave it up to Providence than to struggle with the enormous implications of such a commandment. His father had preached forgiveness. His mother had practiced it. He hadn't been able to forgive the men who'd murdered his father or the ones who'd killed his wife. Nor could he forgive himself for failing his family. He'd chosen instead to uphold the law.

His choices hadn't changed the past. Eventually, the path he'd chosen brought him back to the same confusing place he'd been before. But he wasn't sharing his doubts with a twelve-year-old.

He told Billy what he'd learned from being a lawman. "There's some who don't want forgiveness. They'll keep doing bad things and hurting people unless we stop them."

"Jasper is coming here to turn me in." Billy's hurt expression made it clear he felt betrayed. "I haven't seen him around yet. One of his men told him about the reward and he left. I reckoned he'd come here to arrange a handoff."

A train robber showing up in the headquarters town for the railroad to collect a reward. Now, that would be a bold, crazy move.

Reportedly, Byrne was bold and crazy, but he'd never acted stupid. If he figured on turning Billy in, he'd have someone else collect for him.

"You sure he'll be here?" Frank asked.

"I told you everything I know." Billy rubbed his eyes. "Can I see her now? Mrs. Daines?"

Frank rested his hip on the corner of the desk and considered his next steps carefully. What would Claire do if she knew Billy had returned? She might, in desperation, say something that would get her into deeper trouble. As much as he hated to do it, he had to keep Billy away from her until the hearing. Once Billy was on the stand, Claire couldn't do anything to change his confession.

Frank knew she'd never forgive him for keeping Billy away. Deceiving her again.

He had no choice. If he wanted to save Claire, he had to betray her trust. After that, he would never be able to convince her to marry him, much less love him.

The low feelings he'd experienced earlier were nothing compared to what he felt now.

He fished for the key in his vest pocket. Good thing he still had half a bottle of whiskey left in the drawer.

"I fear you have a weakness."

The memory of Claire's concerned remark stopped him. She was right. If he gave up and gave in, it proved he was weak.

Billy's hopeful expression cinched it.

If this boy could rally the courage to face his demons, so could he. He had to stop reaching for the bottle. Figure out how to help Billy. Find a way to win Claire's heart and be deserving of her love. It might take the rest of his life, but he could think no worthier cause.

Frank tucked away the key, came off the desk and rested his hand on Billy's shoulder. He'd take the boy upstairs, keep watch over him while he got a few hours of sleep and then take him to Mr. Moore. The lawyer would know how to handle it from there.

"Let's not bother her tonight. She's probably asleep. Looks like you could use some food and rest. You can see her in the morning."

CHAPTER 27

From a corner table in the back of the Rail Yard Saloon, Jasper could keep an eye on who came in and who went out. He could also hear the excited chatter at the bar.

Settlers and railroaders made bets on whether *the Black Widow*, currently locked up in the jail, would be charged with murder. If so, whether she'd be sent to prison or hanged. And they called outlaws bloodthirsty.

Jasper turned his glass to examine the amber liquid. His Pa had made better whiskey. He hadn't been patient enough to learn the painstaking process. He hadn't been willing to learn much of anything the old man had tried to teach him because he'd been stiff-necked and stupid.

It was too late for him to change. But he could see to it that Billy didn't make the same mistakes.

Jasper tossed back the whiskey. Once his contact showed up, they could get down to business.

It was risky, to be sure. *Mr. Smith* had warned him not to come to town. But he'd place his own bet that *Smith* would be willing to cooperate with a ruthless man who could bring him down. If the plan worked, he'd collect that reward and get Billy back home, where he belonged.

One of the serving girls, a pert blonde with lily-white skin and a low-cut dress, sashayed by the table. Her nervous glances weren't surprising. Most women had a similar reaction.

He'd been told he had a *mean look* that scared the gentler sex. His raspy voice—a result of being hanged—heightened the impression that he could be a monster. Ironically, those same qualities earned him respect from men. The reputation suited him because he liked to keep his distance. But he couldn't get the information he sought if he sat here alone and kept his mouth shut.

Jasper lifted his empty glass and put on a pleasant expression.

The large-breasted serving girl approached with a wary expression. His sun-darkened skin might've put her off. Despite his white blood, he looked more Indian than Irish.

"You need another drink, mister?" she asked.

"I'd rather have your company." He could be honest about some things.

She tipped up her nose. "We're *decent* girls here."

Jasper swallowed a dry laugh. He hadn't known a saloon girl yet who wouldn't be *in*decent if the price was right. "I just want to talk."

She scooped up his glass. "Let me get you a fresh drink."

He put a three-dollar gold piece on the table. "Sit for a minute. Then you can go get the drink and keep the change."

Her eyes widened with interest. She took the chair across from him. Slid the gold coin off the table and tucked it into her bodice, where it would be warmed by those magnificent breasts.

Jasper's gaze lingered on her tantalizing cleavage before he reluctantly shifted his attention to her face. She was passably pretty, but who cared. With that body, no one would be looking at her face. Later, he'd pull out another gold piece to see if she might relax her high standards. Right now, he'd buy information. "Tell me about this shooting everybody's talking about."

"You ain't from around here, if you don't know."

"No. Passing through." Many travelers passed through the

railroad town, so it wouldn't be unusual for a stranger to show up in a saloon not far from the depot.

Jasper rubbed the bristle on his face. The extra facial hair was a precaution. That decade-old picture on the *Wanted* poster looked nothing like him. He hadn't made the mistake of being photographed since.

A man at the next table shifted his chair sideways. His companion's conversation must've gotten boring.

The blond tart leaned her tits on the table, which made Jasper happy. "The lady who ran the hotel next door shot her husband. Announced it here, in front of everybody, including the sheriff."

The hotel next door, which was the Belmont House, where Billy said he lived. The lady in jail, *the Black Widow*, had to be his guardian.

Why would she claim she'd shot her husband if Billy had pulled the trigger? The boy might've lied to use the shooting as bragging rights. Or, he'd fired the first shot and she finished the job. If that were the case, why hadn't anyone mentioned him?

Jasper shifted forward in his chair to get a better view. "What about the boy?"

"Boy?"

"I heard somebody say earlier there was a boy living there."

"Oh, you mean that orphan they took in. He ran off."

The gal's dismissive tone grated on Jasper. Billy might've been a stray dog, given her lack of concern. "Somebody wants him. There's a reward. Four hundred dollars."

"Yeah, I heard about that." Her faded blue eyes brightened with greed. "Hey, maybe she killed him too, and buried his body behind the hotel. They might give me that four hundred dollars if I dig it up."

"That's foolishness, Essie. She'd never hurt Billy." The remark came from a man at the next table who'd been eavesdropping. His bibbed denims and soot-stained skin identified him as one of the men who fed coal to the big steam engines. He might know more than the serving girl.

"What do you think?" Jasper asked him. "Did she kill her husband?"

The sturdy fireman turned his chair around to join their conversation. "Mrs. Daines is a nice, decent lady. She said the shooting was an accident. I believe her."

Jasper wasn't convinced. Not all women were as genteel as his mother or guileless like his sister. Some were deceitful. "Why is she in jail if it was an accident?"

"They aren't sure it was," Essie offered informatively. "There's some who say she meant to kill him because he sold their hotel."

The man shook his finger in the girl's face. "That's just gossip, gal, and you know it."

Her rouged lips thinned with irritation. "Is not. That's what Mr. Bond says. They quoted him in the newspaper."

Jasper's ears pricked up. He knew that name. "Bond? Isn't he the Katy's general manager?"

"That's right."

"He'll testify tomorrow at the hearing," Essie added. "That's what the newspaper said."

The railroad man huffed at her. "How do *you* know what the newspaper says? You can't read."

"Can too!"

Jasper ignored their bickering. He'd found out what he wanted to know. Billy's name hadn't come up in connection with the shooting, but someone else's had. The railroad boss had gotten involved in the dispute, which might explain why he wasn't here. Or maybe, he was too nervous to show up. Didn't matter. He could be shaken out of his tree later.

"You want to make a bet on the outcome, mister? Or put your money on something else?" Essie slid her arms across the table, displaying her ample gifts.

Jasper experienced a twinge of lust. Just as he'd surmised, the lure of more money was too tempting, even for a *decent* girl. He doubted he'd get any more useful information out of her, but he wouldn't mind a sample of what she offered.

He tucked the next coin in between warm, soft flesh and gave her a smile. "I'll put my money on a sure thing."

He planned to hang around tonight anyway. Find out what Bond had to say at that hearing, and, just as important, whether Billy's guardian got charged with murder. If so, the boy would need another home.

Jasper had held onto his last card. He would play only if it were absolutely necessary. His sister didn't need another burden. However, under the circumstances, she might be willing to take on the boy. Billy could be helpful. He was a hard worker.

On a happier note, if Billy's guardian was cleared and released, Jasper saw no reason why he couldn't corral the wayward orphan and gain the general manager's assistance in collecting a handsome reward.

CHAPTER 28

$\mathcal{N}$othing drew a crowd faster than the possibility of a hanging.

The following morning, the entire town turned out to gawk when Claire left the jail on her way to the hearing. Or so it seemed. She'd never seen so many people on the sidewalk or in the street.

Frank circled his arm around her shoulders, shielding her from the curious onlookers. He was supposed to guard her as his prisoner. Instead, he upheld his vow to protect her, like it or not.

Curious onlookers crowded the entrance to a stone and brick building that housed city offices and a courtroom. Generally, cases here involved land disputes, sometimes thefts. Not too many killings, thanks to their vigilant sheriff.

"There she is! The Black Widow," someone in the crowd called out.

Claire shuddered at the moniker comparing her to a poisonous spider. The newspapers had already pronounced her a cold-blooded killer.

Frank's expression remained closed. Though he could hide his feelings better than most, she'd been married to a man whose dark moods could strike faster than a storm on the Kansas prairie. For her own survival, she'd learned how to translate the physical signs. Her escort's tight jaw and flared nostrils indicated anger. He would strike at anyone who tried to hurt her.

Even if a judge or jury believed her story, doubts would linger. Frank's strong sense of justice would compel him to defend her. He had enough problems as a lawman without being hobbled by her tainted reputation, which would follow her to the grave, regardless of the verdict. She couldn't imagine how she would get along without him, but she wouldn't shackle him to her.

"Move back." With the sharp order and a sweep of his hand, Frank parted the sea of onlookers gathered at the steps leading up to the courthouse.

Claire stared straight ahead on what seemed a long climb.

He closed the doors on the crowd behind them.

Inside the courtroom, every seats was occupied. More people had crowded in to stand along the back wall. The bustling anticipation, overheated air, and the odor of stale perspiration, added to the circus atmosphere.

Claire longed to bury her face into Frank's shoulder. Instead, she straightened her spine and kept walking toward a table near the front. Loud whispers started as she passed by. The Bonds were seated in the second row. Gertrude had dressed for the occasion in dove-gray silk with a matching plumed hat. The odious woman smirked. Her husband stared straight ahead, stone-faced.

Frank handed her off to her attorney. He continued on, up to the judge's bench. She couldn't hear their words, but the judge's face didn't convey an exchange of pleasantries.

"Mrs. Daines?" Mr. Moore pulled out her chair and offered a kind smile. "You're well-rested, I hope."

"Yes, thank you." She practiced lying to see whether she could be believable. She hadn't been able to sleep or eat. Her stomach had shrunk to the size of a peach pit and was presently lodged in her throat.

After arranging her black bombazine skirt, she lifted the dark veil over her bonnet so the air would cool her face. Shortly, she'd put it back. If she had to go up there and talk in front of this crowd, she would need the barrier, and it would make her look more like a grieving widow. Although her grieving had commenced years before her husband's death.

Without her keys to keep her hands occupied, she plucked at the lace on her sleeve. Frank had told her he wouldn't stand by and let her take the blame. He might be sharing his suspicions about Billy with the judge.

He had no proof. She would stand by her version of the facts.

Mr. Moore studied her with a concerned frown. "You don't look well."

Her previous lie hadn't worked on him. She would try again.

"I am not rested." That much was apparent. She had dark circles under her eyes and fatigue and stress were etched on her face. She almost wished Frank hadn't provided her with a mirror. "I am as well as I can be, under the circumstances."

Her lawyer took the seat next to her with his cane propped against the table. "So you know, this is just a hearing. Fairly routine. The judge has read over the statements. He will ask a few questions before he issues a decision."

Claire adjusted her shawl. The air had gotten cooler. Or the chill might be due to her blood turning cold. "If he believes the shooting was an accident?"

"I imagine he'll release you. Accidents aren't crimes."

She fiddled with the black lace at her wrists, keeping her eyes on the judge and sheriff who were still in deep conversation. "What if he doesn't believe me?"

"I'll argue for a lesser charge than murder."

Thank heavens for Mr. Moore. His steadiness had a calming effect on her nerves.

When the judge called for order, the hearing quickly got underway.

Mr. Moore stood first, then helped her to her feet. The buzz of conversation quieted while he escorted her forward. She moved on shaky legs. He slipped his hand beneath her elbow. How did he think he could catch her if she went down? He needed a cane for balance. She murmured her thanks and removed her arm, so as not to burden him.

For some reason, Frank remained next to the judge's bench, almost as if he waited for her. Could he do that? He might expect her to collapse and worried about who would catch her.

She wouldn't fold up. She could do this. For Billy's sake.

The judge's stern demeanor remained unchanged as she approached the bench. Deep grooves creased his forehead and bracketed his mouth. A layer of dust coated his dark suit. The circuit judge had ridden in this morning. He didn't look to be in a good mood. Perhaps no one had offered him breakfast.

She held her hands together to keep them from shaking. "Good morning, sir."

"If you say so, madam. It will be a better morning if we can clear this up quickly. Can you tell me why you're here?"

He had to know the purpose of the hearing. Perhaps this question was put to her to ascertain whether she was clear on the facts. "For... for shooting my husband."

The crease between the judge's bushy eyebrows deepened with displeasure. "The sheriff tells me you didn't fire the gun."

Frank met her gaze without flinching. He'd warned her. She'd expected he would try something like this.

"I-I think the sheriff means I didn't *intend* to fire the gun."

The sheriff's expression remained set in hard, determined lines. "I meant what I said. You didn't fire the weapon that killed your husband."

She put her hand to her chest to calm her racing heart. She couldn't let Frank intimidate her. "I told you that night, I had the gun in my hands when it went off."

"That night you were so addled you couldn't remember where you left the weapon. You still don't know where the gun is or who might have it."

The judge leaned back with his fingers laced over his chest, appearing content to let Frank shoot holes through her story.

A tingling sensation started at the base of her neck. It spread to her scalp, over her shoulders and down her arms. A sign that panic was about to set in. She cast an anxious glance at her lawyer. He'd confirm what she had told him.

Mr. Moore didn't open his mouth. He only looked at her, somewhat sadly.

The truth sent her reeling. Mr. Moore was in cahoots with Frank. They had cooked up some scheme to discredit her. She would fire the lawyer later, after she dealt with the sheriff. "You weren't there, Mr. Garrity. You have no idea what happened."

"*I* do."

The childish voice from the back of the courtroom sent tremors through her.

She whirled around.

Billy stood just inside the door. The deputy accompanied him.

Relief nearly buckled her knees. Thank God, he was safe. Then, anger set it. Frank had sent his deputy out after her son, as if he were a criminal.

Billy twisted his hat in his hands with an apology on his face. His clothes were dirty, but he'd combed his hair and taken time to wash up. As if he'd known he had to look nice for his appearance in court.

She jerked an accusing glare at Frank, then Mr. Moore. The despicable deceivers looked away. They'd plunged daggers in her back. Or through her heart. Which would explain this knifing pain in her chest. They would not get away with this. She would not let them.

"No!" she shouted.

The sheriff blocked her way to Billy. His stern expression made it clear he would not let her pass. "Stay put. Let him come forward."

"How *could* you?" Tears she couldn't hold back sprang into her eyes. He'd known about Billy's return and had held back from telling her in order to set her up as a liar. He'd betrayed her in the worst possible way.

She wanted to strike him. Instead, she begged. "Please, don't make him do this. He's just a child. He hasn't done anything wrong."

"He's not being forced, Claire. He showed up on his own because he cares about you."

Mr. Moore appeared at her other side. "His conscience compelled him. He's a brave lad."

She didn't want him to be brave. She wanted him to be safe.

"What's your name, boy?" the judge called out.

"Billy. My name's Billy Frye." He squared his shoulders. When he did that, he looked taller. Or had he grown in just a few short weeks? He'd soon be as tall as the men on either side of him. He'd become the promising young man she'd seen in him the day he'd come to live with her. But right now, he was still a child. One who needed her protection.

The judge motioned with his hand. "Step forward, Mr. Frye."

Hot tears streamed down Claire's cheeks. "No," she mouthed the words at Billy. "Don't do this. Not for me."

He hesitated. His courage appeared to waver. He glanced to his left at the people spread out along the wall, and surprise flashed across his face. He halted in his tracks.

Claire followed the direction he seemed to be looking.

Amidst the onlookers, a black-haired man in a fringed jacket hunched his shoulders as if he wanted to melt into the wall. The faded bandana tied around his neck made him look like a cowboy, but a holstered gun tied to his thigh suggested a more ominous occupation. Billy's expression said he knew the rough-looking stranger.

Claire's heart hammered a warning

"Jumpin' Jehoshaphat," Frank blurted, before releasing her arm. He moved with long, rapid strides toward Billy. At the same time, he pulled his revolver.

"No." The word came out of her mouth in barely a whisper.

Mr. Moore snagged her elbow with a surprisingly strong grip. She struggled to get away, but only managed to drag him a short distance before he wrapped his arms around her. They were like iron bands.

The stranger came off the wall and made haste to the back door. A crowd pressing in from outside impeded his attempt to escape. He brandished a large revolver. "Get back!"

Cries of alarm broke out. Men and woman cleared the doorway like ants scurrying away from a disturbed anthill. Billy, however, appeared rooted to the floor. He'd be struck if the sheriff fired on the escaping gunman.

Claire, still struggling to break free, unstopped the panic in her throat and screamed. "Don't shoot!"

The gunman vanished out the door. Frank followed. Her cry seemed to snap Billy out of his frozen indecision. He turned and bolted after the departing men.

What was he *doing?* He could be killed!

She jerked away from her captor.

He thrust out one hand to catch himself on the table. "Mrs. Daines, you mustn't leave—"

"Order! Order!"

She heard the banging, the warnings, the shouts, but she ignored the commotion behind her and shoved people aside when they got in her way. She heeded nothing but the frantic voice in her head, urging her to get to Billy before he was caught in the middle of a gunfight.

WHILE THE COURTROOM was in chaos, the outlaw took full advantage of the pandemonium he'd created. By the time Frank got past the panicked observers, Jasper Byrne had made it outside.

Frank swore, dodging people who poured out the courthouse doors. If the commotion followed them out here, he'd lose his opportunity to catch the outlaw without someone getting in the way, and possibly getting shot in the crossfire. He couldn't take that chance.

He threw his arm in an arching gesture meant to stop whoever was behind him. "Stay back."

A few folks listened.

He kept moving with his attention riveted on the gunman.

Byrne ran across the street like a rat scurrying for cover. He dodged between moving wagons and riders, smart enough not to give anyone a clear shot.

The crowd outside exceeded the one inside. Besides the usual farmers and cowboys, there were women and children, far too many people to engage in a shoot-out. The outlaw knew this and would use it to his advantage. He appeared to be headed for a hitching rail in front of a saloon where several horses were tethered. If he reached one, he'd skedaddle before anyone could stop him.

"Look! There he is! Shoot him!" a male voice called out.

Frank resisted the urge to look behind him and take even a second to call down that idiot. He'd catch Byrne without endangering innocent bystanders.

"Everybody get back. Keep quiet. Don't do anything to draw his fire." Frank threw the response over his shoulder. He bent over to keep his head low. If he could get in the right position, he could cut the outlaw down before he got away. If he missed the chance, he'd take his deputy's horse, the fastest in the county. Catch up with Byrne outside of town.

The outlaw might have friends waiting for him.

Damn. There were no good choices.

A small figure in a tan coat shot out into the street, running at a diagonal, nimbly avoiding the horses and wagons that still moved.

Billy. What the devil?

Frank veered into the street after the little fool, who moved faster than a yearling colt. There was no catching him. The boy reached the outlaw before Byrne could untie a horse.

Billy grabbed the man's sleeve.

Frank's heart nearly gave out.

God, no! Byrne would kill Billy before he'd let himself get captured or shot. Didn't matter whether the kid was trying to catch him or escape with him.

A wagon loaded with railroad ties rumbled past. In a moment, the driver would go by the boy and the outlaw. Frank leapt onto the bed and cocked his gun. He'd have one chance. One shot. If he got lucky.

"Billy!"

Shocked by Claire's cry, Frank nearly lost his grip on the side of the wagon.

She ran down the street in a beeline, straight for Billy. A rider wheeled his horse out of the way to avoid striking her. She was blind to everything except that boy.

Frank's heart hammered in his chest. He had to go after her, but he was almost there, seconds from where he could take the outlaw down before Byrne hurt Claire or Billy.

He shouted as the wagon approached the hitching rail. "Claire! Take cover!"

A loud crack split the air.

She stumbled. A gut-wrenching instant later, she fell facedown into the mud. Her black skirts billowed.

Frank leapt off the wagon. Nothing registered in his brain except Claire's still form in the middle of the street. And the utter stillness that took over for the blink of an eye. Then, pain ripped through him as if someone had thrust a bayonet through his chest.

He bellowed like an enraged bull as he raced to Claire's side. Put himself in front of her with his gun raised, prepared to die to protect her.

The outlaw wasn't on or beside the horse. He wasn't in a practiced stance, ready to fire his weapon again. He lay stretched out over Billy, had apparently thrown the boy to the ground. His hat had rolled off and tilted into a muddy rut.

The black-haired devil looked up at Frank. Their eyes met, both confused.

Frank realized with a start the shot had come from behind. He twisted around, searching for the shooter.

A knot of people hovered near a rain barrel beside the boardwalk. Close by, the lawyer, Mr. Moore, wrestled with the Katy's general manager. It looked like...by God, *Bond* had a handgun. No, now, Moore had the gun. He struck Bond on the side of the head and the general manager dropped to his knees.

William Bond had fired that shot? *He* had tried to kill Claire?

Frank stopped up an onslaught of murderous intentions and

holstered his gun. Moore had taken care of Bond. There would be time to deal with him later. Claire needed help.

He leaned over her, frantically running his hands over her back. Where had she been hit? With utmost care, he drew her into his arms and tenderly wiped mud off her face.

"Claire?" he choked out her name.

She didn't open her eyes. Her cheek felt cool, but that could be on account of the damp mud. He searched her face for some sign of consciousness. Her body lay slack in his arms.

Anguish ripped his heart out by the roots. His throat closed up. Some invisible hand crushed the throbbing muscle in his chest. She couldn't be dead. She had to be alive. She had to be. He'd sworn to protect her. He'd given her his vow.

He released a low, brute sound, a tortured groan. "No... NO!" Not again. Providence wouldn't make the same mistake twice. God wouldn't take another sweet woman and leave behind a miserable wretch.

Hushed voices surrounded them. Frank darted a furtive look around, prepared to send them away. Shoot them if necessary. No one would take her away from him.

The people standing around them didn't appear eager to try.

Frank caught sight of his deputy. Gideon had Byrne pressed up against a post. He'd handcuffed the outlaw. Byrne's days as a free man were over. Ironic as hell. Byrne gave up his chance to escape when he threw Billy to the ground and covered him. Another person who'd sacrificed for the boy. Not nearly as much as the woman who'd become his mother.

Frank stiffened as Billy ran up. He knelt. His face so pale it looked whitewashed. "She-she's all right, ain't she?"

The little risk-taker had escaped another disaster unscathed, as usual. Claire hadn't. She'd died to protect him.

Frank sucked in a rough, anguished breath and cradled her to his chest. He couldn't blame others. This was *his* fault. He should've thrown himself at Claire, gone after her the moment he saw her run into the street. Not hesitated for even a second.

Like before. He'd made a calculated decision—the wrong one—and had failed Claire. Just as he had failed Sarah. This time, he'd find the courage to put a bullet through his brain and end his miserable life.

"She's breathing!" Billy cried.

Frank jerked his attention back to the woman in his arms.

Her chest moved. Oh God! She breathed!

He jerked at the ribbon holding her veil and bonnet to remove any possible obstacle to getting air into her lungs. The frilled edges caught on her hair. He stroked the loose strands away from her face and smoothed them back. Her beautiful hair had become matted and wet...

His fingers came away bloody.

"Sweet Jesus," he whispered. A head wound, the worst kind. Even if she survived, she might never be the same.

No, he couldn't think about that right now. Couldn't let her lay here in the mud, bleeding. He had to get her inside. Somewhere she could be tended. "Somebody, fetch the doc."

"I'll get him." Billy jumped to his feet.

Frank scooped Claire into his arms and stood. She moaned when her head lolled against him, smearing blood on his vest. He nestled her closer, tried to make her more comfortable.

Her hair caught on the prong of his badge. The very thing that should protect her only added to her misery. He couldn't seem to avoid hurting her, no matter what he did.

He didn't deserve a woman as fine and good as Claire, even if he was crazy in love with her, and, honestly, had been for some time. This was God's way of punishing him for coveting another man's wife. Even after she'd become a widow, he'd known damn well he had no business pursuing her, seducing her, and taking advantage of her pure heart.

He'd made too many mistakes, had too much blood on his hands. He didn't deserve her.

If God would save her, he'd do anything. Anything.

CHAPTER 29

Frank didn't stop praying from the time he stood up to the moment he pushed the door open at the Belmont House. He shouted at the young man behind the counter. Told him to fetch water and towels and show the doctor in, then headed upstairs Claire in his arms. He knew where to go, assuming the Bonds hadn't moved her things.

"Sheriff, wait. I'll help you." Mrs. Bond dogged his heels as he took the stairs two at a time and headed down the hall. "Mr. Bond feels terrible about what happened. He meant to shoot at that outlaw. He didn't imagine Mrs. Daines would run into the street."

"I don't give a damn what he meant to do. He fired a shot when she was in the way. He shot her in the head, for God's sake. He'll hang if I have any say in the matter."

Frank ignored the horrified gasp. Far as he was concerned, that nasty woman could swing beside her husband. Both of them put together weren't worth as much as the tip of Claire's little finger. He reached the door to her room with Gertrude Bond still trailing behind. "Open it."

"I'm afraid it's locked. I'll go get a key."

"Don't have time to wait." He lifted his leg and kicked in the door.

It gave a satisfying bang. He veered into the bedroom and gently laid Claire on the coverlet.

He glanced over his shoulder. Bond's wife stood in the doorway of the bedroom, looking put out.

"Go check to see if the doctor is on his way. Tell Deputy Branch to find Billy. And get somebody to help undress Claire." He'd do it, but that would be entirely inappropriate and he wouldn't shame her by suggesting it.

"I can help."

Hell no. He wouldn't let that spiteful woman anywhere near Claire. "Go find the cook, Mrs. Kelly. Claire trusts her."

"I have no idea where that Irish slattern might be. But I'll go look for the doctor." Gertrude Bond left on a huff.

Good riddance.

Frank sat beside Claire and took her hand. Cool, but not too cold. Or should her skin be warmer? He had rudimentary knowledge when it came to injuries and illness. Head wounds were far beyond his skills. He leaned down, speaking in a low, but urgent, tone. "Claire? Can you hear me?"

Her eyes fluttered but didn't open. She gave a shuddering sigh. He recalled seeing men struck in the head by shrapnel. Their breathing had been irregular—right before they expired.

Fear shredded his composure. He started to shake.

She had to wake up. She had to be all right. He didn't want to do anything that might cause further harm, but he had to do *something*. He couldn't just sit here, holding her hand, feeling useless.

He focused his attention on removing the pins that held her hair in place. As he separated each lock, he checked to see if he could tell where the bullet had struck. Too much blood.

Bottled up grief pushed the cork into his throat. He stumbled over to the washstand. Poured water from a pitcher with trembling hands. Took a deep breath to calm himself before he returned with the basin and began to carefully clean the hair near her head, using his hand to wash water over it. In moments, the water in the bowl had turned bright red.

The sound of rapid footsteps grew louder. A second later, the compact little cook bustled into the bedroom. "Here, now, Sheriff. Let me do that."

Mrs. Kelly hurried to the bed. The minute she saw the bloody water, her kind features pulled into a look of distress. "Poor lamb. I'll empty this and get fresh."

"We'll need lots of water. Boil it first." A stranger in a dark suit issued the order. He'd entered the bedroom with a firm grip on a beat-up leather case. He looked Frank over with a brisk assessment. "Are you the injured woman's husband?"

"Who are you?"

"Jeremy Stone. I'm a doctor."

Frank had never heard of this Dr. Stone. The pale, slender man didn't look very old or distinguished, or particularly capable. "You new in town?"

"Actually, I was on my way to Texas. I stayed here last night. Mrs. Bond said you need a doctor." Stone set his kit on the side of the bed, removed his coat and rolled up his shirtsleeves. He opened the case to reveal an array of metal instruments. A surgeon's tools.

Frank shuddered with revulsion. Claire didn't need a sawbones. He folded his arms over his chest, disinclined to trust a stranger with her life. "We can wait on Doc Stanton."

"If she has a head wound, you don't have time to wait." Stone's tone was calm, but firm.

He moved Frank out of his way. Then he sat on the side of bed next to Claire. First, he lifted her eyelids with this thumb to peer at her eyes. Then he slowly shifted her head to one side and drew back her hair, examining the area where Frank had washed away blood

Claire's pained whimper sent a knife through Frank's heart. "Be careful," he snapped.

The surgeon didn't even look up. "Doesn't appear the bullet entered her skull."

Frank released a relieved breath. Had she taken a bullet to the brain, it would be a death sentence. "Why is she unconscious?"

The doctor straightened. "I didn't say it wasn't serious. If a bullet strikes the skull, it's like taking a blow to the head. It can cause inflammation in the brain. I'll know more after I get this wound cleaned up."

Frank moved closer. "Will she wake soon?"

"Hard to tell. We'll have to wait and see."

Wait and see wasn't the answer Frank wanted. If Claire didn't come back...

His vision blurred. He blinked, surprised by tears. He hadn't cried when Sarah and the baby had died. He hadn't wept at his father's funeral or even his mother's. He'd been too bitter and filled with regret. Then, he'd met Claire. She had lanced his heart and drained the poison. Thanks to her, he'd gone soft. Now, he couldn't even hide behind his badge.

"You might make yourself useful and see about that water." Stone pawed through his bag. "Also, tell that woman I'll need more towels, pounded ice with salt, vinegar, and soap, so I can wash my hands."

Frank didn't trust strangers, even ones who sounded like they knew what they were talking about. He had no idea where the old doc had gotten off to—maybe delivering a baby or patching up some railroader. He'd fetch this fellow what he wanted and get back to keep an eye on him.

By the time Frank reached the kitchen, Mrs. Kelly had gathered most of the items, as if she'd read the doctor's mind. Frank trailed behind her up the stairs into the sitting room. When he tried to follow her inside the bedroom, she shut the door in his face.

His anger flared. By God, that old woman couldn't keep him out if he wished to be in there, even if it wasn't his place. Fear clawed at his gut. He had to be at Claire's side so he could protect her. What if something happened?

He reached for the knob—then froze. *Fool.* Something *had* happened. When he'd been within a few feet of her. The time to act had been then. There wasn't a damned thing he could do now.

A KNOCK CAME at the door to the suite.

Gideon Branch waited out in the hall until Frank motioned for him to come inside. He removed his hat. "How's she doin'?"

"Not good." Frank allowed the admission. "That doctor says it looks like she got grazed. But she won't wake up."

"Sorry to hear. Got Byrne in jail. And the boy."

Frank paced the length of the sitting room. The outlaw behind bars was good news, but Billy? He should've thought to bring him along. Though he couldn't be certain Billy wouldn't run, and he couldn't concentrate on both Claire and the boy. It was probably best that Billy remained in jail for now. She'd have a fit when she regained consciousness. *If* she regained consciousness.

Regret and fear made a pretzel out of Frank's insides. "Did you arrest Bond?"

"Haven't yet. There's disagreement over what happened."

Not as far as Frank was concerned. "Does he deny he shot her?"

"He admits he fired the gun. Says he was aiming at the outlaw. Miz Daines got in the way. Others around him say the same."

Frank glared at his deputy. "I don't give a damn what anybody says. He shot Claire. We're locking him up. If you don't feel comfortable doing it, I will."

Gideon raised his hand. "Slow down, boss. You go after Bond and somebody else'll get hurt. Don't want to have to put *you* in jail."

Annoyed, Frank made a sharp turn. "You wouldn't."

The deputy's visage became stern. "Yes suh, I would. If you gunned a man down 'cause you got your back up. The reason don't matter. That's the law."

"You're quoting the law to somebody who knows it better than you."

"Knowin' it and abidin' by it are two different things. You're not thinkin' straight. Your mind is in there." Gideon gestured with his chin at the closed bedroom door.

No, not just his mind. His heart was in there, too.

Frank longed to horsewhip Bond before he strangled him. Even though he knew from experience that getting revenge wouldn't ease his pain or help Claire. "I won't let him get away with shooting her."

"Wasn't suggesting it. But I don't see how creatin' a scene is gonna help."

Sound reasoning. Gideon's hallmark. Whenever possible, the former soldier thought things through before he reacted. Once he did act, he did so decisively and without flinching. Frank appreciated both traits.

For years, he'd struggled to master his raging emotions and thought he'd succeeded, until Claire came into his life. He had to restore his control in order to do his job and protect her in the process.

He passed by the desk, dragged his fingers over the smooth surface. The last time he'd been here, papers covered it. He checked the drawers. Empty.

Claire wouldn't have removed all their personal papers before she left. This was Bond's doing. No telling what had been taken, but there could be only one reason why. The papers on the desk or inside might've contained incriminating evidence.

"They've cleared out the desk."

"They?"

"The Bonds." Frank shut the top drawer with a bang. "They managed to get Mr. Daines to sign over the hotel, then moved in while Claire was gone. Looks like they went through the desk and took out all the papers."

Frank quickly updated his deputy on his suspicions about William Bond targeting Claire.

Gideon nodded thoughtfully. "You suppose he thinks the hotel makes lots of money? I hear the railroad's in trouble."

"A hotel won't save the railroad."

"Mm, true. What about his wife?"

"What about her?"

"You think she's involved?"

"She's bound to be. I can't imagine him doing anything without her."

Gideon's eyes gleamed with amusement. "Sho'nough. I'm bettin' she got a whip hid away somewhere."

Gertrude Bond wielding a whip. It fit. Bond kowtowed to his wife. He acted boastful and domineering when he was with other men, but around her he turned docile as a lap dog. She was cruel. Maybe more so than her husband. But Frank had nothing on her, and he didn't see how harassing a woman would get him anywhere.

"We'll worry about her later. For now, find Bond and lock him up. Put him in the overflow cell. The one in the railroad supply building. It's hot in there. He might start talking quicker if he gets to sweating."

"If you say so." The deputy replaced his hat, looking solemn. "The judge wants to know if you're agreeable to movin' ahead with charges against the boy for killin' Mr. Daines."

Billy's series of rash actions had led to a string of events which had ended up with Claire being shot. Now, she fought for her life. The idea of taking a strap to him was tempting, though Claire wouldn't stand for it. Not if she were awake. She'd risked everything —her reputation, her livelihood, and her life—to protect a child that wasn't even hers. But she'd taken him into her heart, and like a mother bear would fight tooth and nail to save him.

She was in no position to help him now.

Frank heaved a troubled sigh. Responsibility for what happened next rested on his shoulders. He could try to delay the hearing until Claire's brother arrived, except the judge had already indicated he wanted a speedy closure.

Delay only postposed Billy's already uncertain future and kept him in jail, where he didn't belong. He needed a home. Family. Most of all, he needed his mother.

"Tell the judge I want to talk to him before he makes a decision."

CHAPTER 30

$\mathcal{F}$rank approached the table where Judge Jessup sat surrounded by old settlers.

"Pull up a chair, Frank. Have you joined the GAR yet?" the judge asked.

"Been meaning to, I'll get the paperwork done this week."

The judge spent the next hour drumming up support for the Grand Army of the Republic, a fraternal organization for Union veterans. He jawed about his intention to run for a senate seat and promised to improve veterans' benefits. He knew his audience. Most of the local settlers were Union veterans.

When Jessup wasn't handing down harsh sentences, he spent his time socializing with former soldiers and reliving the *glory days* when he'd served as attaché to a desk general. He hadn't slogged through the mud and seen disease take more men than bullets, or stepped over bodies strewn across a bloody field, or chased down and executed rebel guerillas. There was no glory in that.

Frank had spent ten years trying to forget those memories and escape the nightmares. But if reminiscing would help him gain the judge's support, he'd do it.

Two hours and many drinks later, the settlers left to go home to their wives. Only the judge and Frank remained. He figured it was time to broach the subject he'd come to discuss. Sure as hell wasn't the GAR or politics.

The judge was a stickler for upholding the law. His toughness on criminals was part of his campaign. Billy had one thing going for him. His youth.

"Are you sure you won't have a drink, Frank?" The judge lifted the bottle and motioned toward Frank's empty glass.

"Not tonight." Frank moved the glass to one side. He leaned his arms on the table. He did *want* a drink. Badly. But he'd decided to *refrain*, as Claire had so delicately put it. In fact, he'd told the Almighty he'd give up anything in exchange for her life. Whiskey seemed a small price to pay.

"I believe I'm done, too." The judge set the bottle down and finished what was left in his glass. "Full docket tomorrow, including the hearing for that young man you've got locked up."

Jessup's remark opened the opportunity Frank had been looking for all evening. "I thought we might have a word about Billy."

"Now, you know I can't render a decision here in the saloon."

"And I wouldn't ask you to. Wasn't sure if you knew Billy's age. He's twelve."

No senate hopeful wanted on his record that he'd sent a child to the gallows. Frank didn't point it out. Jessup was smart. He'd get the idea without being browbeaten.

The judge leaned back in his chair with his fingers laced over his chest, appearing to mull it over. "I didn't realize he was that young. He's an orphan, I understand."

There were some who espoused rounding up homeless children to put them into institutions. Hopefully, Jessup wasn't one of them.

"Mrs. Daines plans to adopt him. She's taught him his letters and his numbers, has worked wonders with him. He hasn't had an easy life. But if you talk to the men at the rail yard, they'll tell you he's a hard worker. I can vouch for him, too. He's not dangerous. He's not a killer."

"He admits he shot and killed a man."

"To protect the woman he considers his mother." Frank went on to explain how ill Frederick Daines had been, how he'd attacked Claire in a deranged state, and Billy had come to her rescue. Frank kept to the truth, yet tried to show Billy in the best light possible.

Jessup listened quietly.

When Frank finished, he waited. The familiar aromas of whiskey and cigar smoke triggered a gut-deep longing. He stared at his empty glass.

He could resist.

The serving girl passed by the table. He waved her away. A few stragglers at the bar craned their necks to look over, as if hoping Jessup would resume buying drinks—he purchased top-rate liquor. Frank signaled them with a slight shake of his head while the judge sat in thoughtful silence.

"Mrs. Daines lied to protect the boy."

"Like any mother would do," Frank pointed out.

Jessup poured another glass of whiskey. Motioned to Frank's glass, which Frank moved over and allowed to be filled. He didn't have to drink it.

"Trying to influence a judge is against the law," Jessup pointed out.

"Just giving you the facts." Frank held the glass. He lightly tapped his finger against the side, fighting the urge to gulp it down.

"I'm not keen to put a child on trial."

Good, the judge was looking for a way out.

"Didn't think you were. No reason it has to go that far."

Jessup nodded, took a sip of whiskey. "An unfortunate accident."

That would be the ruling. Frank released a pent-up breath.

"Who'll make sure he doesn't get into trouble again?"

"Mrs. Daines, once she gets better. She'll keep a close eye on him."

Frank held his breath as Jessup took another drink. He set down his glass, his expression set.

"Not a good solution, Frank. That boy is half grown. He's proved he's too wild for her to handle alone. If he gets into trouble again, she'll cover up for him."

Frank heaved a sigh. He suspected the judge might say that, but he had to try.

"There's a home for destitute orphans. He could go there," Jessup suggested.

"Billy needs a real home," Frank said with conviction. "He'll run away if you stick him in an orphanage."

The judge's mouth turned down in a thoughtful frown. "Based on what I've heard, he's likely to run away from anywhere I put him."

"Not if you put him with someone who can control him." Frank prepared the groundwork for the suggestion that Billy be placed with Henry Stevens. He'd been the one to foist the boy onto Claire in the first place. If Stevens and his wife took Billy in, Claire might get to see him occasionally. It wasn't ideal, but it was better than the alternative.

"You're saying *you'll* take responsibility for him."

Jessup's assumption took Frank aback. He hadn't suggested he would take Billy.

How the hell did he know whether Henry Stevens would? It was a risky bet, and Jessup wasn't the mood to debate. He'd landed on a solution. This could be done and over with tonight.

Frank reassessed. He had the means to support a family. Land. Money he'd saved up that would be good for nothing else. He could provide a better life for Billy, and, at the same time, give Claire the opportunity to be his mother.

He'd sworn he would give up anything so she could live. This seemed a sign, somehow, that God didn't want him to abandon Claire and Billy. The thought took hold and wouldn't let go. He could protect Claire, she would have Billy, and she'd get a husband who loved her with the deal.

He ignored the glass of whiskey. The longing subsided the moment he made his decision. "That's right. I'll take responsibility."

"You sure you can manage a troublesome boy along with your duties?"

His job. That put a damper on the idea. He knew—had known all along—he couldn't bring Claire and Billy into his life without risking their safety, not to mention their happiness and wellbeing. The dangers would always be there, gathering over their heads like storm clouds.

What about the farm?

The soft whisper in his head sounded an awful lot like his mother. She would say something like that. She'd wanted him to return home and take over. He hadn't been able to bear being there before because the place reminded him of his father's useless death. He'd been too angry, filled up with too much bitterness and the need for revenge. All that had been burned out of him some time ago. The idea of returning to the farm held appeal, especially if it meant he'd get Claire in the bargain.

He wouldn't have to chase outlaws and wrestle drunks or wonder when a vengeful bullet might find him. He could take her and Billy home and they'd be safe there. Or safer than they would be if he remained a lawman.

Nothing held him here outside of a sense of duty, and some misguided idea that he had to remain a lawman to make Sarah's death purposeful. Nothing he did could erase his mistakes or change the past. In fact, Sarah would tell him what would make her sacrifice worthwhile would be helping a woman and child who needed him.

"I've got land up near Marais Des Cygnes. I'll take him there. Turn him into a farmer."

The judge sat back as if Frank's statement had truly surprised him. "You'd give up your badge?"

Frank set the full glass aside and leaned back in his chair. The decision lifted a load off his shoulders. He felt easier than he had in years, which told him he'd done the right thing. It ought to relieve Claire, too. All she had to do was marry him to get what she most wanted. Billy.

"It's time I settled down," he admitted. "Let someone else do this job. The town can find another sheriff. Gideon would make a darn good one."

The judge's stern visage softened. His lips pulled into a knowing smile. "You'd do that on account of an orphan?"

Frank hadn't expected to fool him, but he had to talk to Claire first and gain her agreement before he told the rest of the world the good news. "He's a good kid. Just needs more discipline."

"That's right, Frank, and you're the man for the job." Jessup drained his glass and set it down with a thump. He slapped Frank's shoulder. "I'll see you tomorrow. Have Mr. Moore draw up the proper papers. We'll make it legal before I leave town."

CHAPTER 31

*C*laire awoke the next day with a splitting headache. She took even breaths, keeping her eyes closed, and waited to see if her stomach would remain calm. Her mind was a jumble. She'd even imagined her brother sitting beside her, stroking her hair. Something he'd never done that she could recall. And Lucy stood behind him with a baby.

At the sound of a whimper, her eyes popped open. The light stabbed into her head. She moaned in pain and raised her arm to block the rays.

"Close the drapes, Henry. The sunlight bothers her."

Claire peeked from beneath her arm at the woman next to her bed, who swayed back and forth while she cradled a fretful infant. Lucy Forbes? No, that wasn't right. Lucy *Stevens*. She and Henry were married now, and that must be their baby daughter.

A frilly white bonnet concealed the child's face.

Rustling from across the room drew Claire's attention to a man at the window. The light outlined his tall, lean form a moment before he drew the heavy drapes closed.

The room grew blessedly dim.

She couldn't remember when Henry and Lucy had arrived. It hurt too much to think. She struggled to sit up—a dizzying effort—and put her hand to her head. Felt a bandage. "What...what happened?

Her brother slipped extra pillows behind her. "You were shot."

"Shot?" Images flashed through her mind. *Frederick descending into another fit of madness, choking her. Billy with a pistol in his trembling hands.* Her throat closed with fear. Had Billy shot her? No, he'd shot Frederick. Her husband was dead and Billy was...

Oh God, why couldn't she remember?

"Where is he?" Frightened, she reached out to her brother. "Where's Billy?"

"He's safe. You needn't worry." Henry pulled a chair next to the bed, sat down and leaned over to grasp her hand.

The waves of anxiety receded. Billy was safe. Henry had come back.

Wonderingly, she touched her beloved brother's face. He looked much the same as the last time she'd seen him. His dark hair neatly parted and combed to one side. No beard covered his face—or his smile. "Henry, you're really here."

"Where else would I be?" He captured her hand and squeezed. "You should've sent for me sooner." His words reproached her, but his dark eyes shone with warmth and concern.

"I didn't want to cause any inconvenience."

His lips twisted in a wry expression. "You have never been *inconvenient.*"

Oh, that was a lie. She had been *very* inconvenient when her elder brother had been thrust into the role of guardian at age fourteen, and when she'd married a man unable to support her. Henry had been forced to come to her aid. Now, he'd rushed home to rescue her from another debacle.

Memories floated randomly. It was difficult to arrange a clear picture. She recalled her confession. Rueful, she squeezed her brother's hand. "You may change your mind when you find out what I've done."

"You've done nothing wrong, Claire." Lucy shifted the baby to her shoulder. She straightened the infant's gown before patting her bottom soothingly. The baby would be only a few months' old. How surprising that Lucy had been willing to travel. Her ivory skin and golden hair shone with good health. Motherhood obviously agreed with her. "Sheriff Garrity told us the whole story."

Sheriff Garrity. Frank.

Thoughts of him stirred longing and grief, as well with warmth and tenderness, fear and...anger? Her memories jelled. He'd done precisely what she'd begged him not to do. He'd brought Billy before the judge to confess to the crime.

She couldn't remember what happened afterwards. The hole in her memory tripped another surge of panic. She looked at Henry for reassurance. "The judge, what did he rule?"

"I can answer that." Frank seemed to materialize out of thin air. Maybe he'd been in the sitting room. He didn't look nearly as put together as Henry. Dust covered his worn coat and jean trousers. At court, he'd been dressed in a suit. Overall, much cleaner. What had he been doing since? He looked haggard, as if he hadn't gotten much sleep.

She wanted to hold him. She also longed to slap him.

Frank stood behind Henry's shoulder. The two men exchanged a look. Whatever it was the sheriff had to say, Henry already knew.

Her brother patted her hand and then stood. "We'll let you two talk."

Claire's heart fluttered. She didn't want to be alone with the sheriff. Being with him made her want things she ought not think about. "Why do you have to leave?"

Lucy shifted her hold on the baby so she could bend over to kiss Claire's forehead. "Don't worry. We'll be back later. Ginny needs to go down for a nap."

"Genevieve," Claire whispered to herself. It had been in the announcement she'd received in the mail. They'd named the baby after Lucy's mother. "Genevieve Adelaide."

"Big name for a small baby, don't you think?" Her brother teased.

"No. I think it's beautiful." Claire sighed with longing. What she wouldn't give to hold a child in her arms. She would never have a baby of her own. Still, adopting a child, even one half grown, would fill the aching void.

Henry and Lucy left. Frank hovered at her bedside. He turned his hat in his hands. His nervousness made her nervous.

She tried to scoot up on the pillows. Moving took too much effort and made her lightheaded. "What happened? Where's Billy? I need to see him."

"Let's take one thing at a time." Frank set his hat aside and grasped under her arms. She held onto his shoulders as he repositioned her. His hands on her body triggered a starburst of erotic images: tangled limbs, tracing the muscles on his back with her fingers, smooth, bare skin, heated from desire.

She drew a ragged breath. Even a headache couldn't squelch her need for him.

He released her with a slowness that spoke of his reluctance to let go, then took a seat in the vacant chair. Every touch, every intimate kiss branded on her mind, seemed to be reflected in his eyes.

She flushed and lowered her lashes. Utterly absurd, considering how bold she'd been before, to be too embarrassed to look at him. Regardless, she couldn't get past her discomfort. She focused on adjusting the bed sheets, pulled the covers up to her chest, considered drawing them over her head.

He sighed audibly. It was hard to interpret the meaning behind that sigh, especially when she wasn't looking at him. Frustration. Resignation. He could be tired.

"The judge postponed the hearing after all the uproar." Frank spoke as if she knew what he was talking about. She couldn't recall the judge doing anything except pounding his gavel. The pounding continued. In her head.

"What uproar?"

"When that outlaw Jasper Byrne showed up in court and Billy chased after him."

"Billy chased an outlaw?"

Frank shifted forward in his seat. "And you went after Billy. Do you recall being shot?"

Claire pressed her fingers to her forehead and willed the memories to return. She could come up with nothing but a dark, frightening void. "No. The last thing I recall is being in court, my shock when Billy arrived."

"The doctor said that might happen. You'd forget things that occurred right before you got hurt." Frank leaned over and peered into her eyes, as if searching for those things she'd forgotten. "I should've stopped you before that trigger-happy sonofa—" He cut off the curse by sealing his lips in a tight, angry line.

"The outlaw shot me?"

"William Bond."

"The general manager?" Stunned was too mild a word. She had to be missing a great deal more than Frank was relaying because thus far nothing made sense.

"He claims he hit you by mistake when you ran out into the street." Frank's features hardened. "There was a minute when I could've stopped you. I was too focused on Byrne."

Her heart ached for him. He'd tortured himself for not protecting her well enough. "Don't shoulder the blame for an accident. It sounds like you were doing your job."

"I almost lost you," he said harshly. "I won't let it happen again."

Did he truly think he had that kind of control over circumstances?

"You aren't my keeper," she reminded him.

He took her hand, gave it a squeeze. "Rest. Get better. We'll talk about our future later."

What future? She hadn't actually agreed to marry him. Even if she wanted him, he'd lied to her about Billy's return. Granted, he'd apologized, but it appeared he'd turned right around and deceived her again.

"Did you know Billy intended to come to court to confess?"

The guilty look on Frank's face gave her the answer even before he spoke. "He came to see me the night before."

She caught her breath in shock, then snatched her hand away.

Another betrayal. "Why didn't you tell me? Why didn't you let me see him?"

He straightened in the chair, didn't appear a bit remorseful. In fact, his gaze rebuked her. "I knew you'd try to talk him into lying."

Hurt gave way to anger, which made her headache worse. She rubbed her fingers on her temple. "Don't try to wiggle off the hook by using me as an excuse for your abominable behavior. We have nothing further to discuss."

His flat expression closed off whatever he might be feeling. "Yes, we do have something to discuss. Billy."

Fear leapt in her chest. Something had gone wrong. She *knew* there was a reason she hadn't seen him, other than being indisposed. "Henry assured me he was safe."

"He is."

"Where is he?"

"Locked up. So he won't run."

"In jail?" Tears filled her eyes. Her brother had lied to her, as well. Or Henry thought jail was *safe*. Maybe he viewed it as necessary if he thought Billy would flee.

Much as she wanted to, she couldn't leap out of bed and go straight to the judge to make her plea. She'd crawl if she thought she could, but she couldn't. She didn't have the strength, and her head spun. She had no choice but to appeal to the man she most distrusted where Billy was concerned. "Please Frank, do something. Don't let the judge lay charges against him. Don't make him face a trial."

"He won't. The judge dropped the case. He believes the shooting was an accident."

She caught a sharp breath. Had she heard right? "No trial? No charges? He's free?"

Frank's hesitation threw a net over her soaring heart. "Billy isn't agreeable to the arrangement I made with the judge. I told him I'd release him after he promises to abide by it."

Freedom came with strings attached.

"What arrangement?" Her voice came out quavering and weak.

Instead of answering, Frank slipped his fingers beneath her hand to grasp it. He rubbed a circle around the base of her thumb. His comforting gesture increased her dismay because it meant she wasn't going to like his answer. "Claire, the judge won't let you keep Billy."

If he had reached into her chest and ripped out her heart, it couldn't have hurt worse. Billy would be saved, but he was lost to her.

"The judge did agree to let me adopt him. I signed the papers this morning."

Claire's breath left her body. Of all the deals Frank might've made with the judge, this was one she never would've guessed. "But, you don't want children. You said having a family was too risky."

"Things have changed."

"I don't understand."

"The only reason I didn't want a family was because of the career I chose. I'm giving up my badge, going home to the farm and taking Billy with me. It'll be a safer place for him...and for you." He sandwiched her hand between his, the stoicism transformed into urgency, his voice became rough. "Marry me, Claire. Come with us. You can be Billy's mother. We'll be a family."

Despite her confusion and the incessant headache, she could think clearly enough to grasp the reason for his sudden interest in Billy. Astonishment was followed by disappointment, and quick on its heels, anger.

"That's why you adopted him? To coerce me into marrying you?"

The frown he gave her was the same one she'd seen whenever he defended something he'd done that was indefensible. "If you'll stop being mad at me and think about it, you'll see it's the best thing for him. God knows where he might've ended up if I hadn't taken him."

"He might've ended up with my *brother*. Did you even think to ask Henry if he wanted Billy?" Her voice cracked with emotion. "At least Henry and Lucy care about him."

Surprised hurt flashed in Frank's eyes. "I care about him. Wouldn't have taken him if I didn't."

He'd been willing to throw Billy to the wolves before. To save her. He cared for her, if desire could be associated with affection. But he didn't understand love.

"What you care about is getting what you want. You think you know best. You don't give anyone else a chance to offer an opinion. How can I marry someone who doesn't respect me enough to seek my counsel? You'll go on making my decisions and telling me what to do, regardless of what I might think."

She withdrew her hand from his grasp and put her fingers to her head. The throbbing pain was getting worse. Arguing with Frank was less effective than contending with a rock, and she couldn't think clearly enough to figure out how to undo what had been done. "I'm not feeling well. Please leave."

Frank stood up with obvious reluctance. "This isn't what you think."

"You don't know what I think. You didn't bother to ask." The moment she flung the retort, she regretted it. She wasn't usually so spiteful, but her head ached and her heart bled.

He'd stolen her child, and then dangled him before her nose like bait. How could she marry someone so manipulative?

It seemed he might say something more, but then he moved to the door. He hesitated, looking at her as if *he* were the one offended, the one who had been hurt. "I'll be leaving for the farm after I finish investigating Bond. I want you to come with me. I can't make you. Whatever you decide, I want you to know you can come see Billy anytime. You'll always be welcome."

CHAPTER 32

"You're acting like a damn fool." Jasper paced in the adjacent cell and kept on running his mouth. "Be glad they didn't decide to hang you."

Billy turned to the other side of the cot and hunched over. Too bad there wasn't a wall between them. He put his hands over his ears. He didn't want to hear Jasper tell him what an idiot he was and how he ought to be grateful. He'd been stuck in this cell for four days with only his troubled thoughts and an ornery neighbor for company.

Jasper hadn't talked to him the first day. Once he did start talking, he cussed Billy out for chasing after him. Claimed he'd been forced to save a *stupid kid*.

He hadn't forced Jasper to do anything. If anybody was stupid, it was the train robber for showing up in a courtroom. Even a *stupid kid* knew better.

"Shut up!" Billy leapt off the cot. He prowled the cramped cell. Now he knew what a caged wolf felt like.

He also knew he had brought all this on himself. Instead of ending up with a woman who *wanted* to be his mother, he'd gotten stuck with a so-called father who *despised* him. "I don't want to be adopted by the sheriff."

Jasper paced inside the other cell. "Why not? I can think of worse things."

"So can I. But that ain't the point. He doesn't want me."

"He wouldn't take you if he didn't want you." The way Jasper said it sounded like he was explaining something to a two-year-old. Even a baby could see the sheriff was up to something.

"He wants to keep me away from her. He blames me for her getting shot."

The sheriff hadn't said as much. His eyes had done the talking, as he'd knelt in the muddy street with Mrs. Daines clutched to his chest like a limp doll.

"I never meant for her to get hurt. I wanted to protect her." Billy plopped back onto the cot and put his head in his hands. "He *hates* me. I know it. I'll bet he needs somebody to do chores. That's why those other folks took me in. They needed an extra pair of hands."

"You aren't thinking this through, Shorty."

Billy looked up at the hated moniker. "Don't call me that."

Jasper came to a halt in front of bars that separated the two cells. He rubbed his hand against his side where he usually wore his gun and knitted his forehead like he was surprised to find it wasn't there. "All you got to do is agree to go with him. The minute his back is turned, you can run. Go anywhere you please, if that suits you."

How had this outlaw become a legend? He was just a man. Not particularly tall or strong, not even good-looking, especially with that scowl on his face. Plus, he had the character traits of a coyote.

Billy straightened to look Jasper in the eye. "That's just what I'd expect *you* to say."

The outlaw propped his hands on his hips. "What's that supposed to mean?"

"Your word isn't worth spit."

Jasper grasped the bars with a look that said he'd like to get his hands on Billy. "*My* word? You said you wanted to be part of my gang. Then you blew on me. That ain't exactly trustworthy behavior."

Billy glared at his former friend while keeping his distance. "Oh really? Well, what about *you*? You came back here to turn me in for a reward."

"Only if I knew you'd be safe. That's why I took the risk, to make sure of it. I thought they'd send you home. You'd thank me one day. Put a flower on my grave." He walked away, hiking up the waistband of his trousers.

He'd lost weight. He also looked like he hadn't slept much. That made two of them. The deputy had provided a basin of water, but Jasper had overturned it rather than wash up or shave. He acted like it didn't matter. Like he'd given up.

A twinge of guilt made Billy mad. He hadn't asked for any favors. It wasn't *his* fault Jasper had come up here and gotten into trouble.

The outlaw flopped down on the bed in his cell. It didn't have a mattress. He leaned against the wall and propped up one leg. Then he dug a piece of string out of his pocket.

Billy's nerves jangled when Jasper went to winding that string around his finger with this thumb. He'd been doing that for days, winding and unwinding that string. He'd even shaped it into a noose once. Gave Billy the shivers.

Jasper leveled a cold stare at him. "You like it in here?"

"No." He was about to go crazy. Mostly because of Jasper and that string.

"Didn't think so." Jasper unwound the string. "You want the truth? You wouldn't make a good outlaw."

Billy twisted away. He was sick and tired of Jasper's taunts.

"You're too *soft*." Jasper kept on talking like he didn't care that he was being ignored. "And you're a damn sight too *smart* to waste your life and end up in here. But right now, you're being just plain *stupid*."

Furious, Billy whirled around. If he could reach Jasper, he'd punch him. "Don't treat me like I'm a baby."

"Then stop acting like one." Jasper didn't move from his slumped position, yet somehow his sharp look reached right through the bars. "Go with the sheriff. See how things work out. You don't like it, leave and go somewhere else. You have a choice. That's more than you'll have if you stay here."

Billy's shoulders slumped. He didn't want to argue anymore. He didn't understand why Jasper cared about what happened to him. He wished the outlaw hated him instead, because it hurt him to see Jasper sitting there, trapped and waiting to die. It reminded him of a stray dog he'd once seen locked up in a cage. The poor creature had paced and paced until its paws got bloody, and then they'd shot it.

As much as Billy hated to admit it, he owed Jasper his life. He'd gone after the outlaw to capture him. But when that shot rang out, Jasper had shoved him to the ground and fallen on top of him. At first, he'd thought Jasper had done it to save his own skin. It hadn't been until later he realized the outlaw meant to protect him.

Jasper could be annoying as hell. He had also proved himself to be a true friend.

Billy didn't want to lose his friend. He didn't want to lose his mother, either. Mrs. Daines was the only person in the world who loved him. She wanted him to be with her, and he wanted that too. Even more than he wanted to be a locomotive engineer.

He blinked when his eyes burned. Then his nose started to drip. He wiped it with his sleeve. He didn't care if the outlaw saw him cry. "I can't leave Mrs. Daines here on her own. She needs me."

Jasper stared at the string on his finger like he hadn't noticed the tears. "How do you know she'll be on her own? The sheriff said her family was here."

Billy's heart clenched. Did that mean she didn't need him anymore?

The door to the sheriff's office opened. He walked through, followed by two other people.

Billy jumped up, excited, and ran to the front of the cell. "Mr. Stevens! Miss Lucy!"

Miss Lucy tried to hug him through the bars. She turned on the lawman. "Why is he locked up?" she demanded.

The sheriff held Billy's gaze. "He doesn't have to be. All he has to do is promise he'll come home with me, and I'll let him out."

Billy's conscience balked. He couldn't make that promise then not keep his word. Not if he intended to turn his life around and make

Mrs. Daines proud of him. He couldn't run anymore, either. He didn't have anywhere to go. The railroaders wouldn't accept him after they'd heard him confess to shooting his guardian.

Maybe Miss Lucy would take him. Hope swelled in his chest.

The sheriff unlocked the door to his cell. As it swung open, she rushed in and gave him a proper hug, and a kiss on the cheek. She looked so pretty in her bright yellow dress. The brim of her straw hat held up a bird's nest with what looked like a real robin's egg nestled inside.

His heart gave a thump. Even though she was a lot older, he'd been in love with her ever since that day she'd asked him to help her run away to Texas. Then she'd up and married the man she'd tried to escape. Women sometimes did things that didn't make any sense.

Her husband—he wasn't the Chief anymore since he'd left the railroad—stepped inside the cell. He gave it good look over. His nostrils flared like he smelled something bad. The piss bucket—or Jasper. "What's keeping you here, Billy?"

"Stubbornness," the outlaw offered. He hung his arms over the crossbar on the door to his cell. Maybe he thought the sheriff ought to open it. He wasn't going unlock that door even if Jasper stood there all day.

Billy purposely ignored the sheriff. He could act all he wanted like he was a friend. It wouldn't work. "I don't want to live on a farm."

"You might find you like it there." Lucy brushed his hair off his forehead like Mrs. Daines did sometimes. Billy tolerated it from her, but he couldn't think of Miss Lucy as his mother, and her touch disturbed him. It might not work out so good to live with her.

He tried another idea on Mr. Stevens. "I want to work for the railroad. And you promised you'd help me get a job."

Mr. Stevens smoothed his hand over face. He looked different without his beard. "Yes, I did, and you promised you'd get an education and wait until you're eighteen."

"What kind of education can I get on a farm?"

"A good one." Jasper's snide remark made Billy madder.

"You got no rooster in this fight," he flung at his would-be *friend*.

Jasper put his hand to his chest with an innocent expression. "I'm merely supporting Mr. Stevens' astute observation."

Billy frowned. These grown-ups were ganging up on him—even Jasper, who'd started talking fancy for some reason. In desperation, he appealed to Miss Lucy. She was still a better choice than the sheriff. "Why can't I come with you?"

Her sad smile looked the same as the one she'd given him over a year ago, when she'd told him goodbye. "The judge made the decision to place you with Mr. Garrity."

"But *you* could get that changed."

Miss Lucy glanced at her husband with a question in her eyes. He made the tiniest movement with his head, saying no.

His rejection crushed Billy. He thought the Chief liked him. But Mr. Stevens had no use for him either.

"You can leave with me, Shorty," Jasper offered.

The sheriff crossed his arms over his chest like he'd finally had enough. "You aren't going anywhere, Byrne. Not until after your trial. Then I doubt he'd want to follow you to where you'll be headed."

The remark hit Billy hard. He tried without success to block out the image of his friend's body dangling from the end of a rope. Jasper had been hanged before. He would remember what it felt like, and he'd be scared, even if he didn't show it. To be strung up once was bad enough, but twice was a torment nobody deserved.

He looked at Jasper, wanted to say something to make him feel better, but the outlaw had his eye on Miss Lucy. That look he was giving her sent Billy's hackles up.

"Lucy Adelaide, did you come here to give me a kiss?" Jasper's raspy voice made the question sound worse than it was.

Billy gripped the bars, wishing he could pull them open and go teach the outlaw some manners.

Mr. Stevens got there first. "Touch her, and I'll break your fingers."

Miss Lucy's cheeks got pink, but she stood up real straight and faced down the outlaw. "At the moment, I'm here to see Billy. Not you."

Jasper leaned his forehead on the bars and put on a hangdog

expression "And here I thought you'd come to tell me you remembered your promise."

"What promise is that?" Mr. Stevens said in a stony voice.

The outlaw dropped the mopey face. He fixed a cold stare on the chief. "You ought to recall it, seeing as she gave it to me so I'd set you free. She agreed to testify to my good character."

Billy couldn't imagine what Jasper was talking about, unless he was just being a smart aleck and trying to cause trouble.

"I remember," Miss Lucy replied, softly. "And I intend to keep my promise."

Mr. Stevens put his arm around his wife's waist. He looked at Jasper like he wanted to wad him up and throw him away. "She owes you nothing."

"No, he's right. I do owe him. Although I doubt anything I say will help you, Mr. Byrne." Miss Lucy seemed genuinely sad about that.

Jasper lifted a shoulder in a shrug like he didn't care. "Having a pretty lady testify on my behalf can't hurt."

Billy remembered now what they were talking about. Miss Lucy had tangled with outlaws that time when she ran away from Mr. Stevens. Nobody had said anything about it being Jasper. That was a surprise.

Miss Lucy would keep whatever promise she made, Billy didn't doubt that. But would it be enough to save Jasper from the gallows? If he also testified to Jasper's *good character*, the judge might go easier.

"Jasper saved me from being shot," Billy told her.

"That's what I heard. I didn't realize Mr. Bond was shooting at you."

"He meant to hit me." Jasper sounded pretty sure about it. Earlier, he'd said he didn't know who was shooting or why.

"So Bond says." The sheriff didn't sound like he believed it.

Mr. Stevens got a thoughtful look. "How did Bond know who you were?" he asked Jasper. "That picture on the *Wanted* poster looks nothing like you."

The sheriff got a funny expression on his face, like he'd suddenly thought of something surprising. "Have you met William Bond before?"

Jasper didn't answer right away. But when he did, it was with a sly, half-smile, as if he'd hoped someone would ask that question. "We have, a few times. I didn't know his real name until recently. He went by Mr. Smith when he told me which trains carried the payroll."

CHAPTER 33

Frank had intended all along to take Billy to the hotel to see Claire. Now that she was feeling better, he wouldn't keep the boy away.

"How is she? Will she be all right? Is she mad at me?" Billy fired questions as fast as a six-shooter. He'd asked about Claire morning, noon and night, seeming more worried about her than he was about what would happen to him.

"She felt well enough to talk last time I saw her. The doctor says she's healing. She's not mad at you. She asked to see you." Frank didn't add that she'd also told him to haul his sorry hide out of her room the last time he saw her.

He understood her anger at not being consulted. But he'd arranged things so she could have what she wanted most. Once she saw the boy, she would realize that.

As he walked through the lobby, Gertrude Bond sent him a scathing look. She'd already chewed on his ear and swore she would have his badge. The way she said it implied she'd take his balls as well. Thus far, she hadn't been able to make good on either threat.

"As soon as my husband is freed, we'll see to it that you're brought up on charges of unlawful imprisonment," she called out.

Frank smiled grimly. He had the information he needed to see to it that her husband remained in jail for a very long time. But he wouldn't play his hand just yet. Let the Bonds sweat a while longer.

Wisely, Mrs. Bond hadn't made a scene about Claire remaining in her old room. In fact, the haughty woman had told everyone she was nursing *the poor lamb* back to health and harbored no ill will against her. Frank knew better. Gertrude Bond was a vicious, vindictive bitch, and he didn't trust her. He'd seen to it that someone remained with Claire at all times and had hired the former cook to prepare all of Claire's meals. Gertrude Bond seemed the type who might favor poisoning.

Billy had ants in his pants. He raced up the stairs around Henry and Lucy, who had arrived just before them.

Mrs. Kelly let them inside the suite at the same time.

Once inside, Billy hovered at the bedroom door. "Can I go in, ma'am?"

Frank removed his hat, then Billy's, when the boy didn't take the cue. "You forget something?"

Billy spit on his hand and slicked down his hair. "No sir."

He'd remained polite, but there was an edge of resentment to his voice that hadn't been there before. Frank couldn't hold it against him. The boy hadn't been given a say in the matter.

His fierce devotion to Claire and visa-versa could make the situation worse or fix everything. Frank bet on the latter.

"I'll see if the missus is feeling up to company," Mrs. Kelly talked while she hung their hats on a hall tree near the door. "I coaxed her to take a little soup. She says she feels stronger, and insisted on holding the baby."

The cook glanced with concern at Lucy. "I hope you don't mind."

"Not at all." Lucy turned and her husband removed her cloak. "I'm glad she's feeling better."

It had been Frank's idea for them to leave the baby behind while they went to the jail to visit Billy. It was a safe bet Claire loved being an aunt. Frank wasn't so blind he couldn't see that she longed for children of her own. He'd wanted children, too, but had suppressed that soft part of him for so long he'd almost forgotten.

He edged past the cook, who kept eyeing him as if she might slam that door in his face for a second time. "I'll take Billy in to see her. We won't stay long."

"See that you don't," Mrs. Kelly warned, and wagged her forefinger. "I don't want her tired out again."

"We'll make sure she stays quiet," Lucy promised.

That seemed to satisfy the stout little cook. "I'll go downstairs and fetch some tea."

Frank waited while Lucy went in, followed by Henry.

Billy hung back.

What was wrong with him? He'd about torn down the door a minute ago. He might still be uncertain of his welcome. Or did he feel guilty? The same feeling pinched Frank's heart. He hadn't been kind or understanding to the boy after Claire had been shot. His disapproval might've caused Billy to wonder whether Claire was angry, too. He could show a little more sensitivity to Billy's feelings.

Frank opened the door to the bedroom wider and motioned with his arm. "Come on. She's eager to see you."

Claire might not be so eager to see him.

To his relief, she looked much improved. She was sitting up in bed, her color had returned. Someone had helped her wash and plait her hair into a thick braid that hung down over her quilted wrapper. She cradled her niece in her arms, and cooed at the baby.

Frank's breathing hitched. For as long as he had known her, she'd had this effect on him. Desire, yes, but more than that. Need. Along with something that grabbed him by the heart and left him aching and breathless.

He'd been afraid to name this feeling aloud, still couldn't find the right words. But if he didn't say them soon, she might never know how much he loved her.

Instead of running to Claire, Billy hesitated. He eyed the baby as if he expected it might have teeth and claws.

Frank nudged his shoulder. "Go on. The baby won't bite."

"Ain't scared of a baby," Billy muttered. "Just don't like 'em much."

At Billy's voice, Claire looked up. "Billy!"

Her joyful smile lit the room and tugged at Frank's heart, even though it wasn't directed at him. While she cradled the baby in one arm, she reached for Billy. "Come here."

He balked.

Claire's brow knit with confusion, then her eyes filled with tears. "Won't you come give me hug? I've missed you so much."

Dang it, the boy's reluctance had made her cry.

Frank put a hand on Billy's back and propelled him forward. At the nudge, the boy ran to the bed and hugged her.

Claire looked over the boy's shoulder.

Frank's gut clenched at what he saw reflected. Hurt. Resentment. How could she believe he would take Billy away from her, knowing full well how much she loved that boy?

The ache in his chest grew sharp.

Couldn't she see? He'd made a way for all of them to be together, if she would just say *yes*. He'd done everything he knew to do. Well, except tell her he loved her. If he offered his heart and she rejected it, he had nothing else to give.

When the baby whimpered, Billy drew back and eyed the child with a mixture of suspicion and curiosity. He might wonder if the baby would come between him and Claire.

Frank had entertained the same childish thoughts about Billy. He'd gotten clarity over the past week. Love could be a larger tent than he'd previously thought. Room could be made for more without taking shelter away from anyone else.

"Here, I'll take her," Lucy went to the bed and reached for the baby.

Claire hesitated, but then, perhaps noticing Billy's unease, handed the child to its mother. She turned her sole focus on Billy. With a smile, she patted the bed sheets. "Sit here beside me."

That was all the invitation the boy needed. He settled right in. She hugged him again and kissed his dirty hair. He seemed content to put up with her tender mauling for another moment. Then he straightened and adjusted his coat, signaling he'd had enough kissing and hugging—even if he hadn't.

Frank couldn't see the boy's face, but he could see Claire's. She glowed.

By heavens, he had to tell her. Now.

With a few strides, he crossed the room. He looked down at her. She didn't say anything, just returned his gaze, questioning. Or maybe it was yearning. He hoped so.

He glanced over at Lucy, who had the baby on her shoulder, and his throat got tight. The words he'd been searching for finally came to him, but he could barely get them out.

"We could be a family, Claire. I'd give you children, as many as you want. I'd give you anything. Everything." He stood, gazing down at her, expecting that soft look she got in her eyes when he said something that pleased her. If he was lucky, maybe a smile.

Her stricken expression threw him into confusion. She looked as if he'd struck her.

The room went dead silent. Everyone stared at him like he'd lost his mind, and maybe he had. He'd made a terrible mistake in being so familiar with her in front of her kin. Not only that, he'd misjudged the situation, misread her emotions. Claire might want a family, but she wasn't about to start one with him, and it appeared everyone in the room knew it.

Heat crawled up his neck into his face. He backed away from the bed.

Why had it taken him so long to see the best thing would've been to leave her alone? He'd caused her enough trouble and way too much pain because he had put his needs first and hadn't been willing to accept that she might not feel the same.

There was one thing he could do for her that wouldn't require her to talk to him or even see him again. Once he'd squeezed Bond's secrets out of him and made sure the bastard couldn't get near Claire, he would leave town.

And Billy? For now, there was no reason the boy couldn't remain with Claire for a few more days. The judge would understand. But afterwards...

The knot forming in Frank's chest clenched painfully. He didn't want to take her child away. He had no choice. Claire's legal rights had been severed—because of him. He'd struck a devil's agreement without considering the alternatives. He had done this to her.

"If you'll excuse me, I have some business to attend to." Feeling like the world's biggest fool, he turned on his heel and made a quick exit.

CHAPTER 34

*T*he remainder of the day, Claire rested while Henry and Frank pursued justice. At least, that's what she'd been told they were doing. She would've gone to find out for herself what they were up to, but she wasn't allowed out of bed.

The doctor had insisted she remain quiet for another week, more if the headaches persisted. She hadn't told him the pain in her head wasn't half as bad as the ache in her heart.

She touched the tender spot where the bullet had grazed her. Mrs. Kelly had brushed out her hair, cleaned and braided it, and assisted her with washing up. Then her sister-in-law had taken over her care, as if she were a helpless child. Having friends and family around made her feel safe, but also like a failure. They'd swept in to rescue her because she'd managed to get herself into a deep trouble. Worse, she'd lost Billy.

"I'd give you children. I'd give you anything you want."

Her eyes stung. She couldn't marry Frank just so she could become Billy's mother, no matter how tempting. He had lied to her, manipulated her, and Billy.

He'd also been willing to sacrifice his job and to move back to the farm. For her. Everything he'd done had been for her. How could she *not* forgive him when he'd shown her so clearly how much he loved her?

Loved her? Or loved the image he had in his mind of the perfect wife? The kind she could never be.

His halting declaration had been shocking. But oh, it made so much sense. Here was a good man who once had a loving wife with a child on the way. A beautiful life, brutally ripped away. Of course, that's what he wanted again. Somehow, he'd gotten past his fears and rediscovered his dreams, but he hadn't stopped arranging things long enough to find out if she could give him back what he wanted.

A knock came at the door.

"Come in." Claire pushed herself up in bed and straightened her wrapper.

Lucy peeked inside. "Are you awake? Billy would like to see you."

"Certainly."

Billy beamed with pride as he entered, holding the baby on his shoulder. "Look here, ma'am. I know how to carry her, now. She likes me."

Claire exchanged a smile with Lucy. Billy had fallen head over heels for little Ginny.

"She does like you, and she knows you like her." Lucy reached out. "Here, let me feed her and change her. Then, if you'd like, I'll return and you can rock her to sleep."

Billy handed over the baby without hesitation. "She's nicer to hold when she ain't fussy and don't smell bad."

As Lucy left the room, she glanced at Claire with a mischievous gleam in her eyes. "He'd be a good big brother, don't you think?"

Emotions closed Claire's throat. For a moment, she couldn't speak, so she nodded. She longed to give Billy sisters and brothers, to have a family and be a mother. Frank had offered her all that, and more. But what could she give him? He wouldn't be content with raising an orphan. He wanted children of his own and she couldn't produce them.

Billy plopped down beside her on the bed. Lucy had seen to it that he'd bathed and put on clean clothes. His wheat-blond hair needed trimming. Her fingers itched to brush the errant strands off his forehead, but she had pressed her luck earlier with all those hugs and kisses. Instead, she rested her hand on his arm.

"You'd like that, wouldn't you? Being Ginny's brother."

"Is she staying here?"

"That would be nice, but no, not permanently."

"Then, I can't be her brother."

Claire pointed out the obvious option Billy had somehow missed. "You could be her brother if you went to live with Henry and Lucy."

"I want to stay here with you."

His staunch declaration sent a thrill through her. In the time since he'd come from jail to see her, he hadn't said he wanted to remain with her, just that he didn't want to go with the sheriff.

"That makes me very happy." She swallowed a lump in her throat. "I wish you could."

A look of uncertainty crossed his face. "You said you wanted to adopt me."

"I do. More than anything."

"Then how come you're letting the sheriff take me away?" The hurt and fearfulness that came into his expression broke her heart. He'd been abandoned and rejected by everyone in his life. He needed to know he was wanted.

She gripped Billy's hand. "Oh sweetheart, believe me, if I could keep you with me, I would. But I'm not your legal guardian." Her voice cracked as emotion got the best of her. "Mr. Garrity is. And he takes the responsibility very seriously. He's a fine, upstanding man. He'll be a good...a good father."

"Don't need a father." Billy's chin went up at a belligerent angle. "We could leave, you and me. I could get a job and take care of you."

His desperate boast wrung her heart. Billy needed the strong, steady guidance of a caring father more than he knew. God forbid he'd be burdened with the heavy responsibilities her brother had been forced to shoulder at a young age.

"No," she said firmly. "I don't want you to take care of me. I want you to have a good home where you can have a chance to grow up like other children."

Billy looked down at where she held his arm. "If you *really* wanted me, you could marry the sheriff. Come live with us."

"I love you, Billy, I do..." Her chest ached and her throat burned. She couldn't cry. That would distress and confuse him. She swallowed the urge, but gave in to the need to touch him and stroked his hair.

It would be so easy to give in and marry Frank, for Billy's sake. But in the end, she wouldn't be doing them any favors. Billy had seen what hopelessness could do to a marriage. He needed a better example.

Even if she could forgive Frank—and she suspected she already had, because she didn't seem to be able to stay angry with him—her disappointment at not being able to give him what he wanted and deserved would eat away at her soul. Until she despised herself and resented him.

"Sometimes, what we want isn't the best thing for someone else. We have to think of them and not just ourselves. If I marry the sheriff, I could be with you, that's true, but it wouldn't be the best thing for him."

Billy looked crestfallen. "Why not? He likes you. Don't you like him?"

Like him? She took a deep breath. Heaven help her, she *loved* him, despite his insufferable wrangling. He only did it because he was afraid. She understood his fears, might even be able to help ease them, but she couldn't give him children.

"It's not as simple as that. Marrying the sheriff would be a mistake. You'll have to take my word for it. He says I can come and visit you, and I will. I promise. Now you promise me something. Promise to stay with Mr. Garrity and not run away."

The struggle played out on Billy's face. Then he wrapped his arms around her and buried his face in her shoulder. She hugged him and her heart trembled at their combined grief. How could he believe she loved and wanted him if she didn't do everything in her power to keep them together? She couldn't let him go. She just couldn't. There had to be a way.

With tears in her eyes, she held him in a tight hug. "Don't lose hope, dearest. There may be something I can work out so we can be together."

Lucy's remark came back to her, about Billy being Ginny's big brother. Maybe that had been her sister-in-law's way of saying she was interested in adopting Billy. Yes, he would be better off with them than with one parent. And what if they agreed to bring her along?

That would mean she'd have to give up her life, let go of her fight to keep the business she'd struggled to build. Her home.

What life? Even if she won the fight to keep the hotel, it was a means to make a living, not the fulfillment of her dreams. She wanted to be Billy's mother. Being his aunt would be nearly as good. And there was no reason to stay in Parsons—except to see Frank.

Her heart fought the idea. Common sense told her it would be for the best. They could both let go easier if she left. Now that he'd set aside his fears about remarrying, he could find a woman who could give him children and continue to do what *he* wanted to do.

But to go with Henry and Lucy? She'd be a burden. Again.

Not if she assisted with the children. Henry traveled a great deal. He always took Lucy along, and she attended to her writing. They might bring a baby, but as the family grew, they'd need help.

The daydreams lifted Claire's spirits. She and Billy could be together. The arrangement might not be ideal, but it was better than the alternative.

First, though, she had to see if Henry and Lucy would take him. Far more difficult, she had to convince Frank.

THE OLD BUILDING where the railroad had stored construction supplies was little more than a windowless stone oven. As far as Frank was concerned, it was the perfect spot for the railroad's general manager to swelter while he dwelled on his crimes. Bond had baked for a couple days. Now it was time to see if the goose was sufficiently cooked.

Frank undid the padlock on the metal door. He had to duck to get inside the six-by-ten structure. The stench hit him first. A musty smell mingled with the odor of sweat and human waste.

Bond sat in a corner with his arms looped over his drawn-up knees. Didn't look so high and mighty anymore. He lifted his head and squinted at Frank. "You can't hold me indefinitely."

The stint in a smelly hole apparently hadn't taken all the wind out of his sails. It was time to give it to him straight.

"I could lock this door and walk away," Frank said calmly. "Leave you without food or water. By the time some fancy lawyer found the judge and convinced him to let you out, you wouldn't be alive."

"You wouldn't dare." Bond's voice quavered. Slight but noticeable.

"Don't tempt me." Frank left the door cracked to let in light and air. He planted himself in front of it, undid the strap that held his Colt in its holster. Let Bond know he'd shoot him without so much as a blink, if he made the mistake of trying to escape.

Frank hoped he would. Misery and fury had combined into a volatile mixture. He'd combust at the slightest provocation. "You don't cooperate, you don't live. It's that simple. I hunted weasels like you for years. I'm good at covering my tracks. I can make it look like you tried to fight and run."

Bond slowly came to his feet. He brushed the dirt off his fancy suit and smoothed his oily hair. "Why kill me when we could make a deal that would benefit both of us?"

The general manager's blatant bribe tipped the barrel of explosives inside Frank's chest. His fingers closed around the handle of his revolver.

Even in the dim light, he saw Bond blanch. "For Christ's sake, Garrity. You wouldn't murder a man in cold blood." The tremble in his voice made it clear he feared Frank would.

"You have no idea what I'm capable of." The raging beast inside knew. Claire must have sensed his true nature—vengeful, unforgiving

—and that's what kept her from loving him. But she couldn't stop him from seeing to her protection.

"What do you want?"

That should've been the first thing Bond said.

"Explain why you went after Claire. Confess you tried to kill her."

"I did neither."

In two strides, Frank reached Bond. He grabbed him by the throat and propelled him back against the moldy wall. Drew the revolver. He pressed the barrel to Bond's temple, lightly.

The little man's eyes bulged. His mouth gaped like a fish out of water. He smelled of sweat and rising fear.

"You lying little toad," Frank said evenly.

"I-I'm not lying. I wasn't trying to kill her. I shot at that outlaw."

"How did you know he was an outlaw?"

"I recognized him."

"He looks nothing like the poster. That's the only known photograph of him."

If possible, Bond's eyes grew wider.

Frank's hold on the revolver didn't waver. He longed to blow the man's brains all over the wall. But he needed information first. Then he'd decide whether to let the vermin live. There had to be a connection between Caldwell's thievery, Bond's sabotage, and his attack on Claire.

"Byrne signed a statement swearing you gave him information about when the payroll would be in transit. He said you hired him to steal it."

Bond blinked. "That's a bald-faced lie."

"He figured you'd say that. He told me a man came down to the Territory last year and hired him to make trouble for the railroad. Byrne did some investigating and found out his contact was none other than the new general manager. He wanted you to know he was onto you, so he asked you to meet him at the hotel, the Belmont House. A man saw you two together in the upstairs hall and spoke to you. Based on Byrne's description, that man was Mr. Daines."

Frank tightened his chokehold. He kept the gun pointed at Bond's head. "I found two more men who said they'd seen you and Byrne that day, together. They've signed sworn statements."

That was the last card Frank had. But he had won countless games by bluffing.

"And I found something else. Daines wrote a letter about you."

Shocked disbelief filled Bond's eyes, and then tears. He swallowed, hard, the convulsive movement of his throat pressing against the inside of Frank's hand.

"I turned everything over to the U.S. Marshal, along with Byrne's statement," Frank continued. "Byrne agreed to cooperate and give us whatever we need on you."

"I-I'll cooperate," Bond rasped. "In exchange for leniency."

Frank loosened his hold, slightly.

Bond swallowed again. "There's a man in New York, a wealthy financier. He likes to collect railroads. He offered me a great deal of money and a high position if I would make the Katy easy pickings."

A banker. Should've known.

"Keep talking." Frank shifted the barrel of the gun to beneath Bond's chin.

The general manager shuddered. "I feared Mr. Daines might discover Byrne's identity, and I wanted him gone before that happened. That's one reason I bought the hotel. He was supposed to sign it over, but he died before I got the deed. Our lawyer doctored one up. When Mrs. Daines left town, I sent my wife to go through their papers to look for the actual signed documents. I can't believe she missed—"

"You've explained why you'd want Daines gone. After he was dead, why did you care whether or not Claire stayed around if you didn't think she was a threat."

"My wife hates her."

"Why?"

"Gertrude is George Caldwell's aunt. She held Henry Stevens responsible for what happened to her nephew. She thought it would be a fitting revenge to hurt his sister."

"The other reason you bought the hotel." Frank slowly lowered the gun and released his hold on Bond's neck. "You went after her on your wife's say-so?"

The little man coughed, heaved a sigh. "Gertrude can be very persuasive."

Frank holstered the Colt. *Pathetic.* "What does she do? Tie you up and spank you?"

Bond jerked his head up. The startled look on his face was followed by a dark flush. Apparently, he was one of those fellows who liked that sort of thing.

Frank didn't give a damn what those two did in private, but he'd see them both jailed for their scheming. "How did you talk Daines into selling?"

"Mrs. Bond went with me when I met with him. She told him Claire had complained to folks about him and made statements that would lead one to believe she wanted to be free of him. He said she'd changed since coming to Parsons. Blamed her brother and the hotel."

"Bitch," Frank snarled. He grabbed Bond by the lapels and shook him. "What did you two hope? That her paranoid husband would attack her? Because that's what he did."

Bond threw his hands up in the air. "I didn't know what he'd do."

"He took a gun to his room."

"Perhaps to keep it away from his wife?"

"Or use it on her."

Ironic, sad even, that a child had used the weapon against him.

Frank pushed Bond away. His back struck the wall. He didn't make another move. He reminded Frank of a mouse hoping a cat wouldn't notice it was there. "You'll sign a statement and swear to everything you told me. Names, dates, details, everything."

Bond gave a hurried nod. "Will you release me now?"

Frank went to the door. Not on his life would he let the man step out of this cell before he had documents signed and witnessed. He answered a moment before he pulled the heavy door closed. "I won't forget to give you food and water."

CHAPTER 35

Frank secured a table in a far corner of the smoky saloon. He asked for a bottle and removed the cork. The scent of the liquor made his gut churn in anticipation. *Whiskey.* Burning down his throat, filling the emptiness, numbing the pain. He'd become so stupefied he wouldn't have to think—or feel.

He'd gone back to check on Claire, to give her some good news for a change. Bond would not be a problem any longer. Lucy, who'd been feeding the baby, had directed him to the bedroom. When he'd come close to the door, which was opened a crack, he'd caught snatches of a conversation between Claire and Billy. He hadn't stayed around to eavesdrop. He'd heard enough to know his chances of ever convincing her to wed him were nil.

"Marrying the sheriff would be a mistake."

She might as well have picked up a gun and put a bullet through his heart.

He'd just stood there for an awful moment, bleeding. He'd been tempted to storm into the bedroom and demand an explanation.

What difference did it make? He had already asked for her hand numerous times. How many rejections did it take before he got it through his thick skull that she didn't want to be his wife? Sexual desire didn't constitute love. For Claire, it wasn't enough to compel her to tie herself to him. He wouldn't continue to press her. Loving her as he did, he had to respect her wishes and let her go.

He stared at the bottle. Tapped the glass on the table. Before he lost the ability to reason, he had to resolve a question. What to do about Billy? The boy had every right to resent being denied the one person who'd shown him unconditional love. The last thing he needed was to be taken away from Claire. But that's what the judge had ruled.

Frank turned the glass upside down with a hard thunk. He corked the bottle. He'd just have to put up with the pain. He had signed the papers that made him Billy's father. The boy deserved better than a drunk.

Across the table, a chair scraped the floor as someone pulled it out.

Frank raised his eyes with an unfriendly scowl.

Henry Stevens didn't flinch. He apparently didn't value his skin because he took a seat without an invitation. "What are you doing here, Frank?"

"What does it look like? I'd offer you a drink, but I'm not sharing."

"I thought you had to interrogate Bond."

"I did. He confessed."

Surprise flashed across Henry's face. He leaned forward, as if to whisper. It wasn't necessary. There was so much noise in the saloon from the railroaders crowding in after work, no one could hear his own thoughts, much less what someone else said. "Confessed to what?"

Frank ticked off the list on his fingers. "Bankrupting the railroad, taking the hotel, ruining Claire. Said his wife made him do it."

"His *wife?*"

"Didn't ask if she used a whip."

Henry stared at him like he'd lost his mind.

With a weary sigh, Frank explained. He started with Jasper

Byrne's statement and ended with Gertrude Bond's nasty machinations, which ultimately resulted in Daines taking a gun into his room where Billy had found it and used it to protect Claire.

Henry sank back in his chair. "Good God," he breathed. "I knew Frederick had problems, but..." His stunned expression tightened into anger. He banged his hand on the table. "Dammit, I should never have left Claire alone with him."

Frank shook his head. He'd flayed himself for not acting sooner, but knowing Claire as he did, he'd realized it wouldn't have made any difference. "They were married. She considered her husband her responsibility. She wouldn't have let you do anything."

"Well, I can do something now. I'll make sure the judge knows about that bogus deed. The hotel will revert to Claire. I'll find out more about who was supporting Bond. I suspect we'll find more than one hand in the till. Caldwell's relatives, Parsons' friends, more than a few senators..."

Throw Henry a wrench and he'd build a railroad. Give him a problem, he'd come up with a solution. Frank wished his mind worked half as fast. It might work faster if he stopped soaking it in whiskey.

He examined the full bottle. Today, he had to walk away from liquor and never look back. Do his best to be an example and a good father. Claire wouldn't have to worry about that. She could come up to the farm for visits. He'd bring Billy to town. Seeing her and not having her would be painful, but not half as painful as not seeing her at all.

"She'll be relieved to have the Belmont House back," he mused.

The former railroad chief folded his arms across his chest. "Claire doesn't want to keep the hotel. She asked if she could come live with me and Lucy."

Frank sat back, stunned. He hadn't imagined she'd be so desperate to get away from him she would up and leave. "Why would she do that? She wouldn't abandon Billy."

Her brother's silence gave him the answer. The final bullet. She'd been willing to hang to save Billy. It made sense she'd do whatever she thought necessary to keep him, even if it meant leaving everything else behind.

"She wants me to let Billy go with you," Frank stated.

Henry nodded. "But you're his guardian. We'd need your permission."

Frank's natural fighting instinct reared up. If Claire wanted the boy, she could come get him. "I told the judge I'd take him to the farm. Raise him."

Henry rubbed his chin in a thoughtful manner. "You think the judge would stand in the way of us gaining custody?"

They would go toe-to-toe over this. Claire had recruited her brother's support. Henry would meet the challenge, head-on. Just as he met every challenge.

Frank had never run from a fight. But what was the point of fighting Henry? He'd be fighting Claire.

With a last longing look, he set aside the bottle and rested his arms on the table. He had done some selfish things in his time, but taking Billy topped the list. He'd talked himself into it—something he was good at doing—with the same excuse he'd used when he had bedded Claire. He was doing it for her. What a load of malarkey. He'd done what he did because he wanted her more than he had ever wanted anything. Now, it was time to do something for her benefit, and Billy's.

Henry would see to it that the boy stayed out of trouble. Billy would have a good life. Better than what Frank could give him, alone. Would Claire truly be happy with this arrangement? He couldn't read her mind, so he didn't know. But he would give her what she wanted, just as he'd promised.

Frank heaved a resigned sigh. "The judge won't stand in the way. He wants Billy out of Parsons. With someone who can keep him under control. If Claire tags along, he won't care."

Henry studied him for a long moment. Long enough to make him wonder whether Claire's brother would sit there and not say anything. That would be just fine. Conversation was overrated.

"I didn't think you'd give up that easily," Henry said, finally.

Frank lifted a shoulder in a shrug. He didn't care what Henry thought. He was more concerned with what was best for Claire and Billy than he was about being hardheaded. He wouldn't hold onto something that had never been his to begin with. "If I take him, he'll run away again. Then I'll have to go after him."

Henry looked disappointed by his answer. "You don't want to be bothered with raising a child. Is that it?"

Frank would've ignored the provoking question, but it triggered a thought he hadn't considered. Maybe this was why Claire refused to marry him, because she didn't think he wanted children. "Is that what Claire said?"

"No. Funny thing is, she believes you're sincere about wanting a family."

Frank snorted. "She didn't think I was sincere when I told her I'd become Billy's guardian."

"Why did you? What's your interest in Billy?"

Frank fidgeted with the empty glass. He wasn't sure how to answer because the truth didn't show him in a particularly benevolent light. Perhaps Claire still held this against him. If so, he couldn't whitewash it enough to change her mind. "I thought if I could take them to the farm and we could become a family, things would work out better. For all of us."

"You took Billy, hoping to gain Claire in the bargain?"

Frank set the glass down. "That pretty well sums it up."

Henry's lips twitched. He was amused?

Frank wasn't. He'd been stupid to think he could trap Claire. "Did I say something funny?"

"No. It sounds like something I would do."

Being compared to the crafty railroad chief wasn't exactly a compliment.

"I want what's best for Claire. And for Billy."

"And you think being married to you is what's best for her?" Henry darted a brief glance at the bottle Frank had set aside.

Claire's brother had some gumption suggesting he wasn't good enough, even if that thought had crossed his mind more than a few times.

"What are you implying?"

"Nothing, in particular." Henry leaned back. He crossed his leg over his knee and rested his hands in his lap, as if they were having a friendly conversation. "I asked you a question. Do you think she'd be better off married to you, or living with us as a widowed aunt for the rest of her life?"

"What I think doesn't matter. She's not interested in marrying me."

"You've asked her?"

Frank folded his arms over his chest, feeling defensive, which was ridiculous. He didn't have to defend his intentions. "I have. Several times."

Henry bobbed his head. "That's what I thought. I knew you were sweet on my sister. I've known it for some time. Wasn't sure how she felt about it, but I knew she wouldn't encourage you while she was married."

Frank broke out in a sweat. It was late afternoon. More men had arrived and the room had gotten hotter. That was the problem. He wasn't burning up with embarrassment because Claire's brother had guessed his secret infatuation.

"She didn't even know I existed until after her husband died and I had to investigate," Frank said in a droll tone.

Henry tapped his fingers on his knees, silent for a change. He ought to say something, for Pete's sake. An assurance that no one else had noticed the sheriff's attraction to his *married* sister would be a good place to start.

Frank rubbed his hand over his mouth to wipe away beads of perspiration caught in week-old bristle. *Cripes.* He hadn't considered she might've been aware of his interest all along. Probably feared others were, too. "You think she's concerned about what people will say if we got married?"

"If Claire cared about what people thought of her, she wouldn't have confessed to killing her husband."

Frank knew this. He was grasping at straws. That sympathetic look her brother gave him wasn't necessary. He felt foolish enough. Claire wouldn't marry him because she didn't love him. She'd been trapped in one loveless marriage and was wise enough not to get caught in another.

"She'd be better off with someone she loves," Frank stated, belatedly answering Henry's earlier question.

"That's what I think, too." Henry stood abruptly. "Got to get back to the hotel. See you tomorrow."

"Yeah...tomorrow," Frank muttered. He didn't care if he ever saw the blasted fellow again. Just reminded him of Claire, and he didn't need a reminder.

He stared at the full bottle. He could curl up inside and ferment, but it wouldn't do any good. It wouldn't erase this wretched longing. He wouldn't get rid of it until his heart didn't beat any longer. Maybe that day would come sooner versus later if he remained a lawman.

He'd told the judge and Gideon he planned to resign, but no one else knew yet. Without Billy to consider, he had no reason to return to the farm. He'd sell the place. Keep his badge. Do what he knew best. What he'd expected all along he would die doing. There were worse ways to go. Growing old alone being one of them.

The farm would need to be fixed up before he'd get a fair price. He could wrap things up here then go put the house in order. If his parents watched from above, his mother wouldn't be happy, but his father would understand.

He scooted the chair back, left the bottle on the table, and walked outside. The air smelled moist and fresh, like spring. The roses his mother had planted wouldn't bloom for another few months, if the plants had lived.

He wanted to see if they were still there. If the trailing vines had survived, it would be a sign that Claire would be all right. He could let go with some degree of peace. He'd also be able to let go of the farm. Wouldn't be marrying again, so he didn't have anyone to leave it to, and made no sense to let the house fall into ruin and the roses go untended. Some farmer's wife could care for them. Maybe the blood-red blooms and rich fragrance would become a sweet memory for her son.

Frank hated goodbyes, but it was time to say his farewells.

CHAPTER 36

*C*laire remained in bed for two more weeks. Really, the bullet had only grazed her. The worst was how dizzy she felt, the frequent headaches and sensitivity to light. She'd started feeling better after a week, but Henry and Lucy had refused to let her leave her room. *Doctor's orders*, they'd said.

Boredom would have driven her crazy without a baby niece to dote on. Each day, she fell more in love with Ginny, although it was hard to hold a baby without longing for a child of her own. That would never be, so she'd determined not to dwell on what she couldn't change.

She had tried, with less success, not to dwell on Frank's glaring absence. Initially, she'd thought it best if she didn't see him again. Now, she had serious doubts. He had agreed, without a fight, to let Henry and Lucy have Billy. His decision should've made her deliriously happy, not miserable.

According to Henry, Frank had gone north to his family home. He'd decided to sell the farm, and had taken Billy along to help him with some repairs.

What was he *thinking*? He *loved* that farm. She could tell because of the yearning on his face whenever he reminisced about it. The aggravating man hadn't even given her the chance to talk him out of making a huge mistake. He hadn't even come by before he left. He'd just sent a message that he would return with Billy when she was free to travel.

As of today, she was free. Frank would return with Billy on the noon train. She couldn't wait to see them.

She sat at her dressing table and carefully worked her hair over the spot the doctor had shaved. It might've made more sense to shorten the length and let it fall in loose curls, the current fashion. Vanity wouldn't let her. Frank admired her hair greatly. He'd combed his fingers through it with reverence as he'd kissed her bare skin. She trembled at the seductive memory.

How foolish to yearn for what couldn't be, even more foolish to hope. Frank would not want her once she told him she couldn't give him the family he desired. She should've told him of her barren condition before. Her rejection had wounded him. After she corrected his misperceptions, he would understand *he* wasn't the problem and would be able to get past the hurt.

She twisted the heavy length of hair into a chignon before securing it within a snood. Her new hat, a gift from Lucy, had sunflowers and lace ribbons. Proper decorum would have her remain in mourning attire, but she couldn't greet Frank looking forlorn. She didn't want him to think she was miserable about her decision.

A knock came at her bedroom door.

"Claire? Are you ready? They'll be at the station in ten minutes."

Count on Henry to be punctual.

"Just a moment." She secured the cords of a crocheted reticule on her wrist. Took one last look around. Her trunks were packed. She'd arranged to have Mrs. Kelly and her son manage the hotel until a buyer could be found.

The judge had ruled in her favor when she'd contested the legality of the sale to the Bonds. William Bond had been handed over to federal authorities investigating the train robberies. Gertrude had returned to New York, under a cloud of scandal. Claire no longer had to worry about them. Neither did Henry.

They walked out of the hotel together. Much the same as the day when they had first walked through its door.

"You're anxious to get to Texas, aren't you," she asked her brother, as she took his arm.

"I am. We start on a new line this week. I want to be there to oversee the work."

Henry had joined a partnership constructing railroad lines through the midsection of the vast state. If the Katy Railroad wanted to reach the Gulf of Mexico, they would have to deal with him. His dream of connecting Chicago to the Gulf would finally be realized.

She had adjusted her dreams to fit reality. Heartbreaking, but practical.

They started down the wide sidewalk in the direction of the depot. People smiled and greeted them as they passed. Last year, Henry had resigned in disgrace. No one seemed to hold his past against him. Probably because of all the good he'd done while he was here. He had not only engineered the construction of the Katy, he'd designed the town and given large donations to build sidewalks, a school, several churches. He'd also set up a fund for railroad employees' widows.

"Henry, I'm so proud of you." Claire beamed at her big brother. "You've never given up. Nothing stops you. Your persistence amazes me."

He shrugged as if it were nothing. "I'm too stubborn to know when to quit. You inherited the same mule-headed tendency, I'm told. Sheriff Garrity said you chased Billy all the way to Texas and back."

Claire smiled at the memory. "Some might call that motherly love."

Henry was silent for a moment. He seemed to want to say something, but for some reason hesitated. He wasn't usually timid about voicing an opinion.

At the street in front of the depot, he let a wagon pass before guiding her across and inside the spacious depot. Men lined up at the ticket counter while women took to benches, with babies cradled in their arms and toddlers loosely corralled. Henry led her through the building to the back platform where people waited for the next train.

Beyond the depot to the west, beneath a wide blue sky, the prairie stretched out in a vast sea of golden grass. Over the next month, the plains would turn green and be dotted with wildflowers. On farms and ranches, lambs would bleat and calves would prance next to their mothers. Spring brought new life. For some reason, the anticipation of her favorite season didn't thrill her as it usually did.

In the distance, a whistle sounded. Puffs of black smoke appeared in the sky before the train came into sight.

Her heart fluttered nervously. What should she say? She and Frank would need privacy to have the delicate conversation about her inability to conceive.

Henry dipped his head, with his fingers tight on the brim of his bowler to keep the wind from taking it away. He kept studying her.

She released an impatient huff. "For heaven's sake, do say what's on your mind. I've never known you to be reticent."

"Do you intend to turn Mr. Garrity down, should he propose again?"

Claire's breath caught. She hadn't told her brother about her relationship with Frank or his proposals. Nor had she confided in Lucy, believing the less said the better. "Who told you he'd proposed?"

"He told me a couple weeks ago. When I found him in the saloon, deciding whether or not to get sloppy drunk."

Her heart constricted. "Did he? Get drunk?"

Henry shook his head, looking a bit surprised. "No."

She released a sigh of relief. That he might turn to drink had worried her. If he'd resisted the temptation, it showed strength. He would fight his demons rather than give in to them.

"He said he'd asked you to marry him several times, but you refused."

"Yes, well..." She looked down and adjusted the cord on her reticule to avoid meeting Henry's eyes. All the reasons she'd told herself she couldn't marry the emotionally scarred, domineering man had withered and fallen away over the two weeks since he'd been gone. Except one.

She loved Frank Garrity. Regardless of what he'd done, maybe even because of it. He'd risked everything to protect her and give her what he believed she wanted. She would never find another man like him. Regrets over her decision not to marry him would plague her for rest of her life. Still, she had to be strong for both of them. After she told him she couldn't have children, he would agree it was for the best not to marry. That might make it easier to leave. Then again, it might not.

Henry seemed to be waiting for her say something.

"There is a reason I can't marry Mr. Garrity. A very good one." But not something she wished to discuss, even with her brother.

Henry remained so quiet she was compelled to look up through her lashes to see his reaction—a troubled frown. They had rarely discussed her personal life, but if he had concerns, he was usually direct. This time, he left her to draw her own conclusions.

"Are you having second thoughts about taking me and Billy along?"

"No. I'm happy to give you both a home. I just want you to be sure that's what you want." He paused, glancing around as if he didn't wish to be overheard. "Look, it's not my place to say this, but I will. In case for some reason you're not aware, Frank Garrity is in love with you. He doesn't believe you return his affections."

Grief clamped a vise around Claire's throat.

Henry straightened, obviously uncomfortable with his decision to pry. "Very well. I shan't bring it up again."

He removed his hat rather than let the persistent wind snatch it away. Then put his arm around her shoulders to shield her or perhaps offer comfort. He hadn't pressed her to confirm whether or not she loved Frank, and probably assumed she didn't. It would make things easier if she let him continue to think so.

A shrill whistle and rumbling roar announced the imminent arrival of the train.

Claire steeled her spine. She hoped Billy wasn't angry with her.

He hadn't wanted to go with Frank to the farm. Henry had insisted a week's worth of hard work would be good for him and keep him out of trouble while they tied up legal loose ends. She'd agreed. Bedridden, she couldn't keep Billy occupied and boredom wasn't good for him. However, he would be glad to return and ready for a new adventure.

The train squealed and came slowly to a stop, hissing as it let off steam. The grayish smoke momentarily obscured Claire's view of the passenger cars.

Tomorrow, they would leave for Texas. Henry had assured her he would start the adoption process immediately. No one would ever take Billy away. If she couldn't be his mother, she would be content with second best. It was an excellent arrangement for all concerned.

Why, then, did she feel as if she was making the biggest mistake of her life?

CHAPTER 37

Smoke from outside poured in through the open windows and hazed the air in the rail car. It stung Frank's nose and eyes. The smoke didn't bother him as much as the slow-moving passengers in front of him. They were taking forever to get off the damn train.

Over the years, he'd learned to be patient in every area of his life, except where Claire was concerned. He couldn't wait to see her. He had pictured her face a hundred times since he'd left. He heard her voice in the wind sighing through the orchards next to the farm. He dreamed about her every night.

The rose vines his mother had planted next to the house still lived, in spite of years of neglect. In a couple months, they'd produce delicate buds and flower through the summer. Claire had the same fragile strength. Like those tenacious roses, she would survive, without his care and attention. He wasn't so sure he would make it without her.

He tugged on the sleeves of a new coat and adjusted the points on his collar. He'd taken Billy into Fort Scott to buy clothes that would fit him—the boy was growing like a weed—and he'd decided to purchase a new suit so he didn't show up looking like a bummer. He put his hand on Billy's shoulder. "Don't forget your hat."

In his eagerness, the boy had left it on the bench. He snatched it up by the wide brim and settled it on his head. Frank had purchased it for him, knowing he'd need something better than a shapeless piece of felt to shield his face from the Texas sun. He'd also gotten Billy a pair of boots after the boy mentioned his toes were getting cramped in his old shoes.

As the passengers moved at a turtle's pace down the aisle, Frank bent and looked out a window. He spotted Claire on the platform, standing next to her brother. She wore a sunny straw hat tied with a lacy bow, and her outfit was soft gray, not black. No more widow's weeds? That surprised him. It also relieved him because it meant she no longer dwelled on death and loss and the guilt that had plagued her for too long. In fact, she looked so pretty and cheerful, it brought a lump to his throat.

"I see her!" Billy announced. As soon as he reached the door, he thundered down the steps and made a beeline for Claire, straight into her arms.

Her face glowed as she held onto him.

He'd reached her height. If those big hands and feet were any indication, he'd grow into a strapping man once his growth spurt hit.

Billy was a good kid. Smart, curious, eager to learn. And when he let down his guard, he was friendly and likable. Claire had seen his potential and believed in him when no one else would. In turn, Billy was devoted to her, as he should be.

Frank had to admit he'd find it hard to say goodbye. Being a temporary guardian had given him a taste of fatherhood, and he'd discovered he liked it. Very much.

By the time he descended the steps, his stomach had tied itself into knots. He'd come here to hand over Billy and say goodbye, not beg Claire to reconsider. She'd made up her mind. He would honor her wishes. Her happiness was more important than getting what he wanted.

She looked over Billy's shoulder and smiled.

Frank was tempted to take her in his arms and kiss her in front of God and everybody. He'd resist the urge.

"Welcome back, Mr. Garrity." Her voice held a sultry tone. Or he imagined it. Had to be. He'd imagined lots of things over the past couple weeks.

He tipped his hat. "Mrs. Daines. It's good to see you up and around."

"I'm feeling much better."

They stood there, staring at each other like two idiots.

Her brother broke in. "Billy, let's go get the bags. Claire, we'll meet you back at the hotel. We'll be all packed up and ready to leave for Texas in an hour."

Before Billy could object, Henry grabbed his arm and pulled him away.

If Frank didn't know better, he'd swear Claire's brother had done it to give them time alone, which made no sense, considering their last discussion. But why look a gift horse in the mouth?

He offered Claire his arm. "May I escort you to the hotel?"

She curled her hand into the crook of his elbow. "Actually, I hoped we might go somewhere we could have privacy."

Frank's heart flip-flopped in his chest. His wish had come true. She'd changed her mind. No, she hadn't said that. Before he dragged her to him in a fierce hug, he'd better be sure. "Something wrong?"

"No. Not exactly. It's a private matter. I won't keep you long. What about your office?"

"The office? It's not exactly private. We'll go see if Gideon minds being thrown out for a short while."

Outside the depot, the wide street had filled up with buggies, wagons and men on horseback. The rest of the country might be experiencing a financial depression, but Parsons continued to grow. Now that the crooked general manager and his equally crooked wife were gone, the railroad might prosper again.

It wouldn't make any difference to Claire. She was leaving.

Or was she?

Frank shot a furtive look in her direction. A small frown marred her smooth forehead and she'd caught her lip between her teeth. It wasn't the expression of a woman about give a man back his dreams.

She might be nervous.

He guided her through a swarm of farm wives who'd gathered outside the mercantile. The women eyed them and went back to gossiping. He didn't care what they said. Claire didn't look as if she did, either.

"What did you and Billy do at the farm?" she asked.

"Fixed the roof, made repairs to the barn, cleaned everything up. Got a garden planted."

"Did he complain?"

"Not much. He said he'd helped Jasper Byrne work on his farm."

Claire appeared startled.

"Yeah, surprised the heck outta me, too." Frank didn't know Byrne even had a farm. The man gave up nothing about himself. His little friend, however, had been mighty talkative.

What Billy had revealed about the outlaw, combined with Byrne's reaction during the shooting, convinced Frank to do what he could to help Byrne avoid the noose. Although that wasn't something Claire needed to worry about.

"Billy says he won't let anybody turn him into a farmer. He also declared farm work isn't as bad as railroaders make it out to be."

"Are you saying he could be happy living on a farm?"

Was that a question or a challenge?

"He'll be happy living with you. He loves you, Claire." Frank let her chew on that awhile. If she still had doubts, she needed to know that Billy would follow her.

For certain, Henry loved his sister. He wouldn't take the boy away if it were possible for her to be Billy's mother. It would be possible if she married Billy's current guardian.

What the devil was he thinking? He hadn't come back to propose again, and get knocked into a cocked hat with yet another rejection.

Frank opened the door to this office. A shrill voice drifted out. Mrs. Callahan had come to collect her husband—again. Gideon must've locked up the drunk after another brawl. No need to get involved in that right now. Frank pulled the door shut.

"Looks like Deputy Branch is using my office." He eyed the stairway on the outside of the building, which led up to an apartment. Claire might find the suggestion offensive. Unless she'd changed her mind. Before he could change his, Frank motioned to the stairs. "What about my place? It's not much to look at, but it'll be quiet. And private."

Claire's nod seemed a little hesitant. Not a good sign. "This won't take long."

Frank followed her up the staircase, still trying to figure out what she wanted. His baser instincts reacted, tightening his groin. She said it wouldn't take long. She knew if they started *that,* they'd be at it for hours. He couldn't get his hopes up.

He opened the door to reveal a dim room. A small table with two chairs, shelves with a can of peaches. A few plates and cups. No sofa. He ate in this room, slept in the other.

For the first time, he saw his life as a woman might see it. Barren. Sad.

He went to the window and drew back a set of dusty drapes that had been there when he moved in. Light didn't improve the view.

Too late now. He'd invited her in. She knew him. The condition of this place couldn't come as a surprise. He turned a chair around. "You want to sit down?"

She shook her head. Probably entertaining second thoughts about following him up here.

"What can I do to make you more comfortable?"

At her wide-eyed reaction, he wanted to bite his tongue.

"Sorry, what I mean is—"

"Don't apologize." She held up her hand. "As I said, this won't take long. I just wanted to have a word without listening ears or curious stares."

Frank nodded and held his breath.

Claire toyed with the cords on her crocheted bag. When she

wouldn't look at him it meant she dreaded whatever it was she had to say. "I wanted to explain."

Explain why she'd rejected him. That's what she wanted to tell him. He didn't have to hear it. Didn't want to hear it.

"You don't owe me an explanation."

Her head came up. With tears in her eyes. Tears he'd put there.

"Claire..." He moved closer, ventured cupping his hands on her shoulders. He longed to hold her, but not if it made her feel worse. "Don't cry. I'm not worth even one of your tears."

That brought on the flood.

She bent her head and wept silently.

Frank couldn't stand it. He folded her against his chest, desperate to comfort her, yet without any idea of how to ease her distress, other than letting her get out whatever was causing it. "Sweet Claire. Tell me what it is you want to explain. Then you can go back to the hotel and see Billy. He'll make you smile again."

She reached up and grasped Frank's coat lapels as if she needed something to hold onto. "I can't give you...what you want... That's why...we can't..." She spoke in broken, meaningless fragments.

Her grief tore at his heart.

"What're you talkin' about? Are you saying you don't love me? I understand. You don't need to explain."

"No. I *do* love you, Frank. I love you so much it hurts. But I can't give you children."

Frank stared down at her, stunned speechless. Claire *loved* him? So much that it hurt, that's what she'd said. God, he knew the feeling.

Exhilaration rushed through him, so powerful he had to catch his breath. Claire loved him.

But wait, she'd said something else. Something about not being able to have children.

"You refused me because of that? Why didn't you tell me before? I could've put your fears to rest." He grasped her upper arms. "Look at me."

Slowly, she tipped her chin up. Her eyes were bright, her nose reddened. She sniffed. He let go of her long enough to fumble for a handkerchief and hand it to her.

"I love you, Claire. Whether or not you can have children will never change how I feel. Not a lick. I want to marry you, regardless."

Her miserable expression didn't lighten. "You said you wanted to give me children. You want a family, Frank. Don't try to tell me otherwise."

"For *you*, Claire. I wanted to give you children because *you* want them. All *I* want is you. The only family I need is you and Billy. If you want more children, we can take in orphans. There's plenty out there who need a mother with a heart as big as yours. We'll have room on the farm. We can take in as many as you want. A dozen. More, if you like. I'd love raising those kids. With you."

She appeared cautiously hopeful. "You don't care if we can't have our own children?"

He looked her right in the eye and gave her the answer he knew would convince her. "We will have our own children. You told me you loved Billy as much as if you'd given him life. So do I. And we can adopt more. They'll be ours because we'll love them like they are."

The smile that started was tremulous at first, and then grew wider, brighter. She reached up and put her soft hand on his cheek. "I adore you, you wonderful man, even if I don't deserve you."

"No, you don't deserve an ornery cuss. But I hope you'll take me anyway."

Her eyes twinkled with merriment. "Is that another proposal? I've lost count."

"I could go down on one knee."

"Please don't. I'd rather you be standing when I tell you I'll marry you."

Frank's heart took off at a dead run. He cradled her head between his hands and gave her a big kiss. With those simple words, she'd given him back his life, his hopes and his dreams. He wrapped her in his arms and drew her closer. One kiss led to another.

"Sweetheart," he murmured. "Let's go tell your brother we're getting married. We'll go back to the farm. Take Billy with us."

Claire drew back with a troubled frown. She splayed her fingers over his chest. "Frank, Billy wants to go to Texas and be Ginny's big brother. He'll be so disappointed."

"What Billy wants is to be with you, Claire, wherever you are. And we'll get him some brothers and sisters."

"Henry and Lucy are counting on my help."

"They got along without you before. I'm sure they'll do fine."

Frank captured her hand, nipped the tip of a finger. He knew she'd given her heart and wouldn't take it back. She was concerned about the feelings of others, but he couldn't help teasing. "Are you looking for another way out?"

"No, Mr. Garrity. I'll never let you get away." She wrapped her arms around his neck and kissed him with a boldness that thrilled him. He loved the way she gave with her whole self. "When do you want to start adopting other children?" she murmured, in between kisses.

"Whenever you're ready."

CHAPTER 38

Two days later, Billy stood beside Mr. Garrity as his best man, meaning the second most important man in the wedding party besides the groom. He squared his shoulders and stretched as tall as he could. He felt very grown up in a brand-new suit.

The groom kept fiddling with his bow tie. He looked sweaty and nervous. Until Mr. Stevens led his sister into the parlor and said he'd give her away. Then the sheriff started grinning like he'd been knocked silly.

The bride wore her best dress. She'd done her hair up into fancy twists and curls with lots of little white flowers stuck in it. Her maid of honor, Miss Lucy, got all gussied up, too.

Reflected in the mirror over the fireplace were the guests, which included the lawyer, Mr. Moore, Mrs. Kelly and her son, Mr. Tobias and his wife, and the deputy, Mr. Branch. They had big smiles on their faces as Mr. Stevens handed his sister off to the sheriff. The only person who didn't seem impressed was baby Ginny. She'd gone to sleep in Mrs. Kelly's arms.

The preacher said a prayer over the couple and commenced to read a scripture about love. The bride and groom made vows to each other, which included a promise to stick it out until they were both dead. The preacher pronounced them man and wife, and they kissed.

Billy looked away and wrinkled his nose in disgust. A kiss on the cheek was fine. Maybe even a peck on the lips. But he didn't see what grownups liked so much about mashing their mouths together. He had no interest in kissing a girl, anyhow.

"Congratulations!" The preacher told the couple when they finished the mushy kiss.

The women turned to each other and hugged. Mr. Stevens and Mr. Garrity shook hands.

"Thank you for standing up with me." The sheriff pumped Billy's hand with a firm grip.

"Weren't no trouble." Billy had about decided he liked Sheriff Garrity. Actually, he'd decided that before, when they'd worked together at the farm.

Mr. Garrity had claimed he expected *great things* from Billy. No one, except Mrs. Daines, ever expected him to amount to anything. Just knowing the sheriff had high expectations made Billy want to reach them.

He went over to the bride to tell her he was glad she'd married the sheriff after all.

She didn't give him a chance to talk before she hugged him. "You look so handsome."

Billy blushed. He pulled away, but not before he remembered his manners. "Thank you, Mrs., um...." He wasn't sure what to call her. He'd always referred to her as a Mrs. before, but that didn't quite seem right anymore. "Ma'am, you look handsome, too."

The grownups laughed.

Billy's blush climbed higher into his face. "I mean pretty. Real pretty."

"Thank you, Billy. You can call me Ma, if you'd like." The look in her eyes told him she'd like it if he did.

He figured he could get used to it. "Sure. That'd be fine." Uncomfortable with all the attention, he took a step back. "S'cuse me. I gotta get somethin' to eat."

He escaped further embarrassment and made his way over to a table set with little cakes and cookies. Helped himself to a few, saved one for later.

Billy dusted his hands on his trousers and went over to see baby Ginny. "Can I take her?" he asked Mrs. Kelly. "I know how to hold her proper."

"Why, certainly, young man. Here..." The old cook cradled Ginny into his arms and adjusted the baby's white gown.

Ginny woke up and looked at him with wide eyes that were sort of bluish gray. Miss Lucy had said they'd probably turn brown when she was older. Billy wished he had eyes that could change color, but he didn't think his eyes had ever been anything but blue.

He snuggled the baby against him, supporting her spine and bottom with one arm and wrapped the other arm around her as he'd been taught. He walked away from the others so he could talk to her without being heard. They'd all think he was crazy, blabbing to a baby who couldn't talk back.

"I sure wish I could be your big brother," he told her. "But you got to go with your folks, and I got to stay with Mr. and Mrs. Garrity because they want to adopt me. Well, mostly I got to stay because I swore I'd take care of her. My new Ma."

Ma. The word sounded strange on his lips. He hadn't had a mother since he was a baby like Ginny. He'd made up stories to tell people because it embarrassed him that he couldn't remember her. He didn't know if she'd loved him. He knew for certain his new Ma loved him.

He bent his head and lowered his voice. "See, I didn't reckon she'd want me after I shot her husband. But she forgave me. So, if you ever do anything bad, don't forget, your Ma will forgive you, too. You don't have to run away."

Ginny blinked up at him with an awe-struck expression. Heck, she didn't understand a word he said, but she sure was cute.

He grinned at her. Her mouth opened in a wide smile that made him glad—and sad. He would miss little Ginny. His ma had told him about her and the sheriff's plan to adopt more children. That might be okay, if they were as cute as Ginny. Not loud-mouthed and obnoxious like that Mackenzie girl who dressed like a boy.

The baby frowned, then wrinkled her nose and made fussy sounds. She started rooting against his chest. He knew what *that* meant. His face grew hot. "I ain't got what you're looking for."

He took the baby to her mother. "Here, she needs to eat."

Miss Lucy took Ginny and smiled. "Thank you for entertaining her."

"Don't mind." He decided he'd better put a condition on any future offer. "If she ain't hungry or dirty."

Billy looked around. The grownups were talking to the bride and groom. Miss Lucy had stepped out to feed the baby. Tomorrow, everyone would go their separate ways. He'd leave for the farm with his family. Before that, he had something he needed to do.

He had to say goodbye to a friend.

JASPER KNELT to examine cracks in the plank floor for the hundredth time. If he could find something to use to pry them up, he might be able to crawl out through the subfloor. He could do it if the walls weren't bricked. Still might be able to, if he had a tool of some sort.

He knew better than to think the men who'd ridden with him would come to his rescue. The ones smart enough to plan it knew better than to try.

Billy burst through the door leading into the sheriff's office. The boy was dressed in his Sunday best, with his hair combed and oiled, smelling like a five-dollar whore.

Jasper stood and made a mock bow. "To what do I owe the pleasure?"

Billy approached the cell, grinning. "I got to stand up for the sheriff."

"He can't stand up by himself?"

Billy released a loud sigh. The kid didn't appreciate a good joke. "In the *wedding*. He got married and asked me to be his best man."

"You like him better now that's he married?"

"He's tolerable." That shrug meant the sheriff had broken through the boy's hard shell to his soft heart.

"That's an improvement over how you felt before."

"Yeah. He took me up to the farm, made me work, like you did. We dug postholes. Chopped shingles. Replaced a floor in the kitchen. Patched up walls and rails."

Just what the kid needed. Idle hands, and all that.

Jasper rested his arms on the cross bar. "He made you worker harder than I did."

"It weren't so bad. Mr. Garrity told me what it was like to grow up on the farm. He told me stories about his folks and his life, how many men he'd killed—*a lot*—why he'd become a lawman. I never knew he liked to talk so much."

The report relieved Jasper. He'd worried that Garrity might not understand how to father a boy like Billy.

"Did he let you talk?"

"Oh, sure, I told him about all my adventures. He knew how scared I was when I had to go into court." Billy's happy expression faded. "I didn't mean to get you caught."

"You?" Jasper scoffed. "*You* didn't have much to do with it. I got careless." He maintained his prideful stance while the struggle played out on Billy's face.

The last thing the kid needed was the burden guilt put on a body. Not only that, Jasper wasn't about to admit to anyone that he'd been captured by a boy. Even if it was partly true.

"Oh, almost forgot." Billy dug into his pocket. "I brought you a cookie. It ain't much, but I want you to have it. Seeing as we're friends."

"Thanks." Jasper took the treat Billy offered through the bars. He got a tickle in his throat that made him cough. Had to be that. He hadn't gotten choked up over a cookie.

"Miss Lucy says she'll write up a nice letter about you and leave it with the judge. Mr. Garrity promised he'd put in a good word, too. You might not have to stay in jail for long."

The boy kept going on about how they would see each other again sometime in the future.

Jasper didn't point out the obvious. He didn't have a future. Why put a damper on the kid's optimism? He seemed happy, with people who cared about him, which was all that mattered. If fact, it might be only thing that mattered.

In the final accounting after death—if there were such a thing—a few good deeds wouldn't outweigh the bad. Still, Jasper refused to regret his decision to protect Billy rather than run. He'd chosen to run at other times in his life when he should've been brave and honorable. He was tired of being a coward. Most of all, he was tired of running.

That didn't mean he wished to hang—just thinking about it put him in a sweat. He'd hoped to be able to parlay his knowledge about Bond's involvement in the robberies into a pardon. The federal marshal who'd come to see him had nixed that idea. Said he might not be executed if he cooperated, but gave no promises.

Jasper finished the flaky sugar cookie. He didn't let on how desperate he'd started to feel. There wasn't anything the boy could do about it. He did owe Billy thanks for being kind to him. "Appreciate you coming over to see me."

Billy straightened to his full height, which wasn't even to Jasper's nose. It would be too bad if he remained short all his life. "I aim to get you outta here."

If being worked hard, shot at and arrested hadn't cured the boy of his recklessness, maybe a good scare would work.

Jasper reached through the bars and grabbed Billy by his silk lapels. Pulled him forward until his forehead pressed against cold metal. "You ain't doin' nothing of the sort. You try, and I'll take a piece of your hide. Or maybe your scalp."

When he released his hold, Billy didn't run off. He didn't even step back. He just stood there with a sad expression.

Jasper's stomach knotted. He gripped the bars and adopted a stern expression. That seemed to work for the sheriff. "Go to that farm. Grow up. Stay out of trouble."

He didn't add, *make my sacrifice worth it.* He didn't want Billy to feel obligated. He didn't want the boy to feel anything except relieved, and maybe have a fond memory or two.

"They won't hang you, Jasper. All you got to do is cooperate. That's what the sheriff said. If you do, they might let you out of jail."

Only in a boy's dream world would a hardened criminal walk out of jail for merely cooperating. He'd be lucky if he got off with a life sentence. In fact, he might wish they'd opted to hang him. Maybe he could talk them into shooting him instead. He didn't have a death wish, but he had opinions about how he'd rather die.

Billy spirits seemed to perk up. "When you get out, you can come visit me on the farm. Mrs.—I mean, my Ma—says we'll be adopting lots of children. You can help us take care of them."

Jasper got itchy just thinking about children. Look where he'd ended up after getting entangled with this one. "What happens if I don't cooperate?"

Billy scratched his head like the answer puzzled him. "Why wouldn't you? You don't want to stay in jail."

Babysitting or jail?

"Jail don't sound half bad."

CHAPTER 39

May 17, 1874, Marais De Cygnes

A sparkling river bordered the Garrity property on one side, and on the other, forested hills. The farm, a few hours north of Parsons, covered land as verdant and lush as any Claire had seen. Above it all, a bright blue canopy stretched from horizon to horizon. The advertisements sent east to lure immigrants to Kansas must've been referencing this place when they spoke of paradise.

She climbed a hill overlooking the farm and stopped to pluck a handful of wild violets. Although the sun heated her back, its rays couldn't penetrate the neck shade or the wide brim protecting her face. Before she'd moved here, she had never worn one of the massive sunbonnets favored by the settlers' wives. Since then, she had taken to the attire and lifestyle as quickly as Frank had taken to being a farmer.

She shifted the basket on her arm and placed the flowers inside. Other men might think her frivolous for spending time picking wildflowers for their table. Frank had a special appreciation for beauty. Perhaps because he'd seen so much ugliness in his past.

In the field below, her husband labored alongside Billy and the younger boys. The brothers, Samuel and Issac, had been sent west on an orphan train. True to his promise, Frank had made room in his house and his heart for two more children who needed a safe, loving home. He would have room for more.

Her breath quickened with excitement when he spotted her. He started in her direction, leaving the boys to continue their work in the cornfield. His long, confident strides reminded her of the first time she'd seen him. He'd impressed her then as a determined man. She'd learned later just how determined he could be.

"Good morning. You look very fashionable," he teased. He leaned down to brush a kiss on her lips before he tucked her free hand in the crook of his elbow. "Do you need help picking flowers? It's a little early for lunch."

Her heart thumped in anticipation. He'd be so surprised.

"I have something share with you before the boys come in to eat." She led him back to the two-story white frame house with its welcoming porch and the climbing roses his mother had planted and nurtured. "How quickly could you add another room?"

His eyes crinkled at the corners. "Are more children on the way? We should build a railroad station in front of our house. Make it easier to bring them out there."

She removed her hand from his arm and placed it on her flat abdomen. Soon, God willing, her womb would swell with Frank's child. She almost couldn't believe it, but she hadn't had her flow for over a month and a half, and knew something was different. Her prayers had been answered. "This one won't arrive on a train."

His face reflected confusion at first, then surprise when he glanced down to where her hand rested. "How will this one be arriving?"

"By way of a miracle." She'd grown brave enough to believe in them again, thanks to Frank and his love. "I'm with child."

He released a loud whoop, at the same time he lifted her beneath her arms and swung her around. When her feet touched the ground again, he covered her mouth with his. After the kiss ended, he drew her into his embrace to hug her tightly. "Claire, sweetheart. I can't put into words what I'm feeling right now."

She couldn't either. *Joy* was too small a word to capture the expansive emotion that had taken up residence in her heart. "You can show me later tonight."

"I'll do that, Mrs. Garrity. Gladly."

With a happy sigh, she laid her head against his shoulder. *Blessed* also didn't come close to describing how she felt. Somehow, Frank's love had opened heaven's stores. Actually, more than his love. His tenacity.

The determined sheriff had never given up, not even when she'd run away. After she'd run out of hope. He had come after her. Untangled her deception. Dismantled her defenses. Risked his job and his life. In spite of every obstacle, including the numerous ones she'd put in his path, he had succeeded in doing what he'd set out to do. Capture her heart.

FRANK AND CLAIRE are starting a new life together with a growing family and rekindled hope for a bright future. While Jasper Byrne, the outlaw who saved Billy, languishes in jail, regretful, yet resigned to an inevitable fate. Until a woman in disguise offers him a dangerous deal. Will she lead him down a path to freedom or on a journey straight to hell?

FIND OUT HOW THE STEAM! series ends in the last, and most exciting, episode—Lawless Hearts.

MORE FROM E.E. BURKE

*Looking for more dark deceits, daring heroes and scorching love stories? The fifth installment in the **Steam!** series is coming soon. Have you read the first four books?*

Her Bodyguard

Redbird

A Dangerous Passion

Fugitive Hearts

Lawless Hearts

*Four women take their chances in a Bride Lottery on the wild frontier in **The Bride Train Series.***

Valentine's Rose

Patrick's Charm

Tempting Prudence

Seducing Susannah

*Read two bestselling Mail Order Bride novellas that have their roots in the **Steam!** series.*

Victoria Bride of Kansas

Santa's Mail Order Bride

An American Mail Order Bride Christmas Collection

Sign up for my newsletter at www.eeburke.com for exclusive articles and to find out about my new releases.

RESEARCH NOTES

The Civil War had a "long and devastating reach," to quote historian Lesley Gordon,. The impact of one traumatic era on the next runs throughout the *Steam! Romance and Rails* series.

In the 19th century, very little was known about how war and violence could scar minds. Men who exhibited what today would be termed Post Traumatic Stress Syndrome were thought to have character flaws or underlying physical problems. The wives of men who suffered severe breakdowns had little to no support and were faced with committing their spouses to asylums or hiding them away at home, which is the tough decision Claire makes for her husband. The suffering these men's wives must've gone through is difficult for us to understand today. In addition, women had few rights over property or even their own children, which compounded the problems they faced when their spouses were uncooperative or outright abusive.

The towns of Parsons, Muskogee and Denison all came into being in the early 1870s because of the railroad. Parsons was located and built by Robert S. Stevens, the general manager of the Missouri, Kansas and Texas Railroad, and named after Katy President Levi

Parsons. Stevens also founded Denison, which bears the name of the Katy Vice President George Denison.

Muskogee was located in then-Indian Territory (in the Creek Nation), and was considered one of the wildest and most dangerous towns along the line. The boarding house made of railroad cars actually existed and was operated by James Barnes.

In Denison, Sheriff Lee "Red" Hall had the reputation as a tough, effective lawman. He later became a well-known captain in the Texas Rangers.

Special thanks to Jill Marie Landis for her amazing library and even more amazing mentoring, to Linda Broday for her encouraging words and positive vibes, and to Sunny Cole, my coffee buddy and soul sister.

E.E. Burke

ABOUT THE AUTHOR

E.E. Burke is a bestselling author of historical fiction and romances that combine her unique blend of wit and warmth. Her books have been nominated for numerous national and regional awards, including Booksellers' Best, National Readers' Choice and Kindle Best Book. She was also a finalist in the RWA's prestigious Golden Heart® contest. Over the years, she's been a disc jockey, a journalist and an advertising executive, before finally getting around to living the dream--writing stories readers can get lost in.

Find out more about her books at her website: www.eeburke.com.

www.ingramcontent.com/pod-product-compliance
Lightning Source LLC
Chambersburg PA
CBHW060519180626
46817CB00002B/411